Praise for *Garden of the Midnights*

"Hannah Linder's engrossing new ... ger, twisty turns, and sweet, forbidden roman ... o keep you up late turning pages!"

–Julie Klassen, bestselling ... *of Sea View*

"Linder's *Garden of the Midnights* is the best historical novel I've read all year! The unusual plot was more in every way—more than mere romance, more than a history lesson, and more than a usual inspirational. I lived and breathed the story through the excellent sense of place and the compelling characters. The twists and turns had me riveted, and I won't soon forget William and Isabella's story. Very highly recommended!"

–Colleen Coble, USA Today bestselling author and author of *Fragile Designs*

"A uniquely atmospheric novel, *Garden of the Midnights* intrigues from page one and never lets up. Readers will be swept away in the mystery and romance, and find themselves cheering for William and Isabella as they fight for their happily ever after. Hannah Linder's newest is beautifully written and a wonderful fresh take on the genre. One not to be missed!"

–Joanna Barker, author of *A Heart Worth Stealing,*
A Game of Hearts, and *Otherwise Engaged*

"Unexpected twists and turns abound in this sweeping Regency suspense! Hannah Linder's writing is reminiscent of Austen, with fresh storytelling that will keep you on the edge of your seat."

–Kasey Stockton, author of *I'm Not Charlotte Lucas*
and the Bradwell Brothers series

"A beautifully written, evocative love story with pulse-pounding suspense. Prepare to turn those pages as fast as you can."

–Regina Scott, award-winning author of *A Distance too Grand*

"Author Hannah Linder is a masterful storyteller. She did a fantastic job of keeping the spark alive between the two protagonists as danger lurked around every corner. The dialogues were powerful, the descriptions were exceptional, and I greatly enjoyed all the twists and turns. It was a very interesting, original storyline that hooks you from the very first page."

–Laura Beers, award-winning Regency author of *Secrets of a Lady*

"Romantic, original, and suspenseful. Linder's prose is just as lovely as the uplifting themes in this beautiful story."

–Ashtyn Newbold, Regency author of *The Earl Next Door*
and the Larkhall Letters series

GARDEN
of the
MIDNIGHTS

GARDEN
of the
MIDNIGHTS

HANNAH LINDER

BARBOUR
PUBLISHING

DEDICATION

To Jesus, the One who satisfies the deepest places in my soul.

PROLOGUE

Sharottewood Manor
Northumberland, England
December 1787

The time had come.

Edward Gresham leaned out the sash window of his bedchamber, the cold air sending bumps along his skin. He bit his lip against a smile. Open countryside filled his view, glistening with snow. A tiny gurgle of water still sprayed from the icy fountain below. How many years had he waited for this? All his life?

Perhaps at first it had not been so important. Sharottewood had been his father's, and the day it would belong to Edward had seemed too far away to be worthy of thought.

Until he realized such a day might never come if he did not do what was expected of him.

Edward blinked against the snow flurries and tried to push away the unpleasantness of the many raging quarrels he'd endured with his father. He would not be plagued with that now.

Not on his wedding day.

The click and thud of a door turned Edward back to his bedchamber. He pulled the window closed. "There you are, Felix. What time is it?"

His lanky valet drew near with an emerald-green coat draped across one arm and a waistcoat across the other. "Nearly eight, Master Gresham. Are these suitable?"

"Precisely so, but I shall need a fresh jabot." A slight chuckle rumbled out. "I fear I was a clumsy fool this morning and succeeded in spilling my breakfast tea all over me."

A knowing smile warmed Felix's face. "A calamity most grooms are afflicted with, I imagine, Master Gresham." He was just moving behind Edward to undo the stained jabot when he paused. "Forgive me, but I nearly forgot. This came for you."

Edward glanced at the letter.

And froze.

The seal. Tension raced through his body, tightening his muscles, as he snatched the letter from his valet's hand. "Leave me."

"But Master Gresham, the time—"

"I said leave me. At once."

Felix nodded and quit the room.

Then Edward was alone with the intricate red seal and all the searing emotions that accompanied it. *Why now?* He tore open the letter. *After all these months, why should I hear from her today?*

The writing, however, was not hers. The handwriting belonged to her sister. He tripped over the words once, then twice, then a third time. *Constance buried at the churchyard. . .died in childbirth. . .the shame. . .five thousand pounds a year. . .then I shall conceal your secret. . .and your son.*

My son? The room tilted. He groped for his bedpost, raked in air, and crushed the letter within his fist. Constance was not dead. The letter spoke lies. This was some malicious stab of revenge for what he had done to her months before—for forsaking her.

A knot rushed to his throat. He forced his knuckles into his mouth to keep back any sound. Why should he grieve? Why should it hurt like this?

In a few hours, he was to be married. He was to commit his life to the daughter of a squire, a woman of his father's choosing, the only bride who could not only give him happiness but Sharottewood too.

Constance swam before him. Her eyes, bright and young and uncalculating. Her laugh, soft and easy. Her hair, golden and fragranced, like the garden they would slip to so many midnights. They had played and danced and loved in those idyllic, hidden hours.

Until his father discovered them.

Until Edward had to choose between their secret love tryst or his own inheritance.

Until he had to cease coming to the garden at all.

With numbness dulling the pain, he stumbled toward the hearth and leaned his forehead against the mantel. This changed nothing. He had sacrificed too much. He had compromised himself too many times. He had altered the course of his entire life to please his father and gain the only thing that meant anything to him.

Sharottewood Manor.

A bitter taste climbed his throat as he threw the letter into the flames. Sparks fluttered. Warm scents of wood and ash and smoke nearly choked him, scents he determined to henceforth despise forever.

But he could not lose Sharottewood now. Not for scruples. Not for Constance Kensley.

Not even for his son.

CHAPTER 1

Rosenleigh
Leicestershire, England
April 1809

Іt has happened again." William Kensley stood at the entrance of the redbrick stables, mud caking the lower half of his breeches and Hessians.

Mr. Nolan, the stable master, seemed to search William for injuries before he asked, "Ahearn?"

"Lying in the gully."

"Perhaps an accident—"

"It was no accident." Speaking the words unpent some of the fury. William fished the bur from his riding coat pocket, displayed it on his palm, then dropped it. He crunched it beneath his heel. "No more an accident than the other calamities that have befallen me. Excuse me. I must get a gun."

"Mayhap someone else should—"

"No. I shall do it myself." He started back for the manor, the early morning sun cutting through the clouds and stabbing his eyes. The ache spread through him, fissuring through his composure until it turned into rage.

The first few times it had been easier. When they called it an accident that his bed had caught afire, or that his breakfast made him ill, he had believed them.

Until it happened again.

And again.

He brushed the sweat from his forehead and tried to erase his mind of Ahearn's screech as they toppled headlong into the gully. What blackguard would dare do such a thing to the best horseflesh Rosenleigh had ever seen? To any horse?

Indeed, what blackguard would do such a thing to William? What possible gain could anyone have in seeing him dead?

He didn't know. Not yet.

But he would. One way or another, this madness must come to a stop and answers must be given him. He knew just where to go for such answers too.

Whether or not the old gardener would part with the answers was yet to be seen. He never had before.

Reaching the grey-stoned house, with its white-trimmed windows, jutting chimneys, and perfectly trimmed boxwoods lining the front, William burst through the entrance and into the foyer. He rushed through rooms and down halls, grimacing a bit at the trail of mud he was leaving behind for the housekeeper.

At the trophy room, he pushed inside. The room was quiet, spacious, with light slanting through the tall sash windows and brightening the trophies of roebuck and muntjac deer hanging on the walls. He walked for the hearth and grabbed the double-barreled shotgun from above the mantel.

"Going after pheasants, are you, Cousin?"

William glanced to the other side of the room, where Horace Willoughby was slumped into a wingback chair—a decanter of port in one hand, a wineglass in the other. His neckcloth was loose and stained with splotches of drink.

"A bit early for hunting." Horace hiccupped. "Is it not?"

"As it is for drinking."

Horace sprang to his feet, though he seized the arm of his chair to keep from careening. His round cheeks blazed red. "I shall drink if I wish, and I'm bloody-well weary of you plaguing me about it." Shakily, he poured more port into his glass, drained it, then wiped his mouth. "Where are you going?"

"To put Ahearn out of his misery."

"What has happened? What have you done to my horse?"

"He is not your horse." William started for the door. "And I am certain details of his malady would only bore you."

"That horse was Father's."

"Which he gave to me."

"Just because you ride him all across this bloody estate does not make him any more yours than mine. You think you own everything, don't you? Just because you're older. Just because you inherited. You think you can—"

"The horse will be dead, Horace." William clenched the gun and worked the muscle in his jaw. "There is little point in arguing it now."

"I shall argue it if I bloody-well please. Mother shall hear about it too. Get back here, William!"

A glass smacked the door as William reached to open it. Red port dripped down the wood, but he pulled the knob and crunched over broken glass to exit the room.

He turned a deaf ear to Horace's inebriated curses and railings and threats of what his mother would do to William when she heard about this.

He would endure his aunt when he returned.

Right now, he must bury his horse.

William found the gardener where he always found him. Among the flowers, shrubbery, and stone urns, his weathered hands patting soil around a struggling plant.

If anyone could bring the plant back alive, Shelton could.

"Ahearn is buried."

Shelton glanced up at William. A slight tinge of sadness warmed his brown gaze before he turned and nursed his plant again.

William sat on the wrought-iron bench next to him, his clothes reeking of sweat and horse. All his life he'd been coming here—sitting on the bench, or kneeling in the dirt next to the old man, or helping pluck brown leaves from green plants. As a child, William had told him everything. His secrets, troubles, and hurts.

Like the endless times Horace had lied about him. Or the injuries his cousin had inflicted. Or those long, wretched days when his aunt had locked William in a black room because he had finally fought Horace back.

Most of the time Shelton listened and didn't say anything. Most of the time, that was enough.

But not now.

Not today.

"Tell me I imagine these things, and I shall ask you no more." William's pulse quickened. "Tell me they are accidents. I shall believe the words from you."

Shelton angled his face away from William.

"Then tell me *why* they are happening." William stood again, his forbearance draining. "Surely you can tell me that."

"I cannot tell you what I do not know." Shelton sighed and brushed his hands together, dirt flying. "Perhaps you should go away from here—"

"I shall not run from my own land, nor my troubles."

"For a time, it may be best."

"There will never be such a time." William pulled his sweaty hands into fists. "I intend to live and die on Rosenleigh grounds, and whoever thinks they can frighten me away may have to follow through with their 'accidents.'" He started down the path.

"William?"

He turned.

The old man opened his lips, hesitated, then pressed them shut before any words escaped. With sagging shoulders, he returned to a cluster of purple columbines.

Pressure—and hurt—built inside William's chest as he headed for the manor. Shelton was holding something back. Something that could cost William his life.

Why?

William had no sooner washed and changed when a knock came to his door. He swung it open to find fifteen-year-old Ruth on the other side, hands clasped and already blushing.

"Very sorry I be to bother you, Master Kensley. I hope you wasn't resting. Very sorry I am."

"If you tell me why, I might be obliged to forgive you."

"Mrs. Willoughby be wanting to see you, she does. Right away, sir."

Annoyance flickered, but he shoved it back and cleared his throat. "Hurry, Ruth. I must escape. Will you aid me?"

The maid's eyes turned wide as crowns. "Me, sir?"

"We must trade places. Off with your mob cap now, and you must don my tailcoat."

A fierce shade of pink stole over the girl's cheeks, whether from amusement or embarrassment he wasn't sure.

Either way, he laughed and sent her away with the promise he would muster his courage and see his aunt himself. But as he walked through corridors, up a set of mahogany stairs, and into the west wing, his humor faded.

It was a long journey from his bedchamber to hers.

As a child, it had been his nightmare. Sometimes he'd sniffle on the way, blinking fast so he wouldn't have to shame himself with tears. Other times he'd pound his fist into his palm. *Thump. Thump.* Over and over, the sequence as loud and thudding as his own heartbeat.

He experienced no such trepidation now. At one and twenty, he was now inheritor of Rosenleigh after his grandfather's passing three months ago—as much a surprise to him as to anyone else. All his life, Grandfather had hinted that Rosenleigh would one day belong to Horace.

But the will left behind said only that the inheritance was entailed first to the eldest male descendant, then to the next living male relative.

Thus, Rosenleigh was William's. His home. He wasn't just the despicable cousin, the object of his aunt's charity, the unwanted ward they'd all made more than obvious they'd rather do without.

Now, they couldn't do without *him.*

And it infuriated both of them.

At her oak-paneled door, William tapped twice then entered. The bedchamber was damp, the curtains drawn, the air fragranced with perfumes not quite strong enough to overpower the odors of illness.

From the four-poster bed, his aunt's narrow, liquid eyes stared at him.

"Pour me a glass of water, William, if it does not trouble you too greatly."

He moved to the stand next to her bed, poured, then handed her the glass.

She sipped it between wrinkled lips, the longcase clock ticking away seconds, before she finally handed it back and coughed. Her eyelids half lowered. "You truly think you are something, don't you?"

The accusation ground through William, but he worked hard at changing neither expression nor tone. "You wished to see me?"

"Answer my question, you insolent brat."

"I have no answer."

"You must be very proud to force everything away from the ones who cared for you."

"I had no part in the details of the will."

"Didn't you?" Her back arched against the headboard. "All those times you went up to his chamber? A blind old man who found you as despicable as I do and yet you—"

"He was my grandfather."

"You persuaded him."

"I did nothing but offer him company, and even that not very often." William pushed his hands into the pockets of his tailcoat. "Now pray, why did you wish to see me? I must make my leave."

"You shall make your leave when I tell you and not a minute before." Her nose crinkled. "Horace has informed me of your injustice to him today. I might have known you'd go to abusing him. He has nothing at all and you deny him even the right to his own horse."

"Ahearn was—"

"Pay him the animal's worth, if you have any conscience about you. After all I have done for you. Sheltering you and educating you and raising you beside my own son, though I must say you never deserved it. You were a wicked child. It is quite providential your mother died in childbirth, for she certainly could not have loved such a sinful child as you."

He'd heard the words so many times he was dull to them. He focused on holding her eyes and not looking away, his one show of defiance, however small.

"Now get out of my sight."

He left the chamber at her dismissal and rushed in his first breath of odorless air. He shook his mind free of her words.

As if he could ever be free of them.

"Seventy-six guineas." William slid the leather pouch across the dining room table—perhaps with too much vigor, because it slipped over the edge and into his cousin's lap.

Horace grinned and jangled the coins. "I daresay, Mother does have a way with you. Did you have a nice visit?"

William stabbed his fork into his partridge. From the opposite end of the dining room table, Horace's no doubt port-scented breath mingled with the roasted fowl, boiled potatoes, white soup, and baked apples.

He wouldn't let his cousin ruin his appetite though. Horace ruined quite enough without being given that power too.

"I won't have you going to Miss Ettie about me, hear?"

"I have not yet spoken with her today." Besides, when had William ever run to their childhood governess with complaints? She couldn't do anything more about Horace than William could.

"You told her of my drinking."

"I imagine she did not need to be told."

"What is that supposed to mean?"

"That everyone in this house knows how much you drink." William pulled the napkin from his cravat. "For mercy's sake, what are you trying to do? Drown yourself in it?"

"Enough." Horace's bloodshot eyes looked away as he choked the stem of his goblet in a beefy fist. "I have nothing else to allure me in this forsaken place."

"You might go to London for the season."

He harrumphed.

"Or take up hunting. Or riding." William scooted back in his chair. "There are a number of things you could do if you really wanted to, but you don't. You would rather sit about all day and feel sorry for yourself instead of trying to build yourself into the man your father would have wished you to be."

"Leave Father out of this!"

"He would have wished you to—"

"At least my father *wanted* me. Yours won't even admit he has a son. You're just a. . ."

William's heart leapt to his throat as he waited for the sentence to continue. It didn't.

"Finish."

"I have." Horace rubbed a hand to the side of his neck, eyes bulging, then stood. He staggered toward the door—

William rushed to the threshold and blocked him. "My father has been dead my entire life. Explain what you just said to me."

"I am drunk."

"Explain."

"Never mind what I said. I told you. . .I am unclear of mind." Sweat formed along his upper lip, and he wiped it away without meeting William's gaze. "Now out of my way."

William allowed him to leave, but an acrid taste filled his mouth. He tried to push the words away as he returned to his meal. They didn't make sense. There could be no truth in them. His father had been dead the whole of his life, just like his mother.

But his appetite drained and an unsettling fear churned his stomach.

He'd seen Horace lying enough to know when he wasn't.

The nagging thoughts were relentless. Twice in the night William awoke with them, and by the third disruption from sleep, he lit a candle and moved to the window.

He eased open the pane. Fresh night air bathed his face, scented with dew and a nearby lilac plant. Beyond the garden, a blue-tinted layer of fog weaved in and out of the small labyrinth where he'd spent endless hours playing and hiding as a boy.

Too bad he could not hide there now.

How easy it would be to slip into the familiar green maze and pretend the world outside didn't exist. That no one was trying to kill him. That his aunt no longer hated him. That Horace's words, whatever they meant, were not in truth.

He couldn't be certain of anything.

Or anyone.

Even Shelton, the one person he'd always thought would stand next to him, was playing the coward and backing down against the truth. Was the old gardener afraid? Of whom? Horace? William's aunt? Were the two so enraged at his inheritance that they should plot to kill their own flesh and blood?

Whatever he thought of them, he couldn't think that. He didn't want to.

And perhaps that made him a fool.

A soft tap came at his bedchamber door, quiet and timid enough he knew before he swung it open who stood on the other side.

Miss Ettie.

Dear Miss Ettie, with her wispy brown-silver hair and her careful eyes, always looking at him as if he were the one prize she wished she could keep forever. Sometimes, when she thought no one would notice, William saw her slip into that old nursery and close the door, as if by entering the room again she might return to the days when she had coddled and taught her wards.

Indeed, she beheld him that way now. "I saw the light, my dear."

"You should be in Bedfordshire yourself."

"Oh, listen to you." She clucked and pulled her wrapper tighter, the orange candlelight making shadows on her face. "You know I sleep less and less. Perhaps because I have not a young one to chase after all day."

"You may chase after Mr. Nolan's dog, if you like."

He expected a laugh, or at the very least a shake of her head and a smile—but her eyes turned on him with a slant of fear. "William." He knew the tone well enough to know tears were coming. "If something should happen to you—"

"Nothing will happen to me. You need not worry."

"But the horse today. And the other things—"

"Accidents."

"I am not so naive that I cannot see what is happening. You need not pretend for my sake. I know there is danger. Too much danger. You cannot stay here."

"Let us talk about it in the morning."

"No, now, William."

"You know I will not leave. Do not ask it of me."

"At least for a time."

"Not even for that."

Moisture flashed and her cheeks drained white. With a soft hand, she clasped his cheek. "It should not have to be this way." The tears streamed loose. "Heaven knows I cannot lose you, my little William."

He leaned forward and kissed her forehead. "Good night, Miss Ettie."

For several seconds, she did not release him. Then, sucking in air, she walked away down the hall, the candlelight fading back into blackness.

The empty corridor echoed her words, "*It should not have to be this way.*"

But it was.

And he had no intention of running.

"There you are." William leaned inside the rubblestone-and-brick potting shed, Mr. Nolan's dog squeezing in ahead of him.

Shelton rose from the workbench. Morning sunlight fell through the windows, making visible the dark circles beneath his eyes and the grim pull to his lips. As if he, too, had spent a night without rest.

Hurt nipped at William. He tried to push it away and tell himself it meant nothing, that whatever Shelton did, he did for a reason. Whatever he said—or didn't say—had purpose. That was the way of him. This was no different.

Except that it could cost William's life.

As if in scent of a varmint, Mr. Nolan's dog growled and sprang to the corner of the shed, knocking over several potted plants.

William whistled and rushed the animal back outside. "Here. Let me help." He got on his hands and knees beside the older man. They worked in silence, setting the pots upright, cupping damp soil back around the plants, the sun warm on the back of their necks.

"Tell me of my father."

As if he hadn't heard, Shelton continued scraping dirt from the floor. Not until he'd stood to his feet and turned to a shelf of garden tools did he let out a breath. "There is nothing to tell."

"What was he like?"

No answer.

"What did he die of?"

Still, nothing.

William brushed dirt from his breeches as he stood. His heartbeat thrummed his neck. "Why do you not answer?"

"You already know the answers."

"If they are true."

Shelton glanced back at him. Some of William's own hurt, his own confusion, was mirrored in Shelton's gaze.

William nodded and stepped back. "Forgive me. I will ask no more." He pivoted and was crossing the threshold when—

"William."

He paused without turning.

"You are the one who must forgive me." A catch disrupted Shelton's voice. He cleared his throat, moved closer, and rested a hand on William's shoulder. "Meet me in the labyrinth at dark. I shall tell you everything tonight."

Everything. The word plummeted through him like one of Horace's taunts—but worse. How much did William not know?

He didn't arrive for dinner. He didn't even slip down to the kitchen, as he sometimes did when he had no wish to dine with his cousin, for some cold meat and soup.

Instead, he went to her chamber.

The one he avoided.

The one he'd entered only once or twice in his life.

The door whined as he shut himself inside the soundless, floral-papered room. Dust motes filled the air as evening sun spilled in from a crack in the silk draperies.

He was drawn to the mantel. In a gilded frame, his mother's portrait stared across the room, her hair the same deep blond as his, her eyes blue, her lips half smiling and pleasant.

Why was it always so hard to come here?

Maybe because he believed his aunt. Maybe because he'd always imagined the beautiful angel in the painting would have hated him as much as his aunt did. Or thought him wicked. Or lost her smile.

Or maybe because she'd left him.

William stepped closer to the mantel and ran a hand down the dusty, ornate edge of the picture frame. As a child, sometimes he'd lain awake at night and hated her for dying. For allowing him to be both motherless and fatherless in a world so lonely and cruel.

But he was a child no more. He understood the things that had not made sense to him in younger years, and he could no longer bear unforgiveness toward the beautiful woman in the painting for doing what no one could stop.

Dying.

Yet still. His chest tightened as he forced his eyes to meet hers. Coming here was as difficult as it had been then, and for reasons he could not justify, the old hurt still swelled.

He pushed it away and shook his head. He needed to keep his mind clear. The present was troublesome enough without dredging back hurts of the past.

He left the chamber and waited in his own until somewhere in the manor, a longcase clock chimed twelve.

Nervous anticipation surged through him as he shrugged on his greatcoat and slipped downstairs in the dark. Outside, he walked quickly toward the labyrinth.

The moon hung low, the light faint and pale as a slight breeze chased away the fog. Somewhere behind, a scratching noise disturbed the stillness, as if a branch were being smacked into one of the downstairs windows—but he was soon far enough away from the manor that the sound faded.

Sweat dampened his palms. Tonight, he would have answers. He'd had so many questions his entire life, and when he was young, he'd never realized how evasive or inconstant the answers had been.

Now he knew too well.

But all that was about to end. The time for truth had come. And Shelton, at last, was going to give it to him.

At the entrance to the labyrinth, William drew in the cool night air and hurried into the maze. The worn path crunched beneath his boots, an echo in the silence. Were all nights so quiet?

But silence was good. Shelton said so. *"They listen best who have no mouth, and speak loudest who have no tongue,"* he'd always said.

William had never understood the words exactly. He'd only listened. In the end, maybe that's what Shelton had meant after all.

As William turned the last curve into the center of the labyrinth, he spotted the black-stoned bench in the dull light. "Shelton?"

He expected a shadow to emerge from the darkness, for the stooped old gardener to step forward into the moonlight.

He didn't.

"Shelton?" Alarm tingled across William's flesh as he turned a full circle and searched the shadows of the spherical clearing.

No movement. No answer.

Nothing.

Something must have detained him. Something worth more than his promise, his word. And little meant more to Shelton than that.

Unless he was merely late.

Yes, he must be late. He'd fallen asleep, or lingered at the garden, or checked the lock on the potting shed and—

A groan struck the air.

Tension barreled through William as he lunged toward the path adjacent to him and made the first turn.

Then he froze.

Half in moonlight and half in shadows, a body lay sprawled on the ground. Face up. Arms spread. Head lolled to the side, with blood flooding from the crushed forehead.

Shelton. William dove to his knees next to him. Panic struck him, piercing and jagged, like shards of glass splintering into his soul. "Shelton, can you hear me?"

Deep red matted the white hair, leaked down the left side of his face, dripped to his neck and the ground like a torrent of rain.

God, help. William ripped off his greatcoat, staunched the flow with the fabric. "Do not move. I am here. You are well."

But he wasn't. Another wound had ripped open his chest. More blood. Too much to soak into William's coat and too much to stop and too much to live without. *No, no.*

"Leave. . .get out. . ."

"Do not speak." William gathered Shelton into his arms and tried to stand, but Shelton's hissing groan made William lower him back. Nausea punched his gut. His mind reeled. Should he move him? Keep him still? Run for help or stay or—

"Forgive me. . .for the lies." Choked. Deep. "William?"

"Here."

"Leave."

"Shelton—"

"Leave Rosenleigh. Promise." The wrinkled eyelids blinked through the blood. "Tonight. Before. . .before you. . .too. . ."

"Shelton!" William grasped the man's face with his hands. He rasped in air, moved his thumbs, tried to hold contact with a gaze growing dimmer. "Stay with me. Please. Hear?"

"Your father. . ."

"No longer matters. You must not speak."

"Not dead."

"Please. Tell me what to do. Tell me how to help you—"

"Gresham. Your father."

"Shelton!"

"Edward. . .Gresham. . ." The lips stretched open, gasping. Then a noise, gurgling and frantic, as the old man latched on to William's cravat with his fist. "Run. . . Promise."

"I will not leave you—"

"Promise!" With desperate strength, Shelton yanked William closer. Inches from his face. Close enough that the brutal, metallic-sweet scent of his blood took William's breath.

"I promise." The words gutted out of him.

But Shelton never heard them. His grip loosened, his hand thudded back to the ground, and his eyes rolled vacant and sightless into the back of his head.

He was dead.

CHAPTER 2

Mulcaster Square, London
April 1809

T here he is."

Isabella Gresham motioned her lady's maid away from the window, slipped behind the draperies herself, and chanced a glance down to the street.

Below the upstairs townhouse window, a tall stranger alighted from a shiny barouche, dressed in tailcoat and pantaloons that seemed tight against his solid frame. He hesitated before approaching. Angling his head upward, he swept his eyes across the façade of townhouses, skipping from window to window—as if he'd known she'd be watching.

Isabella ducked back, but not before his gaze snagged hers. La, what a shame. She should have known she'd be discovered. Father had likely already filled Lord Livingstone's mind with a perfect and delightful image of her, and on top of that, he would now believe her desperate and silly.

Which she certainly was not.

Well, not desperate, that is.

"Did you see him, Miss Gresham?" Bridget had taken the chair by the hearth, already pulling Isabella's untouched needlework into her lap. If Father knew dear Bridget was the cause of the lovely finished pieces, he would be gravely disappointed.

He would not discover the secret, though, for Bridget would never tell and Isabella's conscience suffered no pains over the matter. If only her maid might perform Isabella's piano-forte lessons too.

"Yes, though I admit I could see very little of him." Isabella went back to the window, confirmed that he'd already been invited inside, and opened the sash window for a breath of fresh air. "I imagine he is much like anyone else. Though to hear Father talk, even the King with all his wealth and decadence would not be a better match."

The slight breeze brushed at her curls, the air smelling of chimney smoke, a fusion of flower scents, and the unfavorable stench of horse dung from the cobblestone street. For all her anticipation of the season, now that it was here, she couldn't help missing their country estate in Northumberland. Life at Sharottewood Manor may be lacking in balls, promenades, theatres, rides in the park, and eligible suitors—though that was more to Father's chagrin than her own—but there was one thing Sharottewood had that London did not.

Clean, fresh, country sea air.

"Then he was not handsome?" asked Bridget.

"From the distance, yes. But I once spied a red-coated soldier on the quay back home and thought him very captivating. Not ten steps closer, I realized my error."

"Oh?"

"He had no teeth."

"Oh."

A giggle tickled through Isabella as she hurried the window shut and whirled back to her maid. "I can sit still not a moment longer. We must decide upon a dress for the ball tonight. Something exquisite that will make even Sophia Kettlewell envious." She threw open her wardrobe doors, pulled out three silk gowns, and hugged them all to her chest as she did a small spin around the bedchamber. "Which one, dear?"

"Perhaps the—"

"And pray, do not choose the white. The embroidery is lovely, but bright color is of the essence."

"Then pink?"

"Pink it shall be." Isabella dropped herself on the bed, stared upward, and let out a sigh. "Bridget?"

"Yes, miss?"

"Perhaps Lord Livingstone *is* handsome. Perhaps he is charming and engaging and just as extraordinary as Father seems to believe him."

"Perhaps so."

"Anyway, I shall meet him tonight. If he is handsome and interesting—and good like Father—the rest does not matter to me."

"The rest, miss?"

Isabella rolled over on the bed, doubtless wrinkling her gowns. The pain struck her again. Dull, faint, and small enough she could push it back before her maid had a chance to notice.

For the thousandth time in her life, she was back at the staircase. Hiding in the late-night shadows. Wrapping her fingers around the wood as the scene played out before her nine-year-old eyes.

Isabella resisted the memory, but it came anyway. Her parents' candlelit faces. The tears. The quiet words they'd exchanged and the hollow realities such words had driven into Isabella's soul.

No, the rest did not matter.

Some girls whispered and dreamed and giggled about the noble prospect of waiting for a match hallowed by true, enchanted love.

Isabella had no such intentions.

She was not even certain such love could exist.

Nothing made sense. Rain slashed down on William, seeping into his shirtsleeves, turning the dry bloodstains on his cravat into pink.

He ripped it from his neck and slung it away from him. The horse plodded onward. Hooves plunking along the muddy, rutted road.

The road taking him from Rosenleigh.

From Shelton.

Numbness chased away the pain, chilling its way into the deep caverns of William's soul. He'd left the body in the darkness. The labyrinth. He should have stayed. He should have buried him. He'd buried Ahearn. Why hadn't he buried Shelton?

The promise. That wretched, demented promise had made William retreat like a coward. He'd told no one. He'd sprinted to the stables, and without awaking Mr. Nolan or arousing a bark from the dog, William had saddled a chestnut stallion named Duke.

Then he'd ridden through the gates. Into the night.

And done the one thing he'd sworn he wouldn't do.

Run.

What is happening? William rubbed a wet, shaking hand down his face. Countryside spread out before him, rolling and green and hazy through the afternoon downpour, smelling earthy and sickening. *My God, please help me. Help me think.*

He needed the fog, the confusion, to leave his head. He needed a plan. A direction. Something tangible he could hold on to and strive for, to keep him from teetering over the abyss of grief.

Leave Rosenleigh. His home.

Find Edward Gresham. His father. *My father?*

How could that be? Why the lies all these years? Why the danger? The attempts on his life? The murder?

His head pounded with questions, too many to cope with. He had answers for none of them and he could not think.

He was cold.

Colder than the rain. Colder than the wet clothes clinging to his skin. Colder than anything he'd ever known in his life.

What am I going to do?

Across the ballroom, Lord Livingstone was barely visible among the feather plumes and colorful dresses crowding around him.

But Isabella had seen enough to confirm her suspicions. He *was* handsome.

"For you, my dear." Stepping closer, Father held out a goblet of lemonade with moisture dots frosting the glass. A smile stretched his lips. "On our next chance alone, I must relate to you the details of my visit with Lord Livingstone. He is a most remarkable young man."

"It seems you are not the only one with such an opinion." Grinning,

Isabella nodded toward the ladies tittering and blushing in Lord Livingstone's presence, just as the orchestra burst into its first reel.

"Can a man help it if he is desirable?" Father said over the music.

"Undoubtedly not." But his lordship certainly did not seem to be doing much to dissuade the attention, either. The last thing she wanted was a dandy who had feigned love to a thousand eager young women who were not wise enough to—

"Isabella." The tone was serious, low, and rare enough to make discomfort push through her.

She met Father's eyes. "Yes?"

"For once in your life, try." Emotion skittered across his face and pushed together his greying brows. He brushed a quick hand down her cheek, chucked under her chin, and walked away.

Guilt flickered through her. Had she been selfish? For three years, Father had been adorning her with the finest clothes, presenting her into society with pride, and nudging wealthy suitors into her path.

All of whom she had turned away. She'd scarcely given them a chance. But how could she?

They were dull, predictable, and far too easily enamored with her. Even though she did not entertain foolish thoughts of love in matrimony, she still could not hold with the idea of being espoused to someone uninteresting.

She sipped the lemonade, cool and tangy, and found a quiet seat upon the green velvet ottoman along the wall. Most days, she would be dancing by now. Or examining the sugar sculptures with her quizzing glass. Or leaning close to her chattering friends as they made blushing remarks about the dandies or told scandalous stories of the girls not present.

But Father's words doused her spirit. *Try.*

In the center of the ballroom, couples joined another set, the orchestra played a familiar cotillion, and the hum of conversation lessened as gentlemen and ladies became engrossed in watching the dance.

"Miss Gresham?"

Isabella twitched in surprise—and glanced up into the face staring down at her.

Lord Livingstone. He was dressed in a double-breasted frock coat, black pantaloons, and a cravat knotted to perfection. His hair and side whiskers were dark, glistening, with a hint of silver at the roots that seemed premature for his young face.

But his eyes were what startled her. They did not ask nor beg to be held—they demanded. Intensity rippled from his being, in a way that was both discomfiting and intriguing.

He turned to Mr. Hornyold—an Oxford man whom Father had once encouraged her toward—and urged him to make an introduction.

Mr. Hornyold frowned but obliged. "Miss Gresham, this is Lord Livingstone. Lord Livingstone, Miss Gresham." Then, as if aware he was no longer needed, he skulked away.

Lord Livingstone stepped closer. "I admit I had ideas of your beauty after spotting you in the window this morning."

A rush of heat moved to her cheeks. Mercy! How bold to speak of such a thing, the rogue.

"But I daresay, you far exceed what I had imagined." Without waiting for her to respond and likely sensing she wasn't sure how even if she could, he held out his gloved hands. "Will you allow me your company and the next dance?"

He asked the question, but with a confidence that seemed to expect only one answer.

She gave it to him, a little to her own surprise. "Yes."

Lights from the windows stabbed the night, glowing orange against a world turning blue and dark.

William approached the timber-framed inn. Wind whistled through the wet trees, misting the air with moisture and sending a chill through him. "Come on, Duke." He led the horse to a one-room stable, the structure as splintered and grey as the inn itself, and left his horse with a scruffy-faced youth.

Then he entered the inn. Harsh lights pierced his eyes—candles lit at the crowded wooden tables, pewter sconces on the dingy taproom walls, a blazing fire in the hearth.

William coughed against the heavy smoke and odor of unwashed bodies. He eased his way through the room without bumping anyone, then pressed close enough to the hearth that the heat burned away some of his cold.

Miss Ettie flashed to his mind. He tried not to think of what she'd said, or how she'd looked when she found William missing. She'd probably gone to the nursery. Locked herself inside. Wept for him, as if she'd never see him again.

But she would. William would be back. Rosenleigh was his—the first thing in his life that had truly been *his*—and as soon as he gleaned answers from Edward Gresham, William would return.

Whether anyone tried to stop him or not.

"A toast, me men!" On William's left, a man clambered upon a wooden chair, sloshing the ale from his tankard as he thrust it into the air. "To the marauders wot been brave enough to take from them that has plenty. Long life to the lot o' them. And long life to me!"

A drunken applause filled the room, loud enough that William's head split with pain. He would have faced the fire again, but something stopped him.

Filthy men, some bearded and most ragged, chortling and emptying their earthenware tankards and shouting and staring at the man on the chair—

Except one.

A man in the corner, elbows on the table, hair bushy under a ratty continental hat, and eyes narrowed enough they might have been closed.

But they weren't. They were deadlocked on William.

"Lodgings for ye, gent?" A small, shorn-headed man approached, wiping his hands on his grimy apron. "Two pence it be, and more if ye be wantin' fed."

William pulled the coinage from his pocket, then followed the man to a doorway, up a creaking flight of stairs, and into an unlit hall.

"Hate to hear them toastin' to the likes o' murderin' marauders, like they be kings and such." The proprietor seemed at ease with the darkness, as he stopped at a door and pushed it open. "Disgrace to crown and country. Drunken fools."

William entered the sparse room, a shiver working through him.

"You want I should bring dry clothes for ye? Hain't got nothing so fancy as those, but they be warm." At William's nod and another coin, the proprietor left, promising to return with food and dry clothes.

Exhaustion pulled William to the edge of the bed. Elbows on his knees, he dropped his face into his hands and willed the pain to leave his head.

And his soul.

Show me what to do, God. Throughout his life, his aunt had taken Horace and himself to a large brick manor. Mostly, William had been forced to stay in the hot carriage, where he'd sweated for hours and tried to entertain himself by twisting the buttons on the carriage cushions—or when he was older, watching the outdoor servants busy with their chores.

But once or twice, his aunt had brought him inside. He remembered well, because it was the few times in his life he remembered his aunt speaking softly to him. She had held his hand, laughed at him, and called him a "darling boy" to the kind-faced Lord Manigan.

The earl had always responded the same, a tender look in his eye, "He is the picture of his mother."

Perhaps if Lord Manigan knew William's mother so well, he would also know Edward Gresham. A faint chance, perhaps, but it was the only one he had.

The stairs creaked again.

William lifted his head as footsteps reached the hall and thudded quietly. Too quietly. Unease sparked through him and he groped for the door to feel for a lock.

None.

He backed up and found the window. He yanked it open and swung a leg out, air trapped in his lungs. Should have lit a candle. Should have braced something against the—

The door burst open. A shot exploded.

William sprang from the window, smacked the ground on his side, and rolled. Breathless from the impact, he scampered to his feet and darted around the back of the inn, ducking under each window.

The stable loomed in sight.

He hesitated at the corner of the inn, but it was too dark to see if anyone awaited him in the shadows. He sprinted into the open anyway.

No shot rang out, and when he stumbled into the stable, even the unkempt boy was gone.

Without taking time to saddle his horse, William leaped on the animal's back and spurred him through the open stable door. The night swallowed them. Duke galloped into darkness.

A shiver raced through William as the lights of the inn disappeared behind him and the severe reality settled in his brain.

Whoever wanted him eliminated was finished playing games. It no longer mattered if his death was deemed an accident.

They simply wanted him dead.

CHAPTER 3

No one had followed him. At least he assumed. He was still alive.

William trotted Duke through the massive brick-and-iron entrance gate. He followed the pea-gravel drive as it curved through green countryside, the rolling meadows dotted with herds of sheep and flower-blooming trees.

He dismounted before the towering brick manor. For all his aversion to running, he easily could have done so now. What would Lord Manigan say to his arrival? Years had passed since his aunt had last brought him. Would the earl even remember? Or see William?

Hunger tightened his stomach, a reminder that he hadn't eaten in two days. Or slept. Or stopped running. If nothing else, perhaps the earl would permit William a chance to care for his horse, maybe even rest a few hours, before he started off again.

Rubbing the grime from his face with his sleeve, he ascended the entrance steps and knocked on the white-painted door. His legs twitched. He glanced behind him twice, scanning the area, just as he'd been doing all night.

Nothing.

No one lurking behind a wall or building or peering at him from beneath a continental hat.

The double doors pulled open. A pristinely dressed butler stared at William. Up and down, his expression dubious, and his fists large enough that if he wanted to grab William by the coat and send him hurling down the steps, he probably could have.

At least today.

"I must see Lord Manigan."

"Impossible."

"It is a matter of great importance. I must see him imm—"

"The servant entrance is around the back of the house." The butler wrinkled his nose. "Although you will find it futile to gain employment, you might persuade one of the scullery maids into sparing you a bite of bread."

Indignation lightninged through him. "I did not come for bread."

"Then it seems there is nothing we might do for you."

"All I ask is that you tell him I am here. William Kensley of Rosenleigh. Tell him—"

"Again, impossible. I must ask you to leave immediately."

"I shall fight my way in if I must."

The giant hands fisted tighter. The butler motioned with his head, then a brawny footman appeared next to him in wig and livery. "An unwise decision, sir, I assure you."

Unwise or not, he had no choice. In one swift motion, he seized the butler's neckcloth and slung him outside, delivering a strike to his jaw and shoving him toward the stairs.

Behind, a blow landed at the base of William's neck. He hunkered, turned, then came back up with a fist crashing into the footman's nose.

A returning blow struck his face.

Then another.

William charged the large chest and barreled the man through the double doors, and they smacked together onto the cool marble floor. They rolled thrice. William was pinned under the huge body, his neck snapping back and forth with each punch, but he rammed his forehead into the footman's and pushed back on top.

He raised his fist for another strike when—

Hands grabbed him from behind. Hauled him up. Slung him back out the double doors, down the steps, and into the gravelly dirt.

William swallowed blood.

The butler stood over top of him, two other footmen flanking each side. "Lock him in the tack room and send someone for the constable." The butler wiped his busted mouth. "This insolent beggar shall be gaoled, if not worse, for such invasion and violence."

The footmen dragged William back to his feet, took him to the stables, and threw him in a dark tack room that reeked of leather, hay, and horse manure.

The door slammed shut.

And locked.

William leaned back against the wall, draping his arms over his knees, dropping his head into his arms. Dull pain throbbed through him, but it was nothing compared to the disappointment racking his brain. What now?

Despite his efforts to keep them open, his eyes drifted shut. He might have missed a chance to see Lord Manigan, the constable may be coming for him, and he might be thrown inside a village lock-up.

But at least he could rest his eyes without fearing a bullet.

That was something.

"I am dreadfully weary, Isabella. Should we not return?"

Isabella did not so much as spare a glance at her companion trudging behind her. Nonsensical girl. Must she always be determined against adventure?

Indeed, if Father wished to invite Lilias Trewman back to Sharottewood after the season, Isabella would despair. She'd have even fewer chances to sneak away and ride along the moonlit seaside, or explore deeper into her caves, or roam the beach for flotsam and jetsam.

Isabella continued her pace until they reached the northwest enclosure of Hyde Park. From here, the Serpentine River, the impressive park wall, and the distant Kensington Gardens were all in view—lovely as anything she'd ever seen.

In London, that is.

Nothing compared to Sharottewood and the seashore back home. *Her* seashore.

"Is it not grandly wonderful, dear?"

Lilias Trewman huffed and collapsed her parasol with a sigh. She fluttered a handkerchief from her reticule. "Exhausting, I say. You know

I've just recovered from the most strenuous cold." She blew her nose. "I cried all day and night yesterday because I could not attend the Sundland ball, even though Mother *did* chide me that tears would only worsen my state. Was it a splendid ball?"

Splendid?

Of that she was uncertain. She had been curiously somber and reflective after Father's reprimand, which was neither usual for her nor him.

But then Lord Livingstone had approached. He was an enigma in every sense and had swept her into more dances than she should have permitted. Why had she allowed him such liberties? Was it Father's quiet admonishment? A sense of guilt and duty?

Or, for once, a true desire in herself?

"Sweet heavens, Isabella. You make me ready to cry again with strange looks like that."

Isabella glanced at her companion. The girl was young, slender, and always modishly dressed—and though education and etiquette were inbred in her, she lacked the pleasing features to make her the object of very many suitors.

Perhaps that could account for her sour temperament.

But with no mother or aunt to fill the role of chaperone and companion, Isabella would have to do with Lilias. At least she was a loyal friend.

"Tell me now what I missed, or I shall simply go mad with wondering."

"You are as wickedly curious as Bridget—except she has the good grace to only look at me with questions instead of asking them outright." Isabella walked closer to the banks of the river, squinting as the bright sun played and danced on the rippling water. "You remember my father's mention of a Lord Livingstone?"

"Of Wetherbell Hall?"

"The same."

"La, yes. Indeed, Sophia Kettlewell wrote me only this morning to tell me of his charms, but that he seemed singularly entranced with one young—"Lilias grasped her arm. "Oh, do you mean to say *you* are the one he danced so many dances with?"

A laugh leaked out. "Indeed."

Lilias groaned. "I knew I would miss something wonderful. Has he sent flowers? Or come to visit?"

"Not yet."

"But I am certain he shall. You are too beautiful to resist. If I were half so lovely, I would have been married three seasons ago. I do hope it is not terrible to say, but I often wonder if you shall marry at all. Indeed, I shall likely write back to Sophia Kettlewell that she has no need to despair over Lord Livingstone's infatuation, for you shall soon put an end to it, I am sure." The girl wiped her nose again with the handkerchief and turned back the way they'd come. "Come along now, Isabella, for I am simply too hot to continue in this wretched heat and. . .why, who is that?"

Isabella tore her gaze from the river.

Approaching fast with a walking stick and a tall beaver hat was the very figure she had danced with the night before.

Emotion bubbled through her. Had he been following her? What sort of thing was that to do? Why had he not done the customary, like sending flowers or visiting her townhouse, instead of lurking behind her like a thief in alley shadows?

Within a few feet, he removed his hat and bowed, leaving her unsure if his actions delighted or unsettled. "Good afternoon, ladies."

Isabella and Lilias curtsied in unison. Neither spoke.

"Imagine the unlikelihood of a meeting such as this." Did he really think she was simple enough to imagine he had not followed them?

She almost laughed or confronted his falsehood in jest—but his eyes pierced through her. Like daggers, they were dark and careful, coupled with an expression she could not read.

And almost didn't want to.

Fidgeting with her glove and looking away, she grinned. "Would you care to join us, my lord?"

"It is my utmost pleasure." He stepped between her and Lilias, offered an arm to them both, and escorted them back through the park as a trio.

Twice, she almost slithered her hand away. She didn't know why. How silly of her. Why should she be afraid of such proximity to the first man who had ever intrigued her?

But his touch was as frightening as his eyes.

An enigma, indeed.

"William Kensley." The name was spoken just the same as when William was a child. The eyes were the same too. Kind and steady and knowing, as if he understood all the things William could not say, just as Shelton had.

Pain gashed through him, tearing anew through fresh wounds. Wounds that still hurt. Would always hurt. Mayhap scar someday, but never go away.

"Sit down, sit down." Lord Manigan gestured across the tall-ceilinged drawing room, where afternoon light brightened the blue lounge and chairs, a harp, a yellow-and-blue Turkish rug, and polished wooden furniture.

A fine change from the tack room.

"You must accept my apologies, dear boy, for the atrocious treatment you have endured since your arrival. I can assure you my butler and manservants shall be dealt with. Had they remembered your name from years past, this would not have happened."

"They could not have known." As the earl took one of the wingback chairs, William took the lounge. His limbs sank deep into the plush cushions, and the last of his energy seeped out of him. "I thank you, my lord, for seeing me."

"Always a pleasure. How fares your aunt and cousin?"

"Well, thank you."

"And Rosenleigh?"

"Well."

The earl leaned forward, eyes narrowing, probing. "And you, my son?"

The question hung on silence. William swallowed hard and looked out the bowed window, where two collared doves fluttered in and out of sight. "I must find a man named Edward Gresham. My father."

"Your father?"

"You are surprised?"

"No." He cleared his throat. "I suppose I should be, but I never quite believed the story of Constance's husband and his death. For despite the gravestone next to hers, I myself never saw the man living or dead. But Edward. . ."

William glanced back at the earl's face. The greying hair, the faint wrinkles, the square jaw and thoughtful look. "Edward what?"

"He loved your mother. I suppose a lot of us did in those days."

"Why were they not wed?"

"Gossipmongers had it many ways. Some said she was not dainty enough for him. Others said he was not delightful enough for her." The earl leaned back into his chair. "But for myself, I always imagined it was a matter of money. Or the threat of scandal. Perhaps both."

"Then my father knew of me."

"That I do not know."

Something coursed through him. Something he didn't understand. Like the queer detachment, the faint bitterness, when he stood before his mother's painting and looked into a face that had left him.

But her abandonment had been without choice.

His father's had not.

"What can you tell me of him?" William asked.

"Very little, I fear, other than the fact that he is a viscount and lives in a country estate called Sharottewood. He is in London at the moment. I can give you the address, for only recently I received an invitation from him to attend a soiree for many of us Tories." The earl rose, crossed the room to a brass-inlaid writing desk, and scribbled words onto paper.

When he handed it to William, however, more than just the address was enclosed. A bank note. "Sir, I do not want—"

"You shall need funds for your journey."

"But I—"

"You have told me very little about your circumstance, my son, and I shall in no wise prod." He pressed his hand to William's shoulder. "But you have arrived at my estate in dire shape. You are weary, haggard, and very much distressed. That much is clear." A squeeze. "Tonight, you shall wash, rest, and eat. The funds are yours."

"I shall repay you with my return."

"I have no doubt but that you will." Lord Manigan smiled. "Now, what say you to a hot meal and a game of cribbage?"

William forced a smile, nodded, and followed the earl from the drawing room. He tightened his fist around the address. Like fire, it scorched his skin, spreading through him in hot and bursting flames.

His father had not wanted him. Had never wanted him.

Mayhap now, however, that was not enough.

Mayhap now he wanted his son dead.

Another minute of this and she'd die.

Isabella rippled her fingers down the length of the ivory keys, pounded the last high note with strength, and zipped from her chair so fast she nearly toppled it over. She was tempted to rip the sheet music for "Robin Adair" in two, the dashed song. Why was Father so insistent she waste beautiful daylight making such raucous noise?

At home, she would have rushed out to the stables. Or begged Bridget into accompanying her in a search for wildflowers. Or trekked alone to the seashore, where she would have unlaced her half boots and ambled across the burning sand.

A sigh filled her. No such diversions were available in London. Tonight, Lord Livingstone had promised to escort her and Lilias to the theatre, where a five-act Shakespearean play was on the program.

But that was hours away. She had need of something to do with herself *now*.

With a listless hum, she roamed through the different rooms—peering into Father's empty study, slipping to the kitchen to tease the ill-humored cook, and visiting her own chamber to find Bridget dozing over more needlework.

Finally, Isabella pulled on a bonnet and went outside, slipped around the small iron fence, and moved beneath a townhouse window. Colorful daffodils, roses, syringa, and cornflowers all lifted their faces toward the late morning sun. Green vines dangled from the flower box, swaying below the window, leaves jiggling like tiny hands clapping their joy.

She plucked a pink rose, careful not to prick her fingers, then turned—

On the walk, a gentleman leaned against a streetlight. His eyes brushed hers.

She whirled around, pretended interest in a drooping cornflower. Then, when ample time had passed, she glanced back over her shoulder.

This time, the gentleman did not meet her gaze. His stance had straightened. No longer leaning against the lamp, he faced the Gresham townhouse with his shoulders squared and his eyes pinned to the door—almost as if it daunted him.

She didn't imagine the man could be daunted by anything, though.

Not by the look on his face. What was he about? Why did he not knock? He was not tall, yet taller than herself or Father, with no top hat and windswept, deep-golden hair. His features were pleasant, jaw defined, eyes darkly lashed and serious.

That is, until they sought hers again. A flicker of amusement entered his gaze, and he acknowledged her gaping with a slight bow.

Isabella frowned, and as he approached, she returned to her flower box with exaggerated concentration. How bothersome of him to laugh at her for staring, when *he* was the one who stood before *her* townhouse without invitation.

Unless he was another prospect from Father. But surely not two at the same time. Had Father forgotten about Lord Livingstone so quickly?

"A wise friend once told me that if you speak to flowers, they shall grow all the better for it. But judging by your great interest in these, they must be speaking back."

Isabella snapped her gaze to him, brows rising. Was he teasing her?

The easy smile that followed answered her question.

And annoyed her further.

"I trust you are come for one of two reasons, sir, either of which shall leave you disappointed." She inched up her chin. "One, to attend business matters with Lord Gresham, whom I fear has been hastened to Bath this morning on a trip of indeterminable days."

"And two?"

"To woo his daughter."

"Who is also on a trip?"

"No. Who has already hopelessly been wooed by another." Well, nearly so. After all, Lord Livingstone *did* garner her curiosity—and that was more than she could say for anyone else Father had tried to espouse her with.

The gentleman's smile widened more fully. "Then I shall waste no more of your time. . .Miss Gresham. Tell your flowers they may carry on." With one more glance, if a sober one, to the townhouse door, the strange gentleman turned and walked away.

Isabella stared after him longer than she should have. Who could he be? And what could he want with Father—or her?

My sister. Like the constant *clip-clop* of the hackney wheels on cobbles, the words clunked over and over. *Sister?* Why had he not considered the possibility before?

William had prepared himself to face the man who had forsaken him. He'd gone through the words in his head. The way he'd look. The questions he'd ask.

But he hadn't been prepared to set eyes on his *sister.* She was small and slender, even when she'd tiptoed to reach the flower box beneath the window. Black ringlets had peeked out from her straw bonnet, and the face that looked up at him had been youthful, flushed, and pretty.

An unbidden ache slithered through him. How often as a child had he longed for someone to play with? Someone who would not strike him? Or run to his aunt? Or chortle from the other side of the door when William was locked in solitude?

He tried not to imagine what it would have been like to have a sister to befriend him.

Or a father to love him.

When the hackney deposited him in front of a white-bricked inn, he paid the jarvey, passed a shingle reading THE SILVER LYNX INN, and entered through an arched doorway. He scanned the public room in one swift glance.

No brooding eyes. No continental hat.

He paid for his room and went upstairs, locked the door, and checked both windows. Nothing stirred below but a swarm of flies from dung piles smeared into the cobbles. The pungent odor intensified with the sight.

Perhaps better lodgings could have been found, but funds were not plentiful.

Nor were they his own.

He would pay Lord Manigan back, though. He would get the answers he came for. He would return to Rosenleigh and see that Shelton's grave was proper and reverent.

But in the meantime, he would learn more of this sister of his.

That and stay alive.

The stranger had come again.

Twice.

The first time, Isabella had been descending the stairs, and on the fourth step down, the butler's scratchy voice and the stranger's steadier one drifted to her ears through the hall. The words were lost on her.

The second time, she had been entertaining Lord Livingstone in the parlor. She'd been close enough to the window to glimpse the stranger disembark from a hackney. Minutes later, he climbed back in and the carriage rolled away.

Lord Livingstone must have detected her distraction, for he'd leaned forward and frowned, teacup clattering back to its saucer. "Something is amiss."

Mercy! Such perception. Was she flattered by his meticulous scrutiny of her—or like everything else about him, was she only intrigued by it? Whatever the case, she'd laughed and called him silly and bidden him to finish his tea.

But today the stranger was back. Yet again. Why?

Isabella pressed herself to an upstairs, rain-drizzled hall window. He must have forgone a hackney today—a poor choice, considering the sudden rain shower moments ago—for he walked the flagway in drenched clothes, brushing water from his sleeves and wiping a wet face.

When he approached the townhouse door, he disappeared from her line of vision.

But not from her line of thought. He was tangled there—annoyingly so—as he had been for the past week. Many men called upon her father. Many called upon her.

But it was the persistence, the look on his face, the way he strode to the townhouse door every other day with his shoulders braced and taut, as if prepared for. . .what?

Such mystery was unbearable. She must satisfy herself, else she'd go mad wondering. "Bridget?"

Her maid emerged from Isabella's bedchamber, wet stains on her pinafore, hands pink from swishing warm water in the copper tub.

"I am desirous to take a walk. You must fetch our bonnets and umbrellas at once."

"But your bath—"

"How much better to take it after our exertion? Besides, I shall look pale and drawn for the dinner party tonight if I do not take on some form of exercise, shan't I?" Isabella turned back to the window, anticipation coursing through her. Below, the stranger was already departing with long strides. "Bridget, make haste!"

They were following him.

And trying very much to appear as if they weren't.

William kept his pace even. Slow enough they might gain on him, yet fast enough they would think him unaware. How could he be anything but?

They had emerged from the townhouse not two minutes after his own departure, and though he'd glanced back only once, he'd found both sets of eyes pinned to him from the shadows of their umbrellas.

Umbrellas they would need, no doubt.

As he crossed Hinckley Court, the street leading from the illustrious Mulcaster Square, he glanced up at the pewter-colored sky. Heavy clouds billowed, made darker by the black smoke rising from townhouse chimneys. The air was moist, tropical, cool to his face.

Then a drop landed on his forehead. Another torrent unleashed.

He ducked to the left under a birch tree, which hovered its leafy branches over a dripping iron fence and bench. Cold seeped through his already-drenched clothes, spurring a shiver through his body.

He should have taken the hackney. He would have.

But something had seemed wrong.

The public room had been crowded this morning. Youths gambled in the corner of the room, hovering beneath a table as if they imagined its four wooden legs would keep them hidden. Innkeepers bustled about with aprons and steaming breakfast plates. Patrons conversed in various groups, the whiff of their unwashed bodies, black coffee, and mutton breakfasts mingling into an unpleasant stench.

Then the jarvey. The one who'd driven William to and from the Gresham townhouse this past week, with his long chin and thin whiskers and yellowed teeth. He'd been leaning against a beam toward the back end of the room, facing a stranger, nodding his head several times.

The stranger wore no continental hat.

But his eyes had found William.

And lingered.

Perhaps it was nothing. His imagination. The result of too little sleep and too much confusion—

"Excuse me."

William turned.

Standing before him, with rain waterfalling over one green and one blue umbrella, were his two indiscreet followers.

Miss Gresham wore a slight flush of pleasure, a small smile, though she seemed less certain of herself than she had upon their last encounter.

The girl accompanying Miss Gresham looked pale and horrified.

"I hope you do not think me brazen, but as you are occupying the only place of shelter to be found, I wonder if we might join you?"

He shifted aside, closer to the bench, allowing both ladies to take a place beneath the boughs. "It seems we have all made quite the fools of ourselves today."

Miss Gresham's face snapped to him. Color flooded her cheeks. "What can you mean, sir?"

Grinning, he motioned toward the downpour surrounding them. "Our choice of walking was hardly sensible."

"Oh." She breathed something between a sigh and a laugh. "Indeed."

Silence fell between them, as thick and pelting as the rain on the stone flagway.

Miss Gresham spun her umbrella slightly on her shoulder, feigned great interest in surveying surroundings she likely already knew by heart, then made several quiet remarks to the girl she called Bridget on the inconveniences the weather sometimes inflicted.

Then, with half-bashful and half-cunning eyes, she lifted her face back to his. "Do tell us, Mr. . . ." She raised a brow. "La, but you have never given your name."

She knew of course that they'd spoken but once—and then without company or any mutual friend to make introductions. But curiosity, which seemed to be the instigator behind her pursuit of him, must have won against her sense of social etiquette.

He bent with a slightly exaggerated bow. "Mr. Kensley at your service, Miss Gresham."

"You know who I am."

"Certainly."

"A wonder indeed, for I have never seen you before, and I certainly did not introduce myself upon our last meeting."

He did not explain away her wonder, though the mystery had been no great one to unpuzzle. After all, no servant would have been dressed as she'd been that first day at the flower box—and certainly no one but Lord Gresham's daughter would speak so.

"Tell me, Miss Gresham." He leaned back against the tree and crossed his arms. "Have you any other siblings?"

"What a strange question. Where are you from, Mr. Kensley?"

"Now I fear that is unfair."

"Sir?"

"To refuse my question and then propose one of your own." The grin deepened until he might have laughed, but he forced back the mirth.

She tilted her head in compliance. "Very well. I have no siblings."

"And I am from Leicestershire."

"What brings you to London?"

"I believe it is my turn, is it not?" When she nodded him on, the humor drained from him, as quickly as the brown water flow raced around the stones and rushed away. "Is your mother yet living?"

The same seriousness tightened her own face. "No."

"I am sorry."

"Thank you. And as for the reason you are in London?"

"A mere personal matter."

"That is hardly an answer, sir."

"With your father."

"Still uninformative."

"Yet I fear it shall have to do for now." He leaned off the tree and glanced at the dubious companion, whom he suspected to be a maid of sorts judging by the pinafore poking out from under her cashmere shawl. "Have you any questions for me, miss?"

The girl's face drained another shade whiter. "Oh no, sir. Not one."

Despite himself, a laugh trickled out. "Then as we have run out of questions"—he glanced to the lightening sky and lessened rain—"and the storm seems to be abating, I shall be on my way. May I escort you back, or will you continue your walk?"

"No, we shall continue our walk." As if she were unwilling for him to imagine he had been the sole purpose for their stroll in the first place. "But there is something you might do for me."

"Oh?"

"I am to have a dinner party this evening, yet the company is at odd numbers. Would you join us and set us to evens?"

"A reward for sharing my tree?"

Amusement crinkled her eyes. "Yes. A reward for sharing your tree."

"Very well. I shall be there."

"Wonderful." Looping her arm with Bridget's, and twirling her umbrella yet again, Miss Gresham walked into the misty drizzle. "Good day, Mr. Kensley."

"Good day." *Sister.*

Lilias arrived much sooner than the others, but that was no great surprise. Where gentlemen or wine were present, Lilias was almost always first to appear, for she did delight in both.

In her red and lilac gown, with her flaxen hair pulled back in a chignon, the girl exaggerated a frown—though her eyes still gleamed with anticipation. "I have yet to see a more wretched day as this. I could neither take a stroll nor post my letter nor paint on the balcony, for it has either rained or hinted of rain, and with this cold of mine I—"

"Never mind all that." Isabella seized her hand and whisked the girl upstairs to her bedchamber. She plopped back to her dressing table, where Bridget resumed rubbing pomade on her hair strands, wrapping them with paper, then pressing them with the hot papillote iron. "You must promise to aid me this evening. I am most in need of your help."

"Do not ask anything strenuous of me." Lilias sat on the edge of the bed. "Remember my cold."

"A certain gentleman will be in attendance tonight. One about whom I know very little."

"Oh?"

"You must be my secret comrade in clever conversation."

"Conversation meant to entrap him?"

"Into lending us answers, yes." As Bridget finished the last curl, Isabella patted them closer to her head, the soft and bouncy tresses tickling her jaw and neck. Through the looking glass, she met Bridget's eyes first. Bridget bit her lip and seemed to plead that Isabella abandon such nonsense.

Lilias, though, communicated no such cautions. From the edge of the bed, she cocked her head and grinned and even wiggled her brows, as if to say that Isabella need not worry.

They would find the answers they were after.

Indeed, Mr. Kensley would not stand a chance.

Uneasiness worked through William as he stood yet again before the

Gresham townhouse door. This time, however, he would not be sent away.

He would be invited in.

Although tutors and books had taught him every social propriety, his aunt had never permitted William to accept any invitation extended to him. He'd been instructed to decline every ball, soiree, and dinner party—while Horace attended alone.

Indeed, William had never even been to London until now. Had he ever traveled anywhere beyond Leicestershire?

Not that he'd minded.

He would have remained on Rosenleigh grounds the rest of his life, working alongside Shelton in the garden, riding Ahearn, teasing young Ruth, calming Miss Ettie's endless worries until she smiled and laughed again. Who would make her smile now? What more did she have to live for but her cold and empty nursery?

With a bitter taste climbing his throat, he lifted the brass ring in the mouth of the lion and tapped it against the door.

Seconds later, the dark-skinned butler ushered him inside. The hall was long and narrow, the lights dim, the air smelling of linseed oil and roses from a hand-painted vase on a stand. He was shown into a green sitting room, where three faces turned his way.

The first was a blond-haired girl perched on the edge of a chaise lounge, with plain features and a demanding, curious stare. The second was Miss Gresham, who rose to her feet and smiled.

The third a gentleman. Tall and broad, dark hair, somber eyes—and a clenched jaw that seemed the result of a sudden and distinct dislike for the newest occupant of the room.

A tight smile spread William's lips. "Good evening."

Isabella swept closer to him, all elegance in her blue evening gown, pearl necklace, and matching earbobs. Cheeriness bubbled from her, like water gurgling from a stone fountain. "Mr. Kensley, do meet Miss Lilias Trewman and Lord Livingstone."

William bowed to both.

The lady rose to curtsy, while the gentleman did little more than nod his head.

In a silence disturbed only by a clock on the mantel, all four took seats. Miss Gresham did her best to instigate conversation, but the room soon fell into silence, as Miss Trewman was too busy scrutinizing William, and Lord Livingstone was too busy glaring at him. Was such discomfort wont for dinner parties? Or was he especially unwelcome?

Perhaps his aunt had done him a service in forbidding him so many events.

At last, two more guests were introduced—a Miss Sophia Kettlewell and Colonel Nagel—after which a footman announced dinner. They followed the servant into the dining room, and each found their chair.

Miss Gresham took the head of the table, with Lord Livingstone to her right, and William was seated next to Miss Trewman, who smelled strongly enough of rosemary that he could scarcely smell the turtle soup steaming from tureens in the center of the table.

Murmurs began to fill the room, silver clinking glass, as the gentlemen engaged the women next to them and all began their soup.

Miss Trewman glanced over at William more than once, as if expecting him to speak. He wasn't certain what to say, however, so he said nothing.

That is, until Miss Kettlewell cleared her throat. "Mr. Kensley, all of us around this table are rather intimately acquainted, having spent more than one season together." She was a handsome girl with chestnut hair and dark-lashed eyes, dressed in vogue, though her sharp beauty was not as soft, delicate, and fresh as Miss Gresham's. "But pray, I fear we have not the pleasure of knowing you at all. Have you been long in London?"

"No, hardly. I arrived nearly a week ago."

"Do you intend to stay throughout the season?"

"My plans are not so determined." He spooned more soup. "I cannot say."

"La, to be a gentleman." This from Miss Trewman. She sighed. "Ladies can never go where they wish, when they wish, and depart just as easily. Everything must be decided for them, is it not so?"

A murmur of feminine agreement arose, though not with much conviction, and Miss Kettlewell skewered him again with another gaze. "I presume pleasures have brought you to town?"

"Matters of personal interest, actually."

At this, Miss Gresham's brows inched up. She'd been watching him since his arrival—quick glances, all hurried away so fast she likely imagined he did not notice.

Even if William had been blind, however, Lord Livingstone was not. His complexion grew greyer and his lips tightened with every glance.

"Who are your connections in London?" asked Miss Kettlewell.

"None to speak of."

"This is a puzzlement. Isabella, darling, you must explain how this came to be." With a smile, Miss Kettlewell turned to her hostess. "He denies any connections—yet here he sits, dining with us, likely laughing at us this very moment. Do explain it, won't you?"

"He has business with Father." The explanation, though clearly one she wasn't satisfied with herself, was spoken with confidence enough to silence Miss Kettlewell.

But not Miss Trewman. "What sort of business?"

All eyes turned upon him.

Clearing his throat, William reached for the platter of lamb cutlets. "You can hardly expect me to discuss matters involving his lordship"—he plopped a cutlet onto his plate—"without Lord Gresham present, can you?"

Miss Trewman huffed. "Oh, how droll. People are always giving me nonsensical responses to my very sensible queries. But tell us more of yourself." Was it his imagination, or did the girl keep slipping secretive glances at Miss Gresham? What had they done—made a pact to puncture him with questions until he bled out all his answers? To what purpose? That they might whisper of them and spread them about through all the silly gossipmongers in their circles?

His stomach roiled against the food. The memories. The cutting shards that had lodged themselves into his chest, until even breathing drew pain.

"Who are your parents?"

Sweat dampened his cravat. "My mother is dead."

"And your father?"

Silence.

He laid down his fork. He had no intention of sitting here and allowing himself to be torn apart. Be hanged if he'd satisfy them—

"Mr. Kensley, won't you pass the sweetbread au jus?"

He glanced back at Miss Gresham. Her eyes were on him again, but with more than curiosity or amusement. Warmth softened her stare.

As if she'd understood.

And put an end to the questions on his behalf.

What was she doing?

As the servants brought in the second course, even Lilias shot her a puzzled glance, as if to ask what in the world Isabella was thinking.

She hardly knew herself. But as the stranger sat in her dining room, two chairs down, with one question after another being hurled at him. . .

Well, enough was simply enough. She desired answers more than the rest of them, but even she could not sit and allow this. His eyes bore grief. She had not noticed until this very moment, but now she saw it so clearly that it could not be undone.

The way the vein bulged in his forehead. The tense bearing. The haunted expression, concealed so well, well enough she would never have noticed had it not been for his eyes.

Under the table, Lord Livingstone's hand snatched hers.

She sucked in a breath and glanced at him.

"You are infatuated."

She blinked at the quiet words, and as the footman lowered a platter of turkey in the center of the table, she made certain no one else had overheard.

They hadn't.

"Whatever do you mean?"

"Your guest. The one of mystery." His fingers tightened around hers. "He has been the object of your interest all evening."

"You are mistaken, my lord." Heat tickled along the back of her neck. She tugged against his grasp, but he did not release her fingers. "I admit to curiosity, but even Miss Trewman and Miss Kettlewell are guilty of those charges."

"I do not trust him."

"Why should you say such a thing?"

"Because it is definite in my mind. I wish you to stay away from him."

This time, she pulled her hand away hard enough for him to let go. Defiance sparked. "You need not take the part of my father just because he is absent. I assure you I am quite capable of remaining far from harm's way."

The skin tightened along his forehead. His eyes speared her, and for the first time, she noticed sweat beads above his lip. He opened his mouth, sucked in air—then turned his profile to her and said nothing.

Isabella flexed her fingers beneath the tablecloth, and for the remainder of the evening, her mind was jostled between the stranger two seats down...

And the stranger sitting next to her.

The night swallowed him. No starlight or moonbeams were strong enough to push through the overwhelming fog. He walked faster in the darkness between streetlamps.

Tonight had been unprofitable. He'd learned nothing of Lord Gresham, and the party had learned much about William. After dinner, the ladies had withdrawn to the sitting room for tea, and the gentlemen had remained at the table while a footman delivered stronger drinks.

William had declined his goblet of sherry.

Colonel Nagel and Lord Livingstone, however, imbibed more than one as they spoke of politics and press gangs and new military developments.

Then, as Lord Livingstone had drained the last drop of his third sherry, he turned to William. Deliberately, throughout the last half hour, the man had avoided William in every conversation, as if to worsen his sense of unwelcome.

Colonel Nagel, a stout gentleman with a greying queue, had done the same.

But in one swift moment, Lord Livingstone's full attention had narrowed in on William with a forceful stare that was likely meant to intimidate.

It didn't.

"At the risk of being disrespectful to the lady of the house, let me impart one warning to you, Mr. Kensley."

William had nodded him on.

"Just because Lord Gresham is away does not mean you may take advantage of his daughter by insinuating yourself into her company. You are, of course, but a complete stranger—and I shall take the liberty of ensuring you remain so."

"My business with his lordship makes me more attached to Miss Gresham than you might think." William had stood and removed his napkin. "As for how well we become acquainted, I believe that decision belongs to the lady herself." He had left then without goodbyes to anyone, and the demeaning threats of Lord Livingstone still rankled his nerves as he walked the streets.

Who did the man think he was? Was Miss Gresham affianced to him? Had Lord Gresham sanctioned such a match?

Yet another reason to dislike his father.

Ahead, windows glowing white in the blackness, The Silver Lynx Inn finally neared. William increased his speed, reached for the door—

"I wouldn't go in there if I was you."

Blood rushing to his face, William jerked to the voice in the darkness. He groped for the gun in his trousers, but a shadow flew forward and smacked the weapon from his hand.

Metal clattered to cobblestones at the same time his heart clattered to a stop.

"Follow me if you wants to stay a-breathing."

"Who are you?"

"Hurry up before I change me mind." After swooping the pistol from the ground, the shadow grabbed William's arm and urged him forward. "Me hackney's waiting over there. Get in and stay low."

That voice. The jarvey?

Panic hollowed William's stomach, but he climbed into the carriage and stayed put when the wheels lurched into motion. This was a trap. Whoever had whispered to the jarvey in the public room this morning had paid him to deliver William in the dead of night.

He could jump out now and face his assailant when he was less aware.

Or he could find out who wanted him dead.

Sooner than he thought, the hackney pulled to a stop in an alley black as sin. The door jerked open and the jarvey scrambled inside, breathing hard, whipping the hat from his head. "You best be thanking me saintly wife for this."

"For what?"

"Your life, for one." The jarvey fidgeted then dropped himself onto the carriage floor. "Just in case we was followed. Don't wants to get me head blowed off for—"

"What's this about?"

"Get down here."

William hunkered beside him, their knees crammed together in the small space. He sucked in air that reeked of grease and musty clothes. "Who paid you to do this?"

"What I gots paid for, I ain't done." The jarvey reached into a pocket, jangled coins in his hand. "Some bloke paid me near a pound to tell him where you go off to every day and what room you be staying in at the inn."

"You told him?"

"The room, I did. Bloke could've figured that out by asking anyone."

"And the other?"

A chortle rumbled out. "Cribbons Tavern, I told him, where you get foxed every day. I never said a word 'bout that fancy townhouse wot belongs to the viscount."

A breath eased out. "Thank you. I shall pay for your secrecy."

"No need. Like I said, you have me saintly wife to thank for this, 'cause every time I do some unchristian deed, she knows it right off and hauls me straight for the clergyman. Taxes a man's patience, that does. Best off just to save a man's life than deal with all the confession and repenting I gots to do."

"Who was the man?"

"Never said his name."

"Did he mention anything else?" William's fingers tightened around the edges of the seats. "Any reason why he should want me dead?"

"Don't you know?"

"No."

"I was pondering all day what it could be. Figured you must o' ran off with his wife or took his gingerbread or something. Whatever it was, good thing I stopped you from going in that room tonight."

"He was waiting for me."

"Saw him going up the steps meself."

"I cannot go back there."

"That's sure as the clergyman's Bible." The jarvey leaned up long enough to glance out the windows, even though it was too black to see if someone had been lurking. "There's a woman I know, kind o' stricken in years and cranky, but she lets a room or two for lodgings sometimes, and if I bring you there tonight, like as not she'll keep you."

William pulled himself back to the seat. "I would be obliged."

"It's nothing too fancy, but you'd be hidden well. Best too you find yourself another hackney from now on, case I'm followed." The man eased open the carriage door, waited, then jumped outside. "I'll be driving fast tonight, so hold on." He tossed something to William's lap. "And here's that. You'll be needing it."

Leaning back into the seat, William tightened both hands around the gun. A sickening anger curled through him, but he tried to push it away.

He was alive. He was escaping.

But he was no closer to knowing who wanted him dead. That thought gnawed at him deeper than his fear.

The chalk dust art on the ballroom floor had long since been destroyed by lively dancers.

Tapping her foot to the Scotch reel, Isabella reached for an iced punch from a servant's silver tray. The cool, fruity liquid chased away the stifling warmth from a room full of fifty guests and an hour of dancing.

The small pleasure dissipated, as thoughts of her own guest from this evening resurfaced. Why had Mr. Kensley departed so abruptly? Without a word to her even? Had he not enjoyed himself at all?

The punch swirled in her stomach. Of course he had not. They had badgered him—and even Miss Kettlewell, who had been oblivious to their plan, had thrown him one question after another.

All of which he seemed loath to answer. Why?

Ah, mercy. She must stop this at once. She had done her best to assuage her curiosity, had failed, and now must accept that she could do nothing more. She was only sorry Mr. Kensley, at the end of her little scheme, had been so uncomfortable as to leave her dinner party without a goodbye to anyone.

She was ashamed of herself.

"There you are."

Isabella jumped at the voice in her ear, turning as her punch sloshed the rim of the cup.

Lord Livingstone, with sweat darkening the tips of his hair, leaned closer. "I hope you are not too much exerted after so sprightly a dance."

"Not at all." She smiled, his breath warming her face, though the need to take a step back overcame her. "Dancing is the greatest diversion from any unpleasant thoughts."

"Which are?"

"You are too inquisitive."

"And you are flushed. Allow me." He took her punch, handed it to a servant, then took her arm. "We must find someplace where you might escape the heat and commotion."

"Ah, but Lilias shall be searching for me. She has retired to the dressing room in hopes a maid might remedy a tear in her hem, but when she is finished—"

"Then allow me to escort you there to meet her."

She almost declined the offer. She should have.

But he left no space for response and whisked her for the ballroom doors so fast she hadn't a chance to collect her thoughts. In the hall, candlelight reflected off gilded mirrors and gleamed on the marble floors, and the air dropped several degrees cooler.

"The dressing room is this way." Their shoes clicked on the floor, and with every step, his grip tightened on her arm.

She walked faster. The hall was empty, save for a manservant who brushed by them then disappeared toward the ballroom.

Lord Livingstone swept her into a three-window alcove.

Air whooshed from her lungs and a protest shaped her lips—

His mouth claimed hers.

Furious shock shivered through her as she pushed at his chest and ducked out of his arms. How dare he! She escaped the alcove, heart hammering, knees weakening as she glanced around her.

The hall remained empty.

No one had seen. How could he do such a thing? Didn't he know how easily such a scandal could leak into whispers that would spread with madness? She would be tainted if such a thing had been witnessed. Father's plans for her would be ruined. Her *future* would be ruined.

"Miss Gresham?"

She had imagined he would follow her, apologize for his untowardness, and beg her forgiveness like a repenting fool.

But he stood still in the darkness of the alcove, shadows playing on his face, eyes blazing through hers without any remorse. " 'Passions are liken'd best to floods and streams. The shallow murmur, but the deep are dumb. So when affection yields discourse, it seems—' "

"Do not speak poetry to me." She raised her chin, mouth burning with the sullying taste of him. "You have compromised me in the most ungentlemanly manner conceivable, and any hope you might have entertained of conquering my heart is finished."

"Not finished, Miss Gresham." A grin crooked his lips. He leaned into the alcove window, rustling the draperies, crossing his arms over his chest. "Only begun."

Heat flaming her cheeks, she glanced once more to make certain no one had seen, then fled down the hall for the dressing room. Inside, she watched a maid weave a needle and thread in and out of Lilias' green satin hem.

The anger morphed into resolution. Upon Father's return, she would make known to him her resolve.

She would never see Lord Livingstone again.

CHAPTER 4

Knocking on this door was becoming so habitual he no longer suffered from frayed nerves.

William took a step back, hands behind his back, and waited until the butler answered.

As always, the dark-skinned man frowned, shook his head, and closed the door. Today, however, it hurried back open.

"Er—you are requested in the sitting room, Mr. Kensley, if it is convenient for you."

That all depended. If Miss Gresham were inviting him in for another round of inquiries, it would not be convenient at all.

The butler's frown went tighter—a feat William would not have imagined possible. "Well?"

"Show the way, dear man." Biting back a grin at the butler's scowl, William followed him into the Gresham townhouse, through the hall, and back into the green sitting room.

Midmorning daylight cast the room into more cheerfulness, although the face staring at William from the chaise lounge was anything but.

"Miss Gresham." He bowed. "I trust you are well this morning?"

"Please, let us both spare ourselves the embarrassment of niceties, Mr. Kensley." She rose, smoothing a plain muslin dress and lifting her gaze to his neckcloth, but no farther. "I fear I was the most unbearable hostess anyone could ever be two evenings ago, and I wonder that you would return here at all."

"I think I speak in truth when I say you were the best hostess I ever had." The only one too, but he would spare her that detail.

His words, regardless, seemed to puzzle her. She cocked her head, black ringlets brushing her cheeks. "You are far too kind."

"Nonsense."

"Even so, please accept my apology."

"Accepted."

"Your business with my father, however mysterious, remains just that. *Your* business. I shall not attempt to pry again, rest assured."

Amusement nudged his lips upward. She seemed a great many things to him—rich, conniving, spoiled perhaps, and certainly no wise judge of suitors.

But she was genuine. Genuine to feelings. *His* feelings. Her apology sprang from no social obligation and her distress seemed only for the thought she had caused some to him.

"And now"—she plucked a stovepipe bonnet from the seat—"Bridget and I are off to visit the poor. I do not suppose you would care to join us? I promise most ardently not to be inquisitive."

A chuckle forced its way out, lightening the pressure that had been stacked in his chest for two days. "With a promise such as that, how can I refuse?"

She was not certain why she had invited Mr. Kensley along, except that she needed some diversion from the disappointed melancholy pressing upon her.

If only Father would return.

If only Lord Livingstone would not.

In the two days following the ball, he had written four letters and arrived unannounced twice. Both times she had told the butler to send him away. Why would his lordship not be put off? Surely if he cared anything for her at all, if he had imagined a future with her, he would not have stooped to such uncouth behavior.

Just her luck, that. To finally find a gentleman who did not bore her into slumber, only to discover the man had uncontrollable passions that might have easily sent her into ruin.

From across the carriage and beside Bridget, Mr. Kensley glanced for the third time out the window. Ever since their departure, he seemed uncommonly alert. Looking up and down the street before handing her into the carriage. Peering out the window with every new street. Sitting stiff and unrelaxed in his seat, as if ready at any moment to spring into action.

But his face denied any such cautions. He turned his eyes to her now, and the easiness of his expression calmed her.

What was it about him?

As much as she tried to tell herself she should not trust him, a mere stranger who could be capable of anything, she could not help but discern a goodness in him. He set her at ease. He seemed light and happy, yet at the same time bore traces of sadness. How could that be?

"Now that you have promised no questions, I feel I cannot ask any of my own."

"You are mistaken, Mr. Kensley. As I have no great mysteries to conceal, I am not averse to inquiries."

"Very well, then. How old are you?"

"Twenty."

"Promised in marriage?"

"No."

"Do you always chew on your lip that way?"

"What?"

"When you are thinking." He leaned back in the seat and some of the rigidness seemed to leave his body. "As you were a moment ago."

As if to betray her, her traitorous bottom lip slid under her teeth again. Did she? One look at Bridget told her she did.

Her maid ducked her head with a smile.

"I suppose it is a habit I must break." Isabella held out her arm to keep the baskets from falling as the coach lurched with a pothole. "Although I do not own to realizing it existed before this moment."

"I suppose none of us are without our peculiarities. Take me, for instance. When angered, I'm prone to stand on my head and recite the Latin alphabet."

Her jaw dropped. Did he jest her?

As if to answer her question, his eyes twinkled with merriment and a small laugh filled the carriage. "It seems you have never seen a man stand on his head."

"Indeed I have not."

"Men do many things women never see."

"Such as?"

"Making fools of themselves mostly. Had you a brother, you might have spent all your years laughing at such follies." Was it her imagination, or did his voice fade lower with the last sentence?

"Miss Gresham." Bridget's very quiet murmur brought Isabella's attention back to their surroundings. They had arrived on Tomfriars Lane, a street on the East End that swallowed the carriage in the stench of dung, desperation, and depravation.

And sometimes death.

Isabella fluttered a handkerchief from her reticule and handed a basket to Bridget, then one to Mr. Kensley, before looping the remaining two on her arms. "Shall we?"

Mr. Kensley hopped out first, handed both her and Bridget to the ground, and apologized for the mud hole already seeping brown water into their hems. Even if he had carried them halfway across the street, however, they could not have escaped such peril.

The street was a river of mud.

Urchins played barefoot close enough to the carriage that the horses pranced at the noise. A ragpicker ambled his way to a grungy pawnbroker shop, and farther up the street, two scantily clad trollops lingered outside a disreputable establishment.

Isabella curled her nose. Why Father insisted they always make these trips was beyond her. What good did a few baskets do in the face of such misery?

"You come here alone?" Mr. Kensley took one of her baskets as they departed down the street.

"Sometimes Miss Trewman accompanies me, other times Bridget. But Father always insists the driver walk with us for protection once we arrive."

Mr. Kensley nodded and did it again—surveyed their surroundings.

What was it he kept looking for?

They stopped at the first two squalid houses, delivering baskets to old Mrs. Whalley, then to the equally old gardener who had once tended their townhouse flower boxes.

Mr. Kensley held a hand to her and Bridget as they crossed the street and navigated behind a crumbling two-story building. Blackened grime dripped down the bricks, and the narrow alley was covered in planks to keep walkers an inch or two above the sewer.

Isabella coughed into her handkerchief, the odor nauseating her stomach. "This way," she mumbled through the white cloth.

They reached the door. The one she was always reluctant to knock on and even less eager to step through.

Today, Mr. Kensley did the knocking. The wooden door creaked with the pressure, as if ready to split in half, then swung open to a little face.

A dirty face.

The child stood in rags that drooped to her ankles, where dirty toes peeked out. Big, round, darkened eyes stared up at them.

"Who is dere, Anna?" rasped a voice within.

"It is Miss Gresham, Mrs. Shaw," Isabella said, "come with a basket of bakeries and preserves."

A wheeze was the only answer, then faintly, "Come. . .in."

Just what Isabella had imagined the woman would say—and hoped she wouldn't.

The three shuffled inside the dank room. No hearth, no furniture, no windows. Just a sallow, shriveled woman lying prostrate in a bed of rags, a couple of wooden buckets that reeked of waste, and three small children pressed together in the corner.

Their frames were skeletal. Hungry eyes cleaved to the baskets, with expressions that cut pity through her chest.

She offered them both baskets and tried not to watch as the children devoured the bread and cakes. When had the situation become so dire?

She had not been to visit the Shaws since last season, but although they had occupied this same filthy room, their clothes had been intact, their Irish spirits had been good, and a few humble beds, chairs, and tables had occupied the space. What had they done? Sold everything they owned for food? Where was Mr. Shaw?

Mr. Kensley bent next to the woman, his knees sinking to the dirt floor. He grasped her wrist, his hand large and tanned next to her bony white one. "She needs a doctor."

"No. . .please. Don't take us now. . .to de workhouse. So close. Daniel. . .coming back." She raised her head, a cough choking through her, sweat dripping down her temples. "Daniel?"

"Lie still and a doctor shall see to you."

"Just ten. . .shouldn't have to go to de sweatshops. . .working, my boy. Where is he?" Another cough. "Daniel. Daniel."

"She burns with fever." Mr. Kensley stood, jaw clenching. "You and Bridget stay with her while I—"

"No." She sucked in air and took a step back for the door. "No, you stay. Bridget and I shall fetch the carriage driver to bring back a doctor." Without giving him time to protest, Isabella seized Bridget's hand and hurried them outside, her heart rattling with emotions she was too unfamiliar with to know how to bear.

She only knew one thing.

She could not stay in that room a moment more.

"How long have you been this way?"

Mrs. Shaw was everything pitiful. Her face bore no color, bones protruded from her skin, and her feverish eyes were ringed with brown, sagging circles. Tiny bugs leaped in and out of her matted hair. "Husband. . .left us."

"I am sorry."

"Emma died."

The words reeked throughout the room. They smelled of death. They lodged themselves into the center of William, burrowed deep, and acquainted him with all her grief.

Grief that resonated with his own.

Emma. He pictured a pretty little girl, much like the one who had answered the door to them, who had suffered the lack of too much.

While others dined and splurged and danced, they were dying.

He didn't mean to hold her hand. He wouldn't have. But ever since he'd felt the weak pulse of her wrist, the thin fingers had grasped him. She mumbled things half incoherent. Worries over Daniel, ten years old, working in the sweatshops. Pleas not to be dragged to the workhouse. Cries for Emma. Little Emma.

Tears pricked at his eyes, but he forced them back. He pulled Lord Manigan's funds from his tailcoat pocket, slid half under the woman's pillow. He wouldn't be in London much longer anyway. He hoped. "There is enough here to make things better."

Her head lolled to the side. "From. . .you?"

"From a friend of mine."

"Who. . ." A cough. "Who are you?"

"No one you need concern yourself with. Close your eyes. Rest." He pulled the blanket closer to her neck, the pungent whiff of urine intensifying. "The doctor shall be here soon and everything shall be fine."

"Bless you." Her strength seemed to be depleted. She closed her eyes and, with coughs rattling her chest, breathed the words "Just have to forgive dem. Even if you got to do it over and over again. . .just got to forgive dem."

He bent closer, unsure if she spoke to him or herself. "Mrs. Shaw?"

"Lot of people. . .hurt us. . .done us wrong. Husband. . .left us. Got to forgive dem. Got to forgive *him*. Over and over and over. . ." She lost consciousness then, and the hand in his finally slackened.

He didn't pull away. Instead, he glanced from her still face to the children devouring bread in the corner, and a strange emotion splintered through him.

After all they had suffered. All they had lost. All the hurt that had been done to them by a husband who could have stayed and met their needs. Why should she murmur of forgiveness at a time like this?

He didn't know. He understood very little of that kind of strength.

But he couldn't help wondering if, should life ever become so bitter to him as it was to Mrs. Shaw, he would have anything that strong inside himself.

"You left them funds." Isabella stared at him from across the carriage, and the compassion she'd been so afraid to cope with spread across his face unabashed.

"How often do you visit the street?" he asked.

"But once or twice a season."

"Left to their own devices, they'll be in the workhouse within a month." His throat bobbed. "Or dead."

Such poignancy unsettled her. She squirmed in her seat. "You talk as if it were our responsibility to aid them."

"Ours and anyone else who stumbles upon their plight."

"You forget there are many such dreadful cases tucked away in London flats or begging on the streets. One cannot help them all."

"One can help some."

"Yes, but—"

"Mrs. Shaw is not so very different from you, Miss Gresham." His gaze held hers, and the gentle seriousness of his voice arrested her complete attention. "We may scorn the poor and lift our noses at them and blame their helplessness on dastardly sins."

Her skin prickled.

"But the truth is they are no worse and no better than we ourselves. They are simply less fortunate."

"Yes." A rasp. "Of course." All her life, she had delighted in looking at all things lovely while skimming past unpleasantries she did not wish to see. She did not enjoy bearing hurts she had so little control of.

Besides that, Father and all her other friends spoke so haughtily of the poor. "Unfortunates who," Father was wont to say, "might have made something of themselves if they were not so afflicted with laziness."

In some ways, she had gone through life adopting such beliefs. Like all her friends, she had skirted past the poor, sniveled her nose at their stench, all while still performing her duties of charity.

But under Mr. Kensley's gaze and still tortured by his speech, part of those beliefs unraveled. Shame pulsed through her.

Straightway, after entering the abode, Mr. Kensley had soiled his clean breeches on the grimy floor. He had held the hand of one who smelled wretched. He had spoken to her, calmed her, addressed her needs, and not wiped his hands of her when he left three hours later.

Indeed, he worried after them still. In all her acquaintances, was there a gentleman who would have behaved this way? And spoken to Isabella in such a manner? Or chastised her in a way that didn't stir anger, but remorse?

The burn of her cheeks must have shown with color, for a smile lessened the severity of his face. "You need not look so dismal, Miss Gresham. Shall I stand on my head for you?"

"Perhaps there is some sort of establishment." She leaned forward. "An aid society of sorts that I might write a letter to and procure a place for them."

"Have you any connections to such a place?"

"Not directly, but there is one my friend Sophia and her family have donated to quite regularly. I believe it is run by a bishop. I shall call upon the Kettlewells at once and see what might be done in way of helping the Shaws."

He did nothing more than nod, smile, and glance back out the carriage window—as seemed to be much more his habit than standing on his head.

But when they arrived at her townhouse and she'd bidden Mr. Kensley goodbye, she could not help feeling that she was somehow better for being with him today.

Indeed, she would not be averse to seeing him again.

Mr. Kensley resumed his visits, though a bit less frequently. When he did call, which was usually in the morning hours, Isabella persuaded him to stay long enough for a chess game or a stroll with her and Bridget in Hyde Park.

He always seemed obliged to join them.

They talked of everything, from nonsense to politics to literature to what it would feel like to travel to Egypt and climb atop the highest pyramid. La, how companionable was his company! She need not conform to any social formalities in his presence, nor did she need to fret over his laughs and smiles as devices to woo her.

If anything, his manner seemed more fraternal than flirtatious. A welcome change from all the male company she had been forced to keep over these last few years. Yet what would Father say?

He would likely bend his brow at her fraternizing with a gentleman of unknown fortunes and no connections. But she could not seem to help herself.

After all, Father *had* left her alone in this townhouse with little else other than Bridget and Lilias to amuse her. Well, and Lord Livingstone, of course.

Father likely had high hopes that, upon his return, he would find her and Lord Livingstone on the cusp of an engagement. Would he be so very disappointed to find that she had stopped seeing his lordship entirely? That she danced not once with him at balls? And that, worst of all, she had thrown away his letters without so much as opening them?

But she would not think of that now. Biting her lip, she lifted her rook up two and over one. "There. See what you can do to escape me, if you can."

Mr. Kensley, with both elbows on the card table, blew air out of his cheeks. "You are merciless."

"And skilled."

"And quite boastful."

"And very much winning." When he made another pitiful move of his pawn, she claimed his queen with her invading rook. "Check. You had better take your king and run, good sir."

"I do not run from anything."

"Oh?"

"I will stand"—he slid a bishop diagonally across the board—"and fight."

She clicked her tongue when he removed her rook from the board. With a mere unnoticed pawn, she conquered his king. "Checkmate."

He leaned back in his chair, raked both hands through his hair, and breathed out a laugh. "Remind me, Miss Gresham, that I have far more important things to do in London than sit indoors and play chess."

"Such as?"

"Sunlight, for one."

"Pray, how does one *do* sunlight?"

He flicked over chess pieces as he stood. "Not by sitting in here all day, that is for certain. Go and get your bonnet."

"Sir?"

"Hurry now, Miss Gresham, or I shall never be able to teach you how to do it."

"Do what?"

"Sunlight, of course."

A laugh trilled out, mostly because she had no idea what he meant but partly because his ridiculous humor was so infectious. She hurried for her bonnet and shawl and against her better judgment did not even seek out Bridget before she went hurrying out the townhouse door with Mr. Kensley. Why did he make her feel reckless? As if they could abandon all rules of society and set off to play?

Now Father really *would* chide her.

They walked together at a brisk pace, her hand looped in his arm, until they reached Hyde Park. But instead of following the footpath, they cut across fresh grass and disappeared from sight or sound of anyone.

Good sense should have warned her against such a thing. Indeed, just Lord Livingstone tugging her into a quiet alcove had seemed alarmingly dangerous.

But no danger could be found in this. If they broke rules of decorum, Mr. Kensley did so unwittingly. How strange he was. He seemed, at times, as if he had experienced very little of society. As if he'd been kept away somewhere and remained unexposed to the ways of the world.

Yet he was so jovial. So amiable. What could she make of such a puzzling persona?

When they reached the shade of an elm tree, Mr. Kensley plopped beneath it and patted the ground next to him.

She shook her head. "I hardly think so."

"What?"

"Can you truly wish me to soil my dress with grass stains? Are you in earnest, Mr. Kensley?"

"Are you so afraid of them?"

"I would not blame my refusing to sit on fears, but rather a healthy sense of practicality."

"Very well." He leaned back against the tree, arms behind his head, and closed his eyes. "I shall enjoy the grass by myself, as you enjoy your practicality." He breathed deep. "You smell that?"

"Smell what?"

"The air."

She sniffed—then, because he was not looking—finally eased herself a foot away from him in the grass. How very impish. If Lilias did such a thing, she would complain of insect bites for weeks. "I fear it smells to me most like any air."

"Yet it lacks chimney smoke and horseflesh, and all the other things of the city."

"You are not from the city, I gather?"

"No."

"Where are you from?"

He glanced over at her, but if he was annoyed that she asked, he showed no signs. "Rosenleigh." His voice turned soft with the word, as if the place meant as much to him as Sharottewood meant to her. "Where the grass is so green and soft that, if you chance to lie down in a patch, it shall bewitch you."

"You sound as if you love it very much."

A nod.

"I wonder that you ever left such a place."

"I wonder too." He leaned forward and grabbed a handful of grass in his fist. He ripped it out. "But I have every intention of returning."

"When?"

"I daresay, are you doing it again?"

"Doing what?"

He nodded to her with a grin. "Chewing your lip."

She hid her mouth with her hand and laughed. "You are terrible to mention it. You are terrible to make me soil my dress too." She hurried back to her feet and brushed off the muslin gown. "And you are terrible to answer my question with a question. Did you not teach me thus yourself?"

He stood and offered his arm again, his grin compelling and playful. "Whatever are you talking about?"

They found the footpath again and strolled back to the townhouse, the warm sunlight dampening her hairline with perspiration. Once inside, she offered him tea and would have led him into the sitting room, but a maidservant approached and handed her a letter.

"For you, Miss Gresham."

"Thank you, Janet."

Isabella shifted away from Mr. Kensley and undid the red seal with her thumbnail. She read over the contents of the letter, double-checked the date, then smiled. "Mr. Kensley, I believe I have the most wonderful news."

He'd been handing the butler his beaver hat, but he turned now and glanced at her letter. "From your father?"

"Indeed. And from the date this was posted, I dare to say he shall likely arrive within three days from now."

His face tightened and the look was back—the one she'd noticed when he first stood before her townhouse, or when his eyes had borne sadness at her dinner party. What kind of business could warrant such a powerful expression?

"Then I shall return to call upon him." Turning, he gathered back his hat and gloves from the butler—but before he exited the door, he glanced back at her. His gaze, now devoid of laughter or teasing or merriment, pulled her in with pleading. "I ask one thing of you, Miss Gresham, and all your servants."

"Anything you wish."

"Do not speak my name to Lord Gresham before I arrive. That is something I should like to do myself." He forced a smile then left.

Isabella clasped the letter to her chest. More than ever, she longed to discover what kind of business he and her father were entangled in.

Judging by Mr. Kensley's manner, it was not business at all.

CHAPTER 5

I already know." Father sat across from Isabella in the sitting room, his large frame nestled deep in the upholstered chair. Grey streaked through his black, perfectly combed hair and he clamped a meerschaum pipe between his lips. For all his trying to look cross, however, he could not quite pull it off.

Isabella was not fooled. "Are you terribly disappointed?"

"Yes. Lord Livingstone is a commendable—and wealthy—young man. I should have been most pleased to see you wed him, and besides that, he wrote me a most gentlemanly letter explaining his fault in everything."

"But he might have ruined me!"

A chuckle broke through Father's feigned scolding. "I should hate to think what the ladies all told their papas of me when I was young."

"Were you quite the rogue?"

"Yes."

"And did you artfully deceive young ladies into stealing off with you in unlit halls, that you might kiss them unawares?"

"That and far worse, I fear."

Isabella smiled. "I wonder that Mother ever married you."

The words were meant in jest, but Father's lips clamped tighter about his pipe. "Such naughtiness was never spent on your mother."

"Well, that is something we can all be grateful for." Isabella stood and walked to the window, where she opened a drapery farther to let in more evening light. The golden rays played on the Persian rug and furniture. "But even so, I can no longer bear the thought of a courtship with Lord

Livingstone. He is far too unpredictable."

"Good heavens, child. Is predictability not the very reason you can no longer bear to court anyone else?"

"Father." She whirled to him with a pleading look—one she'd mastered well enough to know his reaction.

He softened, just as she'd known, with a defeated sigh. "Very well, my dear. If you have no wish to see the prestigious Lord Livingstone again, I shall not be the one to force you. Though I shall warn you, my dear, if you keep this up forever, you shall never—"

The butler entered the sitting room with a quick bow. "Forgive me, my lord, but a visitor is come."

"At this hour?" Father pulled the pipe from his lips. "Good heavens, we are nearly an hour after dinner. Who is it?"

The butler glanced at Isabella, as if in question of how to answer. Then he said only, "He wishes to remain anonymous until he is seen."

Mr. Kensley. For reasons unknown, her heart sped faster. Perhaps because, though she did not know what the meeting was about, she knew it meant *something.* Something important to the laughing, teasing, pleasant Mr. Kensley, who had entertained her so well of late—and whom she could not help but feel a certain attachment to.

Father unbent his knees and placed his pipe on the stand. "Very well. Send him in."

"He wishes a word in private, my lord."

"Very well, very well. I shall wait for him in my study." He and the butler left, and Isabella waited several seconds before she too crept to the still-open doorway.

She drew in a breath and held it as she waited for sufficient time to pass. When the study door thudded shut, when the butler passed by without noticing her, she slipped into the hall and pressed to the outside of the study door.

Her curiosity was to be satisfied at last.

Edward Gresham was everything William had imagined. Tall and broad and dressed in black, well-tailored clothes, every hair in place. The study desk he stood behind was meticulous—the ledger straight, the letters stacked, the surface without ink spills or pencil shavings.

His eyes bored into William. "Well, sir, you have your private audience, even if it is at an inconvenient hour. Now what do you want?"

Want? William's chest suffocated with emotion. All his life, he had wanted a mother and a father of his own. He had wanted a home where he was not afraid of being locked in dark rooms. He had wanted assurance against the cruel, demeaning words always shouted at him by his aunt.

Now, he wanted nothing.

Except answers.

"Well?" Lord Gresham tapped his fingers against the desk. "I have only just returned from a long journey, and I have many pressing matters to attend to—"

"I am your son." The words raked from his throat.

The tapping ceased. Color flushed from Lord Gresham's neck to his cheeks as the longcase clock ticked away the seconds. Fury settled into the man's gaze. "Who are you?"

"William Kensley, son of Constance Kensley of Rosen—"

"How dare you come here." His father stepped around the desk, sweat beading across his face. "How much do you want? How much has she sent you for?"

"Sir—"

"Answer me!"

A tremble raced through William, but he kept the man's stare and pulled himself taller. He spoke with the feigned indifference he'd practiced with his aunt endless times. "No one has sent me, and I have come for naught but answers."

"Answers to what?"

"Why you allowed me to think you dead."

A curse blew from Lord Gresham's lips. "I will not be blackmailed. I will not be interrogated. Get out of here—"

"I will have my word with you."

"You will have nothing from me."

Pain prickled through William as the rejection seeped deeper and wrapped clawlike fingers around his heart. He would have rather kept his father dead. The lichen-covered headstone with the short and kind epitaph *Here lieth the body of a pious man, devoted husband, and loving father.*

He had clung to those words a thousand times.

Loving father.

But they weren't true any more than anything else had been true.

"Get out of here," said Lord Gresham again, with less volume. His blood-red features altered some, and the new look smoldering in his eyes seemed more pleading than anything else. "Have you no inkling what this could do to me?"

"I wish no harm to your reputation, but a dying man has bidden me to find you."

"Dying man? What dying man?"

"The gardener at Rosenleigh."

"I know nothing of any gardener. This is preposterous." His voice boomed again. "I have been true to her terms and faithfully sent the five thousand pounds every year—"

"You paid to keep me a secret?"

"Do not pretend ignorance to me, you conniving and foolish blackguard."

William fended off the insult, just as he did with his aunt. "Never mind all of that. It is not why I have come."

"Then why have you come?"

"Because my life is endangered. I need to know why."

"Endangered how? I know nothing of it."

"The gardener at Rosenleigh sent me to find you. He thought perhaps you had answers that would divulge who would want me dead—"

"He thought *I* wanted you dead, is that not so?"

"Perhaps."

"Well, it is untrue." Lord Gresham stormed to the door, and his hand shook as he clasped the knob. "I have wished you out of my life since Constance's sister wrote me of you. I have paid a great price to keep you away. I have sacrificed more than you know—not just for myself, but for my daughter." Moisture filmed his eyes. "I will not have you destroy me now."

"My lord—"

"Get out of this house, and if I ever cast eyes upon you again, whoever is trying to kill you may not get the chance. I shall do it myself." He slung open the door and waited stock-still, eyes hot and raging, sweat rolling down his temples and down his neck.

William nodded and quit the room, bitterness coursing through him. Loving father, indeed.

She had imagined a hundred things, but never this.

Isabella hugged her arms at the sitting room window and waited until Mr. Kensley's hackney drove away. She squeezed herself, indignation heating her blood flow. She'd been eavesdropping at the study door long enough to hear the abominable Mr. Kensley speak those incriminating words to Father: "I am your son."

The nerve of such a contemptuous lie! To think she had laughed with him, and fraternized with him, and played chess with him, while all along he was. . .

Planning to blackmail us.

A maid had swept into the hall before Isabella could hear more, and she'd been forced to retreat back to the sitting room lest the maid tell everyone what her mistress had been up to.

Now Isabella bounded for the study and found her father at the window, the last burning light of day on his face, shoulders hunched. "Father?"

"Leave me, child. I am in no temperament for anything at the moment."

"I heard."

The confession turned him around. He stared at her, his gaze long and hard and undecipherable. "You should not have listened—"

"I could not help myself. Mr. Kensley has been calling most every other day since you left, and I could not bear the suspense a moment longer." She clasped her hands. "I never imagined he was plotting such a wicked lie against us."

"Wicked lie."

"Father?"

He turned back to the window. Pulled both hands down his face.

"It was a lie. . .was it not?"

"Of course it was."

"Then we cannot allow him to do this. Such falsehoods would bring unbearable shame upon Sharottewood and all our friends and—"

"Yes, yes, I am aware, my dear. I am quite aware." A sigh shuddered the large shoulders. "Please. . .I am fatigued after my journey. Leave me to myself now."

"But what are we going to do?"

"I do not know."

"We must do something!"

"We shall, but the man will not accept money. I hardly know what he wants, and I hardly know what to do." When he commanded she leave for the second time, she departed the study with a knot growing in her throat.

How dare Mr. Kensley waltz in, accept her hospitality, befriend her, then knife her in the back with such a dangerous, treacherous lie. She would not stand for it.

Father may not know what to do.

But she did.

William paced back and forth in his tiny, white-painted chamber. Tomorrow, he must leave London. Coming here had accomplished nothing.

Except causing him to get hurt yet again.

A part of him shriveled as all the hostile words Lord Gresham had spoken to him returned and echoed within the chamber. Why had Shelton sent him here? What purpose was there in this?

None. William was no closer to knowing who wanted him dead or why.

Unless he knew already.

His aunt's face loomed in his vision, with her deep wrinkles and pallid skin and accusing eyes. Yes, she hated him. She had only ever cared for him for five thousand pounds a year. Most of all, she begrudged him Rosenleigh. But enough to kill him? She—who had watched him grow up, raised him along with her own child, blood of her blood? Why could he not accept the thought?

And Shelton.

She would not have permitted the murder of such a faithful gardener, a servant who had been with her so many years. Would she?

How much easier to pretend some unknown father wished him dead. Or an elusive, secret enemy. Anyone but. . .but the aunt and cousin he'd always longed to have love him.

William rubbed his hands over his face and trapped a groan before it escaped. Now what? Go back and confront his aunt, ask if she wanted him dead so that her own son might inherit? Or continue in what Shelton had sent him to do?

Someone rapped on the door.

"Who is it?"

"King George III. Who'd you think?"

William opened the door to his landlady, a squat old woman with a fluffy mob cap and a chin that dripped three layers of fat.

"You gets another caller this late at night and yous can be looking for other lodgings right fast, you can. Now come along before I gets peeved and throws you out now."

William followed her down a narrow flight of wooden stairs, then into a plain parlor with but two chairs and no windows. His landlady left him with the candle and disappeared.

A figure waited in the shadows.

Muscles tight, William strode forward until feeble candlelight uncovered the woman in a blue cloak. "Miss Gresham."

"How could you do this to us?"

So she had come on her father's behalf. Likely to stuff a bank note into William's pocket, swat him on the hand, and scold him to never dare approach his own father again.

William could not be put off so easily. "I do not wish to discuss the matter with you, Miss Gresham. How did you find me?"

"The day you forgot your hat. I had a servant follow you to return it."

"I see."

"You did not answer my question."

"Nor do I intend to. You have no business coming here, and besides that, it is not safe."

"Safety is exactly the reason I have come." Her chin lifted and orange light flickered in her determined eyes. "My father's and my own."

"Have no fear. I shall not be the one to soil your reputation."

"What do you want?"

"This is none of your affair."

"It is very much my affair, as it is my life you are threatening." She drew closer to him, breathing fast, the hood falling from her head. "You must take the money my father offered you and leave."

"You forget, Miss Gresham. I do not run."

"I fear that tactic ended in your demise, if you remember."

"A tragedy which will not happen again." William took her arm and started her for the door, but she shook out of his touch.

"You are despicable and wicked to say such lies against Father."

"You truly believe that?"

"Believe what?"

"That they are lies." He held her eyes and willed her to believe him. He didn't know why, or why it should matter.

Doubt thawed her gaze—though whether in their father or William, he could not tell. Tears flashed. "I hope I never see you again," she whispered. She fled from the dark parlor so fast her cloak billowed after her.

But her hopes were in vain. That much, as of now, he determined. Because Shelton would not have sent William after Lord Gresham if there were not a reason.

William would not quit until he knew what that reason was.

"We are leaving."

"What?" Isabella jerked her gaze to Father across the breakfast table, and the coffee she poured from the silver pot did not quite make it to her cup. Brown liquid splashed to the white tablecloth and scorched her fingertips. She mopped it up with a napkin. "You cannot mean leave London."

"Precisely what I mean. Mary?"

A maidservant rushed to the table, and Father bade her assist with the mess.

Isabella abandoned her chair. She was not hungry anyway. Not now. "I daresay, Father, I think it most craven to. . .to run." Mr. Kensley's words from last night returned to her.

And his look.

The way he'd leaned closer, captured her with probing eyes, as if begging her to trust him and disbelieve her own father.

Which she didn't.

She couldn't.

Even so, she glanced over at Father now and watched his haggard face. His hair, normally so perfect, was a bit ruffled. His expression pinched. His eyes unfocused and red-rimmed, as if he'd spent a night without sleep. All over a stranger's false accusation?

Of course. This was a great, delicate matter. An illegitimate child, even rumors of one, could arouse scandal so fierce they could never return to the good graces of society.

And yet. . .

"I say, child, do not look at me so. You quite remind me of your mother." Father stood and brushed honey-cake crumbs from his tailcoat. Another oddity, as he was never so clumsy. "There is always next season, Lilias is bothersome, and there are no eligible suitors to tempt you anyway."

"Yet if we return back home, there is no telling what Mr. Kensley shall do."

"A chance we must take."

"I cannot see that such a plan shall resolve anything."

"You do not *have* to see." Irritation flamed across his face, and his tone had risen an octave. Something was wrong indeed. He was never cross with her.

Never.

"I am sorry, my dear. All this is just rather. . .inconvenient. If you wish to remain in London without me and finish out the season, you are quite at liberty to do so. You should not be cheated of your time in town on my account."

"It could hardly be charged to your account when none of this is your fault." Isabella stepped around the table and reached for his hand. She squeezed. "If you depart London, I shall go with you."

A smile broke through the shadows on his face. He patted her hand and—with a great sigh—pulled her against him and hugged her longer and harder than he was wont to do. "My dear child. All I do I do for you. Do you know this?"

"You are far too good to me."

"It is my wish that you always have what is *too good* for you." He pressed her face into his tobacco-scented waistcoat. "And I shall do whatever it takes to see that wish come true."

Why did the words make her want to squirm away? And why did they pull her back to Mr. Kensley's eyes, when his gaze had made her half believe he was telling the truth?

Something was amiss.

William strode faster along the line of townhouses, his gaze fixed on one.

From two stories above street level, a maid leaned over an iron banister and whacked at a rug with a carpet beater. Dust showered the air. At another window, a different servant scrubbed the glass, soap suds bubbling and smearing with every stroke of the rag.

William knocked on the door, and when it opened, a lanky footman filled the doorway, white sheets draped over both arms. "Excuse me, but I am here to call on Lord Gresham."

"Too late for that, sir."

"Pardon?"

"The Greshams departed for their estate in the country two days ago. Took three carriages to the port in Kent, then sailed back for Sharottewood Manor by ship."

Disappointment overwhelmed William. He thanked the footman and departed, making his way back to his chamber to gather his things. He should not have waited the two days. He had hoped the small time would soften Edward Gresham to the reality of meeting his son.

Apparently, William had been wrong.

Never mind though.

He would follow by horseback and see Sharottewood for himself. This time, he would not be put off so easily.

Isabella drew back the soft red curtain and peered out the carriage window. Ah, there it was. To the right of the road, the long cliff dropped off into a glistening blue sea. Seagulls soared through the air, waves rippled, and puffy white clouds moved and danced in the sunniest sky. "Father, let us stop the carriage, please."

He must have dozed off, for it took several seconds before he snorted, straightened in his seat, and yawned. "Dear girl, do not be impetuous. You are yet too weak for such adventures."

"But we are only a mile from home, and I should love to walk back along the seashore." She smiled as a dolphin broke the surface of the water then dived away again in the distance. "Besides, I am not so very ill."

She had spent the four days traveling by ship in her cabin, unable to arise from bed, and making frequent use of the bucket Bridget kept by her side. Perhaps Father was right. Her stomach certainly did not feel calm, and the jostling carriage, however uncomfortable, was probably less sickening than a challenging one-mile walk.

Besides, Bridget was exhausted.

Isabella smiled over at her maid, who leaned against the carriage wall in slumber, Hannah More's *Strictures on the Modern System of Female Education* in her lap. The dear, dull girl. Isabella could not derive pleasure from novels, let alone such tedious literature as that.

As the carriage rumbled through the large entrance gates, excitement rippled through her. She scooted to the edge of her seat and was the first to climb out when the carriage halted.

She swallowed in the sight of Sharottewood Manor. With Corinthian columns topped by acanthus-leaf capitals and seraph statues crowning the roof, the stone manor stretched out before them with sunlight glinting on the endless windows. Two impressive stairways led from both sides to the front door, and an equally intricate fountain sprayed water from the center of the large courtyard.

How wonderful it was to be home. She always enjoyed London and anticipated her time there—but if the only joy she derived from such a trip was the elation of returning home, she would ever be satisfied.

Yet this time, something tainted her return. As the servants unloaded her valise and trunk from the carriage, as Father hopped down and stretched, as Bridget clutched her book and yawned. . .

An unsettling twinge pulsed through Isabella. As if they had left unfinished business behind them. As if they had run like cowards.

As if they had done something wrong.

Which wasn't true, of course. If anyone was wrong, it was Mr. Kensley. The sooner she put him out of remembrance, the better off both she and Father would be.

Riding soothed William. He lost all tension to the fresh air and open countryside and *ploppety-plop* of each hoof on the muddy road. He rode through foggy dawns, sunny afternoons, bluing dusks, and halfway into star-filled nights.

Once he stopped at a coaching inn along the side of the road in Lincolnshire. He ate a cold meal of beef, bread, and fruit, then shared a bed with a squirming gentleman before the sound of departing coaches awoke him at four in the morning.

Three more days before he arrived at Sharottewood.

Before he faced his father again.

Overwhelming bitterness flooded through him, and he tightened his fists around Duke's reins. What kind of man hated his own son? What made one of his children dear and priceless, while the other was nothing more than dirt he wished hidden away?

William had not asked to be born into illegitimacy.

The painting of his mother replaced his view of rutted road and rolling meadows. Edward Gresham should have married William's mother. He should have made right the wrong instead of forcing her to feign a marriage with a man who did not exist.

Perhaps if Edward had done his duty, Constance would not have perished in childbirth. Perhaps she would've had a reason to live.

A day away from Sharottewood, William bedded down in a forest along the side of the road. He awoke before daylight, urged Duke to a gallop, and covered the rest of the distance with a bulge of trepidation growing inside his chest.

The road veered along the edge of a forty-foot cliff, where a crashing sea spread out to his right. The air was salty and moist, the sky grey, the wind increasing.

"Almost there, boy." William leaned forward and rubbed the horse's sweaty neck, pride surging at the soft and bulging muscles beneath the thick hide—

A noise cracked like thunder.

Something pricked at his side, a small flare of irritation, as if a pebble had lodged beneath his rib cage. He glanced at himself.

Shocking red formed a circle at his side.

Then thunder again. Or a gunshot. Duke reared and William flew from his saddle, a searing sensation grazing his neck as he tumbled over the cliffside. Craggy rocks jabbed him, ripped him, cut him as he plummeted through the air.

Then his body smacked solid rock. Air escaped, but he couldn't pull it back in, and darkness jarred through him in staggering waves. *I'm dying.*

Oh dear.

The housekeeper, Mrs. Morrey, was three feet away from the front door—her rigid back turned to Isabella as she situated blue delphiniums in a porcelain vase.

Isabella crept with bated breath, clutching her riding crop to her side.

Six more steps. Five. Four. Three until she made it to the door—

"Miss Gresham, I have not yet heard you practicing the piano-forte."

A sigh blew out Isabella's cheeks. If it were not so terribly unladylike, she would have grunted an answer instead of speaking one. "I am only saving the best amusements for last."

Mrs. Morrey turned with a knowing expression. "Indeed."

"I shall be off on my ride and return to fill the entire manor with beautiful songs—"

"You know your father wishes you to practice."

"Yes, but he shall not badger me."

"The dilemma precisely." Mrs. Morrey stepped forward, her thin and wiry frame tense as always, her chestnut hair pulled back into a severe chignon. "Which is why I try my best to do the job myself. You do not wish to be an unruly daughter, do you? If it were not for my guidance, who else would gently yet firmly direct you in the path all fine ladies must follow? Do you not wish to be accomplished?"

"Not particularly. What I wish is to ride my horse."

An annoyed, condescending smile formed on the housekeeper's lips. "Very well. You may, of course, do as you will. I only think it rather a shame that after all your father does for your delight, you would not try in this one way to gratify him—"

"Oh, please say no more. I shall go and practice." Isabella's shoulders wilted as she handed the fussy old housekeeper her riding crop. "But we both know my playing is rather horrid, so do not complain when we all must suffer the unbearable strains." She ambled off to the music room and skulked to the piano, then began the wearisome notes and chords. After a short while, she glanced with longing to the window.

Rain streaked the glass, and thunder reverberated against the panes. Perhaps it would not have been a pleasant day to ride the seashore after all.

Rain slashed down on William in a cold, brutalizing torrent. He must have been unconscious many hours, for the sky teetered on the edge of purplish dusk.

He tried to move. Pain webbed through his side, fierce enough he dropped his head back against the wet rock. Blood puddled beneath him. He swallowed the salty, metallic taste in his mouth and clamped his hand against the bullet graze along his neck.

Bullet. His mind spun. *Shot.* Groaning, he strained to inspect the wound at his side. *Shot twice.*

Pain radiated through his body as he ripped off his cravat and pushed it into the hole along his left rib cage. The white fabric turned pink then red. How much had he bled?

Colors blurred as he squinted through the rain. Six or so feet of harsh, uneven cliff hovered over him. He'd be dead had it not been for this ledge.

He might be dead still, if he couldn't get out of here.

Help me, God. The prayer shook through him as he elbowed himself up and fought the blackness crowding the periphery of his vision. Nausea roiled. He collapsed back and gritted his teeth against pain so intense it stole his breath.

Blackness sucked him back. Voices shouted at him. His aunt, with her knotty finger jabbing into William's chest. *"Wicked child."* Edward, with his booming voice of thunder. *"Get out of here. Conniving blackguard. How dare you. . .dare you. . ."*

Then the shadowed face. The continental hat. The luminous eyes glaring at William with a pistol lifted, aimed, fired.

William flinched, jolting himself back awake. *Help.* With torturing rain stinging his wounds, he dragged himself up. He fell against the wall of the cliff, secured his footing, and clawed upward with torn hands. *Get me to the top.*

He slid back to the ledge but hauled himself up and tried again. *God, please.*

Isabella descended the left side of the exterior stone stairs. Orange and pink streaked the morning sky, and the tropical scents of rain still lingered in the chilled air. Today, she would have her ride.

Whether Mrs. Morrey or Father liked it or not.

She paused at the fountain, squinting through dense fog toward the entrance gate. Who was that approaching?

She would have scuttled on to the stables, as likely any visitor was an acquaintance of Father. She should not like her ride to be delayed by formal greetings to somber-faced gentlemen.

But the vehicle nearing the manor was no shiny post chaise or landau or barouche, but a mere farmer's cart.

And moving fast.

She crunched gravel beneath her riding boots, curiosity mounting. Wasn't the man behind the reins one of Father's tenants? The one who leased a small, eighty-acre farm she rode by sometimes, with a thatched cottage and barley fields?

As the cart came within feet of her, the tenant jerked on the reins and leaped down. He pulled a sweat-stained hat from his head and flattened it against his chest, looking for all the world like a timid mouse ready to be squashed underfoot.

Isabella withheld a smile. "Is there something I might do for you, Mr.—"

"Abram." He bowed. Twice. "Nash Abram, Miss Gresham, and rightly 'morseful I be for bargin' in this way, but. . ."

"But what?"

He wrung the hat in his hands and motioned toward the cart. "Found him, I did, on the way to the village. Lyin' in the road. Dead methoughts. 'Twould have taken him to my own place, but wot with the fancy clothes—"

Heartbeat thrumming in her ears, Isabella hurried around the cart. *Mr. Kensley.*

His body was folded into the small space, with his head pressed into his shoulder and his legs draped over the back of the cart. His flesh was ripped. Blood stained his hair, his face, his neck, his stomach, while clumps of mud clung to his shredded clothes.

Queasiness struck her abdomen. She whirled back around, clamped her hands over her mouth to stifle any sound. This didn't make sense. What had happened?

"Miss Gresham?" The farmer touched her elbow, as if to steady her.

"Is he. . .dead?"

"Not when I loaded him up. Might be now." Distress rippled through the man's words. "Just tell me wot I can be doin' to help. Please."

"Can you carry him?"

"Sure enough." With surprising strength for a man of fifty-some years, Mr. Abram flipped down the back of the cart and hoisted Mr. Kensley into his arms.

They hurried for the manor, up the stairs, through the foyer, panic racing helter-skelter through her limbs. Nothing made sense. What was Mr. Kensley doing here? How had he arrived so quickly from London? How had—

"What is this?"

Isabella froze, Mr. Abram nearly bumping into her as they halted before the winding marble steps.

Father waited at their base. A muscle tightened in his jaw as he swiveled his gaze to the body in Mr. Abram's arms. Rage flushed his cheeks. "Get this man out of my house."

CHAPTER 6

Father, no." Every inch of her body tightened as she matched his stare. "Continue on, Mr. Abram."

Just as she'd known, Father stepped aside, his back pressed against the banister as the tenant lumbered his burden up more steps. Blood dripped from the dangling arms as Isabella started after them.

Father snagged her elbow and pulled her toward him, growling, "What is the meaning of this?"

"I know as little as you."

"I do not want that man in my house. After what he has done—"

"His offenses to us are not so great we can let him die." Confusion, and perhaps disappointment, weakened her knees. This was not her father. The one who chuckled at her and coddled her and read his political pamphlets and smoked his pipe. . .

This was a man she did not know or understand. How could he be so heartless? What was the matter with him?

As if sensing her thoughts, Father released her and marched away, his footfalls echoing across the marble.

Isabella raced up the stairs, clutching the skirt of her riding habit, careful to avoid the nauseating blood trail. She directed Mr. Abram into a guest bedchamber, where he leaned Mr. Kensley within the four-poster bed.

His skin was white as the counterpane.

When a maidservant appeared in the doorway, Isabella beckoned her to fetch warm water, linens, and the entire medicine chest. "And send for a doctor!" She hovered over the bed and peeled back the sticky fabric of his tailcoat then shirtsleeves.

Sweating, she swallowed down more sickness. The gaping hole left his insides exposed, and a fresh flow poured forth onto the clean bed.

Dear mercy, he was dying.

Despite any wrong he had done Father, she would do almost anything in the world to stop that from happening.

A dark room. Solitude again, but this time worse, because he could no longer hear his aunt's footsteps trailing away, or Horace chuckling, or Miss Ettie promising him it would be over soon.

He was alone in the blackness. No one lingered on the other side of the door.

If there *was* a door.

He groped, but everything was heavy. The air was heavy. He touched a hundred things but couldn't feel any of them. Where was the door?

Get me out, dear God. He opened his mouth and his tongue nearly choked him. Thick, dry, swollen. *Please let me out.*

As if in answer, a light hand swept across his brow. Pain prickled through him as the hand pressed harder, dabbing at his hairline, then dragged down the length of his face. He smelled blood, rusty and repugnant. What had his aunt done to him? Or had it been Horace?

He couldn't remember.

The room was too black, too heavy, for memories. He waited in the solitude for so long he thought he'd die if he didn't find the door—then the hand returned.

This time it didn't scrub at him or hurt him. Just fingered into his hair, easy and gentle, as if comprehending his hurt.

As if whispering that he would not be locked in the black room forever.

He looked different now.

For the third time in an hour, Isabella dipped a cloth in the water basin, wrung it out, then placed it across his burning forehead.

With the doctor come and gone, the wounds dressed, the tattered clothes replaced with a fresh nightshirt, he appeared less like some ghoulish creature in a nightmare.

Less like death too.

Yet scratches and cuts marred his face, his neck was bandaged, and an uncommon pallor stole his otherwise tanned complexion.

Pity pooled deep inside her. He could not die. Perhaps she should not feel so strongly. Were it one of Father's friends from Parliament, or even roguish Lord Livingstone, would such fright have washed over her?

She didn't know, nor did she understand her reaction. She stared at him now, watched his blue lips mouth something without sound, and remembered how often he had smiled and teased her in London.

They had been nonsensical together.

In an idyllic way, they had talked and laughed and forsaken the customary conversations for words that were not feigned. Words that meant something. She had been herself in his presence, and when they spoke to each other, they had been real in the fullest sense.

Did she really believe he had betrayed them? Or did she only pretend she did for Father's sake?

Behind her, the bedchamber door creaked open. "Miss Gresham?"

Isabella glanced up and nodded Bridget into the room.

With timid steps, Bridget inched closer. "How fares the poor thing?"

"The doctor has cleaned the gunshots with alcohol and turpentine. The one to his neck was but a graze, and the other not far into his side. He is lucky to have no broken bones."

"Then there is hope of recovery?"

"Yes." She swallowed hard. "Though I daresay but a little."

"Come." Sweet Bridget took her hand, squeezed it, and tugged Isabella. "You must take supper and rest. You have been sitting with him for hours, when a maid shall do just as much—"

"I wish to stay."

Bridget's brows rose, as if with questions.

Questions Isabella didn't know the answers to herself. "He seems to be comforted when I sit with him. A familiar voice, I suppose." Whether that was true or not, it was the only excuse she could think of. "Now go and tell a servant to bring a plate up to me. I shall eat dinner here."

With a sigh she tried to cover with her hand, Bridget nodded and moved for the door. She paused, however, before exiting. "Miss Gresham?"

"Yes?"

"I daresay, you have behaved rather bravely this day. I have never seen you face unpleasantries so boldly and unshrinkingly."

The praise soothed Isabella's distress. She smiled. "You are dear, Bridget. Now run along."

But when the door shut, all her anxieties galloped to full speed yet again. Bridget was right. Isabella had confronted Father, ripped back Mr. Kensley's bloody clothes, stared at his injuries, and never once turned her eyes away from him. What made him so special?

She hoped to goodness her attachment was not linked to him because...

Well, because he'd spoken in truth that day in Father's study.

Because he was her brother.

A kink pulled at her neck as Isabella peeked open her eyes to the blinding morning sun. A groan rumbled through her. Daylight already? How long had she been asleep?

Mr. Kensley's moan urged her from the discomforts of the chair, and she peeled off the dry cloth draped across his forehead. Her hopes sank.

His skin still scorched her fingertips.

All night long, she had sat with an elderly maid, Helena, who had kept fresh water in the pitcher and reorganized the medicine chest, likely to keep from falling asleep.

Now the old woman slumbered in an odd position in the chair by the hearth, her soft snores filling the room.

He moaned again.

Isabella sat on the edge of the bed, reached for his hand, and pressed it against her chest. He was missing two fingernails. As if he'd clawed his way up the cliff Mr. Abram had assumed he'd tumbled down after...

Someone shot him. A shudder darted up her spine, another unpleasantry she desired to look away from—but couldn't. Who would do such a thing? Why would anyone want him dead? He, who was young and handsome and affable?

How terrible it was to see him this way. Helpless and broken. Like the flotsam or jetsam she searched for along the beach, lost and alone, no longer cared for by anyone. Did someone care for Mr. Kensley? Who loved him?

She imagined a thousand people loved him. What with his smile, his pleasant manners, his carefree jesting. Most anyone could find him endearing.

Except Father, of course.

"Let me out." Rasping. Feverish. "Please. . .let me out."

She squeezed his hand against her. "Shhh, Mr. Kensley. You are quite safe now."

His head fell to one side. He breathed heavily, painfully, then squinted glassy eyes into her face. "Miss. . .Ettie?"

The name seemed to give him comfort, so she nodded. "Yes. Miss Ettie indeed."

His eyelids sank shut again, his expression lax, and Isabella tucked his hand back beneath the warm bed linens. She awoke Helena and bade her sit by Mr. Kensley, then departed the chamber with a long yawn.

A hot breakfast, change of clothes, water and soap, and a comb through her disheveled hair were quite in order. She massaged her neck as she turned down the hall.

"Isabella."

The sharp command whirled her around.

Father approached fast, looking as unkempt—and without sleep—as she doubtless did. "You were with him all night."

"Have no fear, for he cannot harm me." She tried to keep the bite from her voice. "Indeed, you shall be comforted to know he can scarcely lift his head."

"This must stop. This *will* stop. I shall not have you sacrificing yourself for the sake of a man who—"

"Has brought your illegitimacy unto Sharottewood?"

Father's chin bunched and lifted. "Then he has been turning you against me."

"On the contrary. He has said not a word."

"I have told you once his allegations were lies. How many times should a father have to defend himself?"

She started away without answer, but he grabbed her arm and eased her back.

"Isabella, my dear, my darling." Remorse bobbed a knot at his throat. "Please, I must have your support. You must obey my wishes concerning this man and do as I say. I want you to stay away from him. Can you not see he has already driven a wedge between us? That he has convinced you of these preposterous lies against me?"

"Are they so preposterous, Father?"

The question hung, dangling between invisible walls of silence.

She saw a hundred things in his expression. Defeat, regret, bitterness, anger, even love—but love for whom? The woman who birthed Mr. Kensley? Had it been before or after his marriage with Mother? Did it matter?

The scene swept her back. The staircase. The flickering candles. The faces of her parents, their whispered words, and the acknowledgment of something that hurt beyond reason.

Isabella pulled herself away from Father's touch. "I am wearied and must find my chamber."

"Will you respect my desire?"

"Ask me to never question you again on the matter, and I shall consent. Ask me to never inquire after your past, and I shall leave it forgotten." She glanced back at Mr. Kensley's door, and a fierce protectiveness rushed through her. "But ask me to leave an injured gentleman friendless in a house where he is hated. . .and I cannot oblige you. While he remains at Sharottewood, I shall tend to him and smile at him and comfort him as best I can. He has suffered much."

"And after he is gone from Sharottewood?"

She hesitated, a pinch in her chest. "Then I shall fulfill your request. I shall never see him again."

Sometimes the door creaked open, as if his aunt had finally heard his moans and released him. Light flittered away the darkness, but everything appeared dim and vague and confusing.

Hands soothed his forehead. Voices hummed. Often, the same pair of gentle eyes stared down at him and seemed to whisper comforts, though he never quite grasped what they meant.

Then the pain would steal him back, the door would slam, and he'd be locked in the blackness he had no strength to fight. How long would he claw to be free like this?

His body twitched. The movement summoned his eyes open yet again, and he focused on breathing easy and slow to keep the aches bearable.

This time, his vision was clearer. He was in a bed. Rumpled white counterpane and dark green curtains. Floral paper-hangings on the walls. Oval looking glass above a mantel. A chair. An old woman, frumpy and stout and situated with her legs stretched out before her.

As she met his eyes, a quick "Mercy, mercy" flew from her lips. She scrambled up and left the room and within seconds returned with someone else.

Someone he knew.

Confusion darted back and forth in his brain, delivering a wretched pounding to his head. What was *she* doing here? In fact, what was he doing here?

Miss Gresham slipped her hand beneath William's neck, pressed a glass to his lips, and eased the cool liquid down his dry throat. Then she settled on the bed next to him, smiling. Why did she smile?

"I hope you know you quite frightened poor Helena out of her wits."

Helena?

"The maid," Miss Gresham explained, as if she'd heard his thought. "She did not expect to find you staring that way. Rather lucid like, you know. But then again, the poor old thing is terribly excitable."

Grogginess weighted his eyelids. He strained to keep them open. "Where. . ." He slid his tongue over his cracked lips. "Where. . .am I?"

"Sharottewood Manor. Have you forgotten then?"

Had he?

"Well, if you do not remember, I dare not remind you. You must think only of pleasant things. You have been four days here, and you are quite safe. Nothing else need matter."

Safe. He latched on to the word, but he wasn't sure he believed it. He hadn't been safe in a long time. *Edward.* His father. Sharottewood. No, he shouldn't be here—

He raised his head and pushed up on his elbows, but a piercing pain struck his side. He collapsed back against the pillows, guided by Miss Gresham's hands.

Her smile stayed in place, a lifeline in a sea of so much agony and dread. "Stay still, Mr. Kensley. You must not move. You must not do anything but regain your strength."

Had he any left, he would have. His eyes shut against his will, but not before he saw a flash of tears in her eyes. Did she cry for him?

Four days later, Isabella entered Mr. Kensley's chamber yet again and walked to the window. She pulled back the green draperies.

The sound must have awakened him, for when she turned back around, he was looking at her. These last few days had quite improved upon him. The scratches and cuts were less severe, already fading back into his pleasant, tanned complexion. His lips had regained color, and his eyes, though often still muddled with laudanum, lacked the dreadful redness of fever. "I hope you have not brought up that dashed chess game again, for I shall have none of it."

"Hardly so." She presented a book from behind her back. "Do you like to read?"

"Not usually." He scooted himself up, wincing. "But I am willing to try most anything. Here, let me see."

She handed it over. "*The Sorrows of Young Werther*. I thought perhaps the agonies of someone else might help divert you."

"A novel then?"

"I presume."

"Have you not read it?"

"No, of course not. I have much greater ways to occupy my mind than novel reading."

"Such as?"

A sudden heat crept to her cheeks. How silly it sounded to say riding the seashore, or walking the beach, or searching for flotsam and jetsam. "Oh, you know." She grinned. "Netting purses, practicing the piano-forte, writing letters, and painting fire screens."

A laugh rumbled out of him. "You are a terrible liar."

"One should never call out a lady on a lie. It is improper." She bent over him and adjusted the pillow behind his back. "There. Better?"

"What *do* you do with your time, Miss Gresham? I must know now."

"You must promise not to laugh."

"Never."

"Or scold me."

"I would not think of it." His look of interest, along with his amused expression, made it easy to sit on the edge of the bed and divulge her faults to him.

"Father and Mrs. Morrey, our housekeeper, find it degradable, as I should be doing things all accomplished ladies do. But my true enjoyment is riding my horse, Camilla, out to the beach. Ever since I was a child, I have delighted in going there. I search the caves, or sit on the rocks, or look for any trinkets washed ashore from a ship." She bit the edge of her lip. Why had she told him such things?

She had never shared such secrets with any other acquaintance. Not even Lilias.

But he didn't condemn, or laugh, or seem at all as if he thought her ridiculous. "Perhaps, if I am ever strong enough to make it out of this dashed bed, I shall have to see the seashore for myself."

"What fun we would have! Riding from one end of the cliffside to the other and—"

His back stiffened. The humor, the pleasure, drained from his face so quickly it took his color along too. "My horse. Duke. I had forgotten—"

"He is well." In this, at least, she could comfort him. "A servant found him two days after you had been brought in, hungry and lathered in sweat, but otherwise unscathed. We have been caring for him in our stables."

Relief sank him back into the pillows. "Thank you." A pause. "For both his care. . .and mine."

"I do not suppose you remember much."

"I fear the memories are rather distorted. I remember waking up in the rain and climbing until my hands bled. Everything else is lost to me." He stared down at his bandaged hands, spreading them open as if in them he might find answers.

"Who would want you dead?"

He blinked hard.

"Mr. Kensley?"

"That is what I came here to find out." A hesitant smile creased his face. "I never quite made it."

"But how should Father know? What does all this have to do with the. . .with the business you discussed in London?"

"Let us not talk of it, hmm?" He nodded to the door. "Now leave me alone so I can torture myself with the sorrows of Mr. Werther, whoever he is."

"But—"

"Remember? If you make me angry, I shall stand on my head."

"In your condition, I should like to see you try." Sighing, she walked around the bed, then looped an arm around the bed poster and cocked her head at him. "Mr. Kensley?"

"Hmm?"

"Have you any other sisters?"

His eyes widened with the realization she believed him. Then he shook his head with a small laugh. "None so merciless in chess as you."

Days passed into more days with very little to distinguish them. Moving hurt. Not moving hurt. Over and over, William imagined ripping away the bed linens, hobbling from the room, finding Duke, and getting away from here whether he perished on the way or not.

Miss Gresham's visits kept him from madness. She brought him books, or a chessboard, or even a drizzling box so he could assist her in removing gold and silver threads from a tapestry. Such tedium. None of the pastimes amused—but then again, he doubted they amused Miss Gresham either.

She likely came for his sake alone.

Because she believed him.

How strange that she did not curse his being here. That she did not look at him with a wrinkled nose of disdain, as if his illegitimacy were a pollution. Instead, she seemed almost as if she. . .well, as if she cared a bit whether he lived or died. Or whether he went mad in this bed. Or whether his pillow was situated wrong and giving him pain.

If he had imagined a sister, he could have thought of no one greater. She was light and happy and innocent and true. She had feelings that were not buried behind a stoic exterior but were displayed without restraint at every change of thought or temperament.

The door pushed open, drawing William from his thoughts. Dusk had already turned the windows a dark blue, and as no one had yet come to light a candle and the visitor did not hold one himself, only a shadow entered the room.

Blood coursed hot and fast through William's veins. The figure was too large, too broad, to be Miss Gresham or Helena or the lanky footman who was sometimes sent up to assist William. If he had to fight for his life again, he didn't know if he'd have enough strength—

"You should never have come here." Lord Gresham's voice. He stepped to the end of the bed, where streams of pale moonlight illuminated his rage-filled face.

William glanced at his father's hands. No gun. William's body relaxed. "There is not much I can do about it now."

"Who endeavors to see you dead?"

"You?"

"If I had wanted you killed, you would not have survived the first day in my house."

Somehow, William believed that.

"I want you gone. I want you away from Sharottewood."

"When?"

The glowing eyes punctured him, and the chin lifted with a disgust so fervent it answered the question without words.

Gritting his teeth, William yanked off the bed linens. Be hanged if he'd stay here a moment longer. He'd crawl his way out if he had to.

His bare feet hit the cold floor and a shiver worked through his legs as fast as the tremble. "Have my horse prepared then. I am grateful for the ministrations I have received and shall not bother you again." He clutched an arm around his side, the throb pulsing his entire body, as he wound around the bed and held on to the edge for support.

Dizziness flashed colors in his eyes as he fumbled to light a candle. His boots. Where were they?

He spotted them in the corner by a chair, stumbled into it, and yanked the clean stockings and Hessians onto his feet. Pain radiated through him in waves. Where had they stuffed his clothes? Perhaps Helena had taken them somewhere else or tucked them in a drawer. Or perhaps they were right before his eyes, and his vision was too blurry and spinning to see them.

Never mind.

William never ran, but he never stayed where he was not welcome either.

He pulled himself up, started across the room on legs that felt like jelly, and kept his gaze pinned to the doorway. His knees buckled, but a pair of hands seized him before he thudded to the floor.

He was led back to the bed. Helped beneath the counterpane, even as his chest hammered erratically and out of control.

The face staring down at him dipped in and out of blackness. "I shall not have a murder charge against me. You shall leave when you are well."

Gratefulness seeped through William, but he could do no more than nod, breathing hard. Perhaps the man was not all devil.

Perhaps, despite everything, he had one small feeling of kindness for his son.

"You have a visitor."

Isabella glanced up from the letter she had been reading, which proved to be nothing more than dreary accounts of all the unpleasantries Lilias was forced to endure in life. The poor girl. Did she ever find *anything* to be happy about?

Besides gentlemen and wine, that is.

Bridget stepped closer to the satinwood writing table in the drawing room. "Miss Gresham?"

"Yes, I know. I have a visitor." Isabella left the letter with another unopened one and tidied the desk. Standing and smoothing her morning dress, she finally turned her full attention to her maid. "Who is it?"

The slight pinch on Bridget's face sent a warning through her. Only one visitor would prompt such a reaction.

"Lord Livingstone?"

"Yes, Miss Gresham. However did you know?"

"Never mind that. You must tell him that I am ill."

"But Lord Gresham already assured him you were in good health—"

"Then tell him I am riding."

Bridget's quick shake of the head assured Isabella that Father had already ruined that escape route too.

A sigh filled her. "Very well. Have him sent in, wait a minute or so, then come and interrupt us with an urgent matter for me to attend to."

"Oh miss." Pink blossomed on Bridget's face. "Please do not ask such a thing."

Good heavens. Was everything against her evading this visit? "Very well. I shall endure it without any help at all." Isabella found a seat on the red velvet sofa with scrolled arms, then watched the door until a servant announced Lord Livingstone.

He bowed upon entrance. He appeared much the same as he had in London, his expensive taste evident in the well-tailored clothes, the pristine cravat, and the gold watch fob looped below his flamboyant waistcoat. "Miss Gresham, you appear the epitome of comeliness."

"Thank you, my lord." She gestured to the chair adjacent to her. "Won't you sit?"

He did so without taking his eyes off her. "I would inquire after your father, but I have already spoken with him."

"So I have heard."

"He appears in the utmost health. He was going for a ride when I encountered him upon my entrance."

"Yes. Father has always been most vigorous in activity."

"A worthy trait."

"Indeed. And your family, my lord?" She struggled to keep a smile in place, though the conversation lacked any originality. "I have not yet heard you speak of them."

"They are well. Thank you."

"Have you siblings?"

"No."

"Father and mother?"

"My mother is deceased. My father is yet living. But let us not talk of such things any longer." He leaned forward, and a cautioning sensation shot through her at the sight of his gaping lips.

The lips that had once claimed hers.

"There can be no confusion as to why I am come."

"On the contrary. I am quite baffled by it, my lord."

"The life seeped out of London the second you departed. I could stay not a moment longer." He pushed to his feet quickly enough to make her jump. "I shall not hide my feelings. I am in love with you."

In love? Her toes squirmed in her slippers as heat burned a trail of embarrassment through the length of her. No one had ever declared love to her. No one had ever even hinted at such a thing.

She would have laughed at them if they had.

But she could not laugh now. Not at a face so serious, so intense, so powerful that she stood without meaning to. "My lord, I—"

"Do not say anything, for I know you would only discourage me." He shook his head and took one step closer. "And I shall not be discouraged for anything. I am quite set on winning you. I came to make you aware."

She clasped her hands in front of her, eyes widening to the point of discomfort. "I do not imagine that I could be won. I am sorry that in such a short acquaintance you should have been afflicted with love, but—"

"Miss Gresham." Fire lanced his words. Another step. They faced each other, close enough he could have reached out and captured her for another kiss if he was a fool. "You apparently have understood none of what I have told you."

"I fear you misunderstand me as well."

"I shall win you. I must have you."

"We do not always get what we wish, my lord."

"I do." His gaze roamed her person before settling back on her eyes. "I attain everything I desire. Good day." With a step back and a stiff bow, he left the room, the door sending a jarring thud throughout the drawing room.

Isabella sank back into the sofa. She glanced at her hands. They shook in her lap. Was she so affected by his declaration of love?

No, his attachment meant nothing. Especially when she did not even believe love existed. Likely, his affection for her was no more than sensual lust and a potent need to obtain that which was not easily had. So why did she shake?

She didn't like to admit the truth to herself.

She was afraid of him.

Chapter 7

"What do you think you are doing?"

William turned from the bookshelf, two books in one hand and his other pressed to his side. The wound throbbed beneath bandages and fabric. "Getting something to read."

"I can see that." Isabella entered in a white dress with a thin bandeau framing her delicate black ringlets. "What are you doing out of bed?"

"I shall have you know"—he turned back to perusing the colorful spines—"that I have been pacing in my room these past five days."

"Well, I shall have *you* know that I did not go through the trouble of saving your life to have you thwart all my progress now."

"Your progress?" He grunted. "I rather thought I was the one doing the healing."

She walked up behind him, snatched his books, and hugged them against her chest.

He turned to her, growling, "See here. It took me a lot of pain to get down the stairs and locate the library, and a good half hour to find something of worth to read."

Her eyes sparkled, but she seemed to be trying very hard to be cross. She took a step back. "I am unaffected by your pleas. Go upstairs now or I shall not return them."

"Fight or run, then?"

"You are too weak to fight."

"And too stubborn to run."

A sigh left her, and a pleading look drew her lips into a pout.

He imagined she used such expressions to persuade her father into consenting to her.

He imagined it worked.

"Well, it so happens I was headed back anyway." He eased himself to a leather chair and sat, controlling his features against the pain rippling through him. "But first, a moment of rest." His scratches and cuts, mere scabs now, did naught but itch his skin. The graze along his neck had long since healed enough to need no bandage, though Helena still rubbed ointment in the crease every morning.

But it was his side that seemed to flare his body with pain. He tried to remind himself it could have been worse. The bullet had gone clean through his skin and not deep enough to do detrimental damage.

Or so the doctor had said.

The blasted hole certainly felt detrimental. How long would it be before he could move without grimacing? Or walk without tiring so easily?

Isabella approached his chair and with a sweet look laid the books back in his lap. "Can I get you anything?"

"Enemies to friends again so soon?"

"Do not tease me. I am afraid for you. It was far too soon for you to descend the stairs and—"

The library doors swung open. Edward Gresham halted so fast his mouth dropped open a second, as his gaze bounced from William to Isabella—then back to William. "You are much improved, I see, to be making tours of the house."

"He was not making tours, Father. Even this has exhausted him."

William pushed back to his feet. "Good day, my lord."

The greeting seemed to anger his father more. He slammed his book to an end table, hardened his jaw, and nodded toward the window overlooking the entrance courtyard. "If you are able, I shall send for a carriage and servant to escort you home."

"I had hoped to depart the same way I arrived, my lord. On horseback."

"Father, he is hardly strong enough for travel—"

"Very well. I shall leave departure to Mr. Kensley's discretion. Excuse me." He left quicker than he had arrived, and Isabella turned back to face William.

"I shall walk with you upstairs. Here. Give me the books and hold on to my arm."

He did neither, but did not protest when her hand slipped into the crook of his elbow. As they passed from the library to the hall, she offered a slight squeeze.

As if in sorrow for Lord Gresham's scorn. As if in understanding of his pains, external and internal. As if in care of him. Sweet, guileless care of him.

The one thing he needed more than anything else.

"I should like to borrow a carriage." William stood fully dressed in his bedchamber doorway, having waited for Isabella's morning visit.

She was punctual as ever. At his words, though, she strode faster down the hall and frowned. "You insisted you should like to leave on horseback."

"I am not leaving yet."

"But the carriage—"

"I want to see the man. The Mr. Abram you spoke of."

Her dark brows lifted. "He is but a mere farmer. He would not expect you to visit, nor would he expect thanks. Especially when you are still so very weak—"

"I don't care if he's a ragpicker or a king. He saved my life. I want to see him."

Isabella hesitated, pink flooding her cheeks as if she understood the haughtiness of her words. Didn't she realize a pauper was of no less value than a man of wealth? Why did it seem as if she always placed the poor beneath her? Were those the morals Edward Gresham had taught his child?

William went back into the bedchamber, retrieved his hat, and left the hall with her following after him.

"I shall go with you."

"I do not imagine your father shall approve." *Their* father, that is.

"But you shall need assistance."

"Hardly." In the last fortnight, he'd been traveling down to the library twice a day, and the journey through the house, each time, seemed to increase his strength. Within days, he would be ready to leave. Perhaps sooner, if the carriage ride went well.

As they reached the bottom of the stairs, Isabella latched on to his arm. "Please wait one moment and I shall gather my bonnet and gloves. I daresay, I shall not consent to sending for a carriage if you do not take me with you."

Conniving little vixen. Did she always get her way?

"Very well." He nodded her away. "Hurry off with you then." Soon they were seated in a phaeton and driving through the impressive Sharottewood gates.

His nerves twitched as they followed the road along the cliffside. He scanned the area. Where had the assailant hidden? Had the man with the continental hat already rushed back to William's aunt and delivered the news?

Or was it Horace who wanted him dead?

William would know soon enough. As soon as he was able to stay atop a horse, he would return to Rosenleigh and do what he should have done all along. Fight without running.

"Mr. Kensley?"

"Hmm?" When she said nothing, he glanced at her. A blue-green sea rippled behind her, and the sweeping breeze stirred the black ringlets at her chin.

"Have I said something amiss?"

"What?"

"To make you angered with me." She swallowed. "Or disappointed."

Did it matter so much to her? His approval or disapproval?

"I did not mean to say anything ill of Mr. Abram," she rushed on, blinking fast. "He seems quite a nice man and there is certainly nothing in the world wrong with being a farmer, and after all, he did save your life—"

"There are too many people who would offer the honorary seat to the rich and the stool in the corner to the poor."

"I have heard the vicar at church read as much."

"A man is not what he possesses but what he does with himself."

"You are right, of course. I shall never forget." She smiled then, as if the admonishment had soothed instead of annoyed her. "You are wonderfully good, Mr. Kensley. If I took a hundred phaeton rides in your company, I imagine I should become a hundred times a better person."

He laughed. "You are nonsense."

"And you are headed the wrong way. This road here." She pointed him in the right direction, and the phaeton rumbled over a less traversed road with mossy stone walls flanking each side. They rode for less than a mile, when a worn thatched cottage, a red barn, and fields of barley filled their view.

After William handed Miss Gresham down from the carriage, they approached the door and knocked thrice with no answer.

William glanced up and spotted a figure wading through the gold-green barley field. The man waved in greeting and minutes later neared the cottage with greater speed than his age should have allowed.

Sweaty and dusty, he was dressed in brown breeches, striped stockings, and black boots, with a course linen frock over his coat. A yellow handkerchief was knotted at his throat, and he pulled a floppy hat from off his head. Thin grey hair, parted severely to the left and draped across his head, couldn't quite conceal the baldness.

Despite his appearance, a pleasantness shone in the sunburnt cheeks and smiling eyes. "Rightly honored, I be, that you should come, Miss Gresham." He bowed, glancing up at William. "And rightly glad, sir, to see the likes of you standin' on two strong feet."

"I am not yet certain how strong they are." William stepped forward and grasped the man's hand. He squeezed. "But I am standing nonetheless, and it seems I have you to thank for that."

"Oh." A shrugged shoulder, a lifted smile. " 'Tween't nothin' I done. Just hauled you in, I did. Ol' Sunshine over there did most of the work, I reckon." He nodded to where a bony horse grazed inside a fence along the barn.

Mirth stirred in William's throat. "Please express my gratitude to Sunshine, then."

"You want to be comin' inside? I've tea I can be settin' to boil and hot milk, if you have it that way, though I don't have no sugar."

Beside him, Miss Gresham flustered. "Oh, really, we must be go—"

"Indeed. Tea would be just the thing." William winked at Isabella and followed Mr. Abram into the small abode. The room smelled of burning wood, yeast from the bread rising on the table, and a unique blend of sweat, straw, and tobacco.

Only two stools occupied the room, so William and Miss Gresham both seated themselves while Mr. Abram bustled about preparing the tea.

Her finger nudged his knee. "Why did you consent?" she mouthed without sound, her nose slightly wrinkled.

William grinned. For all her assurances on their ride here, she now seemed to have forgotten them. This would do her no harm, though. Sitting here in a humble cottage, perched on stools, accepting steaming tea in earthenware cups from a man who practically trembled with excitement.

They drank and talked and laughed for close to an hour. Mr. Abram, in his simple and quiet way, told them of his crops and his animals, all of which had names and rather amusing misadventures.

Miss Gresham said little at first. But as the conversation wore on, she seemed amused by the funny stories and laughed so hard once she dabbed moisture from her eyes. When they departed, she even left the old man with a promise she'd return again sometime, perhaps with a bit of sugar for ol' Sunshine or a new bell for Rosie the milk cow.

Out of sight of the cottage, William leaned forward and urged the phaeton faster. "That was not so unbearable, was it?"

"Certainly more bearable than the visit with Mrs. Shaw." She tugged off her gloves and fanned her face against the heat. "I retrieved a letter from Sophia Kettlewell, who passed along a letter from Mr. Pidcock, the bishop who runs the aid society. He assures that the Shaws are doing quite well, despite a lingering cough in the mother."

"Good. I imagine she will recover soon enough with proper care and food."

"Indeed."

"How do you access the seashore?"

"What?"

"The seashore." He turned the phaeton onto the road along the cliffside. "You know, sand, water, rocks—"

"I know what a seashore *is*." She chuckled. "But why do you wish to know?"

"Why do you think?"

"La, you are exasperating in every sense. I shall show you the path when we reach it." When the cliff faded into a green, sloping hill, she pointed to a footpath winding toward the shore. "But I daresay, you are not well enough for such a formidable trek."

"I tumbled down the cliffside and survived." He dismounted and helped her down. "I think I can survive this." Leaving the phaeton along the road, they eased down the path as slowly as possible, with Miss Gresham clinging to his arm with a grip so tight it inflicted more pain than his side.

"You can let go now." He pried away her hands when they reached the sand. "So this is your seashore."

"Yes." All her admiration, all the joy she'd derived from this place, escaped in that one word. She untied her bonnet. The wind, salty and warm, played at her curls and bonnet ribbons. "Say one thing against it and I shall never speak to you again."

"I have only good things to say." Leaning into a rock, William pulled off his left boot then his right.

"What are you doing?"

"Taking off my shoes."

"I can see that. But why?"

"Take off those half boots and I shall show you."

She glanced down at her shoes, half sunk into the sand, and hesitated. "But I should ruin my stockings."

"Take them off too."

"And go barefoot?"

A laugh filled his stomach. How much she had to learn. How much he could teach her. "Come here." He jogged toward her, bare feet burning in the sand, and motioned her to sit. Then he helped her off with her shoes and stockings, pulled her back to her feet, and turned her toward the ocean.

At the water's edge, she squealed when the clear, foamy tide bubbled up around her toes. "It's cold!"

"Now close your eyes."

"What?"

"Come on. Close them." He squeezed her hand, slid his own eyes shut, pulled them back a step. "You've spent the entirety of your life *seeing* the seashore, but seeing is only half of things. Now *feel* it."

"I daresay, you are mad. I hardly know what you mean."

"Wiggle your toes. Does the sand burn them?"

"Yes."

"Breathe with your mouth open. Taste salt?"

A giggle. "I think so."

"Now step forward. Into the water. That's it."

"But my dress—"

"Dash the dress, silly, and feel the water swirling around your ankles—"

"Ah!" A wave smacked their legs and freezing water splashed up around their knees, seeping into her dress and his breeches.

Laughing, he scooped her up and dragged her deeper into the sea.

"Put me down! Oh dear. It's cold. Freezing. Mr. Kensley, put me. . ." The pleas dissolved into another fit of merriment, and she rammed her eyes shut with water heavy on her lashes. She gasped with each new wave. "You are impossible."

"Now you understand?"

"Understand what?"

"How to *feel* the seashore."

She wiped her eyes, hair sticking to her cheeks, and squirmed out of his arms. She plodded back to the shore, flinging water from both hands. "I understand feeling the seashore as much as I understand doing sunshine."

He splashed her back. "Admit it."

"Admit what?"

"That you have had more amusement ripping off shoes and stockings and drenching your dress than you ever had strolling the shore."

"I do not just stroll the shore. I ride too." She sat, dry sand clinging to skin and fabric. "Besides, I admit to nothing except that you are mad."

"Madness can be a great deal of fun." He took a seat beside her, rolled up his breeches, and leaned back.

She leaned back too without questioning anything. They closed their eyes, the heat drying their clothes, the wind stirring through them enough to keep them cool and comfortable.

"I shall probably attain freckles," she whispered, her voice sleepy and lazy and filled with a sigh. "But somehow I do not mind."

They remained that way for a long time, with seagulls flying overhead, squawking into the roar of water lapping into land. He breathed in the air, the taste so clean it rivaled that of Rosenleigh. Once or twice, he glanced over at her.

Her eyes were closed. Sunlight pinkened her cheeks, and sand stuck to the side of her face and flecked her black hair.

All his life he'd been alone. He'd had Miss Ettie to hug him, or Mr. Shelton to talk to—but the rest of his hours, as he'd ridden Ahearn through the countryside, or wandered the labyrinth, or climbed trees in the meadow, he'd been alone.

Miss Gresham eased that void. His sister. His blood. Someone who cared for him, took his side, and was not so proper or haughty that she could not be persuaded into his mischief.

The filling of that hollow, however, was but a passing pleasure. For amid all their fun today, his energy had increased and the crippling pain had decreased.

He was recovered more than he'd realized.

Which meant it was time he leave.

The next morning, Isabella knocked on Mr. Kensley's bedchamber door earlier than usual. If he could make it to the library and Mr. Abram's farm and the seashore, certainly he could muster enough strength to join them for breakfast.

What would Father say?

That hardly mattered. Father was being unreasonable, unreach-able. . .and unkind. A vice she had never before accused him of. Couldn't he see how unfair all of it was? That she, his daughter, should be treated with such love, while his own son was rejected and disdained?

As she tapped her knuckles against the door with more force, in hopes of awakening him, a maid appeared in her line of vision.

"If you be looking for Mr. Kensley, Miss Gresham, he not be there."

"Oh?"

"He be in the stables, I think, readying his horse to leave—"

Heart in her throat, Isabella sped past the maid and took the stairs so fast Mrs. Morrey would have her head should she see. Leaving? Without so much as a parting word? How could he?

Unbidden tears blurred her vision as she raced outside and ran toward the stables. She drew to a stop outside the door. If he cared so little about his own sister as to depart without seeing her, should she bother?

Before she could decide, the enormous double doors whined open. Mr. Kensley emerged, fully dressed in a green tailcoat, black breeches, beaver hat, and shiny Hessians.

Hessians she had rubbed clean of blood and mud when he'd been thrashing his head with fever.

"Good morning."

She stepped out of his way, his cheerful words stirring her hurt into wrath. She blinked hard enough the tears were gone. The last thing she wanted was to cry before him. "I see you are departing."

"Yes." He moved to the horse's side, no longer facing her, and tightened the cinch. "After yesterday's excursion, I recognized how greatly improved I am."

"A three-mile trip in a carriage can hardly compare to a ride halfway across England."

"I shall manage."

"I see." She wanted to say more but didn't know what. All along, since he'd first arrived, she'd known he couldn't stay. Father hated him. Mr. Kensley was a threat to them, to their social standing, to the reputation that allowed them to walk in anyone's presence with their heads held high.

If word of his illegitimacy was leaked, she would be ruined. Her hopes of a profitable match, one that would please Father, would be demolished.

She knew that. She understood. 'Twas best he should leave. The sooner, the better.

Yet when he turned back around and looked at her, the traitorous tears were back. What fun they'd had. Indeed, she could never go back to the library without remembering the rainy day they'd sat at the window and fingered pictures into the frosty glass, laughing at each other's nonsense. How could she ever play chess again or take walks in the garden or drizzle the old and boring tapestry without him?

And the seashore. A knot grew in her throat, because the seashore would never be the same. "You are terrible." She swung away—

He snatched her hand and tugged her back. "Terrible for what?"

She wanted to tell him this was not the time to grin, or to tease her, or to seem so easy in his manner. But she said only, "Terrible to leave without saying goodbye."

"I have not yet left."

"You would have."

He shook his head. "I was coming to find you as soon as I prepared my horse. Did you think I would thank Mr. Abram for saving my life but not thank my sister?" He pecked a kiss on the top of her head. "Make certain you do sunshine and feel the seashore, hmm?"

"I shall never see you again."

He turned back to his horse, mounted, then glanced down at her without quite meeting her eyes. "For everything, I thank you."

"I am sorry." She followed the horse a few steps. "That it must be this way. That Father is sending you away and—"

"Never mind all that." He grinned once more, sunlight glinting around him, horse prancing in the gravel. "I should have rather had a sister these last weeks than never had one at all. God keep you safe, Miss Gresham." Tipping his hat, he guided his horse toward the gate and rode away.

She watched until he disappeared. Loneliness ebbed through her as she wiped her eyes and ambled back inside the grandeur of the manor house. Strange, how quiet and empty everything already seemed. The polished marble floors, so clean not a footprint could be noticed. The somber-faced ancestors hanging on the walls. The soundless maids, bustling here and there, never glancing up. The breakfast room, where Father smiled at her and continued on with his cup of cocoa and his unwrinkled newspaper.

She'd never realized herself to be so alone until Mr. Kensley came and left. But she'd made Father a promise.

From this day forth, she would never see her brother again.

Chapter 8

For the third time today, William eased himself off Duke and hobbled to the edge of the road. He leaned against a mossy stone wall, hand on his thigh, exhaustion aching in his muscles. Only three days into his journey and he was beginning to wonder if he'd make it.

He plucked a few grass blades. Miss Gresham had been right. A short carriage ride was not quite comparable to a horse ride from Northumberland to Leicestershire.

Miss Gresham. He stayed on the name, amused by the way she'd angered at the thought of him leaving without a goodbye. Then tears had misted her eyes.

Tears for *him.*

Hadn't she cried when he'd been injured? When he'd been locked in the black room, teetering on the cutting edge of death? What made her care for him so?

She'd certainly not inherited her affectionate spirit from her father.

Two images loomed in William's mind. One of his mother, trapped in the framed picture, beautiful and delicate and sad. Then Lord Gresham. Tall, broad, firm, unrelenting, powerful in both voice and look. They had loved each other?

Strange, that. He couldn't reconcile the two images.

Or imagine himself a part of either of them.

Dusting off his breeches, William grunted and pulled himself to his feet. He swung back atop Duke, pain lancing through his bullet hole as he grabbed the reins and tugged them toward the road.

Two, perhaps three days at the most. If he could make it that far, he'd reach home. He only hoped he would not have to fight for his life yet again when he arrived.

"Oh dear."

"What is it?" From across the drawing room, ensconced in his favorite chair, Father glanced up from his own stack of letters. "Miss Trewman is not unwell, I hope?"

"No, she is as well as can be expected." Isabella smirked at the words, then twisted around in her chair at the satinwood writing desk. "It is this second letter which distresses me. Can you guess who it is from?"

"I am sure I would not know."

"Lady Sarsfield."

"Oh?"

"You remember. Her husband, Lord Sarsfield, sits in the House of Commons and is always speaking at those political rallies you bid me never to attend."

"Oh yes. No, I certainly would not have you near such rallies. It is half-witted fools like Lord Sarsfield who disgrace crown and country by trying to pass outlandish bills. Pray, what does his wife want?"

"For me to attend their house party in two weeks. Everyone likely has just returned to their homes after the season, and I suppose Lady Sarsfield cares not a whit that all her guests will have to pack and be off again."

"I imagine most will not mind."

"Well, I do."

Father chuckled. "I daresay, it is not the traveling you mind so much as the lady herself. Is she not the one who—"

"Yes, she is the one." Isabella turned back to the offensive invitation, biting her lip. Last season, the prune-faced woman had accused Isabella in a ballroom full of people of stepping on her ladyship's hem.

Maybe Isabella *had*, quite accidentally of course, but she would never admit such a thing. The fussy old woman deserved a rip in her finery anyway.

"Perhaps you should accept the invitation after all."

The serious note made Isabella glance at Father.

He held a letter open before him, lips pinched, as he leaned forward in the chair. "I did not relate the reasons to you before, as I did not wish anything to spoil your gaiety in London. But the same reason that drew me to Bath, it seems, is calling for me again."

Isabella stood. "What is it?"

"It seems yet another manor house has been raided and plundered."

"How dreadful. I have heard whispers of the infamous marauders. Lilias calls them pirates, though that certainly seems a bit old-fashioned and theatrical."

"Pirates, marauders—whatever they are, they are a threat to any landowner of substantial wealth." Father rose from his chair, crumpling the letter. "This is the second friend they have attacked. I must go at once to Cumbria and offer any assistance I can."

"Of course you must." Isabella sighed. "And though Lady Sarsfield is not my ideal companion, I shall write Lilias and beg her to join me. The diversion will do me good."

"Indeed. You have been. . ." Father hesitated, then offered a smile, as if to take back his words. What had he been ready to say? That since Mr. Kensley had departed, she had been aimless, listless, bored?

The absence of Mr. Kensley had quite the opposite effect on Father. Indeed, he'd quite returned to his normal, cheerful self—every hair back in its place, cheeks healthy, eyes no longer wearied from lack of sleep. Could he so easily put it out of his mind and forget he had a son?

Perhaps the house party would put it out of hers.

Yet somehow, she did not imagine it possible she could forget she had a brother.

The sight undid him.

William rode the last few feet with his shoulders hunched, his hand splayed below his rib cage, the throb in his wound matching the throb of his heart.

Rosenleigh was unchanged. Fog weaved along the grey-stoned house, and pale moonlight reflected off the dark glass windows. He strained his eyes to see if a shadow awaited him behind one of the panes. One with a continental hat.

And a gun.

Be hanged if he cared, at this point. All he wanted to do was take care of his horse, find his own chamber, and fall into bed. He likely would not awake even if someone did creep in to murder him.

With weariness dogging his steps, William went through the motions of brushing down Duke in the stables and feeding the animal in his stall. Then he hurried for the house, entering quietly enough that even Mr. Pugh, the footman, would probably not hear in his nightly guard of the family silver.

The stairs whined with every step. William's skin pebbled as he glanced behind him, then around him, before starting down the hall. Why did the house stir such a sense of unwelcome inside him?

How he had missed this place. Not for the memories, or for the people who inhabited it—but because it was the one thing in the world that belonged to him.

Yet even that felt changed.

With a chill sweeping through him, he creaked open his bedchamber door and stepped into the dark room.

Relief chipped away at his tension. The bed was waiting, unrumpled, just as he'd left it the night he fled. Tossing his hat to the rug, William sat on the edge of the bed and yanked off his boots. He drew back the bed linens—

"Well, well, well."

William jerked toward the voice, chest hitching.

A pair of luminous eyes met his from the other side of the room. Heavy breathing filled the air. The shadowy chair creaked under the change of weight as the black figure rose and staggered. "The long-lost cousin is home."

Chapter 9

W hat are you doing in here?" William stepped away from the bed, hands pulling into fists.

Horace lit a candle. Light flittered across the room and revealed the wreckage—stained goblets on the Axminster rug, crumpled clothes strewn across the floor, empty decanters missing stoppers. What in the name of heaven?

"With you dead, the master bedchamber belongs to me. But you're not dead." Liquor dribbled down his chin. "I should have bloody known."

"Sorry to disappoint." William bent down and yanked two shirtsleeves and a foul-smelling tailcoat from the floor. "I see nothing has changed in my absence. No maid?"

"I don't bloody need a maid."

William threw the clothes over the back of a chair. "Never mind. We shall talk in the morning. I shall occupy one of the guest chambers—"

Horace flung himself in front of the door, arms flattened, eyes wild. "They said you were dead." Lucidity altered his expression, as if he were not so drunk as William imagined. "They said you were—"

"I'm not."

"How?"

"You must have wanted Rosenleigh very much. More than I realized." William ground his teeth. "Out of my way, Horace."

"Then it is true." A laugh came out. Brittle, hysterical—then tears flooded his face. "I lied to myself so many times I believed it was not so."

"What are you talking about?"

"You." Vulnerability quivered the face. "Leaving that way, dying that way. This room." He swung an arm. "I knew all along it wasn't mine, but I listened to her anyway."

Stonelike pressure lodged itself in William's chest. "Aunt?"

"Yes. Who else?" Horace stumbled away from the door and fell into the chair. He leaned forward, face in his hands. "I knew she wanted Rosenleigh. She loves this place more than she ever loved. . .me. But I didn't bloody-well know she'd kill you for it."

"Well, she has not killed me yet." William opened the door but hesitated.

His cousin's form was hunched, shoulders racking, in a way that reminded William of the little cousin he once knew. Not the one who stuck out his tongue, or threw a punch, or ran tattling to his mother.

But the one William would find in the corner of the nursery every once in a while, with his head pressed into his knees. The one who cried because his mother never had time for him. The one who confessed once that William should be grateful. "At least she notices you when she scolds you or punishes you. She doesn't even remember I'm here," he'd once cried.

The same pity William had possessed then formed back in the pit of his gut. He closed the door, raked air into his lungs, and wiped a hand down his tired face.

Tomorrow, he would face the woman who had hurt them both.

Morning chased away the horrors of pain and exhaustion. William washed, dressed, and wolfed down a hot breakfast, though Cook screamed and nearly fainted upon first sighting him.

On his way to the west wing, even Ruth was startled.

The girl fluttered both hands to her mouth, turned three shades whiter, and looked as if she might have slunk to the floor if William had not steadied her. "Oh. . .oh, but you be dead, sir. Mrs. Willoughby said you—"

"A mere miscommunication." William winked. "Either that, or I have come back to haunt the place." When the girl swooned again, William laughed and guided her to a hall chair. "Poor girl. Sit here and rest until you feel better. Do you not know ghosts cannot be touched?"

Wide-eyed, she glanced at his hand on her elbow. The thought seemed to comfort her, but she managed nothing more than an incoherent noise.

"Now, when you have your legs again, go and tell Miss Ettie that I am returned. Break the news to her gently, for I do not wish to catch everyone I encounter." He hurried on to the west wing, and the nearer he drew to the bedchamber door, the more his breakfast roiled in his stomach.

He didn't want to face her.

A thousand times he'd been forced into this bedchamber, where he'd been inflicted with words that had bruised him. Sometimes she'd slap him across the face, her rings snagging his skin and bringing blood. Other times she'd yell for a footman to drag him out and lock him in solitude.

But always, he left injured. Today he was injured before he even entered her presence.

He swept inside without knocking, and as he shut the door behind him, he tried to adjust his eyes to the dimness of the room. The closed draperies allowed in little light. Dust motes floated across the air, landing here and there across dusty furniture.

The bed creaked. "Go and fetch me another quilt. It is damp and cold in here. I told you that, stupid girl."

Staring at the lump under the covers, William crept closer. Poor Ruth. No wonder the young maid was always timid and frightened.

"Girl!"

"I fear she is not well at the moment. She fell ill after seeing me."

A gasp, then the lump rolled over until a sallow, stricken face stared back at him. Shadows hung under the eyes, and the wrinkled lips lacked even the small color they'd had before. "You."

He bowed. "At your service, Aunt."

"What are you doing? How are you here?"

"He was mistaken."

"Who?"

"The man who told you I was dead." William walked to the window, ripped back the draperies. A million more dust motes stirred in the morning light rays. "How long have you been plotting to have me killed?"

"You insolent fool. Shut that drapery. Come here this instant."

"I am afraid not, Aunt. Things do not work as they used to. I am far too big for dark rooms."

She scooted herself up, breathing fast and raspy, snot leaking from her red nose. "What happened? He assured me you were gunshot, that you toppled from a cliffside and your body washed into the sea."

"Things are not always as they seem."

"Do not speak riddles to me! I want to know. How did you escape?"

"Does it matter?"

A series of deep coughs rattled her chest. Then, leaning her head against the headboard in exhaustion, she rasped, "No. It does not matter, I suppose. I should have known a wretched lamplighter from the village could not do as I asked. I should have. . .but no, it does not matter. Even you being alive does not matter, because Rosenleigh still does not belong to you." Her rheumy eyes settled on him. "You really do not know, do you?"

"Know what?"

"You mindless fool. I could have killed you and it would have been a kindness. Then I could have secured the five thousand pounds a year. No one would have ever known. You would have had a burial far better than you deserve—"

"What are you saying?" William braced himself, tried to prepare his mind, but every inch of him needled with fear.

She snarled and laughed. "You are not my sister's son, you wretch. We took you out of a workhouse the night Constance and her child died in childbirth. I raised you under pretense. All for the money. All so I might have the means to get back at Edward Gresham, the fool who chose my sister over me and was willing to pay five thousand pounds to keep you secr—"

"You are lying." William stepped back and shook his head. "They must be lies."

"Ask your precious Miss Ettie."

"No—"

"You know it is true. Filthy little pauper. You are nothing next to me. Nothing next to my son. You look and smell and act like the dirty rats you came from. I hated you from the second they brought your starving little carcass into this house."

Numbness cloaked him and threatened his vision. He backed up another step. *God?* This wasn't true. Shelton would not have sent William after Edward Gresham if the man was not William's father. Shelton would have told him the truth.

Miss Ettie would have told him the truth.

"You owe me everything." His aunt leaned forward, pointing a jeweled finger. "You would have died in the workhouse if it wasn't for me. You would have been like all the other starving little brats, scrounging for food, sleeping in corners, hungry and despicable and rotten." She clasped her chest with more coughs. "Now get out. Nothing here belongs to you. You deserve nothing. Nothing."

"Aunt—"

"I am not your aunt!" she screeched and jerked her fist at the door. "Leave! Leave!"

"One word from you is supposed to satisfy me?"

"It is the truth, you beggar. Why do you think you were so wicked as a child? Why do you think I had to punish you so much? You're the offspring of pigs, that is why. Criminals and prostitutes and. . ." Coughs. "And. . ." More coughs. "Get out! Out!" She doubled over, grasping her heart with both hands, a strangled cry filling the room.

William moved next to the bed, her stench of sweat-mingled rosewater perfume overwhelming. He grasped her shoulders and leaned her back against the pillows. "Can you hear me?"

"Do—not—touch me." Her eyes were closed, features twisted in pain, but she spat in disgust.

The spittle landed on his cheek. Rage burned through him, choking, and he swiped away the moisture with his coat sleeve. He had to get out of here. This room. This place. The lies upon lies. His entire life had been untrue? Everything he believed of himself? Or was Aunt so desperate to see him gone that she'd invent such deceptions?

He turned for the door, but another cry pivoted him back around.

"Help." For the second time she hugged her chest, curling into a fetal position with gasps. "Someone. . .help."

Hundreds of memories flashed through his mind. The many times he had begged her to let him out of the black room. Her ring in his skin. Her spittle on his face. The lies she'd just unearthed and exposed to him.

He didn't want to help her. He hadn't that kind of strength.

He quit the room, slammed the door, but made it no farther than the hall before he sprinted back into the chamber he despised. He tucked the bed linens under her chin, added another pillow behind her head, and brought a glass of water to her lips.

"Help." Her lips mouthed the word without sound. The water sloshed past them but then oozed back down her face without making it down her throat. "Help. . ."

"I am here. Stay still. I shall call for someone to ride for the doctor." When she didn't answer, he yanked the bell pull beside her bed, then marched out into the hall and shouted for assistance. As footsteps announced someone coming, William returned to her bedside.

He took her hand, but the cold, clammy skin startled him. "Aunt?"

She didn't stir, or cough, or spew more hatred, or demand him to get out of her sight.

Nausea pushed through him as he inched his hand to her wrist. No pulse met his fingertips.

Dear heavens, she was dead.

Lilias's head swayed back and forth with the motion of the carriage. "I do hope we arrive soon. The roads these days are insufferably atrocious. Indeed, one more jostle and I shall likely fall apart."

"Do try to stay strong, dear." Isabella reached for her friend's hand and squeezed in mock consolation. "We are not five minutes away now, you know. Surely you can bear it."

As if sensing her sarcasm, Lilias smiled a bit and tried for cheerfulness. "Hopefully there shall be many an eligible gentleman."

"Lilias!"

"I am not ashamed of being on a hunt for matrimony. Some of us *want* to get married, you know."

"I want to get married too." Isabella frowned out the carriage window. Sweeping countryside dotted with bushes, trees, and sheep hurried by. "But in my own time and of my own choice."

"I cannot imagine you choosing anyone. Pray, what are your requirements?"

"Good heavens." Isabella gaped at her friend. Did the girl have any sense at all? "You quite make it sound as if choosing a husband were as simple as ordering a hat. Like going into a millinery shop and saying you require a fair bonnet with blue ribbon and cherries and plums and—"

"La, don't be droll. You are funny. Listen here and I shall tell you what I seek in a husband." The girl settled deeper into her seat and no longer seemed to mind the bumps of the carriage. "Tall, handsome features, a bit plump but not so much as to make me feel insignificant standing next to him. Also very rich and gay. There. What do you think?"

"I think that sounds like half the men of the *ton*."

"All the better. I shall have an infinite amount to choose from."

"And you care nothing for his manner? His temperament?"

"So long as he is not so very disagreeable."

"What if he is dull?"

"Why, Isabella, I am only going to *marry* him, after all. It is not as if I need find him perfect in every sense. Now tell me yours."

"I have none. Truly." Expectation had been ripped from her at nine years old. The words played again. How she had despaired over them as a child, but now she understood them.

Love was social benefits, impressive dowries, and the temporary desire between man and woman. Beyond that, it did not exist.

She would not be so foolish as to pretend it did.

The carriage halted before Isabella was forced to partake of any more of Lilias's nonsense. A footman handed Isabella down first, then Bridget, then Lilias—who scolded the servant for causing her to drop her reticule, while Isabella glanced up at Rockingham Hall.

The cream-colored house towered three stories high, with six stone chimneys and more windows than she could count. Two additional wings flanked the main house. Bushes, life-sized Greek statues, and colorful flowers stirred a sense of beauty and ambrosial smells.

In the lawn to her left, next to the pond and gardens, six or so gentlemen played pall-mall.

"Oh look, Isabella. Can it be?" Lilias pointed. Very unladylike, of course, but Isabella no longer cared when she spotted the object of Lilias's interest.

The air caught in her throat.

In the distance, a darkly clothed gentleman bent down to readjust one of the iron hoops into the grass. With his mallet over his shoulder, he straightened and glanced up.

His eyes found hers. Of course they did. Didn't they always?

"Who knew Lord Livingstone would be here?" Lilias urged the footman to take care with her valise then looped her arm around Isabella's. "We shall have a lovely house party indeed, I imagine."

Isabella suppressed a groan. *Lovely* was not the word she would have used at all. Could she survive Lord Livingstone and Lady Sarsfield both for an entire month?

The house still reeked of death. The rotting scent hung heavy in the air, mingled with all the flowers that had decorated her woolen shroud.

Horace threw his hat as he entered the foyer behind William. The door slammed behind him, the thud sickening and entrapping. "Where are the bloody servants?"

All the way to the graveyard, Horace had remained silent. Then at the burial, as the Anglican liturgy was read in monotone, as the coffin was lowered into a hole next to Constance Kensley, he had spoken not a word. Indeed, had he said anything in the two days since his mother's passing?

Shedding his black gloves and tossing them to the floor, Horace hurried for the trophy room.

William followed him. He balled his hands into fists as Horace slung open the doors of the cellarette and yanked out a full decanter.

He threw the stopper across the room then guzzled port down his throat without bothering to find a glass.

"That will not help."

"The devil it will." Horace kicked the cellarette cabinet back shut, glass rattling and clattering inside. "Leave me."

"I will not see you destroy yourself."

"I am destroyed already."

"There are other ways of bearing—"

"Get out!" Horace slung the decanter into the window. Glass shattered, the sound piercing as a small breeze whistled in. He whirled to William. His legs spread, cheeks blazed, shoulders bunched. "I should have been the one with her. I should have been with her when she died."

Too many emotions battled within William. He didn't know what they were or which ones he should accept or hide, but a churning pity circled his stomach and overrode the others. "She has been ill a long time. It happened fast. You could not have known to be there."

"But you were. It is always you. You she notices and talks of and—" Horace reared back his head with a cry then charged. He barreled into William and they bashed into the wall together.

Pain vibrated through William's body, shooting from the healing flesh of his side, but he pried Horace off with one shove.

His cousin stumbled back. He returned to the cellarette and retrieved another decanter, but he sank to his knees before it ever reached his lips. A sob sputtered out. He gulped a drink to prevent more cries.

"I am sorry, Horace." That his cousin's entire life had been one disappointment after another. That all the boy had ever wanted was a mother's love, which was always just out of reach.

But Horace was a fool to wish for the attention William had received. Being hated with such vehement punishments was far worse than being ignored.

William quit the room, no longer able to bear the sight of one so pitiful. He had avoided Miss Ettie these last three days. He had told no one the cruelties Aunt had shouted regarding his bloodline.

Now he knocked on the nursery door, knowing he'd find the governess inside, dread climbing his body so fast the blood rushed to his head. He didn't want to know. He didn't want to confront her.

He didn't want to hear the truth.

The door creaked open and Miss Ettie filled the doorway. Her face brightened. Just as it always did when she looked at him, or spoke to him, or reached out and petted him. "My dear boy. You cannot know what I endured when I thought you dead. What a miracle it has been to see you these last days, alive and strong."

In testament to her grief, the brown of her hair had streaked with more silver, and her small frame had thinned in his absence. He regretted causing her such pain. If he had stayed, if he had never run, perhaps everything would have been different.

"Come in, please? I know you are too old to play, but perhaps we can sit and talk."

He nodded and entered the musty nursery, with its child-sized chairs and bookshelves and wooden toys, so long untouched. Why did she love this place so much? Why come here all the time with only memories?

She settled into the same rocking chair she'd always occupied before, when he had curled on her lap and she'd read books to him.

Now he leaned against the wall, arms crossed over his chest, and bore his eyes on her beaming ones. "Why did you not tell me?"

"Tell you what, dear?"

"That I came from the workhouse."

He had hoped she would gasp, and shake her head at him, and ask what in heaven's name he was muttering about.

But no surprise overcame her expression. Only dread. "Then she told you."

"Yes."

"I expected she would, yet I had hoped against hope she would not." Miss Ettie fluttered out a handkerchief and dabbed her eyes. "Please sit down, my dear. Sit here before me and take my hand—"

"You knew all along. You lied to me."

"Sometimes lies are a kindness. Sometimes they are a necessity. In this case, they were both."

"And Shelton? He sent me away knowing—"

"Shelton knew nothing. He cared for you like a son, which is why he was always seeking answers he should have left alone. He discovered old letters between your aunt and Edward Gresham, indicating that the man was your father. Perhaps he would have found out more if Mrs. Willoughby had not ordered him. . .killed."

Fury sprang to William's throat. Breathing hurt. Everything hurt. "You would have allowed me killed too. You knew she wanted me dead and you did nothing—"

"I had no choice." Both hands framed her cheeks. She stared at some unknown object across the nursery, rocking back and forth in her chair as if she were lulling a child. "The day I was sent to fetch you. . .I swore upon your life and the holy Bible that I would never tell. Such a vow cannot be broken. Before Christ, I could not break it."

"William Kensley died at birth."

"God rest his soul."

"Who am I?"

A small shrug, a tilt of her head. "I do not know."

The words burrowed into him. As if he'd been gutted of his insides. As if everything he'd believed of himself no longer existed and he was but a hollow creature. A shell with no name, no heritage, no past, no future, no father who hated him and no mother he could stare at in a painting.

"You were but four days old when I arrived at the Greyfriar Street Workhouse in the village. I came at night so no one would see me. They brought you out wrapped naked in a shawl with bugs crawling in the threads and biting your poor skin." Tears welled. "There were bruises too. So young and helpless, and already they were being unkind to you."

"My parents." The words raked past a dry throat. "What of them?"

"The matron knew very little. Only that a woman was found sleeping outside of the workhouse gates, fevered and with child, two months before you were born. No one seemed to remember her name. She died within hours of your birth."

Mrs. Shaw flashed through his mind. Forsaken and abandoned, desperate, lying prostrate and starving with children she had not the means to provide for. He'd pitied her. He'd pitied the children.

He'd never dreamed they were a picture of himself.

Of his own mother.

"You had a chance all the other poor wretches in that place never had." Miss Ettie rocked harder and faster, twisting the handkerchief in her lap. "We brought you home and fed you. But four days into life, and you were already fevered and malnourished. I stayed by your side and nursed you back to health myself. I made you well again. I loved you." The rocking ceased. Miss Ettie glanced up at him with her chin quivering. "God forgive me if that was wrong, if keeping this secret has been wrong, but no matter what evil Mrs. Willoughby used you for, I could not unsee the way I found you in that workhouse."

William stepped next to her. As she'd wanted, he crouched by the rocker and pulled her hand into both of his. His chest ached. "You did right."

"I know you suffered here," she cried. "I know Mrs. Willoughby was cruel to you and Horace was abusing. But surely those are small afflictions compared to what you might have endured—"

"Yes, yes." He nodded, rubbed her hand to soothe her. "Yes, you did right. Do not cry."

"I cannot help it." She pulled his head against her. Her tears wet his hair. "My dear William. . .I am so sorry."

He pulled away from her and stood. Loss settled through him. "I shall have my word with Horace, then depart in the morning."

"Would to heaven you were the child of Constance Kensley. Would to heaven you could stay here and Rosenleigh could be yours. I only want to keep you."

He kissed her cheek and fought the tears trying to surface. "You shall always have my heart." He left the nursery and shut the door quietly behind him, then pushed his fingers through his hair.

He grappled for a plan, for a sense of direction, for anything that would stop the world from spinning around him.

But all he could grasp was the grief ripping through him.

Aunt had been right.

He was nothing after all.

CHAPTER 10

W hatever is the matter, Miss Gresham?"

Isabella took a second glance over her shoulder but relaxed to find the garden's gravel path empty. Good. She had avoided Lord Livingstone most artfully these last three days, and she certainly could not bear the thought that he would sneak up on her unawares.

She gave a reassuring smile to Bridget. "Nothing, dear. Is it not lovely?" She swept a hand across the garden. Everything from the well-trimmed shrubbery to the endless rows of bright flowers, the stone grotto, and the gothic benches alluded to wealth and magnificence.

Though, of course, it was nothing compared to Sharottewood.

And the seashore.

She wished to heaven everything would stop reminding her of Mr. Kensley. Why could she not remove him from herself, just as Father had done?

But she couldn't stop wondering how he fared. Had the journey back to his Rosenleigh been too taxing? Did the wound bleed again? Did he still find occasion to smile, to laugh in that dear way that had brightened her otherwise dull world? And what had he found upon his return to his home?

A chill ran through her. If the person who wished him dead—

"Something is the matter."

"No, dear." Isabella smiled into Bridget's careful, searching eyes, but the truth bubbled at her throat. Why could she keep naught from the maid? "Nothing except. . .my worry for Mr. Kensley."

Bridget nodded, as if she'd known. "You think of him much."

"Too much, I fear. There is no purpose in it." Isabella walked faster down the path, brushing her gloved hand along green leaves. "Father has already made me promise to never see him again. My own brother. His own son. It is not right that we should be estranged to him."

"What is right and what is necessary are not always the same."

"You sound as if you agree with Father."

"Only because it would cost you so much. I should not wish to see you injured."

"Lately, I find it all very deplorable." Isabella plucked a purple bloom from a tall foxglove. "The cruelty of rumormongers and the haughty eye of society, always watching everyone for a blunder they can pounce on."

"I quite agree," rumbled a male voice.

Isabella jumped, the flower falling to the path.

Lord Livingstone emerged from the shadows of the grotto, hat in his hands. What was he doing out here? Waiting for her?

As if sensing her question, he frowned. "I was inspecting this impressive garden and noting the design of this grotto. Perhaps I shall build one in its likeness at Wetherbell Hall."

Isabella tucked her arm in Bridget's. "Then we shall not interrupt—"

"On the contrary. I was just leaving. Allow me." He stepped next to her and claimed her other arm.

Despite his chivalry, the calmness of his voice, he seemed not himself. Not three steps away, he glanced back at the grotto. What was he looking for?

"You are enjoying yourself, my lord?"

"Vastly. Lady Sarsfield is a most gracious hostess."

"Indeed." Isabella spared a knowing grin to Bridget. "I did not realize we shared so many of the same acquaintances. How long have you known the Sarsfields?"

"Not more than a month, I confess."

"What a remarkable impression you must have made. To be invited to their house party on such short acquaintance."

"I desire to make many new friends before I return to Wetherbell."

"You do so with great rapidity. I am astonished."

"You need not be."

"Why not?"

He paused as they neared the end of the garden and removed himself from her touch. He bowed with firm, tight lips and a gaze that rent through her. "I always attain what I desire. Good day, Miss Gresham."

Isabella lifted her chin a notch as he walked away. Partly to hide the tremor that coursed through her, and partly to make known the resolution she would not be shaken from.

In this desire, my lord, you shall not.

William departed Rosenleigh with no more than a knapsack of food, his horse, and the clothes on his back. Twice, he almost looked back.

If he had, he likely would have seen Miss Ettie at the nursery window. Or Mr. Nolan and his dog looking solemn in the stable doorway. Or the new gardener trimming bushes by the labyrinth, doing the work no one would ever do with such care as Shelton.

I am nothing. The words returned at breakneck speed and released poison into William's body. All his life he had disliked his aunt. Perhaps he had hated her.

But now the hatred morphed into something more. This was too much. She had hurt him one too many times. He was glad she was dead. He wanted her dead. But even that was scant punishment for what she had done to him—

No. He tried to push back the thoughts. *I cannot think this way.* He rode faster down the rutted road, knowing Rosenleigh, even if he did glance back, was now long out of sight. His precious Rosenleigh. The only thing that had ever belonged to him, and now he was penniless. A pauper. Nothing.

He rode until he reached the village, then Greyfriar Street, then the enormous black gates of the workhouse. Why should he come here?

He had passed by it a hundred times. He had scarcely ever looked up.

But now he dismounted, looped Duke's reins around the gate, and clenched two bars in his fists. His mother had lain here? Destitute at these gates?

William squinted up at the building. Grey, grimy, with twisting vines crawling up the sides of the walls. A hundred windows peered out of the stone like miserable eyes, all watching him, all haunting him.

An old woman hobbled around the side of the house. She was sallow, thin, and her linen dress was threadbare enough that her white skin was visible at every hole in the fabric. She glanced at William. With a deadened expression, she limped on to one of the entrance doors and disappeared inside.

Her misery stayed behind her and tainted the air.

William breathed it inside him. He tightened his fists on the bars. *God, why?* All these years, he had taken for granted the thought that his mother was the beautiful woman in the painting and his father was good and respected.

Now all he had was this.

A dark, destitute place, with some faint image in his mind of a woman curled at the gates in one desperate attempt to gain shelter for her child. For *him.* This was who he was. What he'd come from.

Nothing.

He climbed back atop Duke and rode away from the place, wishing he could rid the ill-smelling air from his lungs. No matter how far he rode, though, he did not imagine the place would ever get away from him.

They were a part of each other, he and this workhouse.

Part of nothing.

All day long it had bothered Isabella. She didn't know why. Perhaps if it had not been for the look on Lord Livingstone's face this morning, she would have assumed he had overheard her plan to visit the garden and reached it ahead of her, all for the purpose of a chance meeting.

But it was more than that. She was certain.

And her curiosity, at all costs, must be assuaged.

"Miss Gresham, pray, do you play?" With dinner finished and the gentlemen just rejoining the ladies in the drawing room, Lady Sarsfield raised her brows at Isabella in waiting.

Isabella cleared her throat. "I fear I am little more than learning, my lady."

"Oh, how funny she is." From beside her on the couch, Lilias fluttered her ivory fan and laughed. "Do not listen to a word of it, Lady Sarsfield. She plays wonderfully. Much better than me, I daresay. I could never play well with such tiny hands and fingers. It is an intolerable curse, you know. Having small hands, I mean."

"Well, I should very much like to hear you play." Lady Sarsfield motioned to the piano-forte, one whose glistening wood and bright keys rivaled any Isabella had seen.

At the moment, she would not have cared if the thing were made of gold. The last thing she wanted to do was make apparent all the days she'd failed to practice.

"Well? Shall you keep us waiting?" asked Lady Sarsfield.

Several other guests piped in with their own hopes of hearing her. Traitorous Lilias made another praising comment. Of all the times for the girl to be cheerful, why now?

"You can hardly refuse now, can you, Miss Gresham?" From the chair nearest the floor-to-ceiling window, Lord Livingstone narrowed his eyes on her. "Do pleasure us. We all beg it of you."

"Very well." Sighing, she made her way to the piano, nerves already jittering her knees. "But I fear you shall all be gravely disappointed."

Lady Sarsfield looked as if she agreed, while Lord Livingstone left his chair to stand next to her.

All throughout Isabella's song—and the many mishaps she'd warned them of—he stayed close enough that she imagined she felt his breath on her neck. Was he truly in love with her? What would Father say if he knew?

He would surely insist she not dismiss him over one mischievous kiss in an alcove.

Yet it was more than that. She didn't know what, any more than she knew the mystery that enshrouded him as he hid in the grotto, but it was distinct enough she must take heed. Surely that was right, was it not?

Though she could say one thing for him.

He still intrigued her.

With the song's end, the guests applauded with less enthusiasm than they had shown when begging her to play, and Lady Sarsfield promptly complained of a headache and sent her servant for smelling salts.

Isabella rejoined Lilias on the couch. "You are terrible."

Hiding half her face with the fan, Lilias whispered back, "Well, we were in need of some amusement. I could think of nothing better."

"At my expense."

"Oh, you are silly. It did not mortify you so very much now, did it?"

"Next time I shall insist *you* play."

"It would not work." Lilias splayed one hand. "Tiny hands, you know."

After a few more hours spent in dull company, each guest finally retired to their own chambers. Isabella went to the window. Outside, a bright moon lightened the grounds, offering her a perfect view of the garden.

And the grotto.

"I think he was with someone."

Bridget approached with a white nightgown and wrapper. "Who?"

"Lord Livingstone. Today in the garden. I think he was with someone."

"Oh, Miss Gresham. You must not be imaginative. He told us why he was in the grotto."

"I did not believe that a whit."

Bridget sighed. "Here, let me help you with your dress—"

"Never mind that. Where is my cloak?"

"Oh, you cannot be—"

"In my trunk, of course. I shall get it." Ignoring Bridget, Isabella swept to the trunk, rummaged for her cloak, and draped it over her shoulders. She pulled the hood over her head. "Stand in this window here and watch me, won't you? Just in case, you know."

Bridget twisted her hands together at her chest. "Miss Gresham, please do not go out there like this. It is most dangerous. Most silly too."

"I just want to peek into the grotto. I shall likely find nothing." Isabella grinned. "But then again, I *do* have the habit of finding things, don't I? I shall be right back." The cloak billowed around her as she left the chamber, navigated the halls in the dark, and crept down the oak stairway to the ground floor.

No servants lingered about, likely already in their chambers for the night, so she slipped out the entrance doors unseen by anyone.

The walk to the garden took her much longer in the dark, and the moon was not so bright as she had thought it from her bedchamber window. Discomfort fluttered in her chest. Perhaps she should have listened to Bridget. What did she hope to find anyway?

Her insane curiosity would be the death of her.

Her slippers crunched the gravel garden path as she padded deeper into the foliage and past several benches and urns. Then, framed by rosebushes and two Grecian statues, the grotto appeared in the moonlight.

Isabella slipped inside. The temperature cooled in the small stone area, and the darkness deepened enough to chill her. She should have brought a candle. At least then she could have inspected for any sign of—

A shadow stirred outside.

Isabella flattened against the wall, pushing her hand to her mouth, heart staggering. Someone was out there.

Boots crunched gravel, then another shadow moved in the moonlight. Voices, deep and humming, drifted over the air. She strained for words, but they were too low to distinguish.

Then silence.

Coldness rushed through her veins, and she prayed the grotto darkness was black enough to hide her. Perhaps there was no danger. Perhaps she was nonsensical to be afraid. But she would be glad when the boots crunched away again and—

"You can come out now."

Air exploded from her. She stumbled farther into the grotto, but a black figure followed her inside. Lord Livingstone. She recognized the tall frame, the voice, the fear that was already puncturing her calm. "Get away from me."

"I only came to escort you back."

"What?"

"I had forgotten my pipe in the drawing room. I was going to fetch it, when I saw you slip outside, alone in the dark, and conscience would not permit me to leave you unattended that way."

"You met someone." Her chin quivered but lifted. "You cannot deny speaking with someone just now."

"Certainly not. I asked a servant to accompany me in my search of you, in case you were in any sort of danger. When I realized you were not, I sent him back." His hand grasped hers.

She gasped and yanked away, but his grip did not lessen. Instead, he pulled her from the grotto and back into the pale hues of moonlight.

"You mistrust me greatly, do you not, Miss Gresham?"

She pulled free of his touch and marched forward. "I admit that you puzzle me and nothing more."

"Am I such an enigma?"

"Excuse me, but I must get back—"

He jerked her around, pulling her close enough to his face that an inch closer would have released the scream in her throat. "You fear me because I have confessed undying love to you."

"Unhand me, my lord."

"One day it is you who shall confess the love, and you who shall beg for my hand in marriage."

"You are quite mistaken. Now let me go, or I shall scream."

He complied, the faintest grin lifting the corner of his mouth. "I am never mistaken about anything."

"I came to repay you." William sat across from Lord Manigan in the magnificent blue-and-yellow drawing room. As a child, when Aunt had hauled him in here and presented him to the earl like some sort of favor-gaining trophy, all the splendor had made William feel inferior.

The same inferiority welled in him now.

Perhaps worse.

Uncrossing his knees, Lord Manigan reached for a teacup from the short-legged stand. He sipped before he answered. "You found Lord Gresham?"

"Yes."

"He admits to being your father?"

"He is not my father." William worked to keep his voice stoic. "It seems the truth of my birth has long been kept from me. Edward Gresham is no more my father than Constance Kensley is my mother."

Lord Manigan's teacup lowered. "What?"

"My aunt—Mrs. Willoughby, rather—sent a servant to retrieve me from the workhouse." The words burned. "I have no knowledge of my parents, other than their depravity. I was a means of blackmail and that is all."

"I could have sworn." The earl clinked the teacup and saucer back to the tray and stood. "All those years, I could have sworn you looked like Constance. Even the hair. Perhaps a mistake—"

"There is no mistake." William rose too. He faced the man with the tea table between them. "You lent me funds this spring with the knowledge I could repay you upon my return. I regret that I cannot."

"Never mind the funds—"

"I wish to work in your employ until the amount is settled."

"I would not think of it. Preposterous." Lord Manigan cringed and walked across the room toward the bowed window, as if too embarrassed to discuss such a matter. "You are a gentleman, and one I have admired since you were but a youth. I have seen tenacity and goodness in you. I shall not thus degrade you."

"I am not above working with my hands. I cannot be above it. Surely you can see that."

"This is all rather shocking. I cannot believe it." Lord Manigan glanced back at him. Moisture gathered in testament to his compassion.

A compassion William drank in like water, for it cooled the flaming places in his soul. "I hardly believe it myself."

"The funds are yours. Indeed, I shall offer you more."

"I thank you, but I cannot accept. I shall be a burden to no one, and if you do not permit me to serve you here, I shall work elsewhere and repay you then."

Shaking his head, the earl let out a small chuckle. "Tenacity, indeed." He walked forward and reached for William's hand. He squeezed. "Very well, dear boy. I shall employ you, as you wish. But as soon as the debt is paid, you must find a better position. A trade perhaps. I shall assist you in any way I can."

"Thank you, my lord." The loss of pride punctured yet another hole inside his chest. How empty he was. How much of. . .nothing. He turned and started across the room.

"Mr. Kensley?"

He paused at the door. "My lord?"

"Circumstances may have changed for you, but one thing has not. You may depend upon my friendship."

For the second time, the earl's words infused comfort into William's grief. He nodded, unable to speak, and quit the room.

He was homeless and penniless, a blow he'd never once foreseen.

At least he was not friendless too.

"I do not feel I should leave you." Isabella pressed her hand along Bridget's warm brow, concern budding. "How long have you felt ill?"

Leaning back into the chair, Bridget shook her head. "It is hardly cause for alarm. I am only a bit tired."

"And a bit fevered."

"Please, Miss Gresham. This is your last night at Rockingham Hall, and I should not wish to be the cause of you missing it."

"What is a ball to me?" Isabella retrieved a blanket from the bed and draped it across her maid. "I attended so many in London I am sure one more could not mean very much. Besides, it would give me ample excuse to avoid both Lord Livingstone and Lady Sarsfield." Which she was *very* desirous to do.

Ever since the night in the garden a fortnight ago, Lord Livingstone had been strange—even for him. He had spoken to her little but seemed to watch her excessively. What thoughts possessed him behind that mysterious, granite exterior?

"You must be more kind," chided Bridget.

"And you must be more severe. Are you always good and perfect?"

A laugh. "Yes, of course you are. That is why I adore you so." This time, Isabella went to fetch a pillow, but Bridget denied need of it and sat up in her chair with such a look of distress that Isabella frowned. "Pray, do not be unhappy. What can I do to make you comfortable?"

"Please, do nothing more for me. I should not have you waiting on me this way."

"Through many a sickness, you have sat by my bed and cared for me all night. I can fetch you pillows and blankets if I wish to."

Bridget sighed. "If you truly wish to help me, please go downstairs to the ball."

"Would it truly ease you?"

A nod.

"Very well, but you must promise to rest." With Bridget's insistence that she would, Isabella checked her hair again in the looking glass, pinched her cheeks, then went downstairs to find the ballroom already loud with music.

As couples were forming together for the boulangere, Isabella joined Lilias and both accepted the offer to dance from two brothers who had been good company to them during their stay. The rapidity of movement, the endless beeswax candles, and the heat of twenty-some guests all warmed her cheeks.

At the end of the dance, she laughed and accepted lemonade, half listening to Lilias complain about her partner's ferocious speed.

Across the ballroom, a pair of eyes snagged hers.

Isabella hurried her focus back to Lilias. Even exaggerated complaints were better than Lord Livingstone's unnerving gaze.

She danced two country dances, then excused herself to hurry upstairs and see how Bridget fared. The poor girl. How uncomfortable this would make her for their journey home. Unless, of course, she worsened in the night. Heaven forbid such a catastrophe, for then they would be forced to remain here at Rockingham Hall even longer than—

The marble floor echoed more than her own footsteps.

Isabella whirled around. Gilded candlesticks, glowing on stands along the hall, had lightened her way down the hall just seconds ago. Now the candles were doused.

Quiet blackness stared back at her.

Shivering, she reached the stairs and ascended with speed, listening for any footfalls not her own. Who had been behind her? Why had they blown out the candles?

A servant of course. But why go through the trouble of lighting them all, only to blow them out before the ball was finished?

Never mind. It did not matter.

Isabella found her chamber and discovered Bridget asleep in her chair, resting as faithfully as she'd promised. With her head on her own shoulder that way, the poor dear would have the most dreadful pain in her neck when she awoke. Perhaps another pillow—

The door slammed open.

Isabella jumped back, legs hitting the edge of the bed, a scream fizzling into a gasp.

A stranger leered in the doorway. Tall, angular, pockmarks on his weathered face. "Git over there with th' other lassie."

Her breath caught. Who was he? How had he gotten on the grounds? Past the servants?

"Go on with ye." His drawn pistol shimmered in the room's candlelight. "Now."

Isabella moved to the chair, curled her hand around her maid's shoulder just as a *boom* exploded in the distance. Isabella jerked at the same time Bridget squirmed awake.

"Miss Gresham—"

"Shhh. Stay still."

The stranger kicked her trunk lid open with his boot. With one hand steadying the pistol, he rummaged through the clothes, tossing them to the rug, before snarling and reaching for a valise. "Where is it?"

Isabella hesitated.

He whirled. A shot rang past her and shattered the looking glass hanging on the wall, notching her panic higher. Noise meant nothing to him. Alarming the house of his presence meant nothing to him.

Which meant he was not alone.

Or in fear of apprehension. *Dear Saviour, what is happening?*

Stepping forward, he ripped the pearl and ruby necklace from her neck. Pain pricked. He shoved it into the pocket of his dirty oilskin coat. "Where are th' rest?"

She motioned toward the dressing table, unable to speak past the pressure damming her throat.

Bridget was already caving. She quivered beneath Isabella's touch, and her breathing was rapid, rising in volume, close enough to panic that another fright would set her to screaming.

Perhaps both of them.

They had to get out of here.

Isabella glanced to the window as the stranger dumped out the contents of her jewelry box. Two stories down. No balcony. Too far from the door to make it, even if they ran—

"Good." Shoving the last of the jewels into his pocket, the stranger turned back to them. He grabbed the candlestick from the stand. He crept closer. Shadows played on his face, in his eyes, flaming so much fear she had no courage to release it.

A second explosion erupted from downstairs.

God, please. Father's words came back to her. The plunders. The manors. *Please, no—*

He dipped the candlestick to Bridget's dress and flames burst at her knees as he knocked over the chair. Groaning, Isabella swatted the fire away, but in the periphery of her vision, she watched him spring to the draperies and light them too.

More flames. A third *boom*. Glass shattering and a bloodcurdling scream from another nearby chamber. The stranger's gun bore down on them. "Git up with ye."

Bridget scampered to her feet, but Isabella remained on the floor. If he wanted to kill her, he could do it here. Her mouth dried. She focused on the black metal circle of his flintlock.

Until it lifted past her.

Up, up.

To Bridget. Whimpering, screeching, then—

The shot blasted.

Isabella flattened herself to the rug, numbness sweeping over her. Bridget was dead. Murdered. For the pearl and ruby necklace in his pocket. The matching earbobs he'd taken from the box. The coral necklace. The old pendant that had belonged to her mother. The cluster hair comb. Why didn't he shoot again?

She wanted him to shoot again.

Or the flames to crawl closer and devour her.

Anything so she would not have to bear the sight of Bridget crumpled and bleeding, dead for the worth of a few jewels in a box.

But instead of a bullet ripping through her, a pair of hands dragged her up. At first the face, the chamber, blurred. A terror of blackness and flames and smoke.

Then her mind made sense of the madness. A body lay at her feet. A stranger with an oilskin coat and spilled jewels.

"He is dead. We must hurry." Lord Livingstone took her by the hand then reached for someone else.

Bridget. Unscathed and without bloodstains, though her eyelids were half rolled into her head, as if she were losing consciousness.

When she swayed, Lord Livingstone swept her into his arms. "Come. There is a servant stairway at the end of the hall. Follow me." He led them from the chamber, through a hallway dim with smoke, and into a narrow wooden stairway with nary a wall sconce.

The blackness seeped into her. "What is happening?" She tripped, smacked into Lord Livingstone's solid back, but he didn't answer. Her own legs threatened to give out beneath her. She clenched her jaw and dragged her hands along the cold stone walls, trying to keep her balance. "My lord. . .please."

"We are under attack. I know as little as you." At the end of the stairs, he pried open a door, glanced both ways, then urged them into an unlit hall. Within seconds, they ran out a servant exit, where two horses pranced in waiting.

"Make haste." He helped Bridget onto one saddle, then her onto another. "Ride as far as you can. Do not look back."

"But you—"

"There is not time. Not enough horses prepared."

"Ride with me. With Bridget. Please, we cannot leave you."

He hesitated, glanced up at the flaming manor, wiped his forehead. Then he lunged onto the same horse as Bridget and supported her slumping frame with his arms. "Go."

His command drove Isabella into action. Kicking her slippers into the horse's sides, she galloped after him into the night, just as another explosion rattled the air.

She clung to the animal with hair whipping about her face. Cold fear quivered in her bosom. They were escaping, but how many others were trapped in their chambers, or burning, or being slaughtered for mere trinkets and possessions?

This was too unbearable to be true.

The work of demons.

God, help.

A brittle laugh breezed past his lips. So this was it.

The attic bedchamber sported only one bed. Joseph, the footman who occupied it, lay snoring between two chaff-filled mattresses, looking much younger without his white wig.

William pulled off his own wig. He scratched an itch on his scalp and button by shiny button undid his livery. Today, he had served platter after steaming platter to Lord Manigan and his two Parliament guests.

Neither William nor the earl had looked at each other.

Or spoken.

They played their roles well.

William tugged too hard on the last button. It sprang loose and clinked to the wooden floorboards, rolled, fell flat next to the thin pallet. *I cannot do this.* He shed everything but his shirtsleeves then settled onto the floor and pulled the wool blanket over himself.

He should have left this place.

He should have accepted the charity Lord Manigan offered him and spared himself the torture of such degradation.

But he could not. No more than he could have stayed at Rosenleigh, even when Horace permitted him to.

I have very little left. Nothing, in truth. Except his manhood.

He would not lose that to charity or pity or anything else anyone tried to extend to him. He would stand on his own two feet, or he would not stand at all.

He would not run.

Not even from himself.

She'd been shaking for the last two hours. She didn't know why. No chill hung in the night air, and the breeze that rippled over them was warm and smelled of fresh-cut meadows.

Are we almost there? The words stuck in her throat. Partly because she didn't know where *there* was or what would happen when they arrived. Where was he taking them? What would happen to her reputation when word spread about her reckless journey on horseback with an unwed gentleman?

She clenched her teeth to keep them from chattering. This was ridiculous. That she should be cold like this and that she should be worried about rumors when she had narrowly escaped with her life.

A life she owed to Lord Livingstone.

Whether she liked the thought or not.

How had he known to come for her? Had he seen her slip upstairs? How had he arranged so quickly for the horses in such mayhem?

Too many questions thronged her brain, and the fog of them clouded her vision. She focused on his back in the moonlight. His rigid position. Or the horse hooves clomping upon the mucky road. Or her hands, white and cold, gripping the leather reins.

If only she'd listened to Father when he'd told her of such plunders.

If only she'd asked him more questions, learned more of the raids, understood better what had happened tonight. What manner of men could execute such atrocities and not yet be apprehended? Could not the

King put a stop to this? Could no one?

'Twas inhuman.

Unfathomable.

Devilish.

She tried to shake herself free of the screams, but they shrieked within her at every *clip-clop* of the horse hooves.

Ahead, the faint lights of a village glowed dim in the waning darkness. Fog rose from the ground. Faded pink and orange streaked the horizon, and by the time they rode their horses down the cobbled street, morning had dawned enough that any villagers peering from windows might have seen them.

Heaven have mercy. Father might as well forget any profitable marriage now. No one would have her after the tales this would stir.

At a wattle-and-daub inn with three gables and a squat chimney, Lord Livingstone dismounted his horse. Bridget must have been asleep, for he shook her before pulling her down.

Isabella jumped down herself before he could offer assistance. A new shiver ran through her. "Where are we?"

"Nasmyth. Come with me, if you please." Guiding both her and Bridget with a hand to each of their arms, he took them inside the inn. Warm scents of yeast and mutton filled the open taproom, the aroma somehow comforting.

"A private room for the mistress and her lady," said Lord Livingstone to an aproned young woman. "Send a chambermaid up as well to assist them. They shall desire a hearty meal and a fire in the hearth."

Relief trickled through Isabella as she reached for Bridget's hand. She squeezed. "My lord—"

"I shall write to your father at once." He turned to her, his expression impassive yet careful. "He shall retrieve you as quickly as possible, I do not doubt. If you remain in your chamber until such a time, I imagine your reputation will suffer very little. I regret any damage tonight has done you already."

"Nothing can be laid to your blame, my lord." She glanced down at her slippers. Her muddy, wet slippers. "Indeed, we owe very much to you. I am in your debt." She imagined he would agree, or at the very least unleash some disconcerting promise that he would collect on such a debt.

But he only muttered them good tidings, bowed, and departed the inn.

Isabella quivered and rubbed her arms. When the aproned innkeeper led them to an upstairs chamber, she could not help but hurry to the window.

Lord Livingstone was already mounted and riding away, his back straight and unbending as ever.

At the manor, he easily could have escaped himself without hurrying to find her. He could have easily compromised them during the journey. He easily could have used the present situation to soil her reputation enough that a marriage would have been her only option.

But he had done nothing more than rescue her and ride away.

Perhaps she had misjudged him.

Perhaps Father had been right.

CHAPTER 11

November 1809

He did not know what it was he missed. Perhaps the long rides on a steed he knew belonged to himself. Or shutting the door to his own chamber and drifting asleep atop feathered mattresses. Or passing Miss Ettie in the hall, with her smile falling on him or her hand grasping his.

All things he wished to forget.

Needed to forget—if he was to keep his sanity.

Dumping the contents of the last chamber pot into one of the slop pails, William hauled the buckets outside into the biting morning air. The wind cut through his livery, stirring his stained apron. He held his breath as he emptied the buckets into the cesspool, but the stench clung to him as he turned back for the house.

Just like the shame.

Another day of polishing cutlery. Blackening boots. Opening doors, trimming lamps, serving trays, sweeping fireplaces. He'd even lost his pallet in the servant chamber.

For the past month, they'd moved him into the butler's pantry at night, with instructions to guard the silver in the event a thief should prowl upon them unawares.

He slept so little he found himself drifting to sleep on his feet, as he stood like a statue behind Lord Manigan's table at mealtimes.

No matter. The work meant nothing to him. The lack of sleep meant nothing to him. Indeed, he was glad for it. At least amid duties, he had not time to think of his aunt.

Awake, she could not taunt him.

Her prune, wrinkled, lifeless face stared back at him in every window he looked through or every silver pot he polished. She infested him. Crawling into the deep places, stinging where it already hurt, until a bitter poison festered through him. Would she ever stop torturing him?

"Say, Kensley, an errand needed of you." Joseph, the footman who matched William in height, was the only servant who ever conversed with William—though it was usually only orders or obscenities concerning all the fair-faced maids.

The other servants avoided William or treated him with a cautious indifference. Perhaps because they all knew of Rosenleigh, what he had come from—that he had once been above them.

Whatever the case, he endured the tedium of each day without more than a nod or word to anyone. Indeed, he had not met eyes with Lord Manigan in months.

Not that he blamed the earl. Or even the servants.

He blamed no one for what he was, where he was, except the woman who had purposed to destroy him. *"Just have to forgive dem."* Mrs. Shaw came back to him. Words he resisted. Words he didn't want to remember, or believe in, or accept. *"Even if you got to do it over and over again. . .just got to forgive dem."*

He doubted he could, even if he wanted to.

And by all that was holy, he didn't.

December 1809

Isabella slipped off alone, the cheering laughter from Father's many guests still a ring in her ear. Hopefully, Lord Livingstone would not follow. These past months, Father had invited him twice to Sharottewood, and after the noble rescue, how could Isabella gainsay the visits?

Besides, Lord Livingstone always brought word concerning the marauders who had attacked Rockingham Hall. As of yet, they had not been apprehended. She would rest easier when they were. Who was to say they would not strike Sharottewood next? Was anyone safe?

Despite such grave topics, the guests in attendance were in jovial spirits and quite enjoying themselves. Strange how everyone could be so merry and she so sober. Yet was it not always this way? Every dreaded Christmastide?

Lifting the white-beaded trim of her evening gown, she ascended the stairs in dim shadows. Halfway up, she paused. She sank to the step. A thrum started in her temples as she wrapped her fingers around the smooth wooden banister and squeezed.

Mother had been dying.

Everyone had told Isabella it was so a hundred times. The nanny. Father. Even Mrs. Morrey, with a gentler tone than usual.

But Isabella had not understood dying any more than she understood why Mother stayed in bed so often. Why did she stop wearing her pretty dresses and playing the piano-forte in the music room?

But Christmas Day, she'd done something wonderful. She'd come downstairs wearing a dress so bright and colorful it cheered the entire room. With Father smiling at her side and Isabella nestled next to her, they'd sat in the drawing room together and watched the Yule log burn, played games, and listened from the window as wassailers sang to them.

Nighttime came too quickly, and Isabella had been sent to bed. She'd waited several minutes, until her nanny drifted asleep in the chair next to her, then crept back to the stairs, too happy to slumber away the last hours of beautiful Christmas.

That's when she saw them. Standing in the shadows, against the hall window, Mother half wilted in Father's arms as if she'd fainted again. *"I want to know."*

"Eloise, you are upset. The day has been too taxing. Let me help you upstairs."

"I want to know now."

"This is nonsense."

"Edward. . ." She writhed out of his arms. Pressed herself against the window. Balled the drapery in her fist. *"We have pretended very well, have we not?"*

"I will not have you speak this way."

"And I will not die without hearing you say it." Defeat weakened the words. *"Perhaps I cannot blame you. We both knew what we were doing. We lied to each other for very noble purposes, I admit."* She careened, shrank to the floor, the thud quiet and sickening on the marble floor.

Father knelt next to her. *"Let me take you to bed, dear."*

"I suppose a woman can live with lies her entire life. It is not until she dies that she must have the truth."

He hoisted her into his arms.

"Edward."

"You shall feel better in the morning."

"Edward, say it—"

"Dear mercy, what would you have of me? What good is there in forcing me to say I do not love—"

"Do you?"

Isabella had clenched the banister railings and searched his face, already knowing he'd say yes, that he'd assure her.

But his features deadened with a frown, and his voice lacked passion. *"No more than you have ever loved me."*

Now, staring at the same moonlit window and draperies, with the ghostly figures still alive in her mind, Isabella rose from the step. Tears wetted her cheeks. Foolish to cry over that night again. Why had it meant so much to her at nine years old? Why should it mean so much to her now?

Perhaps because that warm Christmastide in the drawing room had been pretend, an act played skillfully for an unsuspecting child. She'd believed their lie all her life until that moment.

Climbing the remaining steps, she brushed the tears from her face. She would not be her mother. She would not live that way. She would not die that way.

She would not expect the kind of love she knew too well did not exist.

January 1810

Numb and listless, William moved through each day, performing his duties without a sense of attachment to anything. He tried not to think. Every memory sucked him further into an abyss he could not climb free of.

Only at night, when he unrolled a blanket on the cold floor of the butler's pantry, did he watch his breath cloud and allow his weary mind to remember. He couldn't bear Rosenleigh, Shelton, or Miss Ettie.

But Isabella Gresham always came to him. Like a warming breeze, she swept over the inert places of his mind, fanning to life a small flame of something. He didn't know what. Or why he should always imagine her.

But the memory of her laugh was soothing. The playful way she smiled at him. The trueness, the tenderness of her many expressions. If only they'd had each other. All those years growing up, if only William had truly been Edward Gresham's son and known the bond of a sister who trusted and needed him.

But she was not his sister now.

She'd treated him with care before, as if he meant something to her. When he'd been injured, had she not cried over him?

That was lost to him too. He knew that. Upon their next encounter, upon knowing the truth, she would become cold and aloof. A stranger to him.

Just as well, he supposed.

But still, he could think of her, could he not? Was there any harm in that? If he didn't dream of something, he would go mad.

Perhaps he was mad already.

A fortnight into the chill of January, William was interrupted from lugging an armload of firewood into the kitchen. The scullery maid bade him see Lord Manigan in his study.

Dread coiled through William as he brushed off his livery and hurried through the house. The earl had been gone since before Christmastide. What could he want with William? Why wish to speak with him now—when he had ignored him since the day William had donned a livery and wig?

Outside the white-painted door, he cleared his throat and tapped.

"Come in, come in."

Forcing his features into stone, William entered and bowed. He waited for an errand, a letter to be delivered or a tray to be fetched.

But Lord Manigan remained standing behind his cluttered desk, his eyes on William, a twinkle in his gaze. "Do relax, dear boy. I am not about to send you on a footrace against a carriage, you know."

Despite himself, a small smile lifted the corner of William's lips. "I am very fond of racing, my lord."

A chuckle followed. "Perhaps another time, then. Sit down there, won't you?"

William hesitated.

"Come now. Are you in my employ or are you not?"

William sat and closed his fists on each knee to keep them from bouncing. Silence swallowed the study, disturbed only by the squeak of Lord Manigan's chair as he sat.

"I have learned that you have been quite diligent in my absence. My steward has been more than impressed with the work you can handle." Lord Manigan pulled out a drawer in his desk, lifted a drawstring bag of coins, and slid it across the mahogany surface. "You have paid your debt in excess, my son. I cannot in good conscience allow you to leave without first recompensing the difference."

"There is no difference. If I have paid my debt, that is all I have done."

"On the contrary. You have done more, and it has been quite well earned."

"I do not need it."

"Do not need it?" Brows rose. "I daresay, such pride is more distasteful than accepting what you have already worked for."

Pride? What pride did Lord Manigan imagine William had left?

"Permit me honesty, son. Will you do that?"

"As you said, I am in your employ."

"This is hardly the same young man I credited with such praise mere months ago. You have changed considerably, and it is not to your credit." A frown intensified. "I have always known you to have a certain exuberance for life, and now I must wonder, is that to die alongside your misfortune?"

"What do you expect of me?" Cold rage worked up from the toes he curled in his boots. "I am merely endeavoring to survive—"

"Survive what, may I ask? Do say it. I should like to understand."

Heat pulsing his face, William stood. "If that is all you wish to discuss—"

"Sit back down."

"I have no intention of enduring this. With all due respect, my lord, you must forgive me if I am solemn of temperament. I have lost everything and everyone dear to me. I have forsaken my home to a cousin who is so indulgent in his own grief that he cannot manage his own health, let alone the care of an entire house. I am changed from a gentleman of stature and significance to a workhouse beggar in livery and wig—and worse yet, I have no family at all." He thumped his chest. "Am I to bear all of this with the same vivacity I had before? Forgive me, but I cannot. It is a feat too great for me."

"Then you are less of a man than I had imagined."

William flinched. Shame speared deeper.

"I can respect a man, to a certain degree, who enjoys life when things are prosperous and he is surrounded by the circumstances that best suit him. But I would admire a man far more if he were to lose all his comforts yet still retain that same joy, because there would be a man who was not shaped by the tempest of the wind, but by the morals of his own inward self."

William's shoulders threatened to cave, but he held them firm by sheer force of will. He nodded, bowed, fled from the room.

The words followed him like a nightmare. One he wanted to run from.

But he didn't run. He faced them, every brutal word, that night in his blanket on the floor. *Just have to forgive dem.* The last thing he wanted to do, but Mrs. Shaw had been right.

Lord Manigan was right.

How long did William think he could go on like this, tangled in his own bitterness, suffocating in pity as if he were the only person in the world to suffer injustice?

His aunt had done him wrong. He would live with those wrongs the rest of his life.

But she had done him good too, albeit unwittingly, because if he hadn't been taken from that workhouse, would he still be alive? Would he have survived? Wasn't the raising he'd been given more than anything he could have hoped for, considering his birth?

Perhaps he owed her more than his forgiveness. Perhaps he owed her his life.

Two days passed before he returned to the study again, this time in his own clothes, with Duke saddled and waiting in the manor courtyard.

Oddly enough, the little bag of coins still waited where Lord Manigan had left it—and Lord Manigan himself was in the same chair with the same immovable expression dominating his face.

William reached for the coins, lifting his eyes to the earl. A grin worked at the earl's lips.

"I shall always say you look much better without a wig."

A laugh stirred within him. "Just when I was beginning to be fond of the thing."

"God be with you, dear boy." The earl rose and clamped his hand on William's shoulder, a sort of pride reverberating in his voice. "I know nothing of your true father and mother, but if they be anything like their son, they are a people to be proud of, paupers or no. Remember that."

Whether the words were true or not, they were healing. "I will."

William departed the earl's presence and rode away from the brick manor, a new purpose thrumming the cage of his chest. He would return to Sharottewood and tell Edward Gresham the truth about his bloodline. He would ease their minds of worry. He would sever the last tie to a life he was no longer part of.

But he would do it with his head held high.

He had no intention of lowering it again.

CHAPTER 12

T his will simply not do." Isabella jabbed her fillet of roasted pork with force. "I am no porcelain creature to be bundled and coddled over, as if I might shatter upon a fall."

Instead of taking her seriously, Father grinned across the dining room table. "Mrs. Morrey is right, of course. If she advises it is too cold to ride in the snow, I quite agree with her."

"But I have nothing at all to do with myself."

"You have your piano-forte."

A mere torture, but she would not tell him that.

"And your dancing lessons," he went on. "And your painting lessons. Your needlework. Your letter writing—"

As if to rescue her, the double dining room doors swung open. The butler entered, features as sour as she felt. What did *he* have to be glum about? All day long he could busy about, tending to something worth doing, running the house with excellence, and stepping outside anytime he wished.

While Isabella was trapped indoors. Insufferable. Why must Mrs. Morrey be so disagreeable? And why must Father always heed her opinions?

Ever since Rockingham Hall, he had been terribly sheltering, even more so than usual.

"A visitor has arrived, my lord."

"I am quite surprised anyone would brave a carriage out in this snow." Father reached for his glass of sherry. "See them into the drawing room and have them tended with warm cocoa and a blazing hearth. I shall join them after my meal."

Who would endure such weather as this for a visit?

Perhaps Lord Livingstone. With his determined heart and serious eyes, she did not fathom a bit of foul weather—or anything else—could deter him from something he'd set his mind to. Surprisingly, she could not be disheartened by such a visit. Indeed, it would be a welcome diversion.

Why was the butler still standing in the doorway?

Father, too, must have been confused. He sat straighter. "Something else?"

"Er, yes, my lord."

"Come now, what is it? I am trying to finish my meal, if you please."

"The visitor, I do not doubt, is unwelcome."

Father stood at the same time Isabella's heart pounced the wall of her chest. It could not be. Mr. Kensley would not have come back. For what reason would he come back unless—

"He will regret this." Father marched around the table, bumping his glass with his elbow, fumes of anger rising as quickly as spilled sherry seeped into the tablecloth.

Before he reached the door, Isabella sprang from her seat and caught his arm. "Father, wait. You must compose yourself."

"I have listened to you regarding that blackguard one too many times."

"All I ask is that you let him speak."

"I have heard enough from him. I have taken enough from him." He shrugged out of her touch. "You stay here."

When he bounded into the hall, however, she hurried after him. Her heartbeat pattered. Why would he come back? Did he not know Father would never allow such a thing? Or would Mr. Kensley use his illegitimacy to attain what he wanted, despite Father's wishes?

In the foyer, Mr. Kensley stood hatless before the closed door. His boots dripped small puddles beneath him, snow still spotted his hair, and his cheeks were a flaming pink. "Lord Gresham." Steady voice, easy, smooth, uncalculating.

"Get out of here." Father's command boomed, echoing between the floor and the lofty ceiling.

"I came for no more than a word with you."

"You can have nothing to say to me."

"On the contrary. I have a great deal to say, and I believe it is a matter of consequence to you."

"Isabella, a private audience at once." Father flicked a hand at her, but Mr. Kensley shook his head.

"What I have to say will be said to your daughter as well as to you."

"I will decide what is spoken before my dau—"

"I am not your son."

A gasp caught in her throat, and she stepped forward, shock pulsing through her. What could he mean? How could that be?

"You may relinquish any fears in my regard. The child belonging to you died with Constance Kensley."

Father's shoulders bunched. "What scheme is this?"

"No scheme, my lord."

"Am I to believe. . .am I to believe that shrew of a woman lied to me all these years?"

"Lied to both of us, it seems. I was taken from the workhouse to fulfill the role of a dead child, in the event she might secure the five thousand pounds a year."

"This is preposterous."

"The truth usually is." For the first time, Mr. Kensley's eyes moved past Father to rest on her. A tiny smile graced his lips—one that seemed more gratitude, more goodbye, than anything else. He reached for the door.

"Wait." Father stepped closer. "How do I know you shall not be back? Or that you shall not spread this wretched story among everyone you meet?"

"Father—"

"Silence, Isabella."

She sucked in a breath, waited for a flash of indignation or hurt to pass across Mr. Kensley's face.

He only smiled. Faint and indifferent.

And brave.

Her admiration of him rose just as quickly as he bowed and exited the doors, a flurry of snow breezing in after him.

He had not thought it possible. To forgive so easily.

All the journey here, and even more so when he'd neared Sharottewood and galloped along the cliffside, the old and familiar animosity flared against the man he'd believed to be his father.

But as he'd faced his lordship this last time, something had stirred again. Mrs. Shaw's words perhaps. The now incessant plea, *"Forgive dem."*

Or maybe it was just the man himself.

William had seen him not as the father who should have been there to raise William—but as a man, nothing more. One who had much at stake, a daughter he adored, a reputation passed down to him for centuries.

Forgiving him was easy.

And freeing.

Untying the reins from a horse-head hitching post, William wiggled his numb toes in his boots. The sooner he reached the village, the better. A warm bowl of mutton and hot milk would be heaven.

"Mr. Kensley!"

He turned, frowned, as Isabella Gresham raced down the left stairs without shawl or cape. When she reached him, her nose was already pink with cold, and she rubbed her arms with both hands. Why follow him?

She seemed at a loss too, as if she were not certain herself. Her eyes bequeathed pity. The last thing in the world he wanted. "You must come back in the house and warm yourself. It is far too cold to travel without respite, and it shall be dark soon."

"Duke would not hear of it." As if in agreement, the animal brayed. "Besides, we shall reach the village before sunset. A room is already waiting for us."

"Does your horse make all decisions for you?"

A grin stretched. "Indeed. Everything from the books I read to the clothes I wear, I leave to Duke's discretion entirely."

She laughed, a light and fading sound, as white snowflakes stuck to her cheeks and hair. But when he led Duke forward, she hurried in front of him, urgency draining the humor. "Mr. Kensley, please spare me a word."

"You are shivering."

"I must apologize for my father. He is frightened, but very unjust and—"

"You need not worry yourself. I bear no ill will against him or you." He nodded back toward the manor. "Now run along inside before you catch your death of cold."

"I cannot see you go this way."

What was she saying?

"If everything you say is true—"

"You doubt me?"

More pink suffused her cheeks. "No, I do not. But as such terrible circumstances have befallen you, I cannot imagine where you might go. . .or what you might do."

He lifted his eyes to the snow-laden gate in the distance. "You need not worry after me. I have funds enough to keep me comfortable and two strong hands to work with."

"If they must work somewhere"—her eyes fell to his hands—"I wish they would work here."

Was she in earnest?

"I know Father. He is angry and temperamental today, but tomorrow he shall feel regretful of his behavior and be sorry he treated you so terribly—"

"It would not work, Miss Gresham."

"But it would! There is a position in need at the stables. I heard it discussed just yesterday. Duke could have his stall, and you the room beside our groom in the upstairs of the stables—"

"I am sorry. It would not work." Gripping the leather reins, William sidestepped her and took a few steps, but she moved to block his way yet again.

"Mr. Kensley."

That was no longer his name, but he had no other, so he said nothing.

"Mr. Kensley. . .if I were to ask but one reward for the service I did you when you were injured, would you grant it to me?"

He wanted to move her aside. Climb atop Duke. Gallop away from this place and never look back.

But something in her eyes, in the pooling tears, the pleading stare, kept him planted. "Name your reward."

"For you to stay."

"Why?"

"I do not know." She glanced down, then over, then back to his face with a sincere flush. "I just cannot bear to see you go. Not this way. Will you stay?"

"If your father—"

"Father shall consent to anything I ask of him. Will you?"

Despite the tightness in his chest, a laugh leaked out. He shook his head at her shivers. "If you run back indoors and plant yourself before a hearth, then yes." He winked toward Duke. "After I consult my horse, of course."

"Where are you going?" Isabella leaned in the open doorway of Father's chamber, the hearth flames rippling light and shadow across the warm room.

Felix, the valet, folded another pair of pantaloons and lowered them into a trunk, while Father dropped his tooth powder and hair wax into a valise. "An important political rally is to be held in Cheltenham next month, and Mr. Perronet has so kindly written me to come and attend."

"That letter has sat unanswered on your desk for a fortnight."

"Where is the other stocking?" Father tossed one across the bed, grumbling.

Isabella spotted the missing one on the floor behind him, swooped in to retrieve it, and handed it to him. "Father."

Still, he kept his hands busy—and his eyes. They looked everywhere, checking everything, without alighting on her face. "Yes, well, I was simply delayed in my response. I owe it to Mr. Perronet to attend. Good man, that fellow. Besides, Mrs. Hannah More shall be speaking."

"You read as little of her lectures as I do."

"Never mind that. I should still like to meet her, you know—"

"Father." This time with force. She reached for his hand and squeezed his fingers, a dull frustration tightening within. "Just because I bade Mr.

Kensley to stay does not mean you cannot."

"Kensley." The name came out too soft. As if the sound were a torture, an aching wound, yet something that used to be beautiful to him. Had Father loved her? This woman who had birthed his firstborn?

Mother's words echoed. The pleading. The longing for what she could not have and must die without. In all the years she'd been hoping for Father's love, had it been futile because he'd already given his heart to another?

That thought lined her stomach with sickness. She released his hand. "I suppose if running away shall make this easier, then you must go at once."

"If you think I would leave my own house on account of that. . .that. . ."

"He did not have to return and tell us, you know."

"Indeed. And he did not have to come and find us in the first place either, but he did."

"Could anyone be kept away from such a curiosity?"

"Let us not discuss it. Felix, not that banyan. It itches me. The other one." Placing both hands on Isabella's arms, he worked his features into a gentler look. "My dear, try to understand. This has all been rather taxing on my nerves, and though I see the justice in providing the man a position, I cannot confess to liking it."

"He has done nothing against us."

"Perhaps not to you."

"Nor you."

Father sighed and patted her arms then pulled her in for a small kiss to her forehead. "You are too good, my dear. Would to heaven I had but a morsel of your kindness."

"I wish you would stay."

"I shall return soon." He managed a smile, though it did not reach his eyes. "And do not worry. I shall instruct Mrs. Morrey not to fuss over any of your rides—or guilt you into any piano-forte lessons you have not the heart for."

"Thank you, Father." She pretended pleasure, even laughed, before she left the chamber and shut the door behind her. Alone in the hall, she blinked fast against the welling tears.

How Father must have loved Constance Kensley. Would he run this way had he not?

William busted the ice from the last water trough then thrust his hands into his pockets against the numbing, tingling cold. Last night, he'd had a room to himself. 'Twas not much larger than the bed it sported, but at least it was not a pallet in the butler's pantry.

He made his way to Duke's stall and rubbed the animal down, hoping to bring back feeling in his hands. When the groom awoke, he'd ask about getting a pair of gloves.

From the entrance of the stables, a rattle filled the cold morning air as Isaac, the stable boy, burst in. "Mornin' to ya, sir." No more than thirteen or so, the boy was wiry and small, with a shock of auburn hair beneath his cap and a spray of freckles on his cheeks. His grin seemed a bit sheepish—just like yesterday, when he'd given William a tour of the stables. "His lahrdship wants a carriage prepared and waitin' for him, he does."

William nodded, and the two set off together to tackle two matching geldings to a yellow-wheeled coach.

"A fine team we make, aye, sir?"

"Aye indeed." William tugged the boy's cap down over his eyes, chuckled, then led the coach out before the entrance of Sharottewood Manor. He loaded the trunk and valise already waiting, both wet with fog, and nodded a greeting to the driver who climbed to his perch.

Then Lord Gresham.

William pushed his hands back into his pockets, fisted them, as his lordship jogged down the steps with his shiny top hat and blowing carrick coat. He glanced at William. His steps slowed and the puffs of breath filled the air quicker.

Then he all but ran down the remaining stairs, shouted something to the footman behind him, and slammed himself into the coach.

A small flame of anger tried to burn William's insides, but he doused it. He had forgiven Lord Gresham for any trespasses. He would not begrudge him one sour look.

Even if it was a demeaning one.

As if William were dirt.

Turning back to the stables, he rubbed both hands down his cold face. He raked biting air into his lungs. *God, why did I stay?*

Of all the places, he should have avoided this one the most. He was too much reminded of the person he'd always thought himself to be, and before whom would he less wish to degrade himself than the man who was almost his father?

He glanced up at the manor, and from an upstairs window, a figure waved at him. Strange emotion flipped his stomach. He did not have to guess who it was, though the glass was too frosted to see more than a silhouette.

Isabella.

His sister who was not his sister.

The reason he stayed, though he hardly understood why himself.

Father was wretched to abandon her this way.

Isabella sat alone in the dining room, every clink of her fork against glassware loud and jarring in a room without conversation. If she had imagined herself bored before Father departed, how much more so now.

For a week, she had tried.

Then she had ignored Mrs. Morrey's unfavorable looks, donned her warmest clothes, and hurried down to the stables to see him.

But he was changed.

Toward her.

The gap between them was cavernous and spanned too great for any bridge. Perhaps she had been right. Perhaps there *were* differences in the poor and the rich—differences that reached deeper than wealth.

He was a pauper.

She was not.

They had no more right to be acquaintances now than they did in London, with no formal introduction and no true connections—or here at Sharottewood, when he had been her secret, dangerously unwanted brother. Why should it matter to her if the stable hand would not meet her eyes? Of what consequence could it be if his smile was no longer compelling and earnest? If he no longer teased her?

The first day, when she'd begged him to stay, everything had been the same between them.

But every day after it was not.

La, but she would drive herself mad this way. They held different stations, and propriety demanded they return to strangers.

But that was just it.

He had never been a stranger to her.

Pushing away her half-eaten plate, Isabella scooted from her chair and returned to her bedchamber. A pile of unanswered letters lay waiting on her desk, Bridget sat mending Isabella's redingote, and a blazing hearth filled the room with light and the scent of burning wood.

Isabella threw herself across the bed and sighed.

If only Father would return. If only winter would be over. If only they could depart for the season and leave behind all this boredom and frustration and loneliness.

She rolled onto her stomach, propped herself up on her elbows, and glanced out the window.

Below, in a slow-falling flurry of snow, Mr. Kensley walked a horse from the stables. He bent down, checked the back-right shoe, then mounted and rode away. If he no longer had a wish to befriend her, why should she try to befriend him?

Even so, she pressed her lips in a line and slid off the bed.

"Where are you going?"

"Outside." Isabella drew a cloak from her hand-painted clothes press then whisked to the door as she draped the garment over her shoulders. "To have a word with Mr. Kensley."

Whether he liked it or not.

CHAPTER 13

The biting air pulled in and out of his lungs, invigorating and refreshing. William galloped so hard the snow kicked up around him and his hair beat away from his face.

Were it not for the groom's achy bones, such an honorable task would not have been given to William. He was grateful it had been. Out here, he could unleash his mind and give free rein to any thoughts he wished.

Except the only thoughts he didn't wish for crept to him anyway. Again. Why did Isabella Gresham keep returning to the stables? What did she wish to gain from her visits?

Mercy knew it was not proper.

Not now.

He'd promised himself to keep his head high—and he had—but this was different. He had his place. She had hers. No matter how much he wished it might be different, it could not.

Besides, she was lonely with friends so far away and roads too rough for travel. But with warmer weather and the start of the season, she would have no use for him and would forget the friendship she longed to return to.

'Twas better they both accepted reality.

After riding down to the seashore, then back up the craggy slope to the road, William slowed the horse to a trot and made his way back to the stables in approaching darkness. Humming, he pushed open the door, then slapped the rear of the animal. "In with you, Browny-the-Beau."

The animal neighed and hurried to his stall, just as a flash of pink caught William's eye in the lantern light.

His chest tightened as Isabella stepped forward. "I rode after you, but Camilla could not catch up," she said.

"Something is wrong?"

"No."

"Then you should not have ridden after me." He went to Browny-the-Beau's stall and started brushing down the chestnut Arabian stallion. "At least not alone."

"You are terrible." Her voice cracked. "As terrible as Mrs. Morrey and Father and. . ." She pressed herself to the other side of his stall, hands clamped on the edge, fire in her voice. "How dare you treat me the stranger, as if I had done something wretched to you."

"You have done nothing against me."

"Then why do you treat me this way?"

"Why should I not?" He dropped the brush, turned to face her, the stall wall between them. "We would be fools to pretend there were not bulwarks between us."

"Because you are no longer wealthy?"

"Yes."

"Because you are Father's stable hand instead of his son?"

The words trailed a line of fire through him. "Yes."

Her jaw jutted. "Then you lied to me." She started away, but he circled the stall and grabbed her elbow.

"How have I lied to you?"

"It is no good to speak of it. I must go—"

"Isabella, please." He realized too late. Why had he spoken her Christian name? When had he begun thinking of her as Isabella instead of Miss Gresham?

Her face colored in the orange glow of lantern light. "You said a man is not what he possesses, but what he does with himself."

"I spoke in truth."

"As a gentleman, you were not too good to aid Mrs. Shaw in her rags and poverty, or visit Mr. Abram in his lowly cottage. Yet you have deemed that I cannot be a friend to you. Why?"

"It is. . .uncustomary."

"No more than your actions to Mrs. Shaw and Mr. Abram." She slid free of his gloved hand. "It does not matter. I misjudged you and thought more of our friendship than I should have." She hugged her cloak tighter. "I shall not bother you again."

He stood braced as she walked to the stable doors, and pride should have allowed him to watch her walk through them without stopping her.

But she was right.

"Isabella."

The door creaked as she eased it open, and a cold wind stirred at her cloak and pink dress.

"Forgive me." He smiled. "And promise me one thing."

"What is it?"

"That you shall retract your promise."

Hidden in shadows and far from the lantern, he could not see her face. "What promise?"

"To never bother me again. I fear I should very much like to be bothered."

"Pray, where are you going now, Miss Gresham?"

"Down to the seaside."

"I daresay, have you not been every day of this week? You must consider your health. The possibility that you might catch cold."

Tying the red ribbon of her bonnet under her chin, Isabella glanced back at Mrs. Morrey with a smile. La, to be so bothersome and dismal. What a pity. Had the woman never been young and restless? "Bridget and I are quite strong. Indeed, we find the cold air exhilarating, do we not?"

Bridget, who was fastening the last button on her velvet pelisse, smiled and nodded. Whether she truly cared for the excursion or not, Isabella would likely never know. But the dear thing was always amiable through every whim Isabella ever hustled her into.

"Do not worry. We shall be back within an hour or two, and I shall dutifully sit in my chair by the hearth and do my needlework." Isabella winked at Bridget, then reached for her maid's hand as they bade Mrs.

Morrey a good afternoon and departed.

Outside, Sharottewood's grounds were brown, grey, and dull, no longer brightened by the glistening layers of snow. The air bit as she breathed it in. She turned toward the stables.

"Miss Gresham, perhaps you should not—"

"Please, I cannot bear it if you scold me too. We need an escort, do we not?"

"Yes, but—"

"I quite detest taking one of the footmen. They watch me with the sort of eyes that make me wonder if they report every one of my actions to Mrs. Morrey and Father."

"You know that is not so."

"I know no such thing." Isabella motioned to the boy outside the stable doors, and he swung them open with a quick bow.

Inside, the familiar mixture of fresh hay, horsehide, and leather filled her senses. "Mr. Ribton, I am quite in need of assistance."

The older man, with his frizzy side whiskers and deep-wrinkled face, dipped his chin in a knowing nod. "Off with you then, Kensley boy."

William emerged from a stall, shook his head with a smile, and saddled three horses with a hum under his breath. She should not have watched him. The way muscles rippled under his sleeves when he swung a saddle over Duke, or the sun-browned color of his hands as he tightened the cinch.

"All ready," he said, handing over Camilla's reins.

They rode at a slow, steady pace, the afternoon sun warm enough that it chased away a bit of the chill. All the way, he hummed a nameless tune. One she'd heard him breathe before. What was it about him she was so drawn to?

Before, she had blamed it on the bloodlines linking them together. What had she to blame it on now?

She did not know and did not suppose it mattered. She enjoyed him. For the past week, she had come for him every day—and together, with Bridget in tow, they had ridden to the beach and trekked down to the water. She had talked, and he had listened. He had talked, and she had listened.

And sometimes they did not talk at all.

Just walked.

Kicking at the sand in search of jetsam or flotsam, as content in each other's company as the seagulls were in the bright blue sky.

"Back to the seashore, is it?"

Isabella nodded, and when they'd eased their mounts down the rocky slope and secured their animals to a fallen tree, she motioned William to follow her. "Over here. I wish to show you something." She did not mean to run, but the sand was packed down solid enough that speed was an easy feat. How many times had she convinced her governess to take her down here, where the sullen-faced woman had perched on a rock while Isabella frolicked by herself?

Indeed, she'd done most everything by herself as a child.

The same throb of loneliness returned to her throat, but for the first time, it seemed more of a memory than a present pain. As she slowed, William stepped in front of her and walked backward.

"Is that it?" he asked, the limestone arch behind him.

"You cannot very well enjoy it that way, unless you have eyes in the back of your head."

He grinned and turned back around, jogging the last few yards toward the human-sized hole in the cliffside. "How much pin money would you bet I could squeeze through that?"

"None." She laughed and leaned her head through the opening, staring out to the rippled beach and ice-blue water beyond. "When I was a girl, I used to play here for hours."

"What did you play?"

"Silly things, I suppose. Sometimes I put sticks in the sand by that rock over there and built a castled fortress."

"To fend off whom?"

"Sea pirates, of course. Then I'd come over here to this arch, and I'd pretend that if I stepped through it, I would come out in a different place entirely."

"What place?"

"Balls, most always. I'd be wearing a lovely dress, just like the ones my—" She cleared her throat and stepped away from the rock, brushing the dirt from her sleeve. "Anyway, I had wonderful times."

They walked back toward the horses, where they could see Bridget in the distance bending in search of seashells.

His steps fell in rhythm with hers. "What was she like?"

"Who?"

"Your mother."

"I was young when she died."

"You must remember something."

A pinprick of pain jabbed her. Beautiful dresses, a pale-faced woman in a bed, a wonderful Christmas, then. . .

"Look." He stilled her arm, his clasp strong, before he released her to lift something from the sand. He brushed it clean with his glove.

A small tiara hair comb with carved coral beads, beautiful despite the rust climbing along the claws.

He pressed it into her hand. "What do you do with all these lost treasures you find along the shore?"

"I don't know exactly. I put them in my trunk or in my drawers, or gift them to the servants."

"And this?" He nodded to the comb. "What shall you do with it?"

"I don't know."

"I think you should wear it." His grin was soft, his gaze penetrating. He seemed ready to say more but instead took her arm and continued their walk down the beach.

A part of her soul flurried. The next time she dressed for an occasion, the old and rusty comb would be tucked into her hair locks.

Indeed, she would keep it forever.

A slight knock rose over the faltering notes of "Minuet and Trio." Isabella glanced to the window, expecting that a branch had smacked it, or that the wind had thrown a pebble into the pane.

But it was William who stared back at her from the other side of the glass.

She shushed him with a finger to her lips, but he tapped all the more.

Didn't he know Mrs. Morrey would hear?

She bounded from her piano bench, slipped to her knees, and eased open the window. "What are you doing?" she whispered. "Mrs. Morrey shall have both our necks if she finds you here—"

"Come with me."

"What?"

He bent closer and cupped his mouth. "Come. With. Me."

"Shhh! I quite heard you. I only meant that you should explain where it is I am meant to come with you."

"Mr. Ribton is without need of me today, and I have spent the morning with Mr. Abram. He is desirous that I should sell his pig."

"What?"

"His pi—"

"Yes, yes, but why?"

"Because the pig is fat, and the fellow is putting together every farthing he owns in hopes of earning fare to America."

"America? Why should he want to go there?"

"To be free." William reached in and captured her hand. "Are you coming, then?"

An unbidden emotion spiraled from the warmth of his fingers around hers. She should have tugged free. She should have gone back to her piano bench. She should have, only. . .

"Well?"

"Mrs. Morrey." Isabella glanced back at the closed music room door. "If I go out, she shall see."

"She is but a housekeeper."

"Who shall have an unfavorable report for Father upon his return."

"Then climb out here." Lifting her hand, William inched back and reached for her. "If you are not afraid to be seen with a stable hand, that is."

She glanced once more at the music room door, a hundred warnings whispering through her—all in the fussy housekeeper's voice. She heeded none of them. Gathering her dress in her fist, she climbed through the window and leapt to the ground, heart racing when William grabbed her hand and started running.

What a naughty, reckless child she was being.

Somehow, she did not care a whit.

"Warm enough?"

"Yes." With the oversized gloves he'd given her, she tucked the grey woolen blanket around herself and grinned. "I have never been to sell a pig before."

Amusement gathered in his throat. "To tell you the truth, neither have I."

"What sport. I daresay, none of my friends shall have a story such as this." She tucked her arm in his—for warmth, no doubt.

His heart thumped. A strange reaction, but one that settled into the pit of his stomach.

"Not that I would tell them. Can you imagine the look on Sophia Kettlewell's face?"

"Yes." A small laugh. "I can." From the bed of the wagon, George Washington the pig snorted in frustration at a pothole, and a chilly March breeze rushed over the land. The air carried brisk smells of land and sea, musky and pleasing scents. Despite the cold, no clouds gathered in the sky, and the sun shone as brightly as it ever did in June.

She smiled up at him. She didn't say anything, and he was clueless as to the reason for such a smile. How quick, thoughtless, and effortless it had been—before she turned back to the countryside, sighed, and leaned her head against his shoulder.

Emotion burned within him. How many kinds of a fool was he? But like a moth flutters to a flame, he could not help himself. She was his lifeline. Just as much as she'd been at Sharottewood, when he'd felt the life trying to seep from his soul, or at Lord Manigan's when a different kind of death had loomed within him.

He needed her.

Needed her childish happiness. Her young and amusing company. Her understanding heart. Why did it seem, though he had scarcely told her anything, that she comprehended all of his hurts?

She healed them without realizing. She healed *him*.

"There." Hugging the too-large coat around her, she pointed to the butcher shop.

On the outskirts of the village, the small brick building sat among weeds and thistles, with wood-framed windows littered with faded caricatures.

"You can stay here if you wish."

"And have only half a story? I hardly think so."

He helped her down, hustled George Washington to the ground, then tugged the pig toward the building despite protesting squeals.

After three knocks on the door, a young-looking man appeared with stained arms and questionable clumps of black and red on his white apron. Pungent odors of warm blood, salt, and juniper berries smacked them in the face. "Help you, gent?"

"I am here on behalf of Mr. Abram. Sent to sell his pig, if you shall—"

Isabella gagged. Twice. She clamped her hands over her mouth but remained standing beside him.

William cleared his throat, lest he laugh. "Mr. Abram said to name your price and—"

With a second gag, she sent William an apologetic look and darted back for the wagon.

Poor girl. A fine story this would make for her. Dragging a hand across his chin, he wiped back his grin, though the butcher seemed on the edge of one himself. They finished the transaction on affable terms, and William patted George Washington's head before the animal was led inside. He rejoined Isabella in the wagon and whipped the reins. "Well?"

"I was wretched. Positively wretched." She spoke while holding her nose, as defeated as if she'd just shattered a lemonade glass in an assembly room at Almack's. "How could I be so terrible?"

"How do you feel?"

"Hmm?"

"Your stomach."

"Oh." She pulled the blanket back around her legs. "Do not worry. I shall not retch on you too." She leaned forward, circling her abdomen. "At least I hope not."

Had she not looked up just then, he would not have been caught.

But her eyes most definitely searched his face. "William Kensley, are you laughing at me?"

He had no rebuttal, and the accusation only lessened his control. A laugh busted out of him.

"How could you? The entire ordeal was insufferable. I have never been so degraded, so intolerably disappointed in myself and in the lack of strength in my own countenance. To think you would laugh at my embarrassment—"

"What other amusement is so grand in this life as laughing at each other?"

"I do not like being laughed at. Stop the wagon this instant."

He pulled on the reins and swept his hand to the road. "By all means, if you should rather walk home, I shall be most happy to tell Mrs. Morrey you shall return by dark, if not dinner."

"Now you are teasing me."

"On the contrary, I am quite in earnest."

She clenched her jaw and glanced the other direction, folding her arms over her chest, features flushed and rosy. An amusing pout, which had probably succeeded in gaining her way from Lord Gresham thousands of times.

Indeed, would probably gain her way with any man.

Including him.

"Shall you travel on without me, or should we continue our way to Mr. Abram's to deliver his funds?"

"Continue," she whispered. Not four miles later, however, before they ever gained sight of Mr. Abram's cottage, she glanced back at him again. Tears pooled in her eyes, and she kept the edge of her lip tucked between her teeth. A habit he'd noticed before. A habit that endeared her to him now. "I *am* sorry for being so terrible, William."

"You were not terrible." He schooled his features against the realization she had used his Christian name, his heart pumping warmth. "Indeed, I would dare to say you were wonderful."

"It is just the sort of thing Sophia Kettlewell would have done. Nearly casting up her accounts and running off that way."

"I do not think so."

"Why not?"

"Because Miss Kettlewell, I daresay, would not have gone to the butcher shop at all." Not with a servant. Not in a farmer's wagon. Not with a pig tied to a rope in the straw-strewn back.

But Isabella had.

For him.

Because they were friends, despite all the differences between them. Differences he should be heeding, if he had any sense. Differences that, sooner or later, would drive them apart.

But he would not think of that now.

He would keep her every last minute he could and worry about the torture of losing her later.

The next day, Isabella dawdled about the house, doing things she ought, pleasing Mrs. Morrey with needlework and mind-numbing piano-forte lessons.

But when the second dinner was finished, she slipped upstairs, changed into a riding habit, and hurried for the stables. The groom half grinned, half scowled when she requested William to accompany her.

They rode for the beach. The wind tugged at her hair pins, the roar of the ocean hummed in her ears, and the taste of salt stayed on her lips. How pleasant all of it was. How wonderful.

And how wrong. She tried to push back the guilt, but it stuck in her middle like a rock lodged into a crevice. What would Father say if he knew she was wasting time on the very one he had run away from?

But it was not a waste. How could it be, when the only thing she thought of, all day long, was seeing William Kensley again?

She glanced at him.

With the burn of an orange sun sinking into the water and glowing over him, he seemed surreal with his blowing hair and flapping coat. Duke's muscles rippled as he galloped. Sand kicked into the air in creamy white sprays. William reached down, patted the animal's neck, then glanced up at her and smiled.

A smile that ran through her. Like lightning. What was the matter with her? She hardly cared. He was the brother, the companion, the friend she had needed the whole of her life.

He was easy in every manner. He was comfortable. He was calm. He was true and real and made her better upon each encounter, in ways she could scarcely begin to understand.

Like yesterday, when they'd gone to Mr. Abram's and sat on stools again in the humble cottage. The old man, with his patched clothes and simple goodness, had shown them a grave through the cottage window. He'd talked of hair the color of honeycombs, eyes the shade of the sky, and a touch so tender it made you near warm enough to need no hearth.

William had looked away a couple of times, perhaps so no one would see. Tears had moistened his gaze. Tears she respected because he had a heart for the old man and the wife who had died and that lonely grave outside the cottage window.

How good he was. How she longed for such goodness in herself. Would to heaven she could have his compassion and his strength and—

"It shall be dark soon." He pulled on Duke's reins, the sky now a bluish dusk. "We had better return."

"Not yet, please." She glanced up ahead, where the limestone arch was just in view. "Let us get down and sit for a moment or two first."

He nodded and they both dismounted, the sand thick and wet as the tide drew closer. They led their mounts to the arch then sat next to each other on a smooth-topped rock.

"It is lovely." She breathed the moist evening air into her lungs. "Is it not?"

"Yes." Hushed. Quiet.

"Tell me how I ought to grasp it."

"What?"

"You know. Doing sunshine, feeling the seashore. . .tell me how I might grasp this evening better, so that I might remember it always."

He leaned forward and drew something into the sand, breathing a laugh, glancing up at her face. He stared for too long and too deep, until a startling sensation awoke.

"Come." He slipped off the rock and leaned against it instead. He patted the ground. "Sit."

She complied without argument. "What is next? Shall we take off our shoes?"

"Too cold for that. Now lie down." Scooting himself forward, he flattened against the sand and placed his hands behind his head. "How is that?"

She wiggled deeper into the sand, every sense alive as the coldness shivered through her. "What next?"

"Look up."

"I am."

"Look harder. You see?"

She squinted into the dark blue sky, where the shadow of a seagull flew overhead and a sliver of a moon appeared from behind a cloud.

"The stars. You see them?"

"No."

"There's one." He pointed to the heavens. "And there. And there. And there."

She followed his finger, giggling at his enthusiasm, until she spotted the first twinkling dot in the inky sky. "La, but they are lovely." And with every passing second, with every deepening of the heavens, they grew lovelier. Thousands blinked down at them, brighter than any she'd ever seen—or had she ever looked before?

She couldn't remember.

She couldn't remember anyone ever asking her to.

"What do you think of that, Miss Gresham?"

"I think it is perfection." A moment she wanted to keep. A sight she never wanted to unsee. Much grander than any ball or new dress or trifling party or—

"Come." He swung himself up, reached for her hands, and pulled her up with him. "You had better dust yourself before we return, lest you appear as if you have met with a tumble from the horse."

She shook the evidence from her hair, wiped it from her dress, though she only wanted to burrow back into the sand a little longer. A weave of emotion tangled through her as she mounted again, each thread different and startling.

One of guilt for doing what Father would disapprove of. One of satisfaction for the end of her loneliness. One of ecstasy for each of the adventures unfolding before her.

And one of confusion. Terrible confusion.

Because the truth of it was she did not view William Kensley as a brother at all.

"Not goin' to bed, then?" Pulling the cap off his head, the stable boy Isaac approached the workbench, both coat pockets bulging.

William scooted over. "Have a seat." In the yellow glow of the lantern hanging from a square wooden post, he handed a second bridle and rag to the boy. Strange that doing simple things, these menial tasks like polishing the red-tinted leather, could feel so good. As if he were accomplishing something. As if working with his hands, here with Isaac, had purpose.

William breathed in the strong, oily scent of his cleaning mixture then sighed. Was it possible he was content here? That without Rosenleigh, without his green countryside, without the labyrinth and the title of gentleman, he was still happy? Or was it only an illusion?

One Isabella had painted for him?

"I walked Browny-the-Beau today. Mr. Ribton said I could, if I finished the rest of me chores."

William focused on the freckle-faced lad. "A fine horse."

"I wish I could ride him like you someday."

"Someday always comes sooner than you think." William grinned when the boy lifted his head, brows rising.

"Ya think I'm near grown, then?"

"If the way you work and eat is any indication."

Dipping his chin to his chest, grinning, sheepish, the boy shrugged. "Mum always told me to eat good. Papa always told me to work good." He dug into his pocket. "Look what I got from Cook. A wee present for fetchin' water for one of the scullery maids. Here."

William pushed the sugar biscuit back. "You eat them both."

"I want ya to have it—"

The double doors whined open from the front of the stables.

Isaac stood, stuffing the treat back in his pocket, as if worried someone had come to retract the sugar biscuits.

"William?"

He stood at her voice. What was she doing here? After dark, no less?

Isaac's shoulders slumped in relief that it was only Miss Gresham. In the past fortnight, she had come every day for their ride along the beach, and though the groom grumbled complaints now and then, no one else seemed to notice or mind.

William knew of one person who would.

"William, are you there?"

Isaac mumbled good night and left, while William set his bridle on the workbench and stepped forward with the lantern. "Over here."

In the darkness, clasping a candlestick, she padded toward him. "I thought perhaps you were already asleep."

"Something is wrong?"

"No." She hesitated. Pulled a green-covered book from the folds of her dress. "You mentioned today that you enjoyed the novels you read when you were injured. I brought you another one from the library. For your evenings."

He had very little time for sleep, let alone reading. He took the book anyway. "Thank you."

She nodded, smiled, but it lacked conviction in her eyes. *Her eyes.* He stayed there, pulled in, sucked into the depth of them without meaning to.

This should not happen.

He knew that.

But he studied every inch of her face, every smooth line and slope, and fought the itch in his fingers to touch them. He wondered how soft her hair would be. Without the pins, without the tight curls. Just down over her shoulders, falling around her face, free and slick and black and—

She turned, but he stepped around her.

"You did not come for the book."

"No." A breath escaped. "I came because of this." She handed him a letter, but he didn't unfold it.

"What is it?"

"From Father. He is returning."

"And?"

"He wishes me to accompany him to London for the season."

"As you always do."

"Yes."

"Then what is—"

"I do not wish to go. I do not wish to leave."

He understood without explanation because his own heart sank. This was insanity. They had played and pretended and eased their shared loneliness, but acting upon such nonsense was impossible. She must go to London. He must stay here. Both of them must fulfill their roles—and even if there were emotions between them, 'twould be better they were doused now than to flame higher.

"You will go as your father asks."

"William, I—"

"You will go." He held her eyes, lifted his fingers to her chin, ignored the jolt of her skin against his. "Now hurry back inside before you are missed."

Her features scrunched, throat bobbed, but she nodded and whisked away.

He clutched the book in a death grip and returned to the bench. Disquiet, perhaps even pain, rippled through him in waves. He had grown more attached than he realized.

Far more.

"This dress, Miss Gresham?" A long pause. "Or shall I bring this one?"

"I quite detest both of them." Isabella curled her legs under her in the chair by her bedchamber window. Outside, grey clouds stirred and churned, as forlorn and disquieted as if they too were forced to do what they did not wish.

Bridget knelt beside the chair, silk and satin dresses hugged against her. "Miss Gresham, do you feel well?"

No, she did not feel well. She felt a thousand things, but not well.

"Are you so very devoted to him?"

Devoted? Isabella turned to her maid, the same thread tightening until it choked. "I am not devoted to him at all." William Kensley was her friend. Her companion. In a world of so much artifice, he was genuine and real, but devoted? How could she be devoted to him?

"Forgive me." Bridget stood, ruffling the dresses. "I suppose I only imagined you were in love with him."

Isabella's breath hitched. She pressed her teeth into her lip so hard she tasted blood and forced her eyes back to the window while Bridget went about packing. *I am not in love.*

Yes, she'd admitted to herself she hardly considered him a brother. He was nearer than that, though how she did not know.

But she did not love him. Not in that way. Not in the way Father should have loved Mother.

"Perhaps this one then, Miss Gresham?" Bridget presented her with another gown, one Isabella used to coo over and twirl in.

She nodded approval without interest. "I am going for a ride." To prove to herself she was not devoted. To prove to herself the lifelong assumption that love did not exist.

To prove to herself that even if it did, she held none for William Kensley.

She simply couldn't.

Seeing her again stirred mayhem in his stomach. She came with no cheerful laugh, and the curls usually so bouncy and tight were as limp as her smile.

In silence, he saddled both Duke and Camilla, but when he led the animals outside, he glanced upward. Heavy, earthy scents of rain hung in the air. "I fear the weather may turn before we are returned."

"We shall not ride long."

He could not gainsay her. Not today when she seemed so uncertain. Was she this grieved to depart Sharottewood? Yet if she loathed the thought of leaving on his account, why would she not look at him?

They rode with the wind in their faces, and she galloped ahead of him instead of matching his pace.

Her hair whipped free of pins. Bumps pebbled his skin as the tresses he'd imagined touching unleashed to the wind, long and tangled and thick.

He tried not to fathom what Sharottewood would be like without her. She'd be different when she returned. He knew that. An eligible bachelor would secure her heart, or a dashing suitor would propose matrimony—and they would never have this again.

Whatever *this* was.

Rides in the still hours of evening. Walks along the seashore. Whispers under the stars. Things that made him forget about everything he'd lost. What did Rosenleigh matter? What did his status matter? Gentleman or pauper made no difference in her presence, because it was so easy just to live for their time together and nothing else.

A fool lump lodged in his throat, just as the first splotches of rain hit his face. He kicked his heel into his horse, trying to catch up with her along the curve of the beach. "Isabella!"

The wind must have snatched his voice, for she continued her reckless gallop.

He hunkered forward and kicked Duke again, this time harder. They needed to return before the rain worsened. He knew too well the agonies of being out here in a storm.

Lightning split the sky, striking the water.

Camilla reared, screeched, but pounded back to the ground with Isabella still clinging to the reins. She climbed off the animal before he could reach her. "She is fearsome of thunder and lightning," she said over the rain. "Ever since she was a colt."

William swung down next to her. "You did not think to tell me that before we left?"

"I hardly realized it would hit so fast. It has been brewing all day long with nary a drop. How was I to know?"

He handed her his own reins. "Ride Duke back and I shall come after you when the lightning is finished."

"That may be hours."

"Never mind that. Hurry off with you."

She blinked against the downpour, hesitated, then turned and walked for the cliffside, leading her horse with her.

He jogged after her. "What do you think you're doing?"

She secured the reins to a dead tree then hunkered under a ledge of the cliff. "I am waiting out the storm."

Frustration expanded across his chest. He joined her. "This is nonsense. You shall catch your death."

"Everyone is always telling me I shall catch cold and die. One of these days I shall do it just to prove them all right."

"My." He shook his head with a whistle.

"What?"

"You are in quite the temperament today, Miss Gresham."

Her chin puckered, as if the words had been a rebuke. "I am sorry."

"No need."

"For not heeding you."

"About the weather?"

She nodded.

He nodded too. Then silence, save for the rain pelting around them and the rumbles of thunder in the distance and the crash of the waves against the rain-splotched shore.

She leaned her head on his shoulder. She cried, though he hardly comprehended how he knew, for he could not see her face and her body did not rack with tears.

The scent of her hair, a unique citrus blend, drifted into his awareness. He wished he could keep the smell. Or a lock of her hair. Or something that would remind him of her the rest of his life, even when she was married and living without him. What was the matter with him? Was he so dependent upon her? Did he need her so much?

Or was it only that he loved her—

Lightning zipped to earth in flashing light, just as Camilla reared again and broke free of the tree.

In unison, William and Isabella lurched forward.

"Camilla, down!" Isabella raced after the animal, but William slung her back from the spray of sand and the rearing hooves.

"Easy, girl." He approached with shuffling steps, speaking soothing words, as the horse finally pounded all four hooves to the ground. He reached for her neck, patted the wet hide, stretched his fingers for the reins—

Another split of lightning. Camilla screamed and bolted, knocking him to the ground.

He scrambled back to his feet fast enough to grab Isabella as she ran after the animal. "Let her go. She is gone."

"I am going after her—"

"Isabella, no." He wrenched her back to face him. "I shall go after her tomorrow. She will not go far."

Rain pelted down on them, heavy on her lashes, mingling with her tears. "You do not understand," she gasped. "Camilla has been with me since I was a girl. I cannot let her go. I will not—"

His lips pressed into hers. Insanity, iniquity, injustice to both of them, but his hands framed both of her cheeks and squeezed. *God, stop me.* But he couldn't stop himself. He drank of her, passion rippling through him as fast as the rain slashed their faces.

She yanked herself free and stumbled back, cupping her mouth with both hands, and faced the water.

His chest roared. His blood coursed hot, despite the cold clinging to his body like the drenched clothes. *Heaven and mercy.* What had he done?

Blinded by the water in his eyes, he ran for Duke, ripped the reins free from the brittle branch, and tugged the horse next to Isabella.

He swung her into the saddle. She didn't protest. She didn't look at him. She only stared ahead, black hair plastered to her cheeks, until he slapped the rear of the horse and Duke carried her away. Minutes later, she disappeared along the curve of the shoreline.

He raked both hands through his hair and groaned. *Dear God, what have I done?*

CHAPTER 14

Isabella slid her hand along the banister as she flew up the stone steps. Another sob threatened to come through, but she swallowed it back. She must get ahold of herself. One would think she had never been kissed before.

But she hadn't.

Not like that.

How dare he. Heat speared her chest and the blood spanned to the tips of her ears. *How could he?* All this time, was that what he had thought of her? How his eyes had seen her friendship?

The greater agony was. . .had she thought of him that way too?

No, no.

She most certainly had not. She did not believe in love, and she certainly had no intention of falling prey to nonsensical emotions. She knew her place well enough. Father's greatest desire was that his only daughter marry well—and it was an obligation she had already determined to fulfill.

Even if she did love William Kensley, the match was impossible.

More than impossible.

Scandalous.

Ripping open the front door of the manor, she stumbled inside and ignored the butler when he asked about her disheveled state. She hurried for the massive winding stairs, leaving a trail of water on the floor, like tears she could shed if she allowed herself—

"Isabella."

She froze three steps up. *Father.* Trying to compose her features, smoothing back wet hair from her face, she turned to face him. Her stomach fell at the sight of the gentleman next to him.

Lord Livingstone.

The last visitor in the world she wanted to see at the moment.

Three hours later, she was seated in a damask chair in the drawing room, clean and dry. Hot soup churned in her stomach. She tried to focus on the conversation, the hum of words between Father and Lord Livingstone, but her eyes kept drifting to the fire.

Heat flamed in her cheeks as stealthily as it flamed in the hearth. She was back in the rain. Cold, wet, shaking, with his hands clamping her cheeks and his lips closing in on her mouth. The memory took her breath.

More than that. It took her good sense. Her reasoning. Her sanity.

"Do you not agree, my dear?"

Pulling herself from the reverie, she focused in on Father's face. His eyes narrowed, as if he sensed she was not herself. "Agree to what?" she asked.

"That sea bathing is most invigorating. We visited the resort in Scarborough two summers past and quite enjoyed ourselves, did we not, dear?"

"You cannot expect me to enjoy memories of swimming in cold water at such a moment as this."

"Quite right. I have forgotten your ordeal today. Are you warm now?"

She assured him with a smile, though it did not lessen the worry line between his brows. "Quite."

"Perhaps a turn about the room might warm you," said Lord Livingstone. He stood and offered his arm. "Shall we?"

A refusal sprang to her mind but did not make it to her lips. She accepted his arm, and together they walked along the perimeter of the drawing room, their footfalls soft thuds against the colorful Axminster carpet.

"That was not Camilla you rode in today."

She glanced at him, startled. "How could you have possibly—"

"I was in the window when I saw you dismount at the stables."

"Yes." She shivered. "Camilla was frightened by the storm."

"A noble footman you must have had in company."

What to say? She glanced back at Father as they turned with the corner of the room, hoping to direct conversation away from today's tragedy. If it could be named as such. "Father is looking well. However did you arrive here together?"

"Is that chagrin I sense?" His dark eyes bore down on her, capturing her, thronging her with guilt. Had he not rescued her at the risk of his very life? In the worst situation imaginable, had he not considered her reputation and aided her without imparting one stain to her respectability?

She owed him much. Besides that, he intrigued her, Father doted upon him, and he was wealthy enough to meet every expectation. Why should she not marry him?

Perhaps she would.

Perhaps she *should*.

"Well?"

"No, I am hardly chagrined."

"Dare I hope my arrival is welcome?"

"Any guest of Father's," she said, dipping her head, "is welcome in my regard too."

"You must know such a speech encourages me."

A warning trickled through her, aroused from all the emotions of the past, but she pushed the notion away. Lord Livingstone was everything she had ever visualized for herself. She had misjudged him for one reckless kiss.

But surely she could forgive that.

Because she needed Lord Livingstone. She needed him to help her collect her sense, remember her place, consider Father, and forget what just happened at the seashore.

Her lips still throbbed.

She doubted she would ever forget.

She had not returned to the stables in the past three days.

Not that William blamed her. He laid fault on no one but himself. Perhaps it was better this way. He had known they could not keep on as they were—at least not forever.

But it hurt.

More than he'd realized. As he lay in bed, with rain beating the roof outside, a strange pain clamped down on him. 'Twas a hollow sickness, like holding Shelton's dead body in his arms or departing the gates of Rosenleigh for the last time. Why had he kissed her?

At least if he had controlled himself, she would have departed for London with a fond memory of him. They could have told each other goodbye with smiles and tender looks.

Now he would have no goodbye at all. He would have nothing from her. Nothing but memories—along with all his other haunting remembrances. Rosenleigh's bewitching green grass, Shelton's quiet ways, Ahearn's rippling muscles beneath William's body, and—

No. Rolling over in bed, he rubbed both cold hands down his face. He would not despair. He could not. All he needed to do was keep his head high and his work done. If his hands were busy, he would not have time for his heart.

Help me, God. The prayer spread warmth through his chilled body. *Help me not to grieve her too.*

"May I come in?" Father's voice rumbled loud in the hush of nighttime.

Without moving from the window, Isabella tightened her wrapper. "Yes, of course."

The door hinges shrieked as he entered her chamber, his tall presence a warming comfort to all her swirling thoughts. Rain pattered outside, just as it had done for three days past, and light from Father's candlestick reflected off the water-streaked window.

Standing next to her, he pulled her against his side. He smelled of tobacco and lemon, a pleasant mixture she'd been inhaling for as long as she could remember. "I fell asleep reading in the library chair and only just awoke," he said.

"Not great praise to the author."

"I saw a light under the door."

"Only because I could not sleep."

He leaned his chin to rest on her head. "When you were a little girl, sleep evaded you because Camilla had taken sick, or because your tutor had been unkind, or because you had eaten too much marzipan and had a toothache."

She chuckled against him. "I remember."

"I always tried to resolve your troubles, did I not?"

"Of course you did."

"Then do you not think I have the right to resolve this one too?"

Sadness vied with shame in her chest, a ruthless battle that kept her eyes glued to the window and not his face. What would he think if he knew what she had done? If he knew the thoughts that kept her from sleep?

She had devoted the last three days to Lord Livingstone's company, but her mind was a traitor. She could not prevent herself from reliving the kiss. The one that never should have happened. The one that would hurt Father—and herself—if she ever spoke of it aloud.

He squeezed her tighter. "It cannot be so very bad, my dear. I am troubled to see you not yourself. What has dismayed you in the short time of my absence?"

"I shall not have you fret over my melancholy."

"Has Mrs. Morrey been imperious?"

"No."

"Has someone written you an unamiable letter?"

"No indeed, Father. Please. I am well. Truly." She pulled away from him and tugged the draperies over the window. "I am quite tired."

"In bed with you then, my dear, and I shall tuck you in as I did when you were a child."

"Father."

"Permit an old man his fancy, will you not?" He smiled, setting the candlestick to the stand while she climbed into the four-poster bed.

Then he hovered over her, drawing the counterpane to her neck, with an expression as fond and concerned as if she *were* a child. "I think perhaps we shall not yet go to London. You are too pale for the journey, and after your dreadful ordeal in the rain—"

"I am not ill, Father, and am of perfect strength. I should very much like to go to London." Indeed, she *must*. The thought of remaining here, with William outside these walls and the seashore close enough to taunt her—

"I have quite made up my mind. I shall not chance your health."

"Father—"

"Please, my dear." His flash of tears startled her. "I did not heed the signs of your mother's declining strength, and by the time I realized her sickness, it was too late to remedy."

She knew the tears were not for Mother, though. Why did that bother her?

"At any rate, you must not despair. I shall invite Lord Livingstone to remain here in our company, and I shall also prepare for a ball here at Sharottewood. Colonel Nagel's regiment is camped outside the village, and with the militia joining us too, I believe we shall have a splendid guest list, despite those who are in London. Does that make you happy?"

No good would come of arguing with him. In matters of health, not even a pout could persuade him. "Yes. That would make me happy indeed." But her quivering voice belied her words, and the second Father departed her chamber, she turned her face into the pillow and wept.

Leaving William and Sharottewood would have been difficult enough. Remaining was unbearable.

What was she going to do?

"Do you always awake looking so perfect?"

Isabella darted a glance about the breakfast room to make certain the footman, who was lowering a platter of buttered toast to the sideboard, did not hear such a remark. The last thing she wanted to be was the subject of servant gossip. "My lord, you should not say such things."

"They do not please you?"

"No." She forked a sausage. "They do not please me."

"Most surprising, as other ladies find such complimentary comments endearing."

"Have you such experience?"

"Pardon?"

"With other ladies." Not that it truly mattered to her. She had seen more than one tribe of conniving mamas and daughters form about him, and it bore no effect on her.

Lord Livingstone smirked as if it did. "You must not be taunted with jealousy, Miss Gresham. My heart, as I have already declared to you, is irrevocably yours."

"You are in error, my lord, as I was not fraught with jealousy. And I fear you are far too bold in your expression of affection—"

"One day we shall not play these silly games." He lowered his teacup, pulled out his napkin, his gaze steady on her face. A nerve twitched his eye. "Shall we?"

Relief marched through her when Father entered the breakfast room, brushing at wrinkles in his tailcoat, though there weren't any. "Ah, I see we are off to a rather early start. What shall the two of you be into today?"

Yesterday it had been battledore and shuttlecock in the yard. The day before, strolls in the garden. The day before that, word games in the drawing room.

"I rather imagined I might take Isabella for a ride." Lord Livingstone tilted his head, and her heartbeat spiked at his proposal. "Provided she is agreeable to the idea, of course."

"You need not persuade Isabella for a ride." Father chuckled as he filled his gold-rimmed plate at the sideboard. "She would rather ride the countryside like a hoyden than remain at home and do her needlework, is that not so?"

"Yes." She crunched her napkin and stood. "But I fear I am not quite up to the exertion today."

"Nonsense, my dear. I daresay, the fresh air would be good for you. The weather is lovely."

"I quite agree. We must insist." Lord Livingstone stood as well, his gaze strong and challenging, as if daring her to refuse.

A sigh left her lips. "Very well. I shall go and change." With a faint curtsy, she excused herself from the breakfast room and bolted back to the bedchamber. She slammed herself inside, breakfast storming within her stomach.

Facing William was something she was not yet prepared for.

Yet it was something she must do.

If ever she was to escape that kiss, she must look him once more in the eye—and convince herself what she felt for him was not love. By all that she valued, it could not be love.

William strode back into the stables, leading Browny-the-Beau beside him. He paused by an empty stall, frowning. Camilla was gone. Had Isabella watched for him to leave before she came for her ride? Did she despise him that much?

"Miss Gresham and her maid come and left, they did."

William glanced at the boy, who was shoveling manure into a one-wheeled cart. "Had they anyone with them?"

"'Deed. A gent." The boy yawned. "Same one what's been takin' walks with Miss Gresham in the garden."

"I see." William kicked plods of mud from his boots, brushed down Browny-the-Beau, then took the shovel from a perpetually yawning Isaac. "Off with you."

"But Mr. Ribton—"

"Never mind him. He should not have kept you up all night for the foal birthing. Now climb into the loft and nap while you've the chance."

Isaac's tired face and heavy eyes grinned. "Ye're a friend to be sure, sir."

William hooked the boy's chin with a light punch. "Go on with you." Ten minutes later, William dumped the last shovel of dung into the wheelbarrow, the foul smell clinging to him as he rolled it through the stable doors.

Afternoon sun bore down on the back of his neck and the warmth tingled his skin. He squinted at the blue sky. The weather was clear for the first time in days, the clouds white and cottony, and a flock of small spring birds, their colored breasts bright against the sky, flew above him.

As much as he resisted, thoughts came anyway. Isabella running to the stables. Laughing. Galloping away with him, as she did every other afternoon, for those idyllic hours when they could be alone.

He still felt her lips. The taste of them. Moist, young, sweet, soft. Everything beautiful. Everything he could not cease thinking about. Everything he loved. *Loved?*

The word smacked him with its ridiculousness. As if a man in his position had any right—

Horse hooves pounded from the left, and without further warning, she appeared around the corner of the stables. She sat straight and erect, drawing back the reins, looking at him, wearing a green riding dress and dainty yellow gloves.

She glanced away so fast he felt slapped.

Her maid and Lord Livingstone halted behind her. "You there, hold the reins."

The sharp command pulled William's gaze from Isabella. Palms sweating, he gathered all three reins while Lord Livingstone assisted both ladies to the ground.

Even then, she turned her face away from William. Could he blame her? Alone, they had been friends. But in prestigious company, who could expect her to acknowledge him? Especially after what he had done?

"You are the one, I presume, who has been seeing to my horse." Lord Livingstone stepped forward, peeling black gloves from his fingers.

"I am."

"*My lord* to you. I shall be addressed properly, do you understand?" The man's chin notched higher. "Have not I seen you before?"

Judging by the way his eyes glinted with amusement, he remembered well enough. Be dashed if William would let the man demean him. Turning, William tugged the horses toward the stable door.

"I am not finished with you, servant."

He halted. Anger ticked through him as he pivoted back around.

Lord Livingstone flicked his riding crop toward his grey horse. "My animal has not been seen to properly. I detected a fur tangle, evidence that he has not been brushed today."

"He was brushed this morning."

"You insinuate I am lying?"

"I insinuate nothing. I am but informing you when he was last brushed."

"This impudence is shocking." Lord Livingstone glanced at Isabella. "Does your father allow such servants who will dishonor his guests?"

Isabella kept her eyes to the ground. "Excuse me, but I must return indoors." With Bridget on her arm, she hurried away without glancing back.

William swallowed past a lump of disappointment. Not that he had expected her to defend him. He hadn't. But treating him as a stranger, not looking his direction, walking away without—

"I have never been so degraded. If you were more my equal, I would demand satisfaction in a duel."

William glanced at the man's face. His eyes burned, feverish almost, and both of his cheeks flamed red. Thunder and turf, he was serious.

Though a duel did not sound exactly undesirable to William either.

"See that the animal is brushed twice a day. I want him walked daily and I want him ridden every evening—though not by you." His lips curled in disgust. "You reek of dung." He marched back toward the manor, muttering under his breath, coattails flapping behind him.

William dragged a sleeve across his sweating face. He caught a whiff of his own clothes and tightened his lips.

He *did* reek—and it was a stench he would never quite be free of.

No matter how much he wanted to be.

How dare he.

Isabella avoided the board that squeaked—evidence that this was not her first time eavesdropping outside Father's study—and leaned close enough to the cracked door to catch Lord Livingstone's distinct voice.

"I rather thought it worth bringing to your attention, my lord. For myself, the insults were bearable. It is only for *your* sake that I raise such alarms, as one can never trust a servant who does not know his place."

"He has always seemed rather even-tempered to me."

"Of that, I would know nothing. Though I do confess to remembering him at your townhouse in London, when he persuaded your daughter into inviting him to a dinner party."

"Isabella did that?"

"Indeed, my lord, and I fear I have but one more caution to mention to you, though I. . ."The words trailed into a sigh of gravity. "Forgive me, my lord. I dare not speak my mind until I am more certain."

"Certain of what?"

"Suspicions which I greatly hope are untrue."

Her heart thumped as she drove her teeth into her bottom lip. He could not possibly know about the kiss. Or the seashore. Or all the other rides. Could he?

"I shall leave you now, my lord, and will trouble you only in asking that you be very cautious. People are not always as they seem, and some have great powers over innocent, susceptible minds. The last thing in the world I would wish to see would be for anyone to take deceitful advantage of you—or your daughter."

With heat curling from her toes to her fingers, she backed away from the door, avoided the loud board, and fled down the hall. She turned into an unoccupied room and closed herself inside.

How dare he accuse William this way. How dare he insinuate she was falling prey to a deceitful manipulation. None of it was true.

William was her friend and nothing more. If it had not been for the misunderstanding, when she had imagined he was her brother, she would likely not even be that. If things had been different, she would not have looked at him twice or spoken to him once.

He was poor. A servant.

She was the daughter of a viscount and well knew her place.

Her knees wobbled and she took a chair by the window, covering her face. The truth was she *didn't* know her place. All she wanted to do was run out to the stables. Her heart throbbed with the desire to burst into Father's study and explain away all the wrong words against the man she—the man she cared for.

Yes, she cared for him. More than she could contain.

If Father knew, he would die.

William had been ordered into the manor house, led into Edward Gresham's study, and scolded for his insolence.

"If you ever behave thus again, I shall release you from your position," his lordship finished, rising from behind an organized desk. Still, he would not look William in the face. "Understood?"

"Yes, my lord." William bowed and left the stifling study. His legs could not carry him fast enough. He needed out of this place. He despised the smells, because they were too much like Rosenleigh.

Clean, airy, with a hint of lavender and linseed oil.

Not dung and horseflesh.

He swallowed another lump of injured pride as he watched mud crumble from his boots and dirty the marble floors. In here, the state of his attire was more apparent. His breeches were stained with oil from scrubbing harnesses and saddles. His woolen coat was frayed at the sleeves. His shirtsleeves underneath still fumed of sweat and horse from the hours he'd spent awake last night with an ailing gelding.

He burst outside and welcomed fresh air into his lungs. One thing he could be grateful for. He had not been forced into Isabella's presence inside the house. The last thing he wanted was for her to see him scolded.

Or for her to see him at all.

Entering the stable, he pulled the door shut behind him and turned for the pitchfork against the post—

"I trust you have now been made aware of your place, servant?"

William jerked toward the voice. He straightened taller as Lord Livingstone exited a stall, complete in a blue frock coat, ruffled shirt, striped breeches, and shiny Hessian boots.

The man's mouth tilted. "I have just taken my horse for a ride. Brush him."

William nodded, blood already boiling, and turned toward the shelf of brushes—

"Speak when I address you."

"Yes."

"Yes who?"

"Yes. . .my lord." William bit the inside of his mouth, jerked a brush off the shelf, then turned toward the stall with the dappled grey horse. A minute more of this and he'd—

No, he would not do anything. He would hold his head high, do his work, and heed Edward Gresham's warning.

Lord Livingstone stepped in front of him, riding crop at his side. "The roads were muddy. Wash his hooves and hindquarters."

"Yes, my lord."

"With warm water."

"Yes, my lord." William started past him—

Lord Livingstone blocked him again. "My boots, too, are soiled. Get a rag and wipe them."

The devil with your boots. William had to bite both cheeks to keep the words back. His hands flexed. Fisted. *God, help me.* Sweat dampened his face as he retrieved the rag.

"Hurry up."

Still, he hesitated. *I cannot do this.* He bent anyway next to Lord Livingstone, swallowed, glided the rag across the mud splatters on the boot tops.

Something lashed across his face.

Fury flared. William sprang up, seized the ruffled shirt, slung the man back into a wooden post. His head thudded against the wood.

"Are you certain you wish to do this?" Lord Livingstone's gasp was hot against William's face, scented with peppermint comfits, a nauseating smell. His eyes were cool, amused, challenging.

Every muscle in William's body itched to unleash the anger. To fight back and satisfy his pride, to gain justice for the mistreatment.

But he freed the man's shirt. He took three steps back, held the infuriating gaze, and braced his feet apart. "Do not touch me again."

A harrumph, as if the threat meant nothing. "See to my horse." He departed, whipping the riding crop in the air until he'd disappeared out the stable doors.

William touched a hand to his left cheek. A stripe stung from his earlobe to halfway across his face, but the greater pain seared in the hollow of his gut.

The last of his pride had just been ripped out of him.

He was not certain he could ever get it back.

"You are unhappy."

"No."

"Does not even the ball excite you?" Alone with Isabella in the drawing room, Father reached for his teacup from the tray. "The invitations have all been sent. We are but ten days away from the event."

The ball meant nothing to her. Before, it would have. Why not now?

Father's eyes seemed to implore the same question. He sank deeper into his chair, sighed, and twirled the silver spoon in his tea. "Inconsequently, I forgot to mention a matter to you."

"Oh?"

"I am releasing young William from his position."

Her teacup crashed to its saucer the same time her heart faltered. "What? Why?"

"It has been reported to me that despite his warning, he has again shown impudence to my guest. I cannot permit such a thing."

"But Father, he was likely provoked—"

"Lord Livingstone is a gentleman of breeding. He would have no gain in tormenting a servant." Father sipped his tea. "Besides, I rather wondered if a situation of this nature might arise. A man raised as William Kensley cannot adjust to a life of servitude, and I cannot afford to accommodate him until he does."

"I think we owe him our patience."

"I think we owe him nothing."

The aftertaste of tea soured in her mouth. A sense of panic swelled inside her. "This cannot be right."

"Dear—"

"You are doing this on account of Lord Livingstone's insinuations."

Father's brows rose. "I see you have not yet outgrown your eavesdropping. But allow me to ease your mind. I put no credit to Lord Livingstone's aimless suspicions, as he is a man quite in love and must be forgiven a bit of jealousy. I, for one, know you far better than that. Do you really fathom I could think *my* daughter capable of affection for a servant?"

She took another sip of her tea, anything to distract her hands, her mind, her eyes. Because if Father looked closely enough, he would know. He would read the guilty evidence in her face. "Excuse me. I believe I shall go and practice the piano-forte."

Father beamed, proud and happy.

He would not be either if he knew that Lord Livingstone's suspicions were true.

She waited as long as she could.

She told herself a hundred times she should not leave her chamber, or slip into her cloak, or hurry downstairs in the darkness.

But minutes later, she stood before the stables anyway. Her limbs shook. She waited several seconds, staring at the doors she was too afraid to open, glancing back to make certain she was not followed. What in the name of good sense was she doing? Was this not the very essence of a scandal?

Yet she could not allow him to leave.

Not without seeing him and speaking to him.

Even if it was goodbye.

She entered the darkness of the stables, but this time, he was not seated at the long workbench with a glowing lantern. Disappointment fissured through her. He must be abed. She was too late. He would arise early in the morning and depart before she had a chance to see him.

She turned back but could not make herself leave. Her heart raced. She felt and bumped her way through the blackness, overturning a bucket of grain, until she reached the splintery door to the harness room.

The smaller room held scents of leather, vinegar, and wood. Moonlight filtered in through a window, brightening a flight of wooden stairs.

She ascended them with bated breath. This was insanity. Father would positively murder her for—

Her foot missed a step. She groped for the banister and caught herself then hurried up the last few steps with greater caution. In the narrow hall, she found three doors. Had not William once mentioned looking out his chamber window?

Which meant only one chamber could be his. The last one.

Drawing her cloak tighter about her, she tapped her knuckles against the rough door and pressed her teeth into her lip.

At first, no one answered. Then soft thuds came from inside the room and the door cracked open an inch or two. "Isaac?"

"No. Miss Gresham."

The crack widened. "What are you doing here?"

"I must have a word with you. I shall not be long." The darkness concealed his features, but she sensed his hesitation. "Please, William."

"Very well. Give me but a minute." He closed himself back in the room then returned seconds later with a lit tallow candle. He led her back down the flight of stairs then guided her along the back wall, where endless tack hung from pegs or rested on shelves.

She took a step back to place distance between them.

Sleep softened his eyes and lent his masculine face a boyish look. Dark blond hair was disheveled across his forehead, and one cheek was pink with a welt. "What is this about?" he asked.

"You must be angry with me. Terribly angry."

He shook his head.

"I have shown you great unkindness. I have been dreadful to you. And now Father is sending you away—"

"You have showed me no unkindness. At least not any that was undeserved." His throat bobbed. "As for what your father has done, it is best."

"How can you say that? You were happy here at Sharottewood." She searched his face with desperation. "Were you not?"

"Let us not pretend."

Air rushed out of her.

"We both knew it could not go on this way. We were not happy. We were dreaming." He glanced away in the candlelight. "We are awake now."

"I should have spoken in your defense against Lord Livingstone."

"It does not matter."

"I should have cried and pleaded with Father until he relented and let you stay."

"Isabella—"

"I will never see you again." More panic smacked full force into her stomach, stealing her breath, until a weakness climbed her legs. "I shall never know where you go or what you are doing. I shall always wonder and never be satisfied. I shall always miss you but never get to—" She lifted her eyes to his lips. She didn't mean to look there, but they pulled at her, like a cord she could not untangle from.

"Even were I to stay, things would be different."

She turned her back to him, lest he witness her lack of composure. Tears rushed hot and salty down her cheeks. Everything was over. All those months of playing and pretending and loving and. . .

No, not loving. Never loving. The rest of the world could claim and testify to such nonsense, but never her. She was far too strong for that. She knew reality because she had witnessed it at nine years old and learned the truth in one heartbreaking lesson. Except now. . .

Behind her, his hands folded around her arms. "You shall forget me."

She shook her head. He was too much a part of her to forget. They were entwined, though how she could not understand. To lose him would end her. She could not bear it. She *would* not bear it. "I shall talk to Father again. I shall persuade him."

"It does not matter. I must leave either way."

"But Mr. Ribton. . .he could not get on without you."

"Isaac shall help."

"He is yet young."

"Isabella, I cannot—"

"Please. Say nothing more." She turned back around. "Let us not even say goodbye." For the second time, she was drawn to his lips. They quivered as hers quivered. They begged to be touched, yet he would never force his kiss upon her again.

That was why she loved him. For his goodness. She tried to retract the thought, but she was already tiptoeing and pressing her mouth into his. She gave him her warmth, her affection, every tender thought and emotion of her soul. She spoke everything she felt for him without words.

His arms pulled her into his chest. His fingers weaved into her hair.

He smelled of wood, hay, and leather and tasted of haunting sweetness. A sweetness that would poison her later. She gasped and turned her face away, but his lips dragged to her cheek, his breath hot against her skin.

A door banged open.

She ripped herself from his arms, tripped backward into a jangling shelf, as a tall figure appeared in the doorway of the harness room.

Several seconds passed in silence.

She was aware of everything. Her tousled hair. The bumps pebbling her arms. William's heavy breathing and the shadow's rigid stance.

Then the figure took one step into the candlelight. "Isabella, go back inside the house." Father's icy voice sent a chill up her spine. "Now."

CHAPTER 15

Shame tunneled through every inch of William. He held himself taller when the only thing he wished to do was bust out of this cursed room. How could this have happened?

He had no right to speak with her.

To love her was madness.

Lord Gresham stepped sideways as Isabella left the harness room. Then the door whined shut. Silence again, the only sound their breathing.

"How dare you." Lord Gresham stepped closer. "How dare you put your unclean hands on my daughter."

Unclean? Because he shoveled dung and cleaned stalls, or because he possessed no wealth?

"I have granted you benevolence. I have provided for you despite the apprehension you brought upon my family. And you repay me by luring my daughter into the dark with you?"

"No harm was wrought against your daughter, my lord."

"You kissed her. That is harm enough."

"I was only—"

"Convincing her to run away with you? Did you imagine I would part with her dowry to a servant, even if you did steal her away to Gretna Green?" Another step. "Or did you even plan to marry her? Did you only wish to compromise her so that you might force me to pay *you* five thousand pounds a year as I paid your aunt—"

"She was not my aunt!" William blew air from his cheeks and stepped back, fury heating his bloodstream into lava. "And I should rather die than take your money or soil your daughter."

"Noble words, Kensley, but they mean nothing to me. I am not so easily persuaded as my daughter. I see you as you are, a predator, and I shall not stand for it."

"You need not worry." William took a step for the stairs. "I shall leave tonight—"

"You are not going anywhere." Edward's giant hands seized William's coat. Seams ripped as he yanked William into his face, nose against nose. "Not until I am finished. Not until I have had my word."

"Then have it." William did not struggle against the hold. He didn't know why. Had it been anyone else, he would have ripped free and landed a punch in the face that leered at him.

But something inside him still remembered Lord Gresham had almost been his father. All the angst of wanting the man to accept him, to love him, rushed back in a torrent.

"How long?" Lord Gresham shook the coat. "How long has this deceit occurred?"

"There has been no deceit."

"Answer me!" Another shake. "How many times has she been to the stable to see you? How many times have you ridden off together? How many times did you degrade my daughter with your kiss?"

"What is finished is finished."

"How can I know that?"

With slow movements, William pried the man's hands away. "You cannot." He started for the stairs and made it three steps up before Edward yelled out to him.

"If you ever return to Sharottewood, if you so much as speak to my daughter again. . .so help me, I shall kill you."

William gripped the wooden banister so hard the splinters dug into his flesh. "I have no intention of coming back."

Isabella pressed both hands against the cool glass of her bedchamber window.

Below in the moonlight, William rode away. She had known he would leave tonight. She had resigned herself to such an ending while she'd hurried back to the house as Father instructed.

But she had done the wrong thing. She should have stayed in the harness room.

She should have stood by William.

Wild, unrelenting emotions choked through her as she backed away from the window with horse hooves still echoing in her ears. Too many thoughts pressed upon her. None of them made sense. None of them matched Father's expectations or her own strong philosophies.

"Miss Gresham, why are you yet awake?" Bridget, clutching a brass candleholder, squeezed through the half-open door. "A commotion outside awoke me. Are you well?"

She was a hundred things but not well. She could not do this. She could not stand here and allow William to be thrown away. Not when she needed him and wanted him and could not bear to wake up tomorrow without knowing he was near.

"Miss Gresham?"

Isabella ignored Bridget and brushed past her as she hurried out into the hall. She ran through the darkness. By the time she reached the top of the stairs, Father was already striding past them below. "Father!"

He paused, his black form casting a long shadow on the moonlit marble floors. "Return to your chamber, Isabella. We shall not discuss what has happened."

"Father, wait." She flew down the steps, panting by the time she flung herself in front of him. She grasped his arms. "You cannot send him away. I beg of you, Father. Send someone after him—"

"The devil I will!" He growled in his throat. "If I thought one member of Parliament knew my daughter had behaved herself unseemly with a servant, I would go upstairs and hang myself."

Anger cut through her. "Is that what this is about? What people shall think?"

"I have worked too hard." Snatching her elbows, he held her at arm's length. "I have sacrificed too much. I have forfeited everything but my soul to keep Sharottewood—and I will not lose what we have built to such a scandalous outrage as this. Do you hear me? I will not!"

She flinched under his yell, but the realization ran with greater ferocity through her veins. "I was kissed in the dark by Lord Livingstone once. You laughed and called it the mischief of young gentlemen."

"Good mercy, the man has manipulated you—"

"Because he is not rich? Because he can no longer afford our pleasures? That makes him less than a gentleman?"

"That makes him dirt beneath our feet." Father lifted his finger to her face. "You are never to speak with him again, am I understood? He is never to return to this place. He is never to pollute this house again." He started past her—

"Father, wait."

Three feet away, he paused without turning.

"I love him." The words wrenched out of her. "I love him."

The next day passed in her bedchamber. She told Bridget she was ill, but the only fever was deep inside her soul. A thousand regrets nicked at her. So many things she might have done differently. If she had remained in the harness room and confronted Father then, would it have changed anything? If she had stood up for William against Lord Livingstone, would it have altered the outcome?

But she had been blinded, just as she had been blinded the whole of her life. Father's coldness toward any beneath him had overshadowed her own vision. She'd been afraid of loving William, afraid of acknowledging her heart, because of the prejudices Father had instilled within her.

Yet it did not matter.

She did not care if gentlemen in the House of Lords or House of Commons whispered over tea about her. She did not care if she was not escalating her wealth in marriage. She did not care if gossipmongers passed her on the street with raised brows and frowns.

Because she loved him. William Kensley. Gentleman or pauper made no difference. She did not love him for what he possessed but for who he was. For who she was when she was with him.

All her life, she had participated in artful conversations, visited proper acquaintances, and made her own aimless circles in society.

William had been real to her. He had listened to her. He had spoken with her. He had taught her how to *do sunshine* and *feel the ocean*. He made life come alive and he made *her* come alive.

She was dead without him.

Rolling over on her stomach, she buried her face into the pillow. Was this not what she had always warned herself against? Was this not what she always mocked? But how could she feel this way if it were not love?

She closed her eyes and was back at the staircase. The ache rippled again. All her life, it had been too painful to admit love could be true—all the while knowing her parents had failed.

She did not understand that night. She did not understand Mother's tears or Father's coldness—or why the love they so desperately needed in each other could not be fulfilled.

She only knew she loved William Kensley.

And one way or another, she would find a way to see him. She must tell him the truth. He had a right to know.

If he would have her, she would leave everything and run away with him.

Because she had no intention of allowing Father to deprive her of love—as he had Mother.

Father was in his study. She knew because she'd hailed a maid and asked her to report his whereabouts.

All yesterday, he had been knocking on her door and asking to speak with her. He had sent up food trays. Once, he'd even ushered in the doctor from the village, but the older physician must have had no grave diagnosis, for he did not return to her chamber.

Certain she could avoid him at this hour of the morning, Isabella hurried for the foyer. She nodded at the butler when he did not immediately swing open the door, as was his custom.

Instead, he cleared his throat. "Good day, Miss Gresham."

She nodded, reached for the knob herself.

But he stepped in front of her, face reddening, features perplexed. "Pardon me, Miss Gresham, but do you not think you should remain indoors? Considering your recent illness, I mean."

"I am not ill. I never was." She frowned. What was this about? "Now, if you will excuse me, I am in a great hurry—"

"I am afraid I am not permitted to."

"To what?"

"Allow you to leave, Miss Gresham." His sagging mouth related his chagrin. "Forgive me, please. His lordship has requested it. Just until you are well, of course."

Discouragement drooped her shoulders. She might have known he would do this. The longer she waited, the more chances William would be gone from the village. Or had he stopped there at all? Had he kept riding, already far enough away that she would never find him?

She would not think that way. She could not.

"What a magnificent surprise." Lord Livingstone strode into the foyer, complete in his tailored riding clothes. "May I inquire after your health this morning, Miss Gresham?"

"No." She started past him. "You may not."

He followed her from the foyer, matching her steps. "I fear I have done something which may have caused you distress."

"Do not think I am unwise to what you have done."

"What I have done?"

"Were you so determined to send William away, my lord?" She paused and stared at him, though if her effrontery embarrassed him, he showed no sign. "You must be madly in love with me indeed to make yourself such a fool."

"I am hardly the fool in this situation." His tone deepened. Eyes flashed. "I have known from the day I arrived you were embroiled in a ghastly affair with the man. I take no shame in admitting I informed your father, night before last, that his daughter had just slipped to the stables in the dark."

Heat pervaded her face. "How could you?"

"Quite easily and without remorse, I admit."

"You are disgusting."

"I would not say such things."

"You have degraded William and you have insulted me. You have inserted yourself in a situation that was none of your concern—and all for naught, I fear, as you are the last man in the world I could ever be convinced to marry."

His chin bunched. "You will not always say such things."

"I shall say that and more if you do not leave me alone." Gathering her riding skirt in her fists, she escaped his presence. Why was she shaking? Why did the man always drain her courage?

And why did his words always seem in likeness to a threat?

"Oh no. I cannot. Please, Miss Gresham, do not ask such a thing of me."

Isabella pulled Bridget to the edge of the bed, where she clasped the girl's frigid hands in her own. Darkness had already fallen, and a strange eeriness swept through the bedchamber as silent as the breeze from the window. "All my life I have been asking things of you. Menial tasks of little importance. And every time you have assisted me with such love and favor I could never ask for more."

Her maid's eyes swam in the candlelight.

"Dear Bridget, you cannot fail me now. Please do not abandon me too."

"I should never abandon you." A sniffle. "But to disobey his lordship—"

"It would hardly be a disobedience. He did not order you to remain within the house; he ordered me." Isabella reached for the sealed letter on the stand. She folded it as small as she could then placed it in Bridget's palm. "Go to all the inns within the village. If he is not there, inquire at the taverns too. They may let rooms."

"Miss Gresham—"

"And take Isaac with you. He shall drive the gig, and I am certain he is fond enough of William to say nothing to anyone else."

"But suppose someone should see." Bridget wiped her eyes. "Before I depart the gates. Suppose his lordship should find out."

"If he does, I shall bear his wrath alone. You need not worry. Father would not be so cruel as to punish you for what I have ordered." Isabella pulled her maid close and kissed her cheek. "Dear, wonderful Bridget. Please be brave. It is only but a letter. You will be courageous, won't you?"

"Yes." The girl smiled, though it quivered, as she stood and rubbed her nose. She glanced at the letter folded in her hands. "Miss Gresham?"

"Yes?"

"Are you certain this shall. . .well, that. . ."

"Am I certain of what?"

"That this is what you want. That such a match could make you happy." Bridget's cheeks dappled with color. "How very much you would be forced to sacrifice."

Her home. Her father. Her standing. All for a love that, only a few days ago, she did not believe existed. Swallowing hard, she guided Bridget to the door and kissed her again. "Godspeed, my dear."

Alone in her room, she swept to the open window and kept her eyes on the stables, watching for the moment Bridget and Isaac stole away. Was she doing the right thing?

William waited until the maid was gone before he undid the folds of the letter. He read over it once, then twice, every stroke of her writing clear and delicate:

> *You must return to Sharottewood. Come the night of the ball,*
> *in six days, as there shall be so much mayhem and merrymaking*
> *that no one shall detect my absence. Wait for me in the garden at*
> *midnight. Please, William. I must speak with you once more.*
> *If you love me, come.*

Love her? He balled the letter in his fist. He strode to the other side of the inn chamber, tossed the letter into the ash pile at the hearth, and then returned to bed.

He would not go. He had already made plans to depart in the morning for Lord Manigan's, where he would resume his position as a footman if the earl would have him.

But he could not go back to Sharottewood. He could never go back. Not because he feared Lord Gresham. Because he feared himself. If he returned once more, if he touched her again, if he kissed her in the darkness of some quiet garden, the temptation to steal her away would be too great. He would forget he had nothing to offer. He would forget he had no future. He would forget his poverty could destroy the beautiful spirit he loved in her.

What could he offer her? In marriage, what could he possibly give her except a servant's chamber and a life of service?

Mrs. Shaw sprang to his mind. He was back in the dank room, where he still smelled her urine and watched her children hunker like skeletons in the corner of the room. Like a twisted nightmare, a different face replaced Mrs. Shaw's.

Isabella wore no glistening silk gown now. Her eyes ceased to glow. No longer was her face full, her cheeks rosy, her hair clean and curled.

Instead, she wore rags that clung to a rawboned frame. The life in her eyes was gone. The hair he loved so much was knotted and limp and filthy, and her only laugh was one of brittle hysteria and hunger.

William gritted his teeth against such horror. He had no means to support himself, let alone a wife and family. He would not chance doing to her what Mr. Shaw had done to Mrs. Shaw.

Or what his own father, whoever he was, had done to William's mother.

No, he would not go to Sharottewood.

He would not see Isabella again.

CHAPTER 16

Have they all arrived?" Isabella pulled Bridget back into her bedchamber.

"Yes, Miss Gresham. I asked the servant who was collecting invitations. Each and every one has been seen into the ballroom."

"I see." She had waited as long as she could. If she did not come down soon, Father would likely arrive to accompany her downstairs himself.

Which she did not wish him to do.

She was not yet prepared to speak with him. Ever since the incident at the stables, a strange and forceful disgust had been forming against the father she had always adored.

But it was more than that.

It was Christmas at nine years old and hiding at the staircase. It was his obsessions. His need to preserve his wealth, his Sharottewood, at any terrible cost in the world. Was he so selfish? Was he so mercenary? If he could not comprehend the sentiments of her heart, could he not at least listen to them?

"Here, let me fix this." Bridget stepped around Isabella and tucked an errant curl back into her coral-beaded comb. The one William had given her at the seashore. "You are lovely tonight."

A small laugh escaped. "Dear Bridget, do not flatter me. Lord Livingstone shall do that quite enough."

"But you *are* lovely. The loveliest thing I have ever seen." Bridget took a step back and smiled. "More so tonight, perhaps, than ever."

"La, you are nonsense." Isabella spun a circle then curtsied with the first true laugh she'd had in days. But as she left the chamber and found her way downstairs, all the mirth shrank back into a frenzy of unpleasantness.

The ballroom was immaculate. Of course it was. Was not everything Father did perfection? The light of beeswax candles glinted off endless gilt-framed mirrors, and the chandeliers hung low enough that their shadows played on the floor. Chalk art, not yet disturbed by dancers, depicted a detailed likeness of Sharottewood Manor.

She frowned at such a display of pride. But was not everything they did intended to flaunt their wealth?

"My dear." Father's voice behind her. "That is a dress very much like one your mother used to wear."

How dare he speak of Mother as if she meant something to him. Her eyes leveled with his—and for once in her life, he did not try to smile away her anger. He matched it.

"Let us take a moment in my study." He took her arm. "Alone."

"I do not wish to discuss anything."

"This infatuation must end, and it must end now."

"Father, I—"

"Keep your voice down." He pulled her farther from the refreshments table, where fewer guests chattered and gathered. "You have never not spoken to me, my dear, and I must admit to being very hurt and disappointed."

"I too am hurt."

"I am doing what is best for you."

"I know my own heart."

"Do you?" He drew in air, as if groping for calm. Then, glancing about to make certain they were not heard, he led her from the ballroom and back into the hall. "On the contrary, you know nothing of your heart, Isabella Gresham." A furious whisper. "You have no comprehension of what you are doing, nor of what you expect of me."

"I expect only to be given a chance to—"

"I have so much protected and sheltered you that you are unwise to anything. You know nothing of the poverty and anguish that exist outside the realms of wealth. Have you any inkling what a life would be like with a man of such meager assets? Do you even realize what you are suggesting I condone?"

The overwhelming emotions provoked by his words drained through her. "I do not wish to discuss it."

"Then we shall not discuss it. Not ever again." His brows jutted. "But know this, Isabella. I would commit murder before I would surrender you to a man of such low degree. Do you understand?"

Pain, confusion, and doubt swept through her. "Yes. I understand perfectly." She returned to the ballroom, focusing on the clash of silk dresses, red military uniforms, and black tailcoats.

Perhaps Father was right. Perhaps she did not know what she was doing.

But as she glanced out one of the windows, where the darkness and moonlight awaited, she knew she would still slip away to the garden at midnight.

She could not have stopped herself if she wanted to.

The dance was taking too long. She moved without care or effort, her only thought the echoing chimes from a distant longcase clock.

Midnight was here.

She tried to tell herself it did not mean as much as she fathomed it did. Had she sense, she would listen to Father. The past two hours, his words had taunted her. *Man of such low degree. . .meager assets. . .you know nothing of your heart. . .unwise to anything.* Why could she not rid herself of the chant?

Lord Livingstone bowed before her as the dance finally ended. They remained standing opposite each other, clapping as the music faded into a cadence of laughter and panted breaths.

"Excuse me." She nodded to him and turned, but he pressed close to her side and followed her through a sea of guests.

Just before she reached the door, he stilled her. "I must have my answer tonight."

"Answer? I was not aware you had presented me a question."

"Marry me."

She nearly laughed, but his solemn face gave her pause. Was he in earnest? After all she had done to discourage him, was he so foolish as to risk his pride on yet another rejection?

"Your hesitation feeds my hope."

"I am only surprised, my lord." She nodded a greeting to Colonel Nagel as he passed. "I would have imagined my answer would now be clear to you."

"Then you are. . ." His forehead tightened. "You are declining my proposal of marriage."

"Yes."

"That is all I wished to know. Good evening, Miss Gresham." With a stiff bow and a perspiring but unaffected face, he weaved his way back through the maze of turbans and feather plumes and curls.

Isabella searched the room for Father. He stood by the yellow ottoman along the back wall, engrossed in deep conversation with a gentleman she was certain she'd seen in London. Likely a man of Parliament. Funny how they all possessed the same beady, intelligent eyes and long faces—so similar to the unpleasant ancestral paintings she used to laugh at in younger years.

She could not laugh at such faces now. She could not laugh at anything.

Not even Lord Livingstone's absurd proposal.

Fleeing the ballroom, she hurried outside and kept to the deep shadows of the manor. Her heart fluttered faster as she drew closer to the garden. How strange and quiet and still it all seemed this time of night, especially after the overwhelming music and voices within the ballroom.

She slipped through the rows with growing anticipation. Perspiration dampened her gloves. Moonlight tinted all the flowers, bushes, and leaves a darkened shade of blue.

At the small garden bench, in the center of the garden, she drew in air. Tears burned and streamed to her lips so fast she tasted salt and anguish.

He had not come.

Now that he could see her, it was more difficult to pull himself away. William leaned farther behind the boxwood, hands curled in his pockets, as Isabella sank to the white bench and covered her face.

He would remember tonight. The way she looked. Young, willowy, in a light blue dress that glimmered with moonlight. That small tiara hair comb decked her hair. The one they'd found together. Her soft sobs lifted into the air, like a song of lament.

She cried for him. Hadn't she done that before?

Yes. Once, when he'd been broken and mangled. Then again the other night, in the dark harness room, when she'd begged him not to speak the word *goodbye*.

He was answering her plea now. He was sparing her.

He was sparing himself.

But he was weaker than he realized. Instead of turning away as he'd planned, he stepped out from behind the boxwood and approached her. How many kinds of fool was he? Why had he come, despite every entreaty within himself not to?

At the sight of him, she hurried back to her feet. "William." She swept against him too quickly and he embraced her before he could stop himself.

"I thought you would not come."

How right she felt, pressed against him this way. Like she belonged here. Like his arms were made to hold her.

"Father is so angry. He says I am. . ." Her whisper faded into his shirt. "I do not know if it is wrong or right, but at every thought of never seeing you again, I cannot bear it."

He pulled her back from him, an arm's length away. His heartbeat ticked away the seconds.

"I never wish to be parted from you." More tears. "Please, I cannot endure it."

We must.

"It matters not what Father says."

He is right.

"We can run away. You can go anywhere and I shall go with you."

Pressure squeezed his throat. He moved his thumbs in tiny circles against her arms, holding her eyes, wishing he could banish the tears he inflicted.

"William. . ."

He did nothing more than shake his head.

Her face crashed. Hurt infested her eyes, overflowed in another rush of tears, and made her tremble beneath the grip he forced himself to release. He did not speak because he could not trust his voice.

He could not trust himself.

Goodbye. With one last long look at her, he headed back through the garden. He crunched the pea gravel with his boots, squeezed through a row of boxwoods, then leaped over the stone fence. He choked the cool, fragranced air into his lungs.

No matter where he went, or how many years stood between them, he would never forget tonight. He would never forget how hard it had been to walk away. He would never forget how much he had loved her. . .how much he would always love her.

God help him and God forgive him for that.

Before, she had been uncertain. Even in her realization that she was in love with him, a small niggle of doubt had weaved itself through her—and she had been unsure if it was madness to allow her heart such liberties with a stable hand.

But it did not matter. She knew that now. As soon as he'd shaken his head and walked away from her, every doubt and confusion and uncertainty had vanished.

She loved him. She loved him from the beginning and end of herself, in more ways than she understood—and the miracle of it was he loved her too.

He never said as much.

Nor did she.

But it was in his eyes and in the shake of his head. He had walked away for her sake. She had begged him for marriage, but he had rejected such a scheme because he had nothing to offer.

He had more to offer than he realized.

He had everything. He *was* everything. He was a king, a prince, a royal knight, a noble gentleman. He was all the things Father was too blind to see, and she would never be able to live without him.

She needed him.

Yet he was lost to her. The power of that, the torture, settled down on her and forced her back to the iron bench. She covered her face for a second time. How could she endure this? How could she ever look at Father, knowing he had not only forced a loveless fate on himself but on her too?

Somewhere near, something snapped and crunched, like footsteps crushing foliage.

She stood, glanced about. The garden was motionless, the shadows deep and unstirring, yet she sensed she was not alone. Was it possible William had returned?

Taking one step forward, she hugged her own arms. She was too afraid to hope. "William?"

"I fear not, Miss Gresham."

She jerked back around. Her heartbeat faltered at the shadow. "Lord Livingstone." She pressed her hand to her chest to still the mayhem beneath her fingertips. "You frightened me."

His eyes were luminous in the moonlight. They smiled. They never smiled.

Something cracked the back of her skull. She must have hit the ground, because small gravel stones pressed into her face and a pair of boots stomped into her vision. Everything blurred. Spun in circles. *What—*

"Get her up. Come."

Pain splintered like lightning as she was dragged upward. She tried to claw. Maybe she did. But the world spun upside down, something wet rushed down her neck, and swirling blackness caved in on her.

No. Her last coherent thought. *Please, no.*

William slowed Duke with a pull of his reins. He swung around in his saddle. There it was again, but louder.

Before, he had thought the distant horse hooves his imagination.

Now they had forms. Ten or twenty indistinct, mounted shadows all galloping in unison.

Leaning Duke's reins to the left, William pressed himself along the stone wall by the road, ready to let the riders past.

But as they neared, they slowed. "That is him!" A muffled shout. Men dismounted.

William stiffened as three strangers lunged forward. He groped for his gun, but before he could aim it, two shadows wrestled the weapon in his hand.

"Release it, gent, if you know what is good for you."

"What is this about?"

Prying the gun from his fingers, they yanked him from the saddle and slung him into the grass, but William bounced back to his feet swinging both fists. He landed a punch across someone's face, a second blow into soft, cracking cartilage. . .

A boot smashed William's face. He fell back, but hands caught him and propelled him forward into another group of shadows. He caught a second boot, this time in his ribs. He doubled over with the third. He hit the ground with the fourth.

Pain weaved in and out of his rib cage as they dragged him back to his feet and pinned back his arms. Warm blood rushed from his nose to his mouth, tasting like halfpennies and salt water.

Then another shadow moved before William. Taller than the rest. Only when he angled his face did the moonlight illuminate him.

Lord Gresham. William's temples throbbed. He swallowed blood. Was the man so angered at William's return to Sharottewood that he would gather all these men to apprehend him?

"Where is she?"

"Who?"

Lord Gresham's hand stung William's cheek. "Do not dare disrespect me now. I will not have it. What have you done with her? What have you done with my daughter?"

Confusion overcame the pain ringing in William's brain. "I do not know what you speak of."

"You were seen going into the garden."

"I was there."

"My daughter was with you."

"Yes—"

"Then where is she?" Edward groped for William's neck, his fingers squeezing, eyes bulging in the moonlight. "She never returned. One of her slippers was found on the path."

God, no. Ice-cold fear spread through William. He could not think any more than he could breathe. He had just seen her. He had just touched her. She had been alone in the garden, but she had been well. What could have happened?

"Answer me, Kensley." The words held death on their tips. The hands gripped his neck tighter, until William had to wheeze in every painful breath. "Answer me!"

"My lahrd, please." A young voice from a horse top. "Please, ya shall kill him."

Isaac. Blackness fluttered before William's eyes then was gone. He drew in air. Slow, easy, grimacing against the ache in his throat.

"I shall ask once more, and heaven help me, if you say nothing, I shall break your neck."

"My lahrd, please listen! It was not him. Someone else. Please listen."

"What?" Edward turned.

The boy must have ridden closer, because his young voice gained volume. " 'Deed, yer lahrdship. I was tryin' to tell ya before but ya would not listen. That be why I followed ya tonight."

"Tell me what?"

"I would not have noticed, except I was outside preparing one of the carriages. William had already come for Duke, he had, when I spotted a gent run into the garden."

Heart skittering into madness, William strained against the arms holding him back. He already knew before Isaac finished.

"It was Lahrd Livingstone."

CHAPTER 17

*T*rapped. The word jolted through her semi-consciousness, but she didn't squint open her eyes. She worked to keep her breathing measured. Perhaps they would not suspect she had awakened.

Whoever *they* were.

She tried to think, to remember, but nothing was clear to her. The back of her head throbbed, as if someone had driven pegs into the base of her skull. *Trapped. Trapped.* Over and over that same word shuddered through her.

She was aware of so much. Too much to comprehend.

Someone's arms were around her, closing her in, and they rode by horse. Coarse, itchy rope bound her hands. She smelled brisk air and peppermint comfits and—

Peppermint. She nearly choked. *Lord Livingstone.*

As if sensing she was awake, the horse beneath them halted. "I trust you have slept well, Miss Gresham?"

Her skin prickled. His tone was so familiar, so unaltered, that she tried to derive comfort from the voice. This was a mistake. She had been injured, but perhaps he—

A rough blow thudded into her shoulder and slung her from the horse. She landed on her back, air whooshing from her, and stifled back a cry.

"Come now, Miss Gresham. It is morning. Must I beg you to open those beautiful eyes of yours?"

She had not realized she was squeezing them shut so tightly. Struggling up on one elbow, she glanced up. Foamy, grey-dappled horse legs. Shiny

Hessian boots. Dusty breeches, a tailcoat made for a ball, and. . .a face that had proposed to her only hours before.

Behind Lord Livingstone, a stranger she'd never seen grinned from his mount—his clothes ratty, face swarthy, head bald and veiny.

Lord Livingstone's mouth twitched, as if with satisfaction. "Do meet an acquaintance of mine. Pike, give the lady your salutations."

The man chuckled through rotting teeth but said nothing.

Limbs shaking, she staggered to her feet and outstretched her bound wrists. "What is this?" She had not meant to divulge her panic, but it shrilled her voice. "What have you done? How could you—"

"This is not Sharottewood Manor." Lord Livingstone dismounted. "I fear you have not the same power here as your doting Father permitted you at home."

Frantic, she glanced about. The road was long and empty, devoid of carriage wheel tracks or other travelers. Trees towered, hiding cottages or farms from sight, if there were any. How far had they gone since she'd lost consciousness at the garden? Where was he taking her?

"I daresay, Miss Gresham, you seem rather out of sorts." He pressed his face into hers, breathed peppermint against her, dipped his lips to hers.

She hit her hands against the side of his face and darted—

He swiveled her back around. Grabbed fistfuls of her hair. Claimed her mouth in a harsh, brutalizing kiss, then slapped her face. "Only one person has the power out here, Miss Gresham, and it is no longer you."

A thousand fears numbed her body and soul.

"I do not wager you remember, but I always attain what I wish." He threw her back atop the horse then climbed on behind her. "If it is not given to me, I take it."

"Are ya hurt, sir?" Isaac stood beside William at the front of the stable, the burn of the morning sun setting his auburn hair on fire.

"No." William flicked off the last dry blood from underneath his nose then accepted the rag Isaac handed him. He wiped his entire face, the coolness a stark contrast to the heat still roiling beneath his skin.

"I did a fair bit of wrong, didn't I?" Isaac slumped against the stables. Around them, military officers prepared their horses, secured their knapsacks to their saddles, or huddled together and spoke in low tones with a few gentlemen not in uniform.

Lord Gresham, nearer to the manor, shouted louder at Colonel Nagel. "Sir?"

William focused back on Isaac. "No, you did no wrong."

"But I should have told sooner. When I saw that man sneakin' into the garden, I should have—"

"You could not have known she was in danger. None of us could." In the darkness, they had forced William back to Sharottewood by gunpoint, where they had locked him in the carriage house until they discovered the whereabouts of Lord Livingstone.

They had found nothing.

Except a missing dappled grey horse, missing jewels and trinkets, and a missing two thousand pounds from Lord Gresham's study.

I should have known. William ground a fist into his palm. Had he not sensed the man was untrustworthy? Had he not known from the beginning he was not as genteel as he appeared? Why had William not warned Isabella?

"You men, get mounted!" Lord Gresham strode for the stables, shouted at Isaac to prepare his horse, and then turned to grasp the hand of the colonel. "You shall not regret this assistance, Colonel Nagel."

The man, rather mousy in appearance with dull grey-brown hair, nodded with a dubious expression. "We can spare no more than a day or two before we must return to camp in continuance of our training."

"That is more than enough time. We shall have Isabella back by then, I am certain."

William slipped back into the stables, and as Isaac was leading out Lord Gresham's horse, William led out Duke. He gritted his teeth as he mounted, loathing in silence the boot that had bruised his ribs—or broken them.

"What do you think you are doing?"

William met Lord Gresham's gaze. "I am going with you."

"You are doing no such thing. Colonel Nagel, have this man locked up until our return. I want him questioned further when I am back."

The colonel frowned. "We have already determined this man did not abduct your daughter, and I daresay, we are much in need of every man we can get. I see no gain in leaving him behind."

"I have no time to argue the matter. Let us carry on." Lord Gresham motioned the men to ride then hurried his horse in front of William's. He seemed as if he were about to say something, a threat of sorts, but then he clamped his mouth shut. He kicked his horse into a gallop behind the rest, and William followed.

"God go with ya, sir!" Isaac's frail voice lifted among the pound of so many hooves.

William waved without looking back. If God did not go with them, they stood no chance of finding her.

He only prayed she was alive and untouched when they did.

Her dry mouth tasted of dirt. She ran her tongue along both lips, trying to ease the cracks, but it did not help. Thirst throbbed at her throat.

If only she had not spit at him.

Two days ago, when they'd been camped along the road and he'd spoken uncouth remarks, she had spewed her disgust at his face.

He had not slapped her again. He had not even discolored with rage. Instead, he had lifted his two-quart wooden canteen, grinned at Pike, and never passed it to her again.

Fogginess hovered over her brain as she allowed her sore body to sway to the motion of the horse. Today, she was with Pike.

His scratchy woolen coat irritated her bare arms, and his ale-scented breath moistened the back of her neck. She tried to keep her head upright. *Stay awake.* She had to remain alert. She had to be ready. At any second, she must be prepared to run, to escape into the trees, to scream at the sight of another traveler.

But there were none. The road was too forgotten.

And she was not certain she could speak, let alone scream, even if she had to. How long had it been since they'd taken her? Sometimes she thought only hours, because everything remained the same.

But night and morning had fallen so many times that it must be days. Three or four. Perhaps more. Her shoulders slumped. Another wave of dizziness.

"Lordy."

The horses must have stopped, because next thing she knew, she was being tugged back to the ground on her stocking feet. Her legs wobbled.

"She be rightly ready to give out, she be."

"We cannot have that, can we?" Arm lacing through hers, as if they were but strolling through Hyde Park, Lord Livingstone guided her from the road. They waded through tall grass, and her vision stilled long enough for the small pond to come into focus.

She swallowed air and staggered forward—

"Just a moment." Lord Livingstone yanked her back, inches from his face. "I might be inclined to revoke your punishment, should you convince me."

Her chin rose. He had abducted her freedom but not her spirit. She would not beg. She would not surrender herself to his desires, despite every unquenchable need to taste water.

"You are not listening to me."

"I have nothing," she rasped, "that would convince you."

"On the contrary. You have something I very much want." He glanced at Pike then back at her face. His black hair hovered half over his eyes, and the gaze that used to intrigue her now held no mystery. He was exposed in the fullest. "You see, my darling, before we are finished, *you* shall beg *me* to marry you."

"Never."

"I would not speak so hastily."

"I would. . .die first."

"You may wish you could." He motioned toward the pond. "Have your drink then, Miss Gresham, but do so quickly. We must be on our way."

She hurried to the edge, dropped to her stomach, and cupped brown water to her mouth. The liquid rushed down her throat, warm yet satisfying, stinging the cracks in her lips.

He hauled her back before she was finished, and she sucked back a protest. She would not have him sense her weakness.

She would not have him know she had never been so desperate and terrified in her life.

William snapped another stick and placed it into the fire as sparks followed smoke into the dark night air. The heat caused perspiration to dampen his chest.

From the other side of the flames, Lord Gresham passed a map to Colonel Nagel. "The fact that we can no longer determine a trail has nothing to do with it. This is the logical location. Where else would he take her?"

"Wetherbell Hall is not an estate accustomed to company."

"Good mercy, man, we are not visiting for tea. They have my daughter!" Edward cursed then raked a hand through his hair as if attempting to gain control of himself. He grabbed the map again. "The elder Lord Livingstone is not a man who partakes in society. I realize that. And in any other circumstance, I would grant him his privacy."

"It is more than a dislike for company, by all accounts."

"You think it matters to me if the man has grudges against England?"

"But arriving with a regiment of redcoats—"

"If you are afraid, Colonel, do not speak in circles." Edward rose to his feet, breathing hard, stuffing the map into the pocket of his tailcoat. "Turn back, and I shall continue on with the others."

Colonel Nagel, rarely aroused by anything, simply shrugged off the comment and glanced into the flames. "No indeed. We shall carry on. I meant only to forewarn you that we are no longer in England, and the Lord of Wetherbell Hall may not be as welcoming as you might hope."

"He can blaspheme the King for all I care, so long as I find my daughter." Edward marched off into the darkness, the echo of his words still lingering.

William stoked the fire with a twig. *Five days.* Sickness swept through him, intensified by the nauseating smell of a roasting hare at another fire.

Five days since she was taken.

The past three, they had remained in England. Today they had followed and lost the trail within the borders of Scotland.

In all their searching, they had discovered but one evidence of her. A slipper.

William rubbed his stinging eyes, poked the fire once more, then scooted a few feet back and pillowed his head with his tailcoat. Even when the rest of the camp grew quiet with snores and heavy breathing, sleep evaded him.

He was far too haunted by her face. Her laughter swept through his memory, young and free and unburdened—and he hurt too much to imagine what she might be enduring. If Lord Livingstone had injured her, if he had laid hands on her, if he had robbed her innocence. . .William would kill him.

Dear God, keep her safe.

Near one of the small fires, a silhouette paced back and forth in the smoky darkness. Lord Gresham, no doubt. Somehow, despite all the bitterness between them, William was comforted by the sight. He was not alone in his love for Isabella Gresham.

He was not the only one who would move heaven and earth to get her back.

CHAPTER 18

Give us answers. The prayer burst in William's chest as the thirty-some men crested the ridge overlooking Wetherbell Hall.

The stone house stood tall against a backdrop of rippling, foggy hills. Fortified towers rose from each corner of the home, and endless mullioned windows glinted with pink morning sun.

Lord Gresham nudged his horse forward. "Let us go."

"Perhaps my men should remain." Colonel Nagel glanced toward the scarlet uniforms and blinding white cross belts. "With his political prejudices, the sight of—"

"Never mind. I shall go myself." Uttering a mild oath, Lord Gresham urged his horse down the hill.

William started after him. Two had more chances of persuasion, and with Lord Gresham's temper against him, he might miss something vital. William would miss nothing.

Near the bottom of the hill, as their paces matched, Edward glanced over and scowled. "Get back up there with the rest of them."

"It is best you do not go alone."

"Do not tell me what is best, Kensley." Despite his words and tone, his face relaxed a little—and he did not argue when William continued alongside him. They crossed the stone-arched bridge over the burn then dismounted within the cool shadow of the house.

Lord Gresham banged on the door. A butler answered, insisted several times that Lord Livingstone was otherwise occupied, then finally relented and allowed them inside. He showed them into a spacious drawing room.

Heavy red curtains hid most of the morning light, though burning silver candlesticks still illuminated the room.

Edward walked to the hearth and leaned his forehead against the ornate mantel. A distant clock ticked by the seconds, the minutes, the hours.

William paced from one end of the room to the next. How long had it been? How long would the elder Lord Livingstone allow his guests to wait, when they had specifically assured the butler of urgency?

Unless he already knew about his son. Could Isabella be here? Were they hiding her together?

"In the name of holiness, what is taking so long?" Edward banged the mantel. He swung a hand toward William. "And do cease your pacing. You are driving me mad."

"I cannot sit."

"Then stand there and do nothing. I would not have permitted your company had I known—"

The double drawing room doors parted, and a large, oval-faced man strode into the room. His hair, frizzing near to his shoulders, was reminiscent of ancient paintings William had spotted on the wall, and even his black coat, though clean and tailored to his form, seemed near forty years out of fashion. "Gentlemen, have seats. Drummond, pour glasses of wine."

"We have not time for refreshments." Edward stepped forward. "I have come to inquire after your son. Is he here?"

"I am a man of principle, sir. I do not desire to receive guests, but if I must receive them, I serve them wine." The elder Lord Livingstone motioned to the chairs. "Sit."

"I do not—"

"We are honored, my lord." William cut off Lord Gresham with a small, pleading glance. He took a chair, and with a heavy sigh, Edward followed his example.

Minutes later, the three men sat in silence, each with antique Roman wine cups filled to the brim. The clock groaned away more seconds.

Edward scooted to the edge of his seat. "About your son—"

"He is well and resting."

"He is here?"

"Indeed. He is always here, as am I." Lord Livingstone sipped at his cup. "Were he up for visitors, I would bring him down now. The lad is quite old enough to sit with his elders and partake of strong drink. I did so at his age. My grandfather brought me into the presence of visitors by the time I was—"

"Your son has been in Northumberland at Sharottewood Manor. You deny this?"

"Yes. I deny it." Lord Livingstone thudded his wine cup to the mahogany stand, his cheeks blazing as red as the liquid. "My son is fourteen years old and has been ill since birth. You may invade upon his private chamber, if you wish to see for yourself."

Confusion swept through William's brain. Fourteen? Ill? Had he more than one son?

"I do not understand." Edward stood. "I met your son in London and welcomed him into—"

"You welcomed Robert Digby, I imagine, not my son. Do not defame the Livingstone name with the deeds of that devil."

Devil. The word burrowed into William's consciousness and quickened his blood flow. He too stood. "Who is Robert Digby?"

"The son of a tavern drunkard. The boy I once hired to feed my sheep." Lord Livingstone pulled a handkerchief from his coat and wiped his face. "And undeniably, the man who has ruined my life."

"If you knew he was imposing upon your son's identity, why did you do nothing?" asked William.

"Very simple." Lord Livingstone leaned back in his chair, eyes heavy and cheeks sagging. He fixated his gaze upon some unknown object across the room. "I once witnessed Robert's father beat him so badly he could not stand to his feet. The child was twelve. After that, I brought young Robert here to Wetherbell Hall and employed him as a servant to assist my shepherds. Trouble followed the lad, but I could never see the justice in sending him back to such brutality." His eyelids half closed. "I wish now I had."

Dread burned through William as he braced the side of his chair. "And then?"

"I suppose when a boy has nothing, he longs to reach for everything. That was the way it was with Robert. Anything he desired, he set his entire attention upon until it was his. First it was but petty matters. An envied coat. A better chamber in the servants' quarters. A position within the house and then. . ."

William swallowed. "And then what?"

The man hung his head. "I should have realized before it happened, but he spent so much time in the village with his ruffians, I had no idea she. . .that a servant could possibly. . ." More color blotched his cheeks. "Over a year ago, Robert and his village cohorts raided my house and fled into the highlands. My daughter went with them. I have not seen her since."

"Why did you not go after her?" asked Edward.

"Digby has chosen his fortress well. He has enough men to defend himself, and anyone climbing the mountain could be spotted and cut down before they ever reached the top."

Silence filled the drawing room, the only sound from the wretched clock marking the seconds and the slow drip of wine to the floor.

Lord Livingstone stood, looking as old and dead as all the ancient paintings he mimicked. "So you see, gentlemen, that is the reason I continue permitting such an impostor to deprecate the Livingstone name. If I have any hope of ever seeing my daughter again, I have no choice."

Edward growled. "But surely—"

"Robert Digby has vowed that he shall kill my daughter if I do not comply, and I do not doubt him. I underestimated him once." The old and stricken eyes grew moist. "I shall not do it again."

Every step drew her muscles into knots of pain. *Keep walking.* She could survive if she followed her own commands. *Do not cry. Do not despair.* Rocks cut through her stockings, numbing her feet. *Keep walking.*

Evening had fallen, darkening the world around them, until it was increasingly difficult to see the trail they followed. Hours ago, at Lord

Livingstone's command, they had dismounted to climb the rocky mountain afoot. Where was this place? Why was he taking her here?

"Miss Gresham." Breathing hard, Lord Livingstone took her arm in his hand. "I trust our little stroll is not too strenuous?"

She ground her teeth into her bottom lip. She tasted blood, but it did not matter. The pain distracted her from his breaths panting in her ear and his cold fingers curled around her flesh.

"Do not be unhappy. We shall arrive presently. In fact"—he quickened his pace—"are those not lights I see, Pike?"

"That they be."

" 'Stars, hide your fires; let not light see my black and deep desires.' " Murmuring more poetry, Lord Livingstone dragged her back up when she hit the ground with her knees. "Come now. Must not give out yet."

Keep walking. The darkness blinded her. She could no longer see and no longer avoid the sharp rocks jabbing her feet or the boulders tripping her legs. Farther and farther, they climbed. She stumbled again. Then again.

Each time, Lord Livingstone yanked her up. By the time they reached even ground, where stone boulders jutted into the air like castle ruins, dizziness swayed her vision.

"After you, my darling." After Pike had squeezed inside a small hole in the rocks, Lord Livingstone motioned her through.

She hesitated then pressed herself into the opening. For a second, she was back at the seashore archway. She pretended all over again. When she stepped through, she would awaken. She would be back at Sharottewood Manor, back at the garden, back at the stables or her bedchamber or—

A bruising shove plummeted her to the other side. She let out a whimper, a chill passing through her as her eyes adjusted to the disorienting lights.

Ragged men emerged from broken huts, some with torches, others with swinging lanterns. Shadows and ghoulish light rippled on their filthy faces. Quiet murmurings and mossy scents of heather filled the air, and from somewhere close, chains rattled the stillness. What was this place? Who were these men? Who was Lord Livingstone?

She jumped when he grabbed her again.

"Men, allow me to introduce you to our honorary guest." He nodded to Pike. "See that our newfound treasures are distributed unto the men, but do so quietly in your own quarters. Do not disturb me until morning."

Until morning. Her breathing hitched as the men parted a path, one she was forced to follow. *God, please protect me.*

In the blazing glow of torchlight sat a small brick house, covered in stucco, with a dark thatched roof. A chimney spewed smoke. At the corner of the house, two grey dogs barked and lunged forward, straining against their giant chains.

"This way, my darling." Lord Livingstone kicked open the door with his foot and swept a hand inside. "Do not mind the dogs. They shall not devour you so long as you are out of their reach."

Please. She pressed her hands against her chest as she entered, the throb of her heartbeat vicious and frenzied. She took in the room in one panicked glance.

Large and open, the floor was covered with colorful rugs and gleaming parlor furniture. A chandelier hung from the ceiling, the windows bore gold-tasseled draperies, and the mantel sported figurines and hand-painted vases.

Then something moved. A woman by the window, dressed in a long cream gown, with limp blond hair that hung to her waist.

"It is but a humble abode, I admit." Lord Livingstone hugged Isabella to his side. "But we are not without our luxuries, are we, Cressida?"

She stepped toward the center of the room. Sweat marks ringed the satin dress, and a face that once might have been beautiful was bloodless, despondent, and thin. Her eyes roamed the length of Isabella then lifted to Lord Livingstone in waiting.

"You are more revolting every time I behold you."

She accepted the injury without so much as a blink.

He slung Isabella to the rug. "Feed my little dove and lock her up. Do not disturb me tonight." Cursing, he stepped across Isabella's body, brushed past the woman, and slammed himself into another room.

Cowardice fissured through Isabella. She could not look up. She could not meet the woman's eyes—perhaps because she was too afraid she would see herself in their haunting depths. What had Lord Livingstone done to the girl to scar her with such agony?

"Your wrists are bleeding." The tone was neither warm nor cold, and the woman made no move to loosen the course, bloody ropes.

Instead, she bent next to Isabella and helped her stand. "I had better lock you up."

William brushed down Duke with his hands, the slow rubbing motion soothing to him. His eyes were bleary, whether from another nightfall or his lack of sleep, he could not tell.

Men whispered and hovered in circles around whist games, sometimes cheering out, other times laughing. The echo of their voices faded on the night wind.

"Kensley." The gruff word turned William toward a figure approaching in the darkness. As the man neared, Lord Gresham's features became more distinguishable. "The colonel has drawn out a map to the fortress. According to his estimations, we should arrive in three days."

William nodded. Three days was hardly anything to cheer over. How many had Isabella been with Lord Livingstone already?

As if sensing his thoughts, Edward frowned. He started to turn but hesitated. Then he faced William again and outstretched a linen-wrapped pastie. "Here."

"I have no hunger, my lord."

"Neither have I." Edward pushed the food against William. "But it is the only way we shall keep our strength. God knows we need that—*Isabella* needs that—more than anything." He walked away with tight, unbending shoulders, and a small trickle of respect ran through the parched places of William's soul. One thing was certain about Lord Gresham.

He loved Isabella as much as William did.

Leaning against Duke, he bit into the cold pastie and forced the nourishment past the lump in his throat. If it was strength Isabella needed from him, it was strength she would get.

That and anything else he could give her. Including his life.

The room was tiny and barren, the only window nailed shut with boards. Isabella pressed herself into the corner. She kept her eyes on the door, waiting for it to swing open, for the woman to sweep in with more soup and bread.

But she never did. The door remained shut.

Sometimes Isabella heard voices on the other side. The soft timbre of the woman's pleas, Lord Livingstone's deeper replies. Other times footsteps thudded near the threshold, but still, no one entered.

Nighttime fell again. Then daytime. Then nighttime. She curled on the floor and pressed her knees into her chest, hugging them to her, as if she were embracing Father or William or Bridget.

"Bridget, dear, won't you bring me something wonderful to eat?"

"What should you like, Miss Gresham?"

"I hardly know. I am positively famished after sleeping past breakfast. Do have Cook surprise me, won't you?"

Hunger gnawed at her insides, like claws ripping and scraping at the empty places in her stomach. She scooted to the bucket they had left, cupped more water to her lips, but even that was nearly gone. Had he brought her here to kill her? Why had he not strangled her in the garden? Would that not have been a kindness?

God, help me. When a thin light of morning streamed through the boards, she pulled herself back to the window. She thrust her fists against the wood, but nothing budged. She lunged her elbow at the center of a board. Not so much as a groan came in response. How did any of this make sense?

Lord Livingstone was supposed to abide at Wetherbell Hall. He was supposed to attend balls and woo ladies and impress matrimonially minded fathers with his wealth and charm.

But he had lied. That much she knew. Had he truly rescued her at Rockingham Hall, as he had pretended? Or had *he* been the one to orchestrate the attack? Was that the reason the marauders were not yet apprehended? Because after each attack, the men dispersed to hide—not in England, as it had been supposed—but here in this forsaken Scottish highland?

Footsteps thumped. A lock rattled, then the door creaked open and the woman named Cressida slipped inside. "Sit down," she whispered. "Before he hears you."

Isabella wilted back into the corner at the woman's command.

"Robert says I might feed you." The woman hurried an earthenware bowl into Isabella's hands then grabbed the bucket and left the room.

Isabella gulped down the cold, chunky liquid. The taste was foreign and dull, but it eased the pangs in her stomach. *Thank You, God.* By the time she had drained the last drop, Cressida returned with a sloshing bucket of fresh water.

Clutching bandages, she bent next to Isabella and glanced at her torn feet. "May I?"

Isabella nodded.

With cool, careful fingers, the woman peeled off the ripped, bloodied stockings and swished a warm rag across the injuries. She bandaged both feet. "You shall feel better now. There is enough water you might wash."

"Who are you?"

"I am no one." The woman spared a glance at the door. "Not anymore."

"Did he bring you this way too?" Isabella's mouth dried. "Did he—"

"I must go." Tragedy loomed in her gaze, distinct enough that it quivered in her voice, like fear or madness or death. "You must be quiet, lest he hear you."

Isabella clutched the woman's hand. The fingers were cold and clammy, but for one brief second, they squeezed back. "Please. . .you must help me." The plea ached from Isabella's lips. Desperation flamed in her chest. "Help me get out of here."

"I cannot."

"Please. . ."

"There is no escape. And if you wish help, you must give it to yourself." Cressida shook herself free of Isabella's grasp, taking the red-stained stockings with her. She paused at the door, hugging them to her chest.

"Your chance shall come tonight."

All day long she waited. She paced along the walls of the room, sometimes biting at the thick rope, other times squeezing her eyes shut and murmuring prayers.

When the cracks in the boards turned black, she sank beneath the window and pulled the comb from her hair. She fingered the rusty claws. *"What do you do with all these lost treasures you find along the shore?"*

William's voice filled the room, as loud and real as if he spoke to her. She was drawn back into too many memories. She was not strong enough for them now—for their poignancy and beauty and magic.

They had loved each other without planning to.

No one had made introductions. No one had whispered how many pounds he made a year and how profitable such a match would be to her. No one had smiled and urged her to dance with him or invited him over for dinner parties or questioned her on whether she found him intriguing.

She had not tried at all. She had not even realized what would happen.

Yet she loved him. His hands, strong and calloused and brown, the way they felt when they touched her cheeks. His hair, windblown and imperfect. His voice. His eyes. His lips. His smile. Everything about him, she loved.

I need you. She needed him now, but even if she were safe in the drawing room of Sharottewood, she would need him—

The door banged open.

Isabella jumped, the comb slipping from her fingers and clanging to the stone floor.

"As you have invited me to your ball, I should like to invite you to my own." Lord Livingstone bowed. "Shall I escort you?"

She stood to her feet. "You have taunted me enough."

"On the contrary. We are just beginning."

"I shall not be degraded."

"You shall be that and worse."

Tremors coursed through her as she clenched her fists and pressed her back into the wall. "Anything you wish from me, you shall have to take. I shall give you nothing."

"I always attain what I—"

"Not from me."

"Time shall change you."

"Time shall change nothing."

His breathing thickened, face reddened, as he stepped toward her. "I would not say such things if I were you."

"Let me go and Father shall reward you." Her voice shrieked. She tightened against the wall, but he edged closer. Her chest exploded. "Whatever ransom, however many pounds—"

"Enough!" He snatched her arm and yanked her toward the door, a furious tremble in his grip. He marched her through the colorful room, the flickering chandelier light, then outside where an enormous fire sputtered and smoked.

"Men, attention." His shout echoed, stilling every man gathered about the fire. "Where Miss Gresham is from, balls are held and attended. I should very much like her to feel at home."

An applause lifted. Bottles raised into the air. From a rock near the fire, a shirtless man strummed the first chord on his lyre.

Then she was slung forward. *God, help.* She fell into someone's arms, beefy and reeking of dead fish, and he spun her several circles about the fire. She pushed at his chest. She turned her face away from his, but someone else ripped her away and nuzzled her neck.

Cold horror rushed through her. She screamed. The music loudened. Clapping, swirling, another pair of arms, another laugh, another foul smell that choked the breath from her lungs.

"Whit's a matter wi' ye, wee lassie?"

"I thought you be lovin' to dance!"

"Och, but give her here to me, Lochlan, 'fore I slit yer throat—"

"Enough." Another voice. One smooth and refined, yet powerful enough that it silenced the jeering and music. Lord Livingstone pried her back away. "We cannot dance and make merry forever. Miss Gresham has something she would like to ask me."

Stillness rushed over the men.

"Let me go—"

He slapped the words from her mouth. Fear weakened her knees as his hand crawled to her neckline and hovered above the fabric. "The men, I daresay, love nothing more than a wedding. You cannot imagine how greatly matrimony would increase one's quality of life." He paused. "Now. Have you anything to ask me, Miss Gresham?"

Sweat formed on her skin. She would not give in. She would suffer, but she would not succumb—

The fabric ripped from her shoulder. *No, God.* Another rip. Terror writhed through her and she crammed her eyes shut as shred after shred of satin exposed her undergarments and skin. A sob escaped. *No, no, no.*

She must have collapsed, because next thing she knew, he was swinging her into his arms and carrying her back into the house. She was returned to the room and the blackness.

"All of this shall end when you ask me to marry you." He threw her against the wall then leaned into her and grabbed her chin. "Have you so much pride that you would reject me still?" When she did not answer, he buffeted her face. Twice.

"Why?" She clawed at his hand, blood on her lips, head dizzy. "Why. . .are you doing this?"

"Because I want you to give what I could very easily take." He struck her to the ground and grabbed another fistful of fabric. The rip was loud and dooming. "You shall beg for my hand in marriage, or you shall rot as a starving animal in this room for the rest of your entire life. The choice is yours, Miss Gresham." He marched to the door. "I shall leave you to your thoughts."

The door slammed shut.

God, help me. She groped for the comb, pressed it between her palms, and curled into a fetal position. Sobs overtook her. *Help me, please, because I am losing strength.*

Creak, creak, creak. Partway through the night, Isabella awoke. Fear sickened her stomach, surging bile to her throat, and she prayed she would not lose the only nourishment she'd been given in days.

As her eyes grew accustomed to the darkness, she stared at the outline of the door, but the noise seemed to come from somewhere else.

Creak, creak. She jerked to face the window.

Pale, thin fingers widened the crack between the boards. A thud. A louder creak. Then the first board fell away and allowed in a cool breeze of air. "Miss Gresham?"

Isabella hurried to the opening.

From the other side, the outline of Cressida's face stared at her. Another board fell free. "Make no noise and come. Hurry."

"But the men—"

"All drunk and slumbering. I have given the dogs meat. Now hurry." The last board groaned and cracked as she yanked it free.

Temples throbbing, Isabella grabbed the edge of the window, hoisted herself up, and leaped down to the other side.

The woman took her hand. The grip was icy and bony, and her fingers squeezed so hard that pain flared. "Whatever you do, you must not stop running. Do you understand?"

"You must run with me—"

"No." Cressida shook her head with violence. "Come."

With a cool wind rushing through them, they lunged through the darkness, hair whipping across their faces. As they rounded the end of the house, one of the grey dogs snapped to attention. His chain clinked. His white teeth bared.

Please, God.

A growl filled the silence, but instead of howling, he took another ravenous bite of his meat chunk.

Relief expanded Isabella's chest. They increased their pace. The house was behind them. The dogs behind them. The dying fire, the broken bottles, a few unconscious men behind them. In mere yards, they would reach the—

A shot exploded.

Cressida was thrown forward, her fingers ripped from Isabella, as the heavy scent of gunpowder struck the air like poison.

No. The panic morphed into grief. Isabella fell next to the body, groped for the face, lifted the woman's wet head into her lap. Blood everywhere. She swallowed back a wave of vomit. *No—*

"I admit to astonishment, Miss Gresham, that you would take a stroll at such a late hour as this."

She glanced up at him, clutching Cressida's body closer to her chest. Every last fiber of courage drained. She shook her head in silence. Over and over and over, but he continued walking toward her.

He raised his gun at her face.

She prayed to heaven he would pull the trigger.

CHAPTER 19

They were so close.

The rocks jutted toward the sky from the top of the mountain, just as the elder Lord Livingstone had said they would. Mist hovered across the valley, climbing the edges of the many mountains like a white shroud of doom.

William's skin chilled with the light drizzle of rain. The distance was unbearable, because he knew not what awaited him. *Dear Saviour, let her be unscathed.*

"I fear this is out of the question." Colonel Nagel urged his steed next to Lord Gresham. "It is no small wonder the elder Lord Livingstone could not retrieve his daughter. Send a regiment up that slope and they would be cut down before they even reached the rocks."

"Some shall make it." Edward ripped off his hat. "Enough to get Isabella out of that place."

"If she so desires."

Sharp anger drilled into William at the same time Edward snapped his head to the colonel. "How dare you imply that my daughter—"

"I imply nothing, my lord. But we must take all possibilities into consideration. As we have heard, Digby has many powers of persuasion. Perhaps Miss Gresham, like Miss Livingstone, ran away of her own accord—"

"You disgrace my daughter once more with such scandal and I shall have satisfaction now."

The colonel tugged at his collar and cleared his throat. "Of course, my lord. I did not mean—"

"I do not give a devil what you meant. Are you sending your men or not?"

"Without knowing how many await us behind those rocks—"

"Answer the question!"

The colonel's thin shoulders deflated. "Forgive me, my lord, but good conscience would not permit me to. I cannot risk the lives of my regiment. Even accompanying you this far has been more than I—"

William spurred his horse toward the mountain before Colonel Nagel could finish his excuses. Fire burned in his gut. What kind of frightened mouse ran from danger when a woman they all knew and respected was in jeopardy? Had the colonel no pride? Had he no manhood?

"William." Lord Gresham hurried his horse next to Duke. "What do you think you are doing?"

"Stay here with the men and make camp. If I am not returned within two mornings, ride for more men—"

"You are not going up there alone."

William wiped rain from his face.

"It is impossible," Edward said. "It is certain death. Ride back with us now and we shall retrieve help. Men who are not women, too afraid to fight—"

"It could be too late." If it wasn't already. "One man, perhaps, can climb the mountain without being seen."

"This is unreasonable madness."

William rode faster.

"You cannot possibly rescue my daughter. You cannot possibly. . ." The sentence lingered and Lord Gresham kicked his horse in front of Duke. The strain of these past days, the lack of sleep, the torture of the unknown—all opened up in his expression and bled from his eyes. "Why are you doing this?"

William squeezed his fingers around the wet leather reins. Too many emotions coursed through him. Reasons he had no words for. The seashore and the scent of her hair and the pulse of his heart at every sight of her.

Swallowing hard, he said the only thing he could think of. "Because I do not run."

Rain slashed harder as William grabbed a rock with both hands and pulled himself up. He had left Duke at the bottom of the mountain, and though a foot trail had been obvious, he had determined he would be less likely noticed if he forged his own path.

Head pounding from exertion, William climbed the steep slope with mud sticking to his clothes. He scrambled up the last few feet, leaned against one of the giant rocks until he caught his breath, then followed the towering stones until he spotted an opening.

The grass was worn away before the hole, as if many a boot had stomped in and out. His nerves sharpened. If he could peek inside long enough to determine the layout, perhaps a plan would come to—

"One step more, gent, and ye'll be gettin' yer head knocked off yer shoulders."

William stiffened, fists balling, as a man leaped out from behind a mossy boulder.

Clothed in nondescript coat and trousers, with a dingy red handkerchief about his neck, the ragged blond stranger lifted a sword. "Thought the likes o' me ne'er saw ye comin', didnae ye?"

"I am come to speak with Lord Livingstone."

"Och, the lordy, eh?" A grin split the man's face. "Ye're a wee bit doaty in the brain, ye are. What ye be wantin' with his lordship, then?"

"A private word."

The stranger stepped closer, sword leveled at William's throat. "Ye ken how to write, do ye?" The point of the blade touched William's neck. "Might be the only word ye can manage, gent, if ye hae no throat."

"Lochlan!" A shout from the other side of the opening. "His lordy wants you should bring the fellow in."

"Hear that, do ye?" The man called Lochlan dragged the point of his sword lower on William's throat, though it did not break the skin. "Come on with ye, and ye had better hope yer private word is a bloody good one."

Chest thundering, sword at his back, William squeezed through the hole. Dull, splintery hovels with sinking thatched roofs crowded along the stone walls. The ground was barren. Disheveled men roamed about—some feeding fires, others digging a hole behind a cluster of lifeless trees, others standing in the open doorways of their huts, seemingly oblivious to the rain blowing in their faces.

"This way." Lochlan jabbed his shoulder blade with the sword.

Pain pinched as William approached the one abode that was not made of broken grey wood. Dogs lunged and barked, but as soon as Lochlan shouted, they slunk back with whines.

William's chest tightened when he entered.

Lord Livingstone—or rather, Robert Digby—sat at a polished writing desk beneath a window, his clothes as pristine as they'd been in London, his position as erect and proper. He glanced up without a rankled expression. "How very kind of you to visit, Mr. Kensley." He stood. "You may go now, Lochlan."

"But Lordy—"

"Do not worry. We are not so rustic in our little village that I cannot entertain a guest." When the door thudded at Lochlan's departure, Digby swept his hand to a decanter on a gilded stand. "Can I interest you in a drink, sir?"

"Where is she?"

"Where are we all, at any time?" He settled onto a settee, crossing his legs. "We are here and there, caught in a realm between heaven and hell. I sometimes wonder if we are in the latter already."

"Where is she?" The words burned out. William stepped forward, fury straining against the thin confines of his patience. "Where is—"

"It is amusing to me, Kensley, that you still assume a manner of pride. You know, of course, I have no intention of releasing you alive."

"Is she?"

"Who?"

"Isabella. Is she—"

"Should you like to see for yourself?" Digby rose and walked toward the window. "Were it not raining, you could see better. Come closer, won't you?"

Pressure slammed William as he approached the water-streaked window. His mind raced with frenzied thoughts.

The men. The lifeless cluster of trees. The digging. The body facedown, dress sullied, skin white against the mud.

"Beast." William lunged at Digby, slammed his back into the window with one swift shove. He bashed the man's head into the pane. Glass shattered. He clamped his hands around the neck and twisted, growled, squeezed—

A door busted open behind and more than one pair of hands ripped William back. They slung him to the floor. Lochlan raised his sword.

"Pike, Lochlan, enough." Gasping, Digby shook his head, glass shards sprinkling from his hair. "Get out of here."

Both hesitated, glanced at William.

"Now!"

They grumbled but exited the house, though William doubted they went any farther than the other side of the door.

Digby motioned William back to his feet. "I underestimated you, I fear, Mr. Kensley. Had I been prepared for your little attack, I would have thrown you to the floor myself."

"The chance is yours."

"Am I to think this a challenge?"

"That day at the stables. You said if I were more your equal, you would demand satisfaction in a duel." William's chest worked up and down. Disgust churned his gut, soured his mouth with a taste so acrid he wanted to spit his repulsion into the face he stared at. "Well, Digby, you are no more rich and esteemed than I am. We are equal now."

"What do you propose?"

Rage shook the core of his being. "A match to the death."

The rain had ceased. For hours, William had been locked in one of the small hovels, a guard at both the window and the door, while he awaited Digby's answer.

As if it mattered.

As if anything mattered.

From his position on the floor, he ran both hands through his hair. He laced his fingers behind his head. Everything hurt. He could not unsee her. He would never unsee her. The body stayed in his mind like the sting of a whip, lashing out pain he had no way to cope with. She was dead?

He tried not to think of Edward Gresham. *"Your daughter is gone. We have failed. She was dead by the time I reached her."* The words carved their way through him.

He would never speak them, though.

He would not have the chance.

By the time the door banged open again, the world had already plunged into evening hues. They shoved him from the hovel to the house, but he kept his eyes away from the cluster of trees.

God, please. He did not want to see again. Even if she was buried. *How could this happen?*

Back within the chandelier lights of the house, Robert Digby stood by a narrow door, hand on the knob. "Leave us, men." They obeyed in silence, then Digby's eyes narrowed to slits. "I have given your match a great deal of consideration, and I daresay, there is only one resolution I can determine." He glanced at the door, hesitated. "You see, Mr. Kensley, it is true we are of equal bloodline—but there is one great difference between us."

William held the spearing eyes.

"You had nothing and accepted such a fate. I did not. Even as a youth, I determined that whatever I desired, I would attain. As you can see, I have." He swept his hand across the room, where endless treasures gleamed in the chandelier light. "There is but one thing I have not yet gained. I had imagined I could break her. That with time and torture, she would relent to my request and ask for my hand in marriage."

Relent. The body flashed again. His blood drained. *Torture.*

"But I have since determined that nothing shall persuade her—and thus, I present my proposition. Tomorrow at first light, we shall have your match to the death. If you win, my men shall be ordered to release you and Miss Gresham both. You may depart without the slightest hindrance from anyone."

William stared at the door, air caught in his lungs, confusion faltering his heartbeat. What was he saying? She was alive? Then who was the woman in the mud?

"But if I am to triumph, Miss Gresham must first agree to the stipulation."

"Which is?"

"To become my wife." Robert Digby flung open the door to a dark room. He motioned inside. "As this is a proposition so greatly affecting both of you, you must be allowed a moment together. But do decide quickly. I daresay, I am very much anticipating the answer."

CHAPTER 20

The darkness swathed them. The door shut with finality, footsteps scuffed at the floor, then silence.

Her limbs shook as she pulled herself to her feet. His presence wrapped around her, soothed everything that hurt, even though she could distinguish little more than his silhouette in the blackness.

Then he moved forward. His hands cupped her face with gentleness that nearly undid her.

William. Her eyes closed against her will. *William.* She was dying, she was destroyed, she was depleted of any strength she had left—but none of it mattered. Everything was better. For one second, for one minute, everything could be good and certain and endurable again.

"Are you hurt?" His arms pulled her into him.

She breathed in the scent of his damp shirt, the familiar earthy smell. Yes, she was hurt—irrevocably hurt—but she was already healing. How could he do that to her? How did he make the terrors subside so quickly?

"Your dress is ripped." Husky, raw. "Has he—"

"He has but kissed me." She shuddered. "Father?"

"Camped below the mountain with a regiment. If I do not return, he shall gather more men and come for you."

How many men would it take? How many could overcome a man like Lord Livingstone?

"We have not much time. He has told you of the match?"

Her comfort fled, like cold water splashing into her face and dripping to her feet. "You should not have come." She pushed away from his hold.

"You should have known it would be this way. You should have waited and arrived with Father—"

"You must agree." When she sank to the corner of the room, he knelt next to her. "We have no choice. At least in this, we have a chance."

"It is not right."

"Isabella—"

"You shall be slain for me, and it is unfair." She turned her face into the cold wall, coaxing air past the swelling fist in her throat. "If you had never come, I would have had hope. No matter what he did to me, I could have imagined one day it would end—that I could see you again and that you would be well—but now I shall have nothing."

"Listen to me." He leaned into her face, hands capturing her cheeks, his breath warm and fast. "I have but one chance to kill that man for what he has done to you. Do not think that I could die so easily."

"I hope they kill me too."

"Isabella—"

"When they kill you, I want to die next to you. I cannot go on in this room. I cannot bear it. I cannot bear to live without you—"

His mouth silenced her. He pressed vigor and strength and assurance into her being, then he trailed his lips to her nose, her cheeks, her closed eyelids. "You speak as a fool, Isabella Gresham."

Tears flooded her eyes as the door creaked open.

Two men entered. With grunts, they seized William by each of his arms and dragged him away from her. Blackness again.

With soundless sobs racking through her, she scrambled to the edge of the door and pressed her ear to the crack.

"Has our darling Miss Gresham agreed to our terms, Kensley?"

She buried her face in her hands as he answered, "Yes."

Daylight streaked the sky in orange and crimson shades, and dark silhouettes of birds fluttered high above them. The burning sun glinted off the blade of the colichemarde smallsword Lochlan handed William.

"Keep it flat to yer leg, gent, unless ye wants the likes o' me to end this duel 'fore it begins."

William nodded, gripped the cold silver hilt, and walked toward the center of the circle. Men gathered on every side, hats shadowing their eyes, many of their arms crossed about their chests in waiting.

A dry laugh pushed at his throat. These men had no intention of releasing William and Isabella, even if Digby *were* defeated.

But it did not matter. William did not expect to come out of this alive. He just wished to take Robert Digby to the grave with him.

At least then she would have more time. As she waited for her father and his men, there would be no one to torture her or demand her hand in marriage or rip away more of her garments.

Two dogs barked as Digby finally strode from the brick house. He was adorned in a double-breasted grey tailcoat, pompous cravat, black breeches, and polished top boots—with a jewel-hilted sword sheathed at his side. He shouted a command back into the house.

A foul-looking ruffian pulled Isabella outside.

William's blood simmered. In the dark room, he had felt her with his hands and imagined her as she'd been in the garden. He had not pictured this.

Her hair, no longer twisted back with curls and pins, hung limp past her elbows. Her underclothes were soiled and ripped, and her wrists were coiled with rope and crusty with blood. But her face, more than anything, arrested him. The hollow paleness of her cheeks. The swollen bruises across her mouth and cheeks. The quiver in her frantic glances—and the strange, pleading way her eyes finally locked with his.

Digby would die for this.

Rage made his hands perspire, so that the sword was slick against his palm as his opponent stepped into the center of the circle. "We are all made aware, I presume, of the prizes that shall be awarded to the winner of this match. Men?"

A grumble of agreement arose.

"And you, Miss Gresham?"

The ruffian at her arm pushed her to the edge of the circle, and without lifting her eyes from the ground, she nodded.

William's breathing quickened. *Dear God, do not let me fail.*

"Splendid." Digby bowed. "Splendid indeed. Kensley, have you any word before we begin?"

He shook his head, stepped forward, lifted his weapon as Digby unsheathed his. The first *clink* of their swords jarred William's nerves into action. He shuffled back and forth, blocking the blows, heart pulsing in his temples.

He knew as little of fencing as he did dueling pistols.

Digby was proficient. That much was certain. Skill and strategy lurked behind each swift thrust of his blade, as men cheered and shouted with madness.

A hissing sound sliced too close to William's face. He lunged forward, clanged his sword against Digby's, then thrust the weapon toward the man's chest.

Digby sidestepped the onslaught, delivering a powerful swing of his own.

Pain slashed William's left arm. He grimaced and ducked another blow. The chanting faded. All he could hear was the next whip of the sword, the jolting clatter as metal hit metal, the squish of their feet in soft mud.

Please, God.

The point of his blade sliced Digby's thigh. The wound must have disoriented him, because he wasn't quick enough to avoid the next blow as it thrust into his shoulder.

A scream. *Isabella.* William turned just as the ruffian backhanded her face. *No—*

Cold metal dove into William's flesh. He blinked hard and stumbled back, pressing a hand into his side, groaning as a gush of blood seeped through his fingers. *God, no.*

He warded off another blow, but his vision blurred. *Clang.* They had distracted him. *Clang.* They had lured his eyes away only seconds, but it had been long enough. *Clang.*

The sword swirled from his fingers and hit the ground.

Agony twisted his insides. *No.* In one swift movement, he groped for it—but another swing of Digby's sword slashed across his chest. He was wet in too many places. The world spun.

"You disappoint me, Kensley." Digby's shadow fell over William as he sank to the mud on one knee. "I had anticipated a much more stimulating opponent."

God, please. Seconds fled. Silence reigned. *Please.* For the second time he reached for his sword and grasped it, and when a cut lashed across his knuckles, he did not let go. He surged the blade into the air.

The weapon must have found its mark, because Digby cried out. He stumbled back. William dove.

His sword plunged into the colorful waistcoat.

William drew it out. Thrust again. Drew it out. Thrust again. Drew it out—

Digby toppled forward, the mud softening the thud of his fall, as a river of blood seeped out from underneath him. His fingers flexed, curled, then stilled.

William flung the sword to the ground. With sweat rolling down his temples, he lifted his eyes to the men circling about him.

If they were going to kill him, now was the time.

He had no more fight left in him.

Everything was still except her heart. Isabella stared at the body in the mud, with his fingers half fisted on the ground and sunlight blinking off the jewels of his sword.

Nausea struck her. She tried to look away from the blood as it ran like trails from his abdomen, but she couldn't. *"I always attain what I desire."* Over and over, the words stung as quickly as William's sword had pierced Lord Livingstone.

He was dead.

The reality pushed back some of her terror as she lifted her eyes to William. Her heart hurt for the slashes of blood across his chest, his arm, his side. He had suffered such wounds for her sake. Indeed, she had inflicted them.

If she had not screamed out, if she had endured Pike's blows without sound, perhaps things would have ended differently.

But perhaps it would not matter anyway. They would both die.

William knew too. He stood in the center of the circle, clutching his side, and glanced about the faces circled around him.

Silence. No one moved.

Pike's fingers sank deeper into her flesh. Had she not wanted it this way? Had she not longed to die next to William? Death would be kind to them. How warm and restful it would be to lose all her hunger, all her fear, into dark oblivion. Just so long as they were together, she could bear anything.

With the sky behind him fading to pink, William stepped over the body and walked toward her. His face was granite, and when he reached for her hand and tugged, Pike released his hold.

They pushed their way through the circle of men.

Her heartbeat buffeted so fast she felt its throb in her fingertips. Her knees shook. She waited for the gunshot to blast her back, or shatter the back of her head, just as it had done to Cressida.

But when they reached the hole in the rocks, no piercing shot hit the air. When they climbed through to the other side, no one shouted or ran after them.

Disbelief moistened her eyes as William increased their speed down the narrow trail.

They had made it out alive.

With the sun's heat burning her face, Isabella focused on not tripping in the oversized boots William had placed on her feet.

They did not speak. Strange that after so much had happened and so much begged to be discussed, they should be silent with each other now.

Perhaps he hadn't strength.

Perhaps she hadn't either.

For the second time, her boots skidded from under her, and she would have smacked the ground had his arms not swept her back up. How long had they been walking? She could not remember. Everything was faint.

Had it been an hour? Two? Had the mountain no end?

"Here." He pulled her down onto a smooth rock alongside the trail, and for the first time, he sank to the ground too.

She wanted him to look at her. She wanted him to climb onto the rock next to her, drape his arm across her shoulder, and let her cry against him as she'd done at the seashore.

But those days were lost to them.

Too many emotions reared themselves in her chest, like a battle that left her heart battered and bleeding. What would he do? Return her to Father and leave again?

With a tight jaw, he untucked his shirt to inspect the wound at his side. Already, the bleeding had ceased. Perhaps it had not been so deep as she had imagined.

Slipping from the rock, she moved next to him and ripped at the hem of her petticoat. "Let me." When he made no protest, she glided her fingers around his waist, wound the fabric against the wound, and grimaced when his blood pinkened the cotton.

She wanted to ask him everything. How much he hurt. How it was that he had come to find her. Why he would be so wonderful as to risk his life for hers, when she couldn't even belong to him.

But she *did* belong to him. She would always belong to him. She lifted her eyes to his face and understood all the exhaustion, all the injury marring his expression. "William." *Please do not leave me.*

He understood, because he shook his head, just as he'd done in the garden.

Her hope sank. Her strength drained. Trembling, she lifted her hand to his cheek, but he caught her fingers before they alighted. The touch burned. *Please.*

Another shake of his head.

Please.

Another.

Please.

He came to his feet, wincing, and guided her back onto the trail.

No. Through a blur, she resumed watching her boots to make certain they did not slip. Every step was heavy. She clung to his hand, fisted her hem, but her knees turned to jelly against her will.

No, no, no.

Numbness coursed through her the way death chills a body. She could not go on. She could not bear anything. Not losing William. Not watching her boots. Not taking another step.

Blackness doused the sunlight. She collapsed, but he caught her in his arms and lifted her from her feet. Her head fell into his shirt. She smelled sweat and blood and the unique scent that so reminded her of the ocean's lulling waves.

Perhaps she was there now. They were doing sunlight and feeling the seashore. Water swallowed her, warm and salty, and swirled her down into the blue depths. She didn't breathe, but she didn't have to.

She floated deeper and deeper. She stayed a long time. Perhaps forever, but then she heard voices. They murmured and shouted, then one was close to her face. One she recognized.

Father.

She didn't know what he said, but she was too weak to swim back to the surface. The arms cradling her fell away. She had no anchor against the tossing waves. *William, please.*

Her last plea, but she knew he would not listen.

Horse hooves echoed into her consciousness just before the sea turned black.

CHAPTER 21

Where am I? The bed linens were soft and heavy, scented with comforting hints of lemon and nutmeg. Several times she awoke long enough to glance about her, but sleep—and perhaps fever—always folded her back into unconsciousness.

Licking her dry lips, she rolled over in bed and flinched when a hand swept along her forehead.

"Is she yet fevered?"

"It must have broken in the night." Thudding noises, a loud *click*. "Give her this essence of camphor and make certain she remains in bed for a week."

"I am beholden, Doctor."

She must have drifted asleep yet again, for the next time she rolled over and opened her eyes, the windows were black and there was but one person present instead of two.

Father.

He slumped in an antique, carved-oak chair pulled next to her bed, his chin resting in his cravat, breathing loud enough to be considered snoring.

She ran her tongue over her lips again. The thirst was painful. She was back on the horse, Pike's filthy arms about her, staring at the water canteen that Lord Livingstone had refused her—

"Dear?"

She must have made a noise, and as Father hurried to her bedside with sleep softening his features, she realized tears streamed to her lips. She mouthed *water* without sound.

Father poured a glass, eased it to her lips, and waited until she was satisfied before setting it back to the stand. "Is there anything else? Are you hungry? Warm?"

The downy bed linens seemed to embrace her, chasing away the tremors racing along her spine. She glanced about the room. The bedchamber was high-ceilinged, colored in gold and burgundy, and rather old-fashioned without losing any opulence. Where was she?

As if Father understood, he sat next to her and brushed away her tears in comforting strokes. "We are at Wetherbell Hall, guests of the elder Lord Livingstone."

A shudder rang through her at the name.

"We shall not speak of it now, but he is not the father of the man who. . ." Father cleared his throat. "In any event, you are quite safe now, my dear. You need only concern yourself with rest."

How wonderful it was. To be safe and warm in a room where candles kept back the darkness. *Rest.* Already, the weight of her eyelids fought her desire to remain awake. The quiet room lulled her. The creaking of the bed. Father's breathing. The wind on the mullioned windows—

William. The name struck with force so great she lifted her head. "William?"

Father eased her back. "You must not distress yourself, my dear."

"Where is he?"

"Isabella—"

"Where is William?"

Father's sigh told her everything. "As soon as he returned you from the mountain, he rode away. Although I would have been grateful for a chance to thank him for his service to us, you must know it is best this way."

She slid her eyes closed. Not because they were heavy, but because she could not bear to see Father's face. He had done this to her. He had taken from her the very thing he had taken from Mother.

The chance to love and be loved.

"My dear?"

She did not answer him. She did not know if she would ever answer him again.

Too quiet. William leaned over Duke, the sway of the horse nearly rocking him to sleep again. He had already fallen twice.

During the journey, he had told himself repeatedly that if he could make it to Mr. Abram's farm, all would be well.

He was not so certain that was true. The old thatched cottage had no chickens clucking in the yard, the red barn doors were shut, and Sunshine did not graze within the small wooden fence.

William dismounted, disgusted by the fact that his weak knees tried to buckle when he hit the ground. He knocked at the door twice. Weariness sagged his shoulders when it did not open to him.

Now what?

Be hanged if he could make it to the village. At least not today. He'd been sleeping on the ground or in the saddle, eating the bread in his knapsack, and, by force of will, remaining lucid against the fever that tried to claim him every evening.

Even if Mr. Abram was gone, William would have that bed and something substantial to eat, if it could be found. The door whined as he threw it open, and frustration mounted as he realized the inside was devoid of furniture.

Except a three-legged stool by the hearth.

William sat and wiped his face. Should this not have been expected? Did anything ever go right for him? What was God doing—sitting upon His throne in heaven and laughing at every new misfortune He placed upon William Kensley?

God had taken Shelton from him.

God had taken Rosenleigh.

God had taken his station, his pride, his security.

Bitter hurt caved in on him as he bent his head forward and stared into the empty hearth. God had taken Isabella too. The one person he wanted more than anything. The one person he needed. *Why?*

"Sir?"

William bounced to his feet and whirled, but his heart slowed when he recognized Mr. Abram stride through the open door.

"Mr. Kensley. I didn't rightly realize it be you." A glowing smile radiated from the man's face as he shut the door behind him and hung his hat on a wooden peg. "You be lookin' for me, then?"

William took another glance about the bare room.

Mr. Abram clucked. "Oh. You be wonderin' about the house, eh, sir? You heard then. Rightly honored, I am, that the likes o' you would come to tell an old man goodbye."

"Where are you going?"

Mr. Abram blinked, as if the question were absurd. "I be leavin' for America, sir."

"When?"

"With the mornin' sun, I'll be travelin' to Ogden Wells. Plan to work out some wages at the docks. The ship be leavin' in a few months from there."

"I see." William blew air from his cheeks and returned to the stool. "I had forgotten."

" 'Tis not the only thing, I reckon."

"What?"

"That you be forgettin', I mean, sir." Mr. Abram stepped forward and rubbed his jaw, eyes a little sheepish.

A small smile nudged William's lips. What a beggar he must look. "I *am* unshaven, am I not?" He stood. "I shall trouble you no longer. I wish you Godspeed on your journey, my friend."

"A friend I am indeedy, sir." Mr. Abram reached for William's coat, hesitated, then peeled it back to see the slashes of dried blood. His head tilted with pity. "And one who is not so hurried for America that he could not be helpin' when needed. Sit back down with you and I'll be fetchin' my blankets and food from the cart—"

"Hardly necessary, Mr. Abram. I shall not detain you from your travels."

"You be putting me in mind of ol' Rosie when she gets something in her brain." Mr. Abram grabbed his hat from the peg and swung open the door. "Just you be sittin' down again, and I'll be returned in a blink with food and blankets. Time there'll be in the mornin' for travel. Tonight, you be needin' a bit o' rest."

William did as he was told, relief relaxing his tired, aching muscles. He wanted to pray that all would be well soon. That he would be strong and his tortured heart would cease to writhe.

But he did not dare.

God might find yet another thing to take away from him.

"I most regret imposing upon your rest this way, Miss Gresham, and if you think it preferable I depart, I shall do so at once." An older, large-faced Lord Livingstone stood at the end of her bed, Father standing next to him. Both wore expressions of gravity. Both waited for her answer.

She had no voice, so she nodded, but the last thing she wished to do was speak to them. Either of them. Why could they not leave her alone?

If only Bridget were here. Dear Bridget. Isabella nearly wept with the thought of her.

"I know this is rather a matter of delicacy, but I wish you to know that with more men brought in to assist Colonel Nagel's regiment, the marauders have been accosted at last."

"You need never have fear of them again," Father said.

Lord Livingstone stepped around the bed. "My daughter has at last been returned to me." A vein bulged in his forehead. "The doctor said we were mere days too late."

The horrors of that moment impressed themselves upon her. Would she ever be free from such memories? Would she ever stop seeing the blood matted in Cressida's hair, or the wretched devils who dragged her body through the mud, and left her lying dead beside a patch of trees?

"I wish to know why she was killed."

Isabella shook her head. Hot tears came again. She could not think of that night.

"If you could but enlighten me. . .if you could but tell me anything she said. . .if she regretted. . ." The man's deep voice shuddered and he leaned over the bed, hands clasped. "Tell me now. I must know."

"Lord Livingstone, my daughter is distraught—"

"And my daughter is dead." Lord Livingstone's mouth twitched as he forced himself to take a step away from the bed.

Pity wrung through Isabella's body as she drew the bed linens closer to her neck. "She. . .was kind to me." Her courage tried to fail, but she spoke the words anyway, turning her face into the pillow. "She died trying to help me escape."

Silence swept through the room for several seconds, then Lord Livingstone departed the chamber.

Father slipped to Isabella's side. He rubbed her face, smoothed back her hair, kissed her forehead in ways that would have solaced her before.

Now his presence did nothing more than add to her pain.

"We shall not speak of it again, my dear."

You forced William away.

"Tomorrow we shall journey home. You shall feel better then."

I shall never feel better.

Yet again he pressed a kiss on her brow. "I love you, my dear. All shall be well. I promise."

He was wrong in every sense. He did not love her. He could not love her. Had he ever loved anyone in his life? Did a man who could feel nothing for his own wife even understand the word?

She did not know. She only knew Father's promise was in vain.

Nothing would ever be well again.

"A mite better you look." In the glow of a single tallow candle, a soft smile crinkled Mr. Abram's eyes. He handed over a gruel of oatmeal boiled in brine. "Here. You best be fillin' your belly with another bowl."

William chuckled as he accepted the steaming earthenware. "If I stay here a day longer, I shall begin to look like one of those paunchy dandies who are always stealing hearts in the London season."

"As I be always tellin' ol' Sunshine, a hearty appetite makes for a merry soul."

Merry? William spooned the warm gruel into his mouth, but it had difficulty sliding down his throat. When was the last time he had been merry? The seashore with Isabella? Or had he only been pretending—because he knew it would soon be ending?

He leaned back against the wall of the cottage, eating his supper and half listening to more of the old man's stories.

Gratitude overwhelmed William, but also remorse. He had not meant to stay so long. Indeed, tonight made five days since he had arrived—and delayed the man's journey.

But Mr. Abram only shrugged, said he had plenty of time to get to Ogden Wells, and insisted he'd rather have a few more days with his wife's grave, anyway.

The time had given William back his strength. He was clean again, his wounds were soothed with herbs and bandages, and his stomach no longer suffered from hunger gnaws. Besides that, Mr. Abram had given him an old shirt, coat, and trousers.

William was a new man.

At least, he wanted to be. He wanted to forget everything, every place he'd ever been, everybody he'd ever loved, and start anew.

"Did you hear me, Mr. Kensley?"

William snapped up his head. "Forgive me. My mind was elsewhere." He lowered his spoon back into the bowl. "And you must no longer call me Mr. Kensley. William shall do well."

"Then Nash you shall be callin' me, Mr.—" Nash grinned with pink cheeks. "I mean, William."

"What had you asked me?"

"Only where you'll be goin' with yourself when I leave come mornin'."

"I have not yet decided." Perhaps back to Lord Manigan, though he grimaced at the thought of resuming his position as a footman. Did he have a choice?

"'Tis a big land, that America." Mr. Abram stood from his stool, stoked the hearth, and stirred the ladle in the iron cauldron. "People wot go there be free, I hear tell. Won't be many a fancy house, nor many a fancy folk, though. Just a lot o' men wot wants to work with their hands."

William set the bowl to the ground. What was he saying?

"Anyway, I'll be goin' outside to say good night to my missus. Last one I'll be gettin' to tell her." He went to the door but glanced back with an uncertain, kindhearted look. "If you was of a mind, I reckon I'd be rightly glad to take you with me."

The invitation swarmed William's brain as the door thudded shut. He had wanted a new start, had he not?

Perhaps this was the chance he needed. Perhaps he should take it.

He was just not certain he wanted to.

Father said little on the journey home. Sometimes he watched her from the other side of the carriage provided them, his gaze sad and searching. Other times he just stared out the window, oblivious to the gold tassel swaying against his face.

He knew something was wrong.

Something was.

Isabella burrowed herself deeper into the quilts wrapped about her. The air was warm, and sunshine slanted through the coach windows, but something about the soft fabric snuggled around her offered comfort.

Heaven knew she needed comfort more than anything else in the world. She hurt everywhere. Her mind, with all its torturous memories. Her wrists, raw with rope burns. Her heart.

Father spoke to her. Some inconsequential thing about how well the roads had held up, despite the past rain.

She closed her eyes and ignored him. The sooner they reached Sharottewood, the better. She needed Bridget. She needed her bedchamber.

As soon as she could lock herself inside, she would.

She did not imagine she would ever come back out.

He never dreamed he would leave.

William jostled next to Mr. Abram on the wooden driver's seat of the cart, Duke plodding along behind them. He tried not to acknowledge the fact that he would be leaving his horse behind.

Yet another loss.

Cannot do it. He tensed his body, ready to reach out and grab the reins, stop the cart, jump down, and ride back.

But he had nothing to ride back to. What was here for him except things he could not have? Did he really want to return to service just so he could be closer to Rosenleigh, a place he had no rights to? Or Isabella, a woman he could never see again?

No. He must do this, whether it was easy or not. He was determined. In America, it would not matter that he was a workhouse beggar. Years from now, he would look back and see that he had left a land that held nothing for him in pursuit of a life full of opportunity.

But as the cart wheeled into the small village of Ogden Wells, as the lights blinked out at him in the evening dusk, his chest suffered blows from his heart.

He was about to lose everything.

God must be laughing again.

As soon as Isabella stepped into the foyer, the sights and smells of familiarity overwhelmed her. She bit her lip to keep back a sob of relief.

Mrs. Morrey, who always beheld Isabella with a cool and disapproving stare, now approached with an almost teary expression. "Miss Gresham, you cannot know how reassured we all are to have you returned to us."

Father took Isabella's elbow. "Take her upstairs, have a bath drawn, and send up tea and soup." As if those things would remedy her. "Then you shall feel much more like speaking again, my dear."

He leaned close to her face, worry creasing his features, but she retreated from his touch. She followed Mrs. Morrey up the stairs. At her bedchamber door, her knees wobbled when she entered.

Bridget was waiting for her.

With a small cry, Isabella flung herself into the arms of her maid, all composure melting. *Oh Bridget.* She sobbed without control. *Dear, wonderful Bridget, whatever shall I do? How can I ever live without him?*

She did not leave her chamber. From the downy folds of her bed, or the striped wingback chair by the window, she watched the window darken and brighten with fading days.

Most always, Bridget occupied the room. She did not say anything, nor did she chide Isabella for refusing to dress and make use of the day. She merely sat by the hearth, read books, or stitched needlework, offering quiet smiles anytime Isabella should glance her way.

Father came every day.

She dreaded his visits as much as she dreaded the fall of night. Both plagued her. She knew she must recover. Whatever darkness, whatever terror had its grip on her must be released.

But she was too hurt to free herself.

In her chamber, she could forget about the seashore. She could forget about the garden. Or would she ever forget? Would she ever stop wondering if things might have been different? If William had held her closer that night in the garden—if he had whispered of running away with her instead of shaking his head that he could not?

William was too good to steal her away. He was too strong in himself. He knew right and wrong too well to do what was untoward, even if he *had* wanted it as much as she had.

She was better for having known him.

She was destroyed for having loved him.

From her seat in the chair, with her face soaking in the afternoon sun, she tightened her hands around the armrests when Father entered the room.

He stood behind her chair but did not touch her shoulder or pat the side of her cheek, as he might have done before. "It has been thirteen days."

Did he think she did not know? That she had not counted every one of them?

"I thought at first you did not speak because of what that blackguard did to you." Emotion tore at his voice. "But it is not he who troubles you, is it, Isabella?" Seconds ticked by. "It is me."

Leave me alone.

He came around the chair and knelt next to her. Tears filled his eyes. Had she ever seen him cry before? "In the name of all that is holy, child, what do you want me to do?"

Leave.

"Is it William? Does he mean so very much to you?"

She turned her face to the window, but he seized her chin in his hand. "Answer me, Isabella." His fingers quivered. His eyes bulged. More tears streamed down a face that bore more wrinkles than she had ever noticed before. "Answer me. . .because I shall go mad if you do not speak. I cannot bear this. My own daughter. My little. . ." A sob engulfed the words, and he grabbed her up into his arms, squeezed with so much angst that her own heart jolted with grief.

No. She pushed out of his hold, escaped to the other side of the room, rubbed her arms with stifled noises. *I only wish to be left alone.* If she had loved William less, she might have forgiven Father this trespass against her heart. She might have wilted into his arms just now, derived comfort from him again, and ceased the hurt she had caused in his red-rimmed eyes.

But his injustice to her was too great.

She had forgiven him for what he did to Mother. She could not forgive him for this.

"I shall bring him back." The door swung open and Father's booming voice echoed throughout the chamber. "If it is the last thing I do, I shall find him and bring him back."

Isabella drew in air. Did he speak in truth? Could he find William again? Even if he did, would William come back?

William climbed into the fishing boat next to Mr. Abram and Mr. Sneyd, the fisherman who had employed them for the past two months. Morning fog blurred the line between sea and sky. The pungent scent of fish tainted the crisp air, though they had not yet caught their first of the day.

The smell, however, seemed to live on them. Like an infectious sickness, it clung to the rowboat, their clothes, even the small room they occupied above the fishery cook room.

"Off to America we'll be soon, then," Mr. Abram told William every morning, cheerful and smiling. "And with an extra few coins in our pockets, besides. But a few more days until we set sail, eh?"

More like weeks, in truth, but William never corrected the old man. Indeed, William tried to think of the departure as little as possible. What would it be like to be oceans away from her? To know that he would never chance upon her someday, or overhear someone speaking her name?

He had wanted to leave it all behind and forget everything.

He was just uncertain he was ready to forget her. Would he ever be ready? He had been a fool to let this happen. All along, he knew she could never belong to him. Why, then, had he allowed his heart to fall in love with the impossible?

When they rowed deeper into the sea to the fishing grounds, William scooted to the end of the boat and attached his hook to the handline. He baited it with capelin, tossed it into the water, then tugged the line up and down to lure in cod.

"Deuce it, fellow, what claptrap," Mr. Sneyd exclaimed. "You'll not talk the likes of me into going to America."

Mr. Abram chuckled. "Mighty lot of land, there be."

"What the devil a bloke like me wants land for? I've fish to take to the market every Friday, and me finks I'm more loyal to crown and country than that." Mr. Sneyd hauled a cod into the boat, uttering a minced oath. "Besides, I couldn't go if I wanted to."

"Why not?"

"Back shore yonder, there's a woman I'm yoked to. She's as plain as a smoothed-out groat and even less agreeable, but I gots an inkling I could never leave her and be happy."

Leave her. William dragged in a cod of his own, the slime fouling his hands the same time a repugnant taste filled his mouth. He would go to America. He would start over.

But the old fisherman spoke truth.

William had no hope of ever being happy again.

"If I may presume upon your conscience, Miss Gresham, I must say it is quite time you cease this languishing about. If you continue to ignore your letters and refuse callers, you shall become known as an invalid. What sort of lady would people think you then?"

Isabella hardly cared what people thought.

Her indifference must have been clear on her face, for Mrs. Morrey's shoulders deflated as she marched closer to the bed. She fluffed the pillow next to Isabella. "I had to try, if not for your own sake, at least for your father's. This ordeal has quite left its mark on him."

Isabella sat straighter. "He is not yet returned, is he?"

"Yes. Late last night."

"No one told me."

"We were asked not to." Mrs. Morrey took a step back and lifted her chin. "It is rather a frightful thing when a father is afraid to face his own daughter."

He was afraid? What did they all imagine Isabella had been these past weeks? Pulling the counterpane away from her legs, Isabella pushed herself to a sitting position. Sweat cooled the back of her neck. "Was there. . .anyone with him?"

Mrs. Morrey frowned. "No. There was not." Turning to Bridget, the housekeeper instructed the maid to select a gown from the wardrobe, heat the papillote iron, and prepare a fresh basin of water. "The very least you can do is look presentable when you greet your father for dinner. I shall tell him to expect you, Miss Gresham."

Isabella did not argue, but an involuntary shiver worked through her. She was not certain she could face Father. She was not certain she could face the news that she would never see William Kensley again.

William leaned against the wall beside the window, glancing out to the port below. The *Royal Montague* bobbed in the crowded blue water, surrounded by small crafts ferrying cargo from the moorings to the wharves. Shouts, sloshing waves, and whistling wind all hummed in his ears like a discordant note. How was the day so near upon him already?

Behind, the chamber door thudded. "Been down to the market to buy us this."

William turned as Mr. Abram unpacked currants, two meat puddings, and a peck of oysters from his leather knapsack.

"All this for two shillings and three pence." He gleamed up at William. "Sort o' a celebration, it be."

William tried to smile, lest he spoil the man's excitement, but his stomach churned at the thought of food—and what awaited them on the morrow.

"I know you be nervous." Mr. Abram walked to William and clapped a hand on his back. They both faced the window, staring out at the square-rigged ship in the distance. "'Tis not easy for a man to leave all he knows."

Tomorrow, the masts would be billowing with wind. The anchor would be hoisted. The shoreline would fade away behind them.

Everything would fade away. His entire life. The last cords holding him to the things he loved—and he was not ready to sever them. *God, how could You take everything?*

Mr. Abram squeezed William's shoulder. "One day, you will be lookin' back and seein' that it was good. That the Almighty be watchin' out for you all along."

He had been watching William. That much was certain. But He had done nothing to stop the tragedies that robbed William of everything.

Indeed, He did not even seem to care.

Mrs. Morrey had been right. The man seated on the other side of the table looked little like the father she knew.

The tailcoat, usually fitted to perfection, seemed loose at his hunched shoulders and chest. More grey had crept through the black of his hair, and his cheeks sagged beneath his eyes—the eyes that held hers with too much fervency to glance away from.

She nodded her greeting then slipped into her chair in front of a full plate. The steam rose, moistening her skin, as a thousand questions tried to spring from her throat. She spoke only one of them. "William?"

"He is gone." Silence fell. Father reached for his glass of sherry, squeezed the glass stem with white knuckles. He opened his mouth as if to explain, to plead that he had tried, that there was nothing else he could do, that she must forgive him—

No. She could not do this. She could not remain in this room. Not with him. Not now. She lunged from her chair, darted through the door, and ran from the manor into the evening air.

Sobs racked through her as she descended the stone steps. She raced into the garden. She should not come here. Not the one place in the world that haunted her dreams as much as the seashore.

But she found the white bench anyway, wilted upon it. All the hurt overflowed. Her eyes stung, her throat ached, and the sense of loss was so hollowing that she felt irrevocably emptied.

"I have something to say to you, and I want you to sit up and listen to me."

She had not realized Father had followed her, and though she wanted to keep her face hidden, she could not disobey such a tone. She faced him with choppy breaths. What could he possibly do or say to make this better?

"I searched for your Mr. Kensley and could not find him. I may never find him. For that, I sympathize greatly with your heart, as I can see now that you did indeed love him—"

"What do you know of love?" Too many years of confusion, of hurt, flew out with the question.

His steady gaze narrowed. "Much more than you know."

"You do not speak truth."

"Isabella—"

"I am not a child any longer. You cannot believe me oblivious to the coldness you held in your heart for Mother. I was there that night."

"What night?"

"When she begged you to. . ." Isabella shook her head, more tears dripping past her jaw. "It does not matter. Please, Father. Please leave me alone."

"You expect me to protest my love for her."

"You need not bother."

"I shall not, for it is not true."

Hearing the words again washed her afresh with grief. "How could you pretend all those years? How could you be so cruel as to feign your heart?"

"I feigned nothing. Your mother knew I did not love her when we married. Indeed, I can say in truth that she did not love me." His eyes moistened as he took one sweeping glance at the twilight garden. "But do not accuse me of knowing nothing concerning love. I know love too well."

"Constance—"

"Yes." A heavy breath. "Yes, Constance." He stepped to a rosebush, plucked one of the vibrant red petals, and crushed it in his palm. "I know love so well it makes me sick when I wake in the morning and leaves me bereft when I go to bed at night."

Isabella stood. "If this is true, why did you not marry her?"

"She was beneath me. For almost three months, that did not matter. I met her here, in this garden, every midnight. My father discovered us. He threatened that if I did not marry the squire's daughter, I would inherit nothing."

"Then you. . ." Why was it so difficult to speak the words? "Then you ceased to come to the garden."

"I came once more. I lost control of myself. I loved her in every forbidden way. . .and I did not know she became with child until the day of my wedding nine months later."

Evening shadows thickened. Bushes and flowers stirred in the silence, smelling of things lost and hearts unsettled.

Isabella shuddered. This did not change the reality that he had not loved her mother. But he had loved and he had loved deeply. The same sharp, unrelenting pain that throbbed in her chest had throbbed in his these twenty years past.

Somehow, that bonded them.

"I made my choice here in this garden. I do not know what my life would have been had I married the woman of my heart. I do not know if the poverty would have destroyed us, or if having. . .having each other would have been enough." He glanced at the ground, the bench, then back to her face. "But it is the choice I made, and God forgive me, it is the choice I live with. I had no right to make that choice for you."

The bulwarks crumbled, and she pressed herself against him. She longed to say something, but nothing came. What could they say—either of them? That she was sorry? That he was?

What was finished was finished.

They were half themselves and half what they had lost in this garden.

"For as long as you wish it of me, I shall keep searching. Perhaps one day I shall find him."

She nodded, gratitude wiping clean any remnants of anger or resentment. "I know you shall find him," she whispered. "But you must not leave until you are rested. I shall not see my father wearied to death." Wiping her eyes, she took his arm, leaned her head against his shoulder, and followed him back through the garden path in the last hints of daylight.

As they returned to the manor, her spirit knew a small touch of comfort. She understood everything now.

Memories of the dark stairway would not haunt her again.

William slammed himself outside, his pulse maddened. Regret already sank to the pit of his stomach. Why had he lashed out?

He had partaken of Mr. Abram's celebration with feigned smiles and forced enthusiasm. For three hours after, he had listened to the old man crow about America in their small chamber, until the simple words pounded into William's temples like nails.

He groaned and started down the street in the lamplit darkness. He should not have lost his temper. He should not have retorted with something sharp.

No doubt, Mr. Abram was confused and hurt. William had dampened the man's dreams.

But if William heard one more word about America tonight, he would lose control of himself. Walking faster, he shoved his hands in his pockets and scooped a few cold farthings and sixpences into his palms.

He almost laughed when he remembered Rosenleigh. The master bedchamber that had belonged to him. The stables full of gleaming horses. The labyrinth. The garden. The two-story house.

All that had belonged to him. . .and now he had farthings and sixpences.

From the fog, the worn façade of a brick tavern gleamed into the night. He told himself to walk past the building, but for once, he did not listen to his own sense of reason. Why should he? What had morals ever gained him before?

The low-timbered room reeked of smoke, and the overwhelming odor of unwashed flesh wrinkled his nose. From one corner of the room, on a makeshift stage, two scantily dressed women swung at each other with wooden swords.

The crowd cheered. A few coins were tossed to the stage.

William shoved his way to the rectangular bar, his conscience already forming perspiration. "Ale, please."

"Please?" The obese woman, whose bosom was not quite concealed by her thin fichu, barked out a laugh. "Wot you think this is, guv'nor? Westminster Abbey, eh wot?"

He glanced back to the stage at the loud smack of wood. One of the females lay sprawled on the ground, blood oozing from her temple.

The crowd's laughter rose in glee.

"Don't pay no mind to the likes of them, guv'nor. The little devil trollops come 'ere every night, they do, to beat each other silly and rake in a few coins."

He swallowed when the woman pushed the pewter tankard across the bar. He cupped it in his hands. This was for Shelton. This was for Rosenleigh. For his aunt. For Lord Gresham. For the loss of Isabella. For the *Royal Montague* and the faraway country of America.

He brought it to his lips and tasted the foam. More than anything, he wanted to do as Horace had done. He wanted to lose himself in rebellion and oblivion. He wanted to escape.

He wanted to hurt God for hurting him.

"Wot's a matter, guv'nor? Ain't you never been an elbow-crooker before?"

He slammed the tankard back to the bar, paid the lady, and fled from the suffocating building. He marched through the fog with a knot growing in his chest. Everything blurred until he reached the wharf, where his vision centered on the dim silhouette of the ship.

God, why?

He stepped to the edge of the wharf, where black water lapped up to wet his boots. He dragged his coat sleeve across his eyes, ashamed of the tears. *Why did You take everything from me?*

Mrs. Shaw came back to him, as she always did. He saw her feverish eyes and heard the croaking voice, *"Just have to forgive dem. Even if you got to do it over and over again. . .just got to forgive dem."*

He had not allowed the words to go unbidden. He had learned from them. Indeed, he had forgiven his aunt for her deceitful cruelty, and he had forgiven Lord Gresham for his rejection. But in the name of heaven, when was it enough? How many times was he expected to accept whatever was done to him and forgive?

I cannot. He lifted his face to the sky. Endless stars blinked down at him. *God, I cannot forgive anyone else again. I have not the strength.*

He was weary in every place imaginable. He teetered on the brink of destruction and madness and rage and confusion and. . .

He wiped his eyes a second time. He despised the tears but could not stop them. *If only You had let me keep Isabella, I could have endured the rest.* Had he not tried to keep his chin lifted and his head held high? Did God see nothing of his efforts? Did God not know that since the first blow, William had done his best to continue doing right?

A shudder ripped through him and he contemplated leaping into the black water and swirling to the bottom. But even there, he knew the words would follow him.

They always did.

"Just have to forgive. . .even if you got to do it over and over again. . ." A soundless sob shook him. He shut his eyes. *God, I cannot.*

Yet he could. He must. He knew that.

Indeed, he *wanted* that.

For many hours, he remained standing on the edge of the creaking wharf, staring out across the dark waters to the outline of the ship. The words did not come with ease. He had to coax them from the deepest, broken places of his soul.

Not until the sky began to lighten in the horizon, not until the heavy fog of morning lifted into the air, did the prayer finally break: *God, I forgive You.*

With one last glance at the ship, he turned and walked back down the wharf, the pressure finally diminishing from his chest. *I forgive You, and I will serve You.*

Even in America.

Even without everything he loved.

William pressed against the gunwale of the ship, ropes and cables rattling in the wind as the white mast filled with air. He breathed in salt and seaweed.

The Ogden Wells port had shrunk in the distance, and all the sailing vessels and rowboats were but specks. *God be with thee, my country.* From Nash's accounts, America would be beautiful with her rugged plains and snowcapped mountains. Perhaps she was.

But William would always remember the quiet English countryside, where the grass was so green it was bewitching. He would remember the seashore. The limestone archway and the—

He shook his head and squeezed the cool gunwale with tight knuckles. He had promised himself he would not think of her.

She belonged to England. She belonged to the genteel society, the luster of shining things, the protection and assurance of a secure life. He tried not to remember how fulfilling it had felt to clasp her against him. To run his fingers through her hair, to breathe of her air, to watch her eyes fill with tears and know they were a voiceless token of her love for him. Had they ever spoken the words?

Perhaps it was better they had not. Perhaps that would make it easier to forget.

"Eh, fellow. Smoke?"

A scrubby-faced sailor leaned his back to the gunwale and proffered a cheroot cigar.

"No thank you." William forced a smile. "I was just going belowdecks." He navigated his way to the lattice hatch, pulled it open, and descended the rope ladder. He found Nash Abram pulling himself into a green canvas hammock—but he slid back out and landed on the gritty floorboards with a thud.

William bit back a laugh. "I daresay, these shall take a bit of getting used to, will they not?" He helped the man back to his feet.

"Righty sure, that be." Nash rubbed his behind, his face a little flushed, though the fall did not diminish the grin that had been in place all day. "Yours be over there."

William nodded. His stomach already roiled from the constant rocking. He could not imagine what a night in a swing would do to him.

"You be hungry?"

"In truth, no."

"You didn't be eatin' your breakfast this mornin', so I saved you this." Nash dug into his knapsack then opened up a linen of boiled beef and cheese. "It be cold, but a sailor give it to me on account of a sickness comin' on him fast."

William accepted the food and would have turned to his hammock, but something in the old man's expression gave him pause. "Is anything the matter?"

A frown lowered both of his brows, and he hesitated before he sighed and reached back into his knapsack. He held out a wrinkled letter.

"What is this?"

"For you."

William smoothed out the wrinkles, heart skipping a beat at the familiar writing. *Miss Ettie.* "Where did you get this?"

The man's shoulders drooped. "From someone wot was sent to find you."

"When?"

His eyes fell.

"Nash, when?"

"Day after we arrived in Ogden Wells. I reckon the man had followed us there from my farm at Sharottewood, he did. Said he was paid a right fine penny to bring it to you."

William ripped it open, a throb in his fingertips, as he hurried in each word:

My dearest William,

It is my most earnest prayer that this letter finds you. I beg God you shall not be grieved by what I am about to say. Since your departure, much has changed in the course of life here at Rosenleigh. Master Willoughby, if I may be so bold, has indulged himself far worse in drink. He has cumbered and vexed the servants badly, and has even been so unkind as to send many of them away. In truth, I contemplated departing myself. There is little here for me, except the nursery, but I fear I cannot hide in memories forever. A sennight ago, Master Willoughby was worse than I had ever seen him. He shattered every window in the trophy room and quite left the room in complete disarray before he ran out of doors without shoes in his banyan. I followed after him, as I could not bear to see him behave so unseemly, and when he mounted one of the roans from the stable, I pleaded with him to come back inside. He did not listen. I cannot say for certain, but I believe in my heart that Master Willoughby knew he would ride to his death that night, for after they found his body the next morning, I discovered a letter in the trophy room. Enclosed are his words.

William unfolded the second paper with an ache pulsing through him.

William,

I quite detest you for leaving. I know it is just the sort of bloody thing I deserve, but if you had stayed, perhaps things might have been different. I cannot bear it here. I shall go mad and murder all the servants if I do not do something. I cannot stop thinking of Mother. You may laugh at this, but you never laughed before, so I shall say it. She never loved me. I was always terrible in hopes she would scold me, as she scolded you. But she did not. You are the only one who ever cared enough about me to reproach my vices. I cursed you for it, but in truth, it was the only thing in my entire life that offered me security. Without it, I am lost. Grandfather always meant for Rosenleigh to belong to you, and so it shall be. Forgive me for every appalling thing I have ever done to you.

Your cousin, Horace

At the bottom of his letter, Miss Ettie had scrawled one last note: *In testament to his words, Master Willoughby did indeed will the estate to you, dearest William. With everything inside me, I beg you to return. I need you too.*

Heart throbbing to his throat, William turned back to the rope ladder. Disbelief made his stomach sink. Could this be true? Rosenleigh was his?

"William, wait." Nash snatched his arm, eyes bulging and teary. "Wot it be, sir?"

"I must go back." William was surprised at the steadiness of his voice when his chest was bursting with mayhem. He could not think. He could not process everything.

Sorrow filtered through his reckless thoughts, as the same pity he had always known for Horace came back in overpowering waves. If only something might have been different. If only Horace had listened, years ago, when William had begged him against strong drink.

"I didn't want to be keepin' the letter from you." Mr. Abram pulled the cap off his head, thin hair askew. "It was just that. . .that I wanted you to be comin' with me so bad that I. . ."

"It does not matter." William patted the man's arm, too touched by the genuine care to be angry. "I must make haste. Forgive me. Goodbye, my friend." He hurried up the ladder, flung open the hatch, and seized the first sailor he found. "I must speak with the captain. Where is he?"

"What for?"

Frenzied emotions shook William's voice. "I must get off this ship."

Chapter 22

Father was home again.

Isabella looped her bonnet ribbons into a bow under her chin and walked faster, the afternoon sun suffusing her cheeks with heat. She bit her lip. She must not succumb again. For Father's sake, for Bridget's sake, for Mrs. Morrey's sake—for her *own* sake.

But ever since Father's dismal news last night, angst had burrowed inside of her and threatened to bring back the blackness.

She would not allow such a thing. If that meant doing what hurt most, then so she must. She would face the seashore for the first time without him. Would that free her? Somehow, would facing her greatest pain lessen its power?

She was not certain anything would.

But she had to try.

When she reached the rugged slope, she drew in a breath of courage and eased through the tall grass. The second her boots met sand, she tugged at her bow. She ripped off the bonnet, slipped out the pins, allowed the wind to whip her hair.

Then she crept to the edge of the water. She pulled off her half boots and stockings and lifted her dress to her knees while the foamy water cooled her bare feet. *I am doing it.* She slid her eyes shut. She breathed as deeply as he'd ever told her to. She wiggled her toes into the sand. She turned her face up to the sunshine. *All the things you taught me, William.*

Perhaps coming here had been a mistake.

Doing sunshine and feeling the seashore was unimaginably heartbreaking when she was experiencing it alone.

Trepidation soared through William at the first sight of Sharottewood Manor. He leaned forward to rub Duke's neck. After he'd rowed from the ship to the Ogden Wells port, he'd paid Mr. Sneyd double to get his horse back. God had returned Duke and so much more.

He glanced down at his clothes—the knotted necktie, the navy tailcoat and gray waistcoat, the tailored pantaloons and new boots. By all appearances, he was a different man than the one who had been here before.

But inside, he was the same. He was still the William Kensley who was born in a workhouse and knew how to serve in the stables—the man Edward Gresham hated.

Wiping sweat from his hairline, he led Duke around the gurgling fountain. Hammers pounded at his temples. What would his lordship say when he realized William had not forgotten his daughter?

Worthless fool. Repulsing beggar. The insults flung into his mind, accompanied by an image of Lord Gresham's raging eyes and heated face. Did William truly think he could stride in here and attain the man's blessing?

Perhaps he should have waited. If he had watched for Isabella to ride out alone, he could have spoken with her and proposed matrimony to her ears alone. They could have run away together if her heart was still his.

But that was wrong.

He would do things right before God, as a gentleman, or he would not do them at all.

After tying Duke to the horse-head hitching post, William ascended the grand staircase and knocked at the door and took a step back. Seconds later, the butler showed him in, albeit with a nonplussed glance at William's clothes.

"This way. . .eh, sir." He led William to a hallway, disappeared into a room, then strode back out with a motioning arm. "His lordship shall see you in his study now."

William braced himself, just as he'd always done upon entering his aunt's chamber. Whatever accusations Edward heaped upon him, he determined to remain uninjured. How many minutes would he have before Edward shouted for a servant to haul him away?

As he entered, Lord Gresham leaped to his feet from behind his orderly desk. His jaw slackened and deep lines formed on his forehead as sunlight from the window shone on his face. "William."

"I ask nothing more than a word with you."

Color flooded the man's cheeks. He moved around the desk.

The silence propelled William forth. "I realize and respect the abhorrence you had for a match between your daughter and myself. I had no means to provide for her."

"William—"

"Please, allow me to finish."

"But—"

"Please, my lord. I must say this." William's voice throbbed. "Since I last saw you, my situation has altered greatly. I now own a small estate in Leicestershire, Rosenleigh, and I—"

"You have my blessing."

William blinked. "My lord?"

"You wish to marry my daughter."

"Yes."

"Then you may do so as soon as the banns can be published and read. You possess both my blessing and my enthusiasm." Was that emotion wobbling the man's tone?

William took a step back. Confusion webbed through him, tangling him in too many thoughts to sort through. "I do not understand."

"You must go to her at once. She has taken a small excursion to the seashore."

His limbs were frozen, his boots stuck to the wooden floorboards. What had changed? He had not yet fully explained the inheritance, his change in position, and already Lord Gresham consented? Was it possible?

As if sensing the questions, Lord Gresham took one step closer. "We are all allotted our treasures in life, and I daresay, there is much from which we derive pride and satisfaction." Fervency rippled from him, a pulse of regret. He shook his head. "There is but one thing that truly completes us. I shall not rob my daughter of what I have lost myself."

William's heart thumped for several seconds before he nodded. "I thank you, my lord. I shall go to her at once." He turned for the door—

"William."

Pausing, he glanced back over his shoulder.

Edward Gresham stared at him. A flicker of something moistened his eyes, some indistinguishable emotion—almost a glint of admiration or affection, if such a thing were possible. "You are not my son, Kensley." The tears rimmed. "But I should have been most proud if you had been."

A long-unmet craving was sated. William did not know what to say, nor what to do, so with nothing more than a second nod, he fled from the study.

He would carry the words with him as long as he lived.

The last thing she wanted was to cry again. Father would know. When she returned to the dinner table, when she pasted on a smile and tried for a cheery tone, he would see her eyes and know the truth.

But there was little she could do.

She hurt.

Deep in the caverns of her soul, where other emotions were too weak to reach, she fissured in a hundred more places. She missed him. How was it possible to long for someone this way? To need them so much you were blinded to everything except their memories?

Standing back to her bare feet, she brushed sand from the white muslin folds of her dress. She ambled along the water, her hem wet and clinging to her ankles, until she paused near the giant limestone archway.

She approached when she should have run away. Touching the rough rock, leaning into the opening, she closed her eyes and wished she could step back into another time.

The day she followed him through Mulcaster Square in the rain.

The afternoons they whiled away with chess or walks in Hyde Park.

Those quiet, pleasant evenings when they rode along the shoreline, and that first startling moment when he'd folded her into his arms and kissed her.

She would never marry. The resolution vibrated through her as she smeared away another tear. No matter if Father never found William. No matter if she never received a letter from him or saw him again in some London street or village walkway.

If she could not belong to William Kensley, she would belong to no one—

"Lose these, miss?"

She jumped, hand flying to her chest, as she pivoted to the voice.

A dream stood facing her, one real and distinct enough she might have imagined him true. With dark blond hair tousled across his forehead by the ocean breeze, William Kensley dangled her half boots from one hand.

His complexion was tan, cheeks pink from sun. He wore plain but well-tailored clothes—more evidence that he was a dream—and the corner of his lips lifted with a smile.

She longed to reach out, to touch him, but she was too afraid the vision would disappear.

He stepped closer, close enough the wind carried his calming smell. Her breath caught. Could dreams affect her senses? Or did she only imagine that too?

"I spoke with your father." Deep, husky. The smile was gone and so was the dream. He was as real as the thunder in her chest. "He said I might come down here to find you and. . ." His head tilted and his eyes were soft, waiting, uncertain.

A salty gust whipped her hair in front of her face. She brushed back the curls, anything to distract herself as she tried to sort through the endless questions. "You came back."

He nodded.

"Why?"

"You know why I came."

"I thought you were gone."

"I almost was."

"We searched everywhere. I thought I would never see you again. I

301

thought you had forgotten already—"

"Much has happened to me since our parting." He shook his head, stepped closer, grasped her fingers. The warmth of his skin against hers ignited fire in her veins. "I have never forgotten you."

"William—"

"I had no right to speak this before, and perhaps I have little right now. I have caused you unpardonable pain. I have brought nothing but misfortune to your home and to your father." He tugged her to him. With stricken eyes, he leaned over her face, a tremble in his voice. "You told me once that you could not bear to be parted from me. Now I confess as much to you."

"What are you saying?"

"I love you." His hands grasped her face. "I love you so much it is pain to me."

"As it is to me."

"I wish to marry you." His forehead pressed against hers. "I promise to provide for you, but I am not rich. I have no bloodlines to boast of. I was born in a workhouse, and my parents are of unknown—"

"It does not matter. None of that matters." Tremors coursing through her, she reached up on her tiptoes and tangled her lips with his. She tasted of a man good, strong, noble, wonderful. She cried against him. "Someone very dear once told me that it is not what a man possesses but who he is." She pressed her cheek to his wet one, closed her eyes. "And he told me when I go out of doors, I ought to do sunshine. And he taught me how to feel the seashore by taking off my shoes and wiggling my toes in the sand—"

"You are too wonderful to be true."

"I love you."

"You are God's kindness upon me."

"I love you." She buried her face in his neck as he lifted her from her feet and spun her in a small circle. No one had ever held her this way. No one had ever resonated so much love for her. No one had ever felt so right against her. "And I shall go on loving you as long as I live. I never wish to lose you."

"You need not worry." He kissed her forehead, her cheek, the corner of her lips. "I shall never be lost again."

That promise chased the last shadow from her soul. From the edge of her vision, she caught sight of the limestone archway. For many years, she had imagined what it would be like to step through the hole into another world, another time, another place.

For the first time, she did not wish to step through the hole at all.

Indeed, she would be happy exactly where she was forever.

EPILOGUE

Rosenleigh
July 1814

Sunlight warmed the back of William's neck as he unbuttoned his tailcoat with his eyes closed. "Five, six, seven." He peeked long enough to see a flash of yellow. "Eight, nine, ten. Are you ready?"

Grinning, he started through the well-trimmed labyrinth, the temperature cooling in the shadows of the bushes. He took the same path he always did. Around the first bend, he halted but pretended not to see the tiny creature crouched in the corner of the bush. "Where could she be?" He spun around, as if frantic. "Oh dear. I shall never find my Emmaline."

"Me here!" His three-year-old daughter leaped to her feet, hands springing up in delight. She raced for his legs and embraced him with all four limbs, her blond curls bouncing. "Play again, Papa. Again!"

He laughed and scooped her up. "Papa must return indoors. Besides, I know one little girl who must take her nap."

"Me no like naps." Her round cheeks flushed with displeasure, and her bottom lip protruded. "Please play again?"

"Miss Ettie would not be very happy with us."

"Yes, she will." Emmaline tilted her head, eyes wide as she tried to convince him. "She will just be happy because. . ." Nothing grand must have come to her, because she began playing with his neckcloth and said instead, "Please?"

A laugh rumbled out of him. He threw her up in the air, caught her, then settled her onto his shoulders as he walked back to the house.

Fondness warmed him as her tiny fingers grasped his ears. Was there ever a more impish little child? Or ever one so perfect?

Inside, Miss Ettie was already waiting on them in the foyer, hands crossed over her chest. "My, my. Just look at your dress, Emmaline. We shall have to bathe and change you before we can even think of settling you down for sleep." For all her attempts at being cross, a sweet glow brightened the woman's eyes. She glanced up at William, shook her head in mock disbelief at the child's untidy state, then took Emmaline's hand with motherly care. "We must come along to the nursery now, my dear. If you are especially good, perhaps I shall read you another story before I tuck you in. Would you like that?"

"Me wants to play outside."

William grinned as Miss Ettie gave another soft answer. The sadness that so long had haunted the woman's expression was gone. She was needed now. She was happy again.

The nursery was no longer old, dusty, and forgotten.

Turning to the maid Ruth, who was adjusting purple sweet peas in a vase, William asked about his wife.

"She be in the bedchamber again. Not feeling well at all, poor thing."

"Thank you. I shall look after her." William strode through the house, up the stairs, and to the closed door of his bedchamber. He entered without sound, lest she be asleep.

"William." Lying overtop the counterpane with pillows behind her head, Isabella laid aside her book.

He grinned. She must be gravely bored indeed to be entertaining herself with a novel.

"Do come and sit beside me, won't you?" She patted the bed and sat up. "You look as if you could use the rest."

He wiped a sheen of sweat from his forehead, settled on the bed next to her, and slipped his arm behind her back. "Our daughter wants for no vitality."

"How many hours of playing this time?"

"Nearly three."

Isabella laughed and nestled into him. "You are terrible to indulge her so."

"Perhaps." He glanced at her swollen abdomen, and all over again, a sense of pride struck him. "How do you feel?"

"A little tired."

"Ruth deemed it more serious than that."

"Only because she quite spoils me. Indeed, all of you do. One would think I was a complete invalid with the way you all set about fussing over me." She sighed and, with her head still in the crook of his shoulder, worked to undo the neckcloth about his neck. "How silly that you wear this thing on a day so warm."

"I received a letter from your father."

"Truly?"

"He wishes to visit by the end of the month."

She tossed his neckcloth off the bed. "How wonderful. He shall arrive just when our little son does."

"Son?" William stared at her stomach. "You sound as if you are certain it shall be a boy."

"I am."

"Isabella."

"No, truly. A woman can sense such things, you know." Her soft, cool fingers slipped to his neck, then his cheek, caressing him. "And I know what we shall call him too."

"Have I no say?"

"None at all."

"I am not certain I can stand for this." He nibbled her fingers until she laughed. "Very well. What shall we call our son?"

"Shelton."

His heart took on a strange beat.

"Shelton Kensley. What do you think of that, my dear husband?"

Unbidden, moisture blurred his vision. He captured her hand. He kissed the slender fingers, smelling her sweet hair, squeezing her warm body closer against him. The unborn life between them gave promise to their future. "I think," he whispered, "that I am overwhelmed with love for you." He dipped his mouth to hers and roved across her lips with precious desire. "I have never been more happy in my life."

ACKNOWLEDGMENTS

This book is the harvest of endless tender smiles, loving words, hard-working hands, and faithful hearts. I'm so grateful for the friends, family, and fellow industry professionals who have made *Garden of the Midnights* a reality. Many thanks to:

Mother, who believed in this story from the beginning. Thank you for encouraging me through all the edits and rewrites. I could not have persevered without your enthusiasm and cheer. I love you.

My agent, Cynthia Ruchti, for coming up with exciting new ideas, offering spot-on guidance, and always being so quick to answer my questions with sweetness and grace. Forever grateful for you, dear friend.

Granddaddy, for reading every single story I ever write. Thanks for giving me all my "romantic ideas". . .ahem, or not.

The publishing team at Barbour. Rebecca, Ashley, Shalyn, Becky, Ellie, and Laura—you're all amazing.

Daddy, for being my "marketing manager" and always thinking up new ways to get my books into the hands of more readers. I can't tell you how grateful I am for your support.

My little sister, Millie, for assuring me that—despite the fact that you adamantly do not like to read—this book is "really good." Thanks, my love.

My brother, Wyatt, for having the same whimsical, romantic notions as I do. We're more alike than anyone notices.

My church family, for reading my books and coming to church with all your guesses on who-dun-it and who-marries-who.

All the fellow writer friends who have made this journey sweeter. Marcus, Steve, Vincent, Kyle, Erica, and so many more. Infinitely grateful for the role each of you have played in my writing career.

And as always, my Jesus. The lifter up of my head. The song of my soul. The friend who listens to every care and makes everything okay. I love You more than I could ever hope to express. Nothing could be better than being Your child.

Hannah Linder resides in the beautiful mountains of central West Virginia. Represented by Books & Such, she writes Regency romantic suspense novels filled with passion, secrets, and danger. She is a four-time Selah Award winner, a 2023 Carol Award semi-finalist, and a member of American Christian Fiction Writers (ACFW). Also, Hannah is an international and multi-award-winning graphic designer who specializes in professional book cover design. She designs for both traditional publishing houses and individual authors, including New York Times, USA Today, and international bestsellers. She is also a self-portrait photographer of historical fashion. When Hannah is not writing, she enjoys playing her instruments—piano, guitar, ukulele, and banjolele—songwriting, painting still life, walking in the rain, and sitting on the front porch of her 1800s farmhouse. To follow her journey, visit hannahlinderbooks.com.

OTHER BOOKS BY HANNAH LINDER

Beneath His Silence

Second daughter of a baron—and a little on the mischievous side—Ella Pemberton is no governess. But the pretense is a necessity if she ever wishes to get inside of Wyckhorn Manor and attain the truth about her sister's death. Lord Sedgewick knows there is blood on his hands. Lies have been conceived, then more lies, but the price of truth would be too great. All he has left is his son and his bitterness. Will Ella, despite the lingering questions of his guilt, fall in love with such a man? Or is she falling prey to him—just as her dead sister did?

Paperback / 978-1-63609-436-6

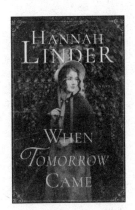

When Tomorrow Came

Nan and Heath Duncan, siblings abandoned by their papa and abused by their guardian, have no choice but to survive on the London streets. When a kind gentleman rescues Nan from an accident, the siblings are separated and raised in two vastly different social worlds. Just when both are beginning to flourish, their long-awaited papa returns and reunites them—bringing harsh demands with him. Soon dangers unfold, secret love develops, fights ensue, and murder upsets the worlds Heath and Nan have built for themselves. Will they be able to see through to the truth and end this whirlwind of a nightmare before it costs one of their lives?

Paperback / 978-1-63609-440-3

COMING SOON FROM HANNAH LINDER

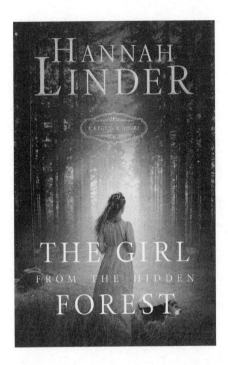

The Girl from the Hidden Forest

After being kidnapped from her safe but lonely life in
Balfour Forest, Eliza Ellis, the long-lost daughter of a viscount,
is brought back to a father she doesn't remember and a manor
that intensifies her childhood nightmares. But when she realizes
the danger isn't just in her dreams, she must uncover the horrendous
memories trapped in her mind, even if divulging that truth could
cost her the man she loves—or both of their lives.

Paperback / 978-1-63609-833-3

JOIN US ONLINE!

Christian Fiction for Women

Christian Fiction for Women is your online home for the latest in Christian fiction.

Check us out online for:

- Giveaways
- Recipes
- Info about Upcoming Releases
- Book Trailers
- News and More!

Find Christian Fiction for Women at Your Favorite Social Media Site:

 Search "Christian Fiction for Women"

 @fictionforwomen